—THE—
WOLF
TREE

The Clockwork Dark
The Nine Pound Hammer
The Wolf Tree

—THE—
WOLF
TREE

—JOHN—
CLAUDE BEMIS

RANDOM HOUSE
NEW YORK

Text copyright © 2010 by John Claude Bemis
Jacket art copyright © 2010 by Alexander Jansson

Published in the United States by Random House Children's Books, a division of Random House, Inc., New York.

Random House and the colophon are registered trademarks of Random House, Inc.

Visit us on the Web! www.randomhouse.com/kids

Educators and librarians, for a variety of teaching tools, visit us at www.randomhouse.com/teachers

Library of Congress Cataloging-in-Publication Data
Bemis, John Claude.
The Wolf Tree / John Claude Bemis. — 1st ed.
p. cm. — (Clockwork dark ; bk. 2)
Summary: Ray Cobb and the rest of the Ramblers must cross into the Gloaming and destroy the Gog's Machine, which has started to spread a darkness over the land.
ISBN 978-0-375-85566-5 (trade) — ISBN 978-0-375-95566-2 (lib. bdg.) — ISBN 978-0-375-89311-7 (e-book)
[1. Orphans—Fiction.   2. Brothers and sisters—Fiction.
3. Characters in literature—Fiction.   4. Fantasy.]   I. Title.
PZ7.B4237Wol 2010
[Fic]—dc22
2009018950

Printed in the United States of America

10 9 8 7 6 5 4 3 2 1

First Edition

To
Claud T. Smith
Thelma M. Smith
William Y. Bemis
Elsie F. Bemis

CONTENTS

—THE—
WOLF
TREE

CONKER BROUGHT THE NINE POUND HAMMER DOWN ON The Pitch Dark Train's *boiler. The train erupted into flame and rocketing debris.*

Jolie fell.

Just before she hit the water, she lost hold of Ray. She plunged into the river, and with the splash came a powerful surge of relief. She had returned to the water where she belonged.

For so long she had been hidden aboard the Ballyhoo, *the medicine show's train. For so long she had been prisoner to the fear that the Gog would capture her, to have her siren voice, and use the enchantment as a means of controlling people, of drawing servants to his monstrous Machine.*

She had at last reached the blessed, true waters of the

Mississippi River. Now she was free to return to her swamp far to the south.

Then she remembered Ray.

The swift current whipped past Jolie, scattering her tangled hair and gown. She arched in the water, kicking fiercely as she swam back for him. Heavy chunks of metal ripped from The Pitch Dark Train plummeted around her in the murky water. She looked all around through the gloom until she spied a shadow below her. It wasn't sinking like the train's debris, but drifting with the current.

Ray!

Kicking her way closer, she saw a hand, the skin a deep brown. Her chest constricted painfully.

It was not Ray; it was Conker.

She could not believe what she saw. The train had erupted volcanically. He should have been blown apart by the blast. As she turned his enormous body over in the swift currents, she saw he had not even been burned.

How was this possible?

She listened to his chest, but no heartbeat could be found. "Conker, dear Conker," she whispered as she clung to her friend's broken body.

Something tickled her neck. Jolie pulled back and saw a charm hanging on the end of a necklace: a rectangle of beaten copper.

She had seen the necklace before, but where? She had never known Conker to wear any jewelry, not like Redfeather.

Redfeather! This had been his necklace. When she had

been rescued from the Gog's train, Ray and Si had been able to walk through a burning field to reach her by holding Redfeather's necklace.

The copper had protected Conker from the immense heat of the exploding train. The fire had not burned him to death, but the impact of the explosion was more than any man could survive. Any normal man . . .

But Conker was not any normal man. He was John Henry's son.

Holding on to Conker as the swirling current carried them through the river, Jolie put her hands to his face.

She had never encountered a shipwrecked sailor, as many of her siren sisters had, but Jolie had been told how to preserve the life of a human. She called out to the river, to the ancient grandmother of the waters, asking for this life not to be taken.

Covering his nose, she placed her mouth to his and blew, filling his lungs with her air.

A tremor came over Conker's body. Jolie put her ear to his chest and listened. It was hard to discern but she heard it: a heartbeat.

He was alive, although just barely. He had sustained injuries to his body from which no man should be able to recover. Her sisters had told her of a place, a spring that might save him if she could ever find it.

But where was Ray?

Jolie looked back into the murk of the river. The swift and scattering currents of the water had pulled her and Conker far from where they had landed.

"Ray." She spoke to the waters. "I know that you will not understand where I have gone, but trust that one day, I will find you."

Jolie wrapped one arm around Conker's waist. She let the rush of the river speed their journey. Following the waters that came together from across the vast continent, Jolie ushered Conker's broken body away.

FLICKERS OF EMERALD BUDS WERE EMERGING ON THE mountainside. Marbled swirls of receding snow and wet black earth still lingered in the shadows of the forest. The sun shone with a clear, white brilliance as Ray Cobb crested the range.

Cool air blew up from the coves, and Ray pulled the doeskin robe tighter around his neck as he climbed. He had grown taller and leaner over the past year. His face was sunspeckled, and his curly mass of brown hair was jagged and uneven from the haphazard trimmings of a knife. Although his linen shirt and wool britches showed considerable wear, Ray had kept them patched and travel-worthy.

He saw no others as he traversed the Great Smoky Mountains; in fact, the wilderness was so remote that he had seen no living person in more than a month. Aside from winter birds, foraging deer, and reclusive creatures venturing from their dens, Ray's shelter—deep in the maze of evergreen-crowned ridges and cascading waterfalls—had been a place of quiet isolation.

Ray crossed an icy black creek. He was nearly there.

The sunlight dimmed as ghostly fingers of clouds moved across the mountain. The chestnuts and hemlocks moaned around him. Ray followed no path or track, nor did he need one. Stopping in the shelter of dark trees, he dug the water-skin from beneath his shirt where the heat of his stomach kept the water from freezing.

As he took a long drink, he saw movement out of the corner of his eye. He turned and whatever it was disappeared into a thicket of rhododendron. Ray's hand slipped to the knife on his belt. "Hello?"

He inhaled, trying to catch a defining scent. But the air was too cold and the wind in the stand of trees too turbulent.

Ray continued walking, scanning for movement. Leaves rustled and then a snort came from the deepest nest of rhododendron. His hand at his knife, Ray crept forward. As he reached the dark green shrubs, a squeal rang out and low black forms rushed out at him. A heavy beast swiped his knee, knocking Ray to the ground. He rolled over and watched several stout feral hogs flee into the forest.

Ray laughed and chased after them. "Hey," he called. "Not so fast."

The hogs swirled about the trees, their white eyes rolling around in their sockets.

"Hey! Come on now. You know me. Come on back," he called, but the hogs disappeared through the bracken and wilting ferns.

When Ray reached the muddy trail coming up the mountain, he spied one of the hogs sitting in the bottom of one of the deep wagon-wheel ruts.

Ray cocked an eyebrow at the hog. "Hungry?" He reached in his pocket and took out a piece of dried venison pounded with checkerberries and wild ginger. He held the pemmican out, waving the stiff strip before its nose. The hog rose from the rut and took the jerky, grunting as it ate with noisy relish.

"There you go," he said. "That a boy." Ray squatted at the beast's enormous face. Motioning with his hands and touching the hog at its ear and at the edges of its mouth, he instructed the hog in what simple vocabulary Ray had learned. Foxes and raccoons and their kin were easier than hogs, but he was best at speaking to birds, especially crows. Fortunately this hog seemed smart, and Ray felt it was following his crude instructions.

Ray untied his sun-faded bandanna from around his neck and knotted it around the hog's fat throat. The hog blinked several times at him and turned.

"That's right," he added as the hog trotted away. "Get on to Shuckstack. Let them know I'm back."

A year ago, they had followed Nel up into the Smoky Mountains and built a home at Shuckstack Mountain. Ray and Sally, Redfeather and Marisol, Buck and Si, Nel and the twelve orphans. The wilderness was everything Nel had promised: a place where the children rescued from Mister Grevol's *Pitch Dark Train* could grow up in peace.

Nel had taught them how to live in the wild. Not just survive, but live fully and happily. But Ray wanted something more. He wanted to be a Rambler. There were skills the old pitchman could offer, but Nel had forgotten his deeper Rambler powers. Ray needed to learn from others.

Mother Salagi's cabin on the Clingman's Dome was nearly two days' journey from Shuckstack Mountain. During Ray's first winter wandering alone in the mountains, he found the ancient seer. Mother Salagi taught Ray some animal speech and a smattering of hoodoo charms.

But neither she nor Nel could teach Ray how to become a Rambler. In order for Ray to really learn, he needed to be alone. He needed the solitude of the wilderness. Ray would wander from his friends and family at Shuckstack into the craggy cliffs and deep coves off and on throughout the year— each season offering its own lessons. He traveled far, seeking out medicine men and root workers who could pass on some nearly lost knowledge or skill.

He wore a toby around his neck. When he first met Mother Salagi, the old seer sewed spells into the red flannel pouch to protect its contents. And as Ray journeyed, learning more and more, the toby grew heavy with charms: nine shoestring-shaped roots, a twig of elder, a twist of rue, Hobnob's dandelion flower, goofer dust, a ball of bluestone, a pair of Indian-head pennies, a tin of saltpeter, and assorted other herbs and objects. Among them, he also carried the golden rabbit's foot—his father's hand.

And in time, without ceremony or decoration, Ray knew he had become a Rambler.

As he passed the first of the bottletrees, the lodge came into sight. The sun had dropped below the ridgeline. Ray thought nothing was more beautiful than returning to Shuckstack in the half-dark, its golden windows illuminated from within by the firelight, and the sound of all those chirping voices bouncing off the mighty trees nestled up against the millpond.

He was home.

Ray saw that preparations had begun for Nel's eighty-first birthday party. Several canvas tents had been erected, reminding him of smaller versions of the one that had been used by the medicine show. A small corral had been built since he last left, most likely to house the horses of the coming guests. Sniffing toward one of the outbuildings, Ray could smell several deer, salted and hanging from the rafters and awaiting the feasts.

The hog trotted from around the barn, the bandanna no longer around its neck, and dashed for the trees. The front door of the lodge swung open. Dmitry, who was ten, and one of the oldest of the children rescued from Mister Grevol's train, ran out onto the long porch stretching across the front of the lodge. His eyes widened as he saw Ray. He held up the bandanna as he shouted, "He's home!"

Mattias was out the door next. The two boys raced down

the stairs into the yard, running to meet Ray. Voices, cheerful and curious, emerged from within Shuckstack's lodge. Figures pushed their way out from the doorway, some coming down the steps to beat Dmitry and Mattias to be the first to greet Ray, others waiting along the rails of the porch.

Ray heard his name over and over, picking out each speaker: Si, Nel, Marisol, Buck, Felice, Naomi, Rosemary, Oliver, George, Dale, Preston, Noah, Adam, Carolyn, and Sally.

They were all there.

Each and every one.

All but Jolie.

The lodge on Shuckstack Mountain had once been a sawmill, abandoned decades earlier. When Nel led them up the mountain the summer before, all that remained was the stone foundation beside a crumbling dam on the creek, a broken waterwheel, and a heart-pine floor buried under the collapsed frame of the mill. Although more than half of the nineteen hands had been children, they had cleared the rubble, cut the logs, and built a home.

As Ray came up the stairs to the porch, the children battled fiercely to greet him, to take his things, to ask if he'd seen any panthers this time, to pull him this way and that as each wanted to show him some new toy or to tell stories of what he'd missed over the winter.

Quieting the row took an irritated roar by the ragged-faced cowboy Buck, followed by the old pitchman Nel's gentler, "Give him a moment's repose to settle in. Recede! Regress! Rosemary, Carolyn, stop pulling at his arms. Poor Ray looks half-frozen. Yes, yes, there will be time to beguile Ray with your salamander soon, Adam. Come over to the fire, Ray. Naomi, fetch Ray some supper. Back away, Dale. . . ."

Soon Ray was sitting before the blazing hearth in the den that stretched across the main floor of Shuckstack's lodge. He had a plate on his knees and sopped at the last of his beans and orpine drippings with fried acorn cakes. Mattias and Dmitry took turns telling a story about a black bear that had chased them from Two Eagle Mountain.

Listening to the boys' story, Nel leaned back in his chair, crossing his legs at the ankle so the mahogany peg rested on the wrinkle of leather at his boot. He grinned widely behind his briarwood pipe. Peg Leg Nel was lean and strong for being on the eve of eighty-one. Ray felt if it hadn't been for the pompadour of silver-white hair, he would never have guessed him to be that old.

The children were scattered on the floor or in the hand-fashioned chairs and benches of split logs. Marisol, raven-haired and lovely in her spangled dress, listened with the smallest, five-year-old Noah, nestled in her lap. Her copper-head, Javidos, coiled down in Noah's lap, but the boy showed no more fear of the fat, blond-and-brown striped snake than if it were a kitten.

Beside Buck sat Si with a blanket to her chin. She was so bundled up, Ray half imagined she was bound for some escape routine as she'd done in the medicine show. But when he noticed the dark circles under her eyes, he realized she must be ill.

Sally had settled beside Ray on his bench, her arms locked in his and her eyes growing animated as Mattias and Dmitry recounted each exciting moment. Ray thought how much she looked like Ray's and her mother. Over the past year, Sally had sprung up skinny like a poplar sapling. Her small upturned nose was sprinkled with freckles, and her eyelashes fell across her cheeks when she blinked.

Nel's barking laugh pulled his attention back to the story. "How did you learn to do hoodoo, Mattias?"

"From Ray," Mattias answered. "He tried to show us the spell a while back. But it didn't work."

Dmitry, whose hair, even his eyebrows and lashes, was so blond as to be white, chimed in, "Well, we couldn't remember if you were supposed to put the goofer dust in the jar first or scoop the footprint dirt first."

"Besides," Mattias said, "the bear was charging too fast and then we—"

"Footprint charm," Nel interrupted once more, looking at Ray. "Where did you get ahold of goofer dust?"

Mattias and Dmitry stopped with mouths left expectantly open to continue as soon as Ray finished his reply. "From that root worker I met down on the Pamlico."

Deep folds of wrinkles tightened around Nel's eyes, and he seemed to struggle to hold his smile. "Of course. . . . He showed you the charm also?"

Ray replied, "No. Mother Salagi taught it to me."

Nel's fingers went reflexively to his neck, to the amulet he wore. The silver fox paw had once been his leg, before the Hoarhound severed it and his Rambler powers were lost.

"Oh. Well. Of course." Nel waved with his hand to turn the attention back to Mattias and Dmitry. "Resume your yarn, boys."

As Mattias and Dmitry both exploded to recount how the bear had chased them across Hanson Knob, Ray glanced down at Sally. Her mouth was pursed as she leafed through the book in her lap. *The Incunabula of Wandering.*

"What are you looking up?" Ray whispered.

Sally closed the book, with her hand still marking the page. "Nothing." She smiled and turned her attention back to Mattias and Dmitry.

Eventually the story concluded. A few of the children acted out the dramatic episode, some playing the bear, others vying for the roles of Mattias or Dmitry. Marisol whispered to Javidos, and he slid up her arm to her neck. She rose with the already sleeping Noah in her arms. "It's getting late. Everybody off to bed."

There was a general grumbling until Marisol added, "We've got a busy day tomorrow. Lots to do and our first guests may arrive."

At the anticipation of strangers coming for Nel's party, the children broke into excited chatter. Carolyn helped Marisol shepherd the children up the stairs to the loft. "What story do you want tonight?" Marisol asked.

"The one about the giant vacaroo!" Preston shouted.

"Ismael is a *vaquero,* not a vacaroo," Carolyn, the oldest of the rescued children, said.

Marisol brushed them forward. "You're not tired of Ismael yet?"

"No!" the children cried together, even the older ones. "Ismael the vacaroo!" they began to chant.

"*Vaquero,*" Carolyn tried to correct.

"Say 'good night,'" Marisol said.

Marching in a line to the toasty loft above, the children chirped out good-nights to Ray and Mister Nel and Si and even Buck.

"Finally some peace," Buck grumbled as the last footsteps disappeared overhead. Ray smiled, thinking how often he had seen Buck showing one of the children how to whittle a duck call or string up a reed fishing pole.

Nel plucked his pipe from his mouth and gestured with it toward Si. "Your tonic? Did you remember—"

"I drank it with dinner," she said, pulling the blanket up around her shoulders.

"Tonic?" Ray asked. "You're sick?"

"Just a little injury," Si said.

"She was stabbed," Nel said gruffly.

"What!" Ray sat up. "Who . . . how did that happen?"

Si shifted uncomfortably and looked over at Buck, who was rubbing his hands before the fire, his long black-and-silver locks hanging over his eyes.

"Long story, Ray, but it was over in Knoxville," she said. "Buck and I went to trade some ginseng roots and some of

Nel's tonics for supplies. I guess the short of it is that they don't care much for my kind."

"Could have been any of us," Nel said, to which Si gave a snort.

Ray tilted his head. "What do you mean, Si?"

"Chinese girl carrying a purse full of coins. You get a couple of buckaroos wanting some easy liquor money . . . Buck was finishing up the trade, and I went out to buy some peppermint sticks to bring back as gifts. Should have known not to take a shortcut by the river. Luckily, Buck got there in time."

Ray couldn't believe it. Si stabbed! And for just a few coins. It had been a long time since Ray lived in the city. He had been to Knoxville twice, and it was nothing compared to where he had grown up in lower Manhattan.

"Dark times," Nel said, shaking his head. "I don't know what's come over folk today, but we're lucky to have this place, very fortunate to have Shuckstack, far away from the growing madness."

Buck raised his head. "Your sister saved her," he said, his dry voice cracking.

"Sally?" Ray asked. "What do you mean?"

Nel nodded. "Amazing girl, your sister. Buck got Si back up here. He'd cleaned and dressed the wound as good as one could desire, but a fever took Si. I tried every herb and concoction I knew, but she was getting worse. We had nearly given up hope when Sally came up with the answer. A simple flower. The Gertrude's Diadem. I've never worked with them before. They're very rare. But Sally was convinced it would cure Si. She found the flower. I made a tea of it. Si was better within hours. It's a wonder, Ray. A true wonder."

Ray blinked with surprise. How had his sister known to use that flower? She knew little about surviving in the wild. She had no idea how to make a fire or how to feed herself in the forest.

Unlike Ray, who had journeyed far and deep in the wild to become a Rambler, Sally spent little time away from Shuckstack. More often than not, she could be found reading the treasured book that had belonged to their father, *The Incunabula of Wandering*. How she could understand the strange, obtuse prose—or was it poetry?—Ray could not fathom.

Sally was convinced the book could explain what had happened to their father. Why he was missing even after Ray had rescued him from the Hoarhound. Why he had not found his children yet.

Si stood with the blanket draped about her arms. "I should get to bed." She seemed momentarily unsteady and grasped the back of the chair. Buck rose, but Si brushed him away. She caught the sympathetic wince on Ray's face and said, "I'm okay. Don't fret over it. Glad to have you home, Ray. Good night."

They bade her good night, and Ray watched as Si slowly ascended the creaking stairs.

Buck leaned closer to the fire. He shivered, crossing his arms and rubbing his hands briskly across his elbows. Nel tilted his head back, drawing deeply on his pipe and sending steamboat puffs drifting above his fleecy white head. Ray allowed the sweet, familiar scent of the tobacco to drive away the thoughts of Si's injury.

Ray broke the peaceful silence. "How about Redfeather? Will he be back for the party?"

Nel blinked. "Oh, no. He's still out in the Indian Territory. It's too far of a journey for a party, and he needs to continue his learning."

"Learning?" Ray asked. "I thought he was just traveling. Who is he learning from?"

"A Cherokee elder," Nel said. "An old friend named Water Spider. He left these mountains a lifetime ago when General Scott drove the Cherokee west at bayonet point. We had many adventures together as young men. I haven't seen him in decades. When Redfeather wrote that he was visiting the Territory, I told him how to find old Water Spider."

Buck prodded the logs in the fireplace. "And how did your winter go?" he asked before dropping back into his seat.

"I wasn't able to cross," Ray said bluntly.

The lines in Buck's ragged face tightened, but Nel remained placid, sucking at his pipe.

"Give it time, Ray," Nel said. "You'll learn."

"Time?" Buck growled. "We don't know how much time—"

"Buck," Nel said in a low reprimand.

"No. He's right, Nel," Ray said. "I've got to find a way and soon. Mother Salagi said so."

"Did she?" Nel asked.

"It's the Machine!" Buck said through gritted teeth. "I've been telling you this, Nel."

"Yes, yes you have, but I don't share your pessimistic paranoia."

"Paranoia? That Machine is still out there."

Nel frowned and shook his head. "But its maker is not. The Gog is dead, Buck. He's dead and we're all fortunate for . . . for Conker's sacrifice. The Machine is no longer a threat to us."

"That's not what Mother Salagi said," Ray said. "I visited her on my way home. She has been casting bones, searching for answers with her charms. She hasn't figured out what's happened to the Machine, but she fears it's still powerful. Even without the Gog! She sees danger ahead—"

"Well, we've got Shuckstack," Nel said, stomping his peg leg to the pine floor. "Why do you think we built this place? Why did I bring them all here? We're safe. This place. These mountains. The children, all of us. We're protected."

Buck's jaw ground back and forth. "But *they* aren't. The others out there. What good is it for us to hide when others will suffer? Don't you see what wickedness the Machine is hatching? Killers! Thieves! The men who stabbed Si . . . their viciousness is the work of the Machine's growing madness."

"There was evil before the Gog built his Machine." Nel scowled.

"Not this kind of evil—" Buck began.

"You're quick to call the action of others wicked, Buck!"

Buck's mouth held open. His pale, blind eyes narrowed.

Ray blinked hard, shocked by the outpouring of emotion from the two men.

After a cold silence, Nel waved his upturned hands to Ray and then asked Buck, "What do you want me to do?" His hands shook and a tic flickered in his left eye. "I lost Conker. I won't lose any of the others."

Buck stood and stormed out the door. The cold wind whipped sparks up from the fire, and as the door slammed, the lodge shook.

Nel exhaled slowly until he steadied his trembling. Ray waited, knowing this was not the first argument the two men had had over this subject.

Nel leaned forward, pushing his long fingers through his mane of snowy hair. Finally he looked up at Ray. "What are you going to do, son?"

Ray's shoulders drooped. "I don't know, Nel."

"Mother Salagi. Did she offer you any counsel?"

Ray wanted to embrace Nel as he had when he was younger. He wanted to tell Nel to forget about Mother Salagi and the Machine and Conker. He wanted the old man to smile, to give Ray a pinch on the ear, to tell him a joke. The weight and anxiety held by this father to all of Shuckstack's children caused Ray's eyes to burn.

"She only said to keep the foot safe."

Nel nodded. "Are you leaving us?"

"No," Ray quickly said. "I'm staying here."

Nel blinked as a guarded smile touched the corners of his mouth. "Good. Good."

He pushed on his knee to rise. Then he clapped a hand on Ray's shoulder. "I'm sure you're ready for your bed, and I'd better go assuage our Eustace Buckthorn."

"Nel," Ray began, dropping his voice to a whisper. "What happened in Knoxville? Did Buck kill those men?"

Nel pinched his fingers to the bridge of his nose, massaging the loose flesh where his silver eyebrows met.

"It's not just that, Ray. It's worse. There was a policeman who came upon them. Si was badly wounded. Buck needed to get her back to us. You know how he is when he's in a rage. It was unfortunate that the policeman came at that moment. Horrible. Buck made a mistake, Ray. He regrets what he did. . . ."

As a young man, Buck had accidentally shot his brother. This had devastated Buck. It had driven him to become an outlaw before Nel and the Ramblers had helped him. And on the Gog's *Pitch Dark Train*, Buck had shot Seth, not meaning to kill him but thinking the boy was attacking Ray. Seth had been trying to protect Ray from the Gog, trying desperately to undo his betrayal. Ray had told Buck that the Hoarhound killed Seth, not the cowboy's bullet. The lie lay wedged in his conscience like an old wound.

And now an innocent policeman . . .

"There's no undoing what's been done. Ray, you won't say anything to the others? They don't know. I'm not sure if Si even remembers what happened."

"I won't."

"Good, good." He patted Ray on the forearm and added, "Get some rest." Nel's peg leg tapped its way across the wooden floor to the door and out onto the dark porch.

Ray rose to climb the stairs, for his bed up in the loft, for sleep he desperately needed. But as he turned, his eyes fell on the wall at the far side of the long den. The fire in the hearth was flickering and dying, and the far wall was nearly in shadow. Wavery ember-light reflected off a handle's outline.

The Nine Pound Hammer's broken handle hung alone and reverently on the bead-board planks. The iron head was missing, lost in the murk of the Mississippi River.

Ray had learned many powers, ones even the Ramblers of John Henry's day would have admired. But one skill eluded him: he had not yet learned to take animal form. If he was to reach the Gloaming, he would need to learn this skill.

Nel had explained that the Gloaming was a spirit world, a place existing as a shadow layered upon this world. A place of great power, few could enter it. Indian holy men found doorways on occasion. As Ramblers learned how to take animal forms, they discovered that they could cross as well. Understanding the influence the Gloaming had over mankind, the Gog built his Machine in its vast depths.

Long ago, Ray's father, crossing as a rabbit, led John Henry into the Gloaming, where John Henry destroyed the Machine with his Nine Pound Hammer. With this hammer that now hung broken before Ray.

Hiding behind the name of G. Octavius Grevol, the Gog rebuilt his Machine and began collecting the unwanted, the unnoticed, gathering slaves to tend his dark clockwork. Sally and the children now living under Nel's care at Shuckstack had been among his captives. Fortunately, Ray and Si and Conker had rescued them.

And with his father's hammer, Conker had sacrificed his life destroying Mister Grevol on his *Pitch Dark Train*. But the Gog's Machine remained, along with its terrible power.

Ray reached out, the tip of his finger touching the worn wood of the handle. Conker, his dear friend Conker . . . Ray lowered his hand.

The Nine Pound Hammer was broken. Even if Ray could cross into the Gloaming, even if he could learn to take animal form and somehow find the Machine, he had no idea how to destroy it without the hammer.

Ray was splitting logs with Mattias when the first guests arrived. The day had warmed, and the sun was shrinking the snow into patches and puddles in the yard. With his sleeves rolled up and shirt unbuttoned, Ray sweated with the effort of the ax. Mattias positioned the next piece of hickory on the fat stump, and Ray brought the ax down with a crack.

As Ray lifted the ax for the next swing, Oliver dashed past, followed by Naomi and Rosemary. "You're supposed to be helping get ready for Nel's party!" Ray called.

The three disappeared around the lodge, and Ray heard the voices of the children abandoning their chores to greet the arrival. Mattias gave Ray an expectant look.

"Go on," Ray chuckled, and Mattias raced to join the others to see who had arrived.

Ray cleaved the ax into the stump, planted his hat on his head, and buttoned up his shirt before following. Nel came down from the porch, clapping his hands together and laughing, with Buck behind him.

Ray joined them and the children as a Nissen wagon, pulled by a pair of mules, came up the path. Driving the mules was a stout man with a wagging walrus mustache. At his side sat a younger version of himself—slender and sporting a mustache that was only beginning to droop at the corners of his lips. In the back of the wagon sat another young man and a plump woman, wispy hair escaping from her bonnet.

"Ya, mules," the stout man barked as he snapped the reins. "Ya! Almost there."

"Ox Everett." Buck greeted him. "You drive mules just as mercilessly as you do the *Ballyhoo*!"

"Come up through near ten miles of mud and slush," Ox grumbled as he brought the wagon to a stop in the middle of the swarming children. "Shuckstack ain't the easiest place on earth to reach."

"And we like it that way," Nel said, extending a hand for Ma Everett to step down.

"My, Nel," Ma Everett chirped. "Looking ten years younger every time we visit."

"You're too kind, my dear. Eddie, how are you, son?"

Eddie Everett extended his hand, which Nel shook heartily, adding a slap on his shoulder. "Fit and fine, sir. Glad to be here again."

The older Everett son, Shacks, helped his father down

from the wagon and then drove the mules to the barn. Ma Everett went around to each child, distributing hugs and kisses and compliments like bits of candy.

Eddie found Ray. The younger Everett had a few patches of coal soot behind his ears and in the creases of his neck and face, but otherwise he was much cleaner than Ray had ever seen him.

"Wait till you see all the food Ma had us haul," Eddie said. "Going to be a feast like you've never seen."

"That's good," Ray said. "There's quite a guest list! Half of them I've never heard of before."

"How does Nel know so many folks?" Eddie asked.

Ray shrugged. "Been around eighty-one years. I guess you get to know people."

Finished with her greeting, Ma Everett called for all the children to follow her to the wagon to begin unloading it. Eddie had not been kidding about the amount of food. With arms filled, the group marched around to the back of the lodge and into the cellar kitchen. Soon the larders were overflowing with sacks and jars, tins and boxes.

"Ma Everett!" Marisol called as she came from her room next to the kitchen.

"Marisol." Ma Everett cupped her hands to the girl's face. "Lovelier than ever."

"Thank you." Marisol smiled.

"Now, dear, we've got our work cut out. Take that sack of corn and start grinding it. Then we'll need to find the flour. Where's the box of apples? My, my. So much to do. After that corn's ground, we'll need to soak it in spring water. . . ."

The kitchen became a cyclone of activity, with half the children helping and half getting swatted by Ma Everett's apron for getting in the way or sticking their fingers in batters and bowls.

The day continued with everyone, including Nel, busily making preparations—cooking, cleaning, chopping wood, washing linens, stringing up decorations. Ray helped Shacks and Eddie nail together makeshift tables and benches until well after dark. With some of their beds lost to the Everetts, several of the children slept on pallets on the floor.

Coming in by the fire for their meal, the Everett boys ate quickly and headed up for bed. Even Nel and Buck made it an early night. Ray sat a little longer in the toasty den, and soon Marisol came up from the cellar kitchen, her dress dusted with flour and speckled with grease.

"The woman's a slave driver," she groaned as she dropped into a rocking chair.

Ray laughed. "Ma Everett knows how to take charge."

Marisol slumped her head wearily to the side to look at Ray. "How many more days until the party?"

"Two."

"I'm not going to survive. I've got to get to bed." She pried herself up, lifting Javidos to her shoulder, and headed for the stairs.

"Good night," Ray said, but Marisol only grunted.

Ray put another log on the fire and settled back into his chair. He did not realize he had fallen asleep until Sally whispered, "Ray."

Ray jolted and blinked. "Sally. You're still up?"

"I couldn't sleep." She slid one of the benches over beside Ray and sat down. "I'm so excited! It's going to be some party, don't you think?"

Ray gave a yawn and stretched out an arm.

Sally kicked her feet out to rest on Ray's leg. "All those people who knew Nel when he was younger."

"Hmmm," Ray murmured, only half listening to her as the warmth of the fire threatened to draw him back into sleep.

Sally twirled a curl from her temple. "Maybe some of them knew Father also."

Ray sat up a fraction, his eyes meeting Sally's.

She let her gaze lower. "I wish Father could be here." She pulled her feet off Ray's leg and picked fretfully at a stitch in her thick woolen socks.

"Sally . . ." Ray hesitated.

She pulled at the bit of thread but didn't answer.

"Sally, I spoke with Mother Salagi about Father," he said.

She cocked her head as she waited for him to continue.

"She's cast bones and consulted bullbats and burned frankincense with black salt—"

"And what, Ray?" Sally asked. "What are you trying to tell me?"

"She can't see him," Ray said. "He's beyond her sight."

"What does that mean? Is Father in some sort of danger?"

Ray took a deep breath. "He's not coming back, Sally. I don't know what happened to Father, but he's not coming back."

"I don't understand!" Sally snapped, her nose wrinkling

and her long eyelashes beading with tears. "Does Mother Salagi think he's dead?"

Ray waved a hand for her to lower her voice. "She doesn't know but she suspects—"

"He's dead!" she struggled to whisper. "You think Father is dead?"

Sally stared at Ray, her wide eyes lit by the firelight.

Ray said slowly, "It's just, Sally, that if Mother Salagi can't find out what happened to him and he hasn't come back to us, is there any hope of finding him?"

Sally stood and brushed her knuckles across her eyes. She held out a hand to pull Ray up from the chair. "There's always hope, isn't there?"

He wrapped his arms around Sally and hugged her.

For the last year, Ray had held hope for many things coming to pass. His father returning. Learning to cross. Finding Jolie again. But hope had brought none of them.

The following day crackled with the excitement of the impending party. Strings of acorns and cedar greens and bunches of white and purple berries from the forest hung from the ceiling. The main floor of the lodge was rearranged to accommodate all the tables for the feast. Down in the cellar, the black iron stove needed constant feeding as Ma Everett and her kitchen crew baked pie after pie.

More guests arrived, some in wagons like the Everetts, others on horseback, and still more on foot. By the end of the day, the celebration had begun, even if unofficially.

Some of the guests were neighbors, people within a few days' journey of Shuckstack, whom Nel and the others had befriended while trading tonics in the local stores. They were hearty mountain folk or Cherokee whose kin had escaped the Removal to the West. There were veterans both black and white who had served with Nel and Ox Everett in the War. Some had come from as far away as Minnesota and the Gulf Coast. An elegantly dressed couple was introduced to Ray as the descendants of the Abolitionist family in Ohio who had befriended Nel in his younger days. Root doctors and gypsy Travelers arrived, dressed in wild outfits. The lodge was over-flowing by nightfall, and many guests erected their own tents by the millpond.

At first the Shuckstack children were excited by all the visitors, but as the crowd increased, the kids grew shy, tucking close to Ma Everett's skirt or to Marisol or Nel. As the instruments came out—for it seemed nearly every other arrival brought something to play, from fiddles to tin-sheet drums to strange instruments from foreign lands—the children grew friendly again and danced in big, galloping circles.

"We've got to get these children to bed!" Ma Everett announced well after midnight. "Tomorrow's a busy day. Marisol, round them up."

"I'll help you," Ray said quickly.

Later, after Ray got the children to bed and lay down on his own mattress, he could still hear the droning accordions and chanting choruses reverberating off the mountainside and up to the stars.

* * *

The following afternoon, with a light snow falling, Nel's eighty-first birthday celebration officially began. The food was all cooked, the final decorations placed, and the children washed and dressed in their best clothes. Fortunately for Ray, Si had picked up a new linen shirt for him on a recent trip into town. Ray tied a kerchief around his neck and joined the others downstairs for the meal.

Ray felt that all of Ma Everett's hard driving was worth the result. The tables were pushed together in one enormous row across the den but were dwarfed by the feast of food laid out upon them. There were roasted haunches of venison and turkey, plates of cornbread and buckwheat cakes, every imaginable vegetable and root—both wild from the mountainside and grown in the gardens of the guests—next to tangy pickles and salted pork. It took much growling from Buck to keep the small hands settled in their laps until Nel blessed the meal and thanked all the guests who had traveled near and far to be with him.

Ray sat between Sally and a Cherokee elder. "Won't forget what Nel did for me," the silver-headed man said as he jabbed at a piece of vinegar-soaked greens. "Summer of fifty-five. The Ripe Corn Moon, if I recall. Hunting this big old black bear with my sons. She tore a chunk out of my side with her claws before I took her down. Right fortunate Nel was visiting Thomas Black Beaver at the time. My sons got me into the village, half-emptied of all my blood. . . ."

Across the table, Si abruptly stopped chewing.

"Nel fixed me up good," the man said, raising his cup of

sassafras beer in Nel's direction and saying something Ray couldn't understand.

Nel laughed from the end of the table and replied back in the man's language.

"I didn't know Nel spoke Cherokee," Sally whispered to Ray.

"I've learned all kinds of things about him over the past two days," Ray said. "Did you know Nel once fell over a waterfall?"

The Cherokee man laughed. "On a horse! Did you hear that part?"

"No!" Si said, leaning over the table to hear better.

"Nel came up at the bottom, but the horse never did. Horse belonged to his friend Chestoa. Doubt he ever forgave him for that. That was back in the old days, before . . ." The Cherokee looked embarrassed and called to Ox to pass him the roasted groundnuts.

"Before what?" Sally asked.

The man glanced at Nel and, seeing him engaged in conversation with the Ohio couple, whispered, "Before he lost his leg in all that John Henry business." Looking warily again at Nel, he added, "Ain't been the same since then. Lost his Rambler powers, you know."

Ray wanted to ask more but sensed the man's reticence to continue. "Who was Chestoa? A Cherokee?"

"No, a white man. My uncle helped him uncover the Elemental Rose. Chestoa was a Cherokee nickname my uncle gave him. Means 'rabbit.' What was his real name? I'll think of it."

Sally, her eyes bright with curiosity, asked, "Was it Bill Cobb?"

"Oh, yeah," the man said, turning to Sally. "Li'l Bill. You heard of him?"

Ray answered, "He's our father."

The Cherokee paused, giving Ray and then Sally a deep look and rubbing his jaw. "He was a good man. Powerful Rambler." Then he called down the table, "Nel, whatever happened to that little sorrel horse you used to own?" And the conversations turned from one story to another and then another.

After dinner was finished, the dishes were cleared and the tables moved to the porch. The oil lamps hanging from the rafters were lit. Gourd banjos, fiddles, and all manner of instruments were brought out of cases and sacks, and the players formed a half circle against the wall, talking to one another about which tunes to play. In the end, they deferred to Nel, since it was his birthday. Nel took his harmonica from his pocket and tapped it to his knee before saying, "How about *Ruckus Juice Stomp*!" As he began the melody, the hodge-podge band struck up behind him.

Ma Everett grabbed people's hands and pulled them to the dance floor. As the dancers squared off, she shouted out steps for them to follow. Ray tried to get Si to partner with him, but she said she was still feeling weak from her injury and settled next to Buck on a bench.

Ray danced with each of the younger girls: Naomi, Carolyn, Rosemary. He and Marisol passed several times on the dance floor, occasionally getting a few moments to dance together before partners were switched again. While wide, laughing mouths shone from the faces around the room, Ray noticed Marisol forcing a smile each time he looked at her.

When he discovered she was no longer on the dance floor, Ray thanked Sally for the dance with a silly dramatic bow and went to look for Marisol. He found her in the next room, moving plates into a tub of soapy water.

"Hey, there'll be time for cleaning up in the morning. Don't you want to dance?"

She dropped a handful of knives with a splash. "Somebody has to start on this cleaning."

"You can do it tomorrow," Ray said.

Marisol frowned. "And the day after that and the day after that . . ."

"What's the matter?" Ray asked.

Marisol tossed more silverware into the tub. "Nothing."

"Is it Ma Everett? I know she's been a little hard, but there's been a lot to do to get ready for the party."

Her cheeks grew red. "It's not Ma Everett. You . . . you wouldn't understand, Ray." She pushed past Ray as she strode out the door.

He followed her, passing from the thick warmth of the lodge into the drifting snowflakes on the porch. Marisol was in the shadows at the far end past the stacked tables, her hands clutching her bare elbows against the cold.

"You're right," Ray said. "I don't understand. Tell me what's going on, Marisol."

She turned, her lovely face more calm, but her almond eyes black and rimmed with tears. "It's my life here. Don't get me wrong. I love Shuckstack. But you, Ray . . . you get to wander off into the wild for months on end. You're learning all these things. You're becoming a Rambler. What am I doing?"

"Is it the show?" Ray asked. "Do you miss performing?"

"Sometimes." She shrugged. "But it's not just that. Look at Si. Even she gets to travel off with Buck."

"And what happened to her?"

"I know. That was horrible. But this . . ." She gestured to the lodge, to Shuckstack, to her life and what it had become. "This is not all I want. I need to get away."

Ray looked at his feet. "Are you going to leave? Is that what you're saying?"

"No!" Marisol put her hand to her temple. "No, that's not what I mean. I knew you wouldn't understand." She turned away, gripping the railing with clenched knuckles.

Ray saw goose pimples prickling across her arms in the cold. He was cold, too. He wanted to go back in, join the laughter and fun of Nel's celebration. But he knew whatever had boiled up in Marisol was something that had been coming for a long time. He had never fully appreciated all the responsibility that rested on her shoulders.

"What if you went with me sometime?" Ray asked.

Marisol lifted her head, thinking for a moment before turning. "Do you really mean that?"

"Sure. Why couldn't you come with me next time?"

"You don't think Nel would mind? You wouldn't mind?"

Ray smiled with a shrug. "I didn't know you wanted to. I

could take you over to the gorge. The laurels will be coming in soon and—"

Marisol's attention caught on something over Ray's shoulder. A man with a dark beard mounted the last step up to the porch. He shook the snow from his wide-brimmed hat.

"This Joe Nelson's place?"

Ray looked out in the dark and saw a horse tied up to a sapling in the yard. He had been so intent on his conversation with Marisol that he had not heard the horse's footsteps in the snow.

"Can we help you?" Ray asked.

"I sure hope so. Name's Herman Bradshaw. I come all the way from Kansas to find a Mister Joe Nelson. If he's the Rambler that Water Spider says, he's the only one who can help me."

Bradshaw broke into a fit of coughing such that he doubled over. Marisol went inside and soon Nel stepped out onto the porch after Buck and Si.

"Mister Bradshaw," Nel said, talking over the music and laughter flooding from the lodge. "Won't you come inside? You've traversed a fair distance, and we've got food and a warm fire."

Bradshaw twisted his hat in his hands and said, "I appreciate it, but I didn't come here to interrupt your party."

"We realize that it's not your intent, but you're here and it's late, so why don't you come in?"

"Frankly, what I've got to speak of ain't fit for the joy of that room yonder."

Nel turned to Si. "Will you get Mister Bradshaw a plate and some warm cider to drink? Bring it down to my room." Nel turned back to the man. "Let's go downstairs. There's a stove you can warm yourself by, and we can talk."

Nel led them down the stairs to an outside door to his room in the cellar. Ray followed with Buck and Marisol. Nel lit the stove and offered Bradshaw a chair. In the yellow glow of the room, Ray noticed how strangely discolored Bradshaw was. Ray had never seen anyone the unnatural shade of Mister Bradshaw. His white skin had an odd gray tint like paper turned to ash.

Nel asked, "Why have you come so far to find me, Mister Bradshaw?"

"If I were to tell it proper, it would take us all night, Mister Nelson. And I feel sore that I've taken you from your party, so I'll tell you as briefly as I can. I know you're friends with Water Spider of the Oklahoma Cherokee. I live up in Kansas, but he and I have become acquainted over the years. He says you're the only one who can help me."

"With what?"

"The Darkness." At these words, Bradshaw broke again into a terrible, hacking wet cough.

Something about the way he said the word drenched Ray in iciness.

Before Nel could continue, Si came down the stairs with the food and cider. Mister Bradshaw, released from the fit, wiped at his mouth and nodded his thanks to Si as he took the plate and mug. For a moment a curious expression passed over his brow as he seemed for the first time to notice the strange group of people all listening expectantly to his story.

Nel leaned forward from his stool. "What do you mean, the darkness?"

Mister Bradshaw set the plate on his lap, already forgotten as he collected his thoughts. "Where to begin? I come from Omphalosa, Kansas. Smack in the middle of the state. Came out there with my brothers when it was still just a territory. We made a good life for ourselves. Good, honest people there. Built a respectable town.

"I reckon we first noticed it around New Year, just over a year ago. With the passing of the winter solstice, days should have been lengthening. On the prairie, you count on the land and the weather for survival. You notice that kind of thing. Each day the sun set a little earlier, when it should have been later. And dawn just extended more and more into the morning."

Mister Bradshaw rubbed his clenched fist in his other hand as he continued. "By summer, we knew something was powerful wrong. The sun wouldn't rise until nearly eleven o'clock. Just pass in a low arc across the horizon and then drop again by two. By October, the Darkness set in for good."

Mister Bradshaw gauged the faces around him. Nel chewed on the end of his unlit pipe. Buck cocked his head. Ray, Marisol, and Si frowned.

"I suspect you take me for a fool or a madman, mayhaps. I ain't, but I've no way to assure you of that except through my words. Some from our town traveled out from time to time, visiting acquaintances, trading goods. They found the same. It weren't near the same complete darkness that had covered Omphalosa, but it settled in bit by bit. A darkness spreading over the towns of the prairies! You head out for a hundred miles any direction of Omphalosa and you'll see the growing dark.

"Can you imagine eternal Darkness, sir?" Mister Bradshaw asked, looking at Nel. "And cold. It's turned our flesh this fearsome shade. I had to leave. Fever took me after I left. No doctor can cure it. It's a slow, lingering killer. I'm afraid I've got it."

Nel's eyes widened with apprehension, and Mister Bradshaw waved a hand. "Don't worry, sir. It's not contagious. It comes from being in contact with the Darkness. Your people are safe.

"As I was saying, Omphalosa ain't the same town I helped settle years back. People are scared, powerful scared. Preacher says the Darkness and the discoloration of our skins are plagues. A curse laid upon us by God for our wickedness. We are good people, as good as you'll ever meet. But something about the Darkness, sir, it's turned us. Family against family. Brother on brother. Fingers pointing. Accusations swirling about what others done to bring the Darkness on us.

"My brother got shot 'cause some folks said his black dog was seen wandering around the churchyard by his house. A dog! What kind of foolishness is this, I ask?" He spread his hands with the question, then, shaking his head, dropped his arms to his knees. "Superstitious idiots. I knew it had to be something else, but I weren't going to stick around to find it out."

"You said you knew Water Spider?" Nel asked.

Bradshaw sat up straighter. "Right. Water Spider. I met him trading horses. We hit it off, you could say. Like to play cards and such whenever I'm over his way. I rode out to consult him. The Darkness didn't reach as far as the Indian country, but he was already aware of it. Got an Indian boy with him said you raised."

"Redfeather." Nel nodded.

"The boy was about to come back here, he says, to tell you about it. I told them I'd had enough. I'm heading back to my people in Virginia, but I needed to find you and deliver the news. Redfeather says you can help."

Mister Bradshaw coughed deeply, finally seeming to remember the mug of cider cooling in his hand. He drained it in a long gulp.

"That's a strange story, Mister Bradshaw," Nel said. "I know you've come far out of your journey to relay it to us. But . . . I'm not sure what we can do for you—"

"You ain't doing it for me," Mister Bradshaw answered quickly, wiping his mouth with a handkerchief. "I'm finished with Omphalosa. I feel the effects of the Darkness. It pulls on me. I've got this terrible urge to return, and many days in my travels I had to force myself not to turn back west. It works on you. The Darkness draws until I feel like some reverse moth—not longing for the flame but for the dark beyond.

"I had to leave before . . . Going to start me a farm and

hope the Darkness don't reach the East. But it's the people in Omphalosa. There's still good people there. It's them you'd be helping. They ain't all like the ones that shot my brother. And if somebody don't help them, there's to be a lot more burying before it's all done."

Nel turned to Buck, whose silver-streaked locks nearly hid his closed eyes.

"Sir," Ray began tentatively. "Were there any strangers in your town back when the Darkness started?"

"Strangers? There's workers for the mill, and I guess there's always the rare traveler passing through."

"Men wearing bowler hats?"

Mister Bradshaw snorted. "I don't keep track of the fashion of everyone who sets foot in Omphalosa."

"Ray," Nel said, frowning.

"You know what I'm asking, Nel," Ray said, his voice respectful and calm.

"There could be another explanation for all this," Nel said.

Then Buck said to Mister Bradshaw in his gravelly voice, "I think what young Ray is asking is, are there agents who ever work in Omphalosa?"

"Agents? Like Pinkerton detectives?" asked Mister Bradshaw.

Buck nodded.

"Well, there's a man who built a mill a decade or so back. That's why them foreign workers been coming in. He had a few detectives overseeing the construction to make sure there weren't no local trouble with the business being started."

Nel gripped his knees, glaring at Buck and refusing to look at Ray.

"Come to think of it," Mister Bradshaw began, but broke into a wracking cough. "Those Pinkertons . . ." His coughing got louder and his face turned a darker gray. "Those agents . . . ," he tried again, but could not get the words out.

"They . . . they . . ." Bradshaw slipped from his chair, but not before Ray caught him. Bradshaw's horrible cough grew deeper and wetter.

"Marisol!" Nel barked, getting to his feet and clapping his hand against Bradshaw's back. "Get that jug of water."

Marisol rushed to grab the crock and filled Bradshaw's mug. But Bradshaw could not drink the water, his coughing grew so fierce.

"The agents . . ." He choked again. Before he brought his handkerchief over his mouth, a splattering of blood hit Ray on the back of his hand. Bradshaw looked up at Ray and choked, "They . . . wore . . . bowlers."

Bradshaw's eyes rolled, and he passed out.

"Ray, Buck," Nel ordered. "Get him on that cot. Bring me damp rags."

Ray stared at the speckle of blood on his hand.

"Ray!" Nel barked.

Ray touched his finger to the blood.

"What is it?" Nel asked.

Ray looked at Nel in shock, dabbing his finger across the blood. He sniffed it and held his finger up. The smear was not red, but dark, inky black. "His blood . . . it's oil!"

~3~

WINTERGREEN

BY THE NEXT MORNING, THE GUESTS HAD ALL HEARD about the man burning up with a strange fever. Nel tended him, trying tonic after tonic, sending Dmitry or Mattias out to find this herb or that root. But no matter what Nel tried, Bradshaw got worse as the day went on.

Bradshaw, no longer conscious of where he was or the people around him, began periodically screaming. The guests anxiously started leaving, and soon all were gone but the Everetts, who agreed to stay and help distract the children by taking them fishing or anything to keep them away from the lodge, where Bradshaw's terrible cries unnerved them all.

As evening fell, Bradshaw finally quieted. Ray helped Nel, as they put cloth after wet cloth on the man's burning forehead. Bradshaw's vision failed, and he stared blindly at the ceiling mumbling about the Darkness. By midnight, he was dead.

* * *

Ma Everett fried up fish for supper the following night. It had been a long day. Mister Bradshaw was buried on a knoll beyond the millpond, and an unsettling quiet descended over the residents of Shuckstack. As Ray sat down at the table, weary and exhausted, he noticed that Nel had not joined them.

To be certain, someone would have to see this Darkness. That would mean going west. All day—as he had helped Buck dig Bradshaw's grave, as he had covered the man with earth—he had been thinking about the strange story. With sick reluctance, Ray realized there was nobody else from Shuckstack who could go. He had to find out. He had to go to Kansas and investigate the Darkness.

The following morning, Ray was helping Mattias and Sally till the garden plot. The topmost crust of earth was still brittle with frost, but below, the dark, moist soil crumbled easily around their hoes. As Mattias and Sally discussed what vegetables to plant, Ray saw Nel walking along the far bank of the millpond.

"I'll be back," Ray said, leaning his hoe against the split rail fence that bordered the garden.

When Ray rounded the millpond, Nel had already disappeared into the forest. He was easy to track. Ray scanned the brown carpet of leaves until he found the circular breaks made by Nel's wooden leg. He knew he was following the right path, as ferns, flattened with Nel's passing, were slowly rising back into place. Soon Ray caught up with Nel kneeling to collect a bright cluster of wintergreen.

"Making a Gambler's Hand Rub?" Ray asked.

Nel shook the loose dirt off the roots and wrapped the herb in a wet cloth before placing it into his sack. "No, Missus Maynard's still got plenty on her shelves." Nel took Ray's hand as he stood. "Have you noticed any cinquefoil around?"

Ray nodded. "I think there should be some over this way." He led Nel toward the creek that fed the millpond. Pushing back the leaves and ferns, Ray exposed the early shoot of a plant with five leaves. "Five-finger grass?"

"That's the one," Nel said. "Still too early for the flowers, but take some of the leaves."

Ray plucked the small leaves. "Cinquefoil's for gambling also. You planning a card game with Mister Everett?"

Nel chuckled. "You've picked up a thing or two from me about my tonics. I'm glad I've taught you something. No, these aren't for me. Wintergreen and cinquefoil are good for gamblers' luck, but they're protective herbs also. Good for those making long journeys."

Ray turned sharply. "Are these for me?"

Nel's careworn face tensed as he nodded. "To protect you from the Darkness."

Ray didn't reply. Nel continued walking, looking around at the trees. "The ash tree," Nel pointed up the slope. "Also good for safe travel. Ensures that those who leave will also return."

Ray followed him. "I didn't think you'd want me to go."

"I didn't. I don't." Nel pushed a hand to his knee above the wooden leg as they climbed through the forest. "But we have no choice. Ray, I didn't want to believe that the Machine was still powerful. I believed . . . I hoped that with the Gog's death, the Machine was, for all good purposes, dead with him. All I've wanted is for you and the others to be safe here at Shuckstack."

He sighed before continuing. "But that's changed. Bradshaw brought a piece of the Darkness, a sign of the coming threat of the Machine, to our very doorstep. It fills me with a deep and weary sadness, Ray, but I have to finally face the truth."

Ray was not sure if he felt relief that Nel finally agreed with him or sad that he was right all along about the Machine's threat. "What do you want me to do?"

"Go first and find Redfeather and Water Spider. I trust Water Spider's counsel. He is wise, and I'm sure he has been looking into what is at the root of this Darkness. Meet with him. Then find out what's going on in Omphalosa. Investigate the town and the Darkness. See if these agents are really Bowlers or ordinary Pinkertons. Be careful. No unnecessary risks. I want you two to come back safely—"

Startled, Ray asked, "I'm not going alone?"

Nel's wooly brows lowered over his eyes. "I'm sending Marisol with you."

"Marisol?" Ray asked.

"Yes. She was the one who convinced me that you two needed to go investigate the Darkness. She said you'd already discussed it, and that she was joining you."

Marisol! With all that had happened, Ray had forgotten about his promise to Marisol.

"You act surprised," Nel said.

"I am," Ray said as he followed Nel through the forest. "I told her I'd take her with me on a trip, but that was before Bradshaw arrived. I didn't mean to take her on something like this. What about Buck? Why can't he help me?"

"Buck can't risk leaving Shuckstack now. He's wanted for the murder of a law man. He can't go, not with a bounty on his head."

"Si, then!"

Nel shook his head slowly as he placed the cinquefoil and wintergreen in a small pouch. "I wish she could. She's still too weak, Ray. If she travels now, if she comes in contact with that illness from the Darkness, she might not recover. It's too much of a risk. No, Marisol will go with you. I wish she didn't have to, but it is the best of a bounty of bad options."

Ray looked down at his feet as he walked.

"Have faith in her, Ray," Nel said. "I think we have all underestimated Marisol. I especially have been guilty of it. She will prove herself."

Nel reached the ash tree. He bent to collect several of the leaves lying on the ground. Crushing them in his hand, he sprinkled them into the pouch.

"Ray, the Nine Pound Hammer is broken. And so we have no means to destroy the Machine. You've become a powerful Rambler. But make no mistake, son, you cannot destroy the Gog's Machine."

Ray considered this for several moments before replying, "Then who will, Nel?"

Nel handed the pouch of protective charms to Ray. "That is an important question, isn't it? I'll seek Mother Salagi's counsel. Come on. Let us get you ready for your journey."

"When I said you could come with me sometime, I meant *here*," Ray said. "Just out into the mountains for a few days."

Marisol had her dresses and supplies spread out on her bed. Javidos coiled on her quilt and darted his tongue at Ray. In the next room, the kitchen was noisy with the voices of the children and the clattering of Ma Everett cooking supper.

"He wouldn't have wanted you to go otherwise," Marisol said.

"I don't need Nel's permission."

Marisol opened the clasps on a floral-patterned valise. "You needed his blessing. Now you'll both feel better about your going."

"But why do you want to go?" Ray lowered his voice.

Marisol cut her black almond eyes at Ray as she folded a dress to place in the valise. "Don't you remember what we talked about?"

"Of course, but—" Ray shifted.

"Don't you think I'm brave enough?"

"Yes, but—"

Marisol aimed a finger at his nose. "I was there when we faced the Hoarhound. I was there when we fought the Gog's agents on the *Ballyhoo*. I have courage, Ray."

"That's not what I'm saying."

"Then what are you saying?" Marisol asked, putting her

hand on her hip. At Ray's hesitation, she added, "If you don't want me to go, just say so."

"I just want you to be sure you know what we might be facing."

"I know, Ray. As well as you, anyway."

Ray shrugged. "Then I suppose we'll leave in the morning."

"I'll be ready." She nodded and turned back to her packing.

Ray passed through the kitchen to go upstairs. He traveled with very little, but he decided to gather what few supplies he would need. "Supper'll be ready in about half an hour," Ma Everett called as he ascended the stairs.

At first Ray thought the loft was empty, but then he noticed Sally at the far end reading by the solitary window. Coming closer, he saw *The Incunabula of Wandering* open in her lap. Sally seemed frozen, almost as if she were in a trance, the way she always appeared when she read the book. She turned the page with a quick flick of her hand, and then returned to her statue-like state. She did not even realize Ray was standing behind her chair until he brushed his hand across her hair.

"Ray!" She looked straight up and then pulled herself around sideways in the chair.

Ray's eye fell on the open page, to a long poem.

"What are you reading?" Ray asked.

"Oh," Sally said, tracing her fingers along the lines. "It's this song, called the Verse of the Lost. And look here. It says something about the Elemental Rose in this line. Remember what that Cherokee elder said? Father helped figure out what the Elemental Rose was." Sally eyes shone with wonderment. "What do you think the Elemental Rose is?"

"I wouldn't know, Sally. I've never understood poems very well."

"The Verse of the Lost isn't a poem," Sally continued. "Not in the real sense. I just want to figure out what Father was—"

"Sally, I need to tell you something." She opened her mouth to continue, but Ray spoke first. "I'm leaving in the morning."

Sally's eyelashes batted against her cheeks. "What? Where are you going?"

"Kansas."

"Th-the Darkness," she said, her voice pitched with anxiety. "I heard Si talking to Buck about it. They said the Darkness killed Mister Bradshaw!"

"Don't worry," Ray said, touching a hand to the toby beneath his shirt. "Nel made me a protective charm. I'll be fine."

She grabbed his hand, squeezing it hard. "But why are you going, Ray? Is this about the Machine?"

"We have to find it—"

"But you need to cross to reach it." Sally spoke rapidly, desperately. "Can't you stay here and keep working on learning how to take animal form? You don't have to go out there to learn to cross. Once you learn, then you can just cross from here. You could find the Machine from anywhere. Then you can destroy it. You don't have to go out to that Darkness."

"It's not like that, Sally," Ray said, moving around until he knelt before her, resting his arms on her knees, holding her hands. "Do you remember last fall when I went down to Georgia?"

Sally lifted her chin with the slightest nod.

"I met a Creek Indian, Aunt Harjo. Her grandfather was a Red Stick, a powerful medicine man. She said her grandfather had learned how to take animal form and to cross into the Gloaming. She told me from what she understood that places within this world corresponded to particular places within the Gloaming. And to move within the Gloaming was to move within a world that followed no map. If I'm to reach the Machine, I must cross at the location where Grevol placed it. I have to find its source in our world first."

"Kansas," she said softly. "You think the Machine is in Kansas?"

"We'll find out."

She leaned forward, hugging him tightly. "I don't want you to go," she whispered.

"I'll be okay." Ray held her a moment before saying, "I need you to do something for me, Sal."

She pulled back. "What? Look something up in the *Incunabula*? I could find out if—"

"No, it's something I need you to keep." He opened the buttons at his collar and pulled up the toby. "The rabbit's foot."

He took out the golden foot. Mother Salagi had told Ray to keep it safe. He could not risk bringing it with him into the Darkness. If the foot was to be safe, it should stay at Shuckstack.

"Remember what's in this rabbit's foot?" Ray asked.

"A lodestone?"

"From Father. He gave it to me before you were born, the last time I saw him. He told me the lodestone would lead me back to him. It did. It led me to him when it became the rabbit's foot. Now I'm giving it to you so you'll know that I'll return safely. Will you keep it safe?"

"Of course." She leaned forward once more, hugging him, squeezing him like she wouldn't let him go. "I'm scared," she said.

"Don't be."

Her soft cheek was pressed against his. She smelled of Shuckstack, of a nice wood fire and spring flowers and the spicy herbs drying in Nel's room. She smelled of the sweet smell of his home.

"But Father . . . ," Sally whispered. "He never came back."

"I'll come back."

She released him enough so that she could see his face, her large eyes searching his. "You will? You promise?"

Ray put the rabbit's foot in Sally's cupped palm, closing her fingers over it. He squeezed her hand. "I promise."

THE SLEEPING GIANT

CONKER SLEPT AT THE BOTTOM OF THE WELL.

Five fathoms deep and filled with clear green spring water, the well was known to the sirens as *Nascuits ai Élodie* or Élodie's Spring. It was a place of healing—secret, secluded, and sacred.

Élodie's Spring lay in a recessed marsh surrounded on three sides by rock outcroppings. To a wanderer, the base of the bluff would look overgrown with a wild tangle of ferns and cattails and the skein of jeweled spiderwebs. No spring could be seen bubbling from the rock. And even if a wanderer had chanced upon the overgrown corner of the wild, he or she would have felt inexplicably compelled to continue traveling. Unless that traveler was a siren.

When Jolie had at last found the spring, she had pulled Conker's body down into the healing waters. She wove a blanket of reeds to cover him and pinned the edges with large stones to keep him from floating to the surface.

There he slept. Jolie did not know how long it would take for him to heal.

When she had first reached the spring, the woods were green with high summer. Soon autumn fell, and red and copper leaves blanketed the silver outcropping surrounding the well.

Jolie watched and waited, swimming down several times each day to check on Conker. He slept, and she could only hope he was healing.

The winter brought little snow but cold nights, and Jolie often slept in the spring's waters by Conker's side. His body was beginning to mend. She could feel it as she touched his chest and muscles and bones. But he did not wake.

And at last—after so long on Jolie's lonesome watch—spring arrived. And with it so did her first visitor.

Electric green leaves wove a canopy over the well. In the shade, Jolie sat mashing cattail tubers that she had boiled for her evening meal. Something or someone was watching her.

Were the months of isolation driving her to invent worries? She considered it even as she listened for a footstep or a snap of a twig. All she heard was the chatter of the birds, the cedar waxwings and martins, gathering at the siren spring's headwaters.

She turned her head a fraction and sniffed as she continued to crush the warm white tubers with the whittled spoon. She could smell nothing unusual to the sheltered spring. Her senses told her that something had approached the well, but maybe it was just a deer or wandering bear. It couldn't be a person.

With a forked stick, she lifted hot rocks from the fire and dropped them into the water-filled bladder at her feet. The heat lifted the aroma of the cooking fish, and she inhaled hungrily.

At the quick snapping of bracken several yards away, Jolie turned. A blurred form burst from the underbrush and leaped upon her. Ferocious instinct took over and Jolie fought, kicking up with her bare feet, tearing and slashing with her fingernails. The attacker growled at the blows, and the two thrashed until Jolie was pinned at the elbows, her face turned into the earth as the attacker held Jolie by her tangled hair. The hard edge of a blade pressed against Jolie's throat.

As a final defense, Jolie began the high, warbling song sirens used to control others. The blade was released from her throat as the attacker gasped, *"Sirmoeur!"*

Jolie turned her head and looked up.

She was tall, taller than Jolie, and a few years older. Her hair was golden red, almost to the point of being pink where the sun shone through the wisps. Her skin was pale, silvery. But unlike Jolie's skin, hers shimmered iridescent, like the belly of a trout, swirling and shifting with faint hues of red and green and blue when she moved.

The siren scrambled off Jolie, throwing the blade to the side as she passionately took Jolie in her arms and pulled her into an embrace. "*Sirmoeur!* Jolie, *meu sirmoeur!*" she cried over and over.

"Sister?" Jolie was startled to hear her siren tongue. "It is you, Cleoma?"

"Yes, yes, Jolie. You are alive!" Cleoma said. "I thought we had lost you. Forgive me for hurting you. Are you injured?" She ran her fingers over Jolie's forehead, where a pink welt was rising and blood speckled where she had been scratched.

Jolie was too surprised to feel where she had been struck. She stared at her siren sister, thinking she must be some delusion that would vanish if she blinked. But Cleoma was real. She was here, in front of Jolie against all reason.

"No, I'm fine," Jolie choked, half laughing, half sobbing.

Cleoma took Jolie's hands in hers as she said, "I had no idea it was you. I was coming to *Nascuits ai Élodie,* when I saw someone hunched over a cook fire. I thought the well's blessed waters were violated. But it is you, *meu sirmoeur!* Jolie, my sister."

"Are the others with you?" Jolie said, looking eagerly to the bracken where Cleoma had emerged.

"No, I am alone," she said. "I have come for the waters, to bring them back to our sisters in the Terrebonne."

"They have returned from the open sea?"

"Yes, we learned of the Gog's death and have come home. But listen—something terrible has happened."

"What is it?" Jolie asked.

Cleoma sat back on her heels. She spread her hands

across her gown, the woven grasses not nearly so frayed as Jolie's. "A sickness is spreading among the sisters. It began with the elders, but now even the young and strong are falling to it. Isabeau was the first to take the fever. She would not eat or swim. We gave her boneset and honey in hot water, but the fever did not break. Then she lost her sight. Soon others were sick, too."

"Dear Isabeau!" Jolie gasped. "Is she . . ."

"She has returned, Jolie," Cleoma said. "Inez and Breaux, too. But before they died, when the fever drove their minds where they could no longer recognize us, each mumbled over and over about 'an eternal night'—the world covered in an endless dark. Whether it was the blindness or a vision of something more, we could not tell."

"No." Jolie brushed her hand against the tears. "What is causing this fever?"

Cleoma took a deep breath, putting her hand over Jolie's. "Before it began, our sisters who eventually got sick traveled up the Mississippi to the Missouri River and then the Platte. They were drawn by a strange call. We were not sure what was summoning the sirens, but a group followed it. I did not go. None of the younger sisters did.

"They returned with a strange tale. They encountered a place with an odd half-darkness. They never knew what was causing it, maybe an eclipse, maybe smoke. Or maybe it was something else. We have not discovered if the darkness carried a curse, but the well's waters must be able to stop the sickness. That is why I must hurry back. I must bring the waters to those who can still be saved."

Cleoma ran her hand gently across the tears on Jolie's cheeks. Then her pale-silver eyes widened as a curious expression came upon her face. "But why are you here at our spring, Jolie?"

Jolie rose and took Cleoma's hand, leading her to the mouth of the well. "Come, *sirmoeur*. I have something to show you."

As night fell and the ocean of stars drifted above, Jolie and Cleoma shared the fish and cattail tubers before the fire. Jolie finished telling her sister the long tale of her time with Nel's medicine show and their encounter with the Gog. Cleoma often turned her troubled gaze back to the well.

"But how do you know he will awaken?" Cleoma finally asked when Jolie had finished. "It has been nearly a year."

"He has started moving lately," Jolie said. "When I first brought him here, his body was broken. Now he is mended, blessed are the waters. I think it will not be long until he wakes."

Cleoma's brow twisted and her lowered eyes narrowed. "Then he may no longer need you guarding over him, Jolie. Come back with me to the Terrebonne."

Jolie's stomach felt as if she had swallowed the hot stones that had cooked their dinner. "I cannot."

"Why not?"

"Conker is my friend. He will need my help when he awakens."

Cleoma's eyes saddened. "I know your sisters would want badly to see you again, Jolie. They need you. I need you." Cleoma leaned closer to Jolie. "Return with me so we can tend to them in this dark time. Do not abandon them, *sirmoeur.*"

An old anger rose in Jolie. When she lifted her eyes to her sister, Cleoma flinched.

"*Sirmoeur,* you call me!" Jolie hissed. "You, dear sister, accuse me of abandonment? Who abandoned me almost two years ago, Cleoma? Who left me alone in the Terrebonne when the Gog's Hound was hunting us?"

"The Rambler men . . . they were protecting you."

"The Hound killed them all. Only Buck saved me."

Fear crackled in Cleoma's face. "You know we could not have taken you with us, Jolie. You are not like us. Your father was not song-bound. Your mother violated tradition when she took him. You could not survive in the open sea. We . . . we had no choice."

"No choice?" Jolie whispered. "You had a choice and you made it. Conker had a choice on the Gog's train. He could have made it to safety, but he chose to save me. I had a choice when I found Conker in the river. I took him here. I have tended and watched over him for this past year. I will not leave him now."

Cleoma's lips trembled as a long silence passed between them. "You are right," she said at last. "If what you say is true, only Conker can destroy the Gog's terrible engine. I should not ask you to leave him."

Cleoma got to her feet. She pulled the skins, filled with the spring's waters, over her shoulder. "The journey home is long, and who knows how many of our sisters will perish before I return. I hope you will forgive us, Jolie. We never should have left you."

Jolie stood. The long-festering resentment that had so swiftly erupted was dissolving. Jolie's heart grew sick at the thought of Cleoma leaving, sick with desire to be once again among her sisters.

"I do forgive you," Jolie said softly. "If you had stayed with me, the Hound might have captured you, and who knows what the Gog would have done with you. I have been angry with you and our sisters for too long, Cleoma, and I want no longer to hold it."

Cleoma pulled her knife from her belt of braided grass. She handed it to Jolie. The blade was gray and pink, a long conch shell filed to a sharp edge.

"Take it," Cleoma said. "I am swimming quiet waterways back home. Where you are going, you will need it more than I."

The whorl was covered in a tight wrap, and Jolie's fingers closed tentatively around the handle. A siren's knife was one of her few worldly possessions. When she was with her sisters, Jolie had not been old enough to need one. She knew Cleoma must have spent a long time seeking the right shell with the proper weight and patiently crafting the weapon. Jolie had never known a siren to give away her knife. Even the dead returned to the sea with the knives tied to their hands.

"Thank you," Jolie said. "I will return it to you one day."

Cleoma nodded and embraced Jolie, kissing her several times before turning to go toward the stream.

"Be swift," Jolie called to her sister. She wanted to send some message with Cleoma, but she was already gone. The dark waters left no ripple to show her passage.

For several days, Cleoma traveled. The stream from the well became a creek, and after a time, it met a river. When she could swim no farther, she found a bed of soft grasses down at the river's bottom. She did not allow herself to rest long, and when she woke, night had fallen.

She emerged from the water to hunt a quick meal before continuing. In the reeds growing along the river's edge, she left the waterskins, wanting to keep her hands free as she hunted. As she came up into a forest thick with the sound of frogs and insects, she smelled the men—two of them—before she saw their campfire.

Through the dense shadows of the trees, the glow of their fire formed a balloon of flickering orange. She could not see the men from her distance, and considered returning to the river to swim past them and look for food elsewhere. But she wondered: if the men were already asleep, it might be easier to steal a meal from their cook pots. This would be the quickest option, so she crept closer, her bare feet making no sound as she drew near their camp.

She could not see the men until she was nearly to the edge of the fire's light. The two men were awake. An animal, reduced to little more than blackened bones, was mounted on a spit over the flames. The men ate greedily, tearing the meat off in their teeth and licking at the grease dripping from their hands. Their rough appearance—each man wore a pistol or two at his belt, and the handle of a knife protruded from one's boot—told Cleoma these were not simple farmers out on a hunting trip. These were dangerous men. She began to back away toward the creek.

When she had gone a few steps, she turned to run, but slammed abruptly into the chest of a third man. He had her by the arm before she could escape.

"Don't you make a noise," the man whispered. "It's best my boys don't know you're here."

Cleoma's breath drew in quick gasps and she tried to back away. But as she did, the man's grip tightened. She struggled, digging her fingertips into his arm, but when the edge of a long razor touched her stomach just below her rib cage, she stopped her fight.

Where had the man come from? How had she not heard him moving in the forest behind her?

She stared up into the man's penetrating face. He had a square, chiseled jaw and cheekbones: a black man who wore a neatly trimmed mustache just above his upper lip. His clothes were fine, unlike those of the other two, and he wore a crisply creased gray Stetson hat, as handsome as any constable's.

"There's no need for any singing neither," he said. "See, I know you're a siren, and even though I ain't never met one of you, I know about your songs."

Something was wrong with the man, Cleoma knew this. She could sense the presence of the two men behind her by the fire. She could sense other animals—night birds, bullbats, creeping opossums, even the men's horses—nearby. But this man might as well have been a tombstone for all the life she could sense in him.

"What's your name, siren?" he asked in his slow, soft voice.

Cleoma hesitated. She was confused by the almost casual cordiality of his inflection. Maybe he would not hurt her. Maybe he just wanted to scare her and then he would let her go.

"Cleoma," she answered.

"I'm Stacker, Stacker Lee," he said. "See, Cleoma, when I was birthed, I had me a caul over my face. You know what that means?"

Cleoma shook her head, her lips clenched tight.

"It means I know things. I was born with a certain sight. Always been blessed with perceiving things, if you follow me. Take your intentions, for instance. You're hoping to save someone."

Cleoma tensed, and Stacker smiled.

"See? I was right. Let me tell you something else I know. I know that if I keep following this river up to a creek, I'll find a man. I've never met this man. Don't even know what he looks like. But I'll know him when I find him, 'cause he's the son of John Henry. There ain't no mistaking that, is there? Did you, Cleoma, come from upstream?"

Cleoma looked from Stacker's passive face to the razor at her gut. She nodded.

"And did you, Cleoma, encounter a man that could be John Henry's son?"

Cleoma shook her head. For a moment, Cleoma was

uncertain whether Stacker had understood her or whether he knew she was lying. He held his blank stare for several terrible moments before his gaze relaxed.

"You know why I'm looking for this man, Cleoma?"

Cleoma tightened her lips as she shook her head again.

"This man, who is John Henry's son, has his father's Nine Pound Hammer, or so I've been told. If I can bring this hammer back to my employer, he will generously return something he never should have taken from me. I bet you'd never guess what he took. Want to guess?"

Cleoma's breathing got quicker and she pulled experimentally at his grip. A dry smile curled at the corner of Stacker's lips. "Not until I've finished my story, Cleoma. So you don't want to guess? I'll tell you. My employer took my heart. That's right, my heart. I know what you're thinking. That I don't mean this in the literal sense, but, dear Cleoma, it will surprise you to know that when I say this man took my heart, I am not speaking poetically."

At this, Stacker tapped the blunt end of the razor to his sternum. "Clockwork. That's what I've got now—a chest full of clockwork." An expression of sadness flickered in his eyes for a moment, but Cleoma did not know if it was for her or for himself.

"I want to be a man again. I want to be alive again. To feel things as a man should. I can have my heart back if I bring the Nine Pound Hammer to my employer.

"I'm telling you this, Cleoma, because I have heard about the waters of the siren springs. They can heal anything, can't they? Well, if you know of such a place"—he brought the razor up and flicked his thumb gently across the edge—"or you were in possession of such waters, I would be most grateful. If it can rid me of this clockwork curse filling my chest . . . well, Cleoma, you would save me a further trip up this river. I wouldn't have to find this son of John Henry, or his damned hammer. You could save me, Cleoma."

Stacker waited, the cold expectant stare boring into her. Did the man know she had the waters, hidden in the reeds just at the river's edge? No, he would not need to torment her if he did.

She could give him the waters—for he was right, the waters could cure him, as they cured any affliction except death—but then she would have to go back. The time spent swimming back to Élodie's Spring might cost the lives of some of her sisters, and it might also bring harm to Jolie and the giant sleeping in the well. She knew she could not trust this Stacker Lee.

"Well, Cleoma?" Stacker said, sticking out his tongue to the edge of his narrow mustache.

Cleoma tried to take a deep breath, but she could only gasp with fear and confusion. How could a man have a clockwork heart? But she knew his words to be true. She knew it because she could not sense Stacker as alive, like she could the other men or the animals of the forest.

That Stacker was not lying frightened her most.

She had to get away. She had no other choice. She said quickly, "I cannot help you. I do not have any of the waters." Then she released her song, piercing and shrill. A song that had held a herd of deer motionless when she hunted. A song that had charmed a dozen fishermen as she passed by their boat.

As Cleoma began to pull from his grasp, Stacker clinched her arm tighter. "That is really regrettable," he said. "I want to be . . . I just want to remember what it's like . . ."

He waved the razor swiftly across her throat. Cleoma had no time to cry out, no time to feel pain. She sank to the ground.

". . . to be a man again." Stacker looked down at Cleoma's still face and folded the blade of the razor into its pearl handle and dropped it into his pocket.

—5—

ÉLODIE

TO HIDE THE HARSH GLARE OF THE FIRELIGHT, JOLIE buried the coals of the cook fire. They would remain hot under the earth until morning. The stars overhead were bright enough to cast a shadow, and she gazed up at them for a long time.

Her sister Cleoma had been traveling for many hours now. Jolie imagined following Cleoma, swimming free in the creek and following the waters back to her Terrebonne home, where she wanted desperately to return. Had the fever spread? Would Cleoma need help tending the sisters? How many lives could extra hands save? Maybe Cleoma had been right. What would she be able to do for Conker—if and when he finally awoke?

This gnawing sense of regret brought a sudden weariness, and Jolie retired to the well. She pushed back the plants and dropped into the deep, black waters. As her body drifted down, she closed her eyes and felt the spring soothe away her troubled thoughts. After a short time, sleep came over her. She sank to the bottom of the well.

A cold hand clamped around her ankle.

Jolie's eyes sprang open. She screamed a fountain of bubbles and kicked, but another hand clutched her leg and pulled her down. Great balloons of air ascended from the dark below.

Conker!

Shaking off sleep and fear, Jolie ran her fingers down to Conker's hands, following them over his arms until she had a grip around his shoulder. She kicked and clawed the rocks lining the well to bring him up. As they broke the surface, Conker gave a great cry.

"Conker! It is me," she said, holding him afloat and reaching for the edge of the well. "Can you see it is Jolie? I have you."

He choked and sputtered and bobbed back down. Pulling him by his massive arm, Jolie coaxed him to clutch the well's rock lip.

"Can you pull yourself up?"

Conker did not answer.

Jolie rose from the water and broke back the stems of the overhanging plants hiding the well. In the dim starlight, she saw his eyes, wide and searching and full of fear.

"Take my hand. I will help you up."

Conker did as she said. Jolie pulled with all her strength until the giant planted his feet on the rock and stood up from the well. His legs gave out as he rose, and he crashed down into the bracken.

"You are weak, Conker," she said, kneeling by him. "You have been asleep a long time. Rest here before you get up."

Conker was crouching on his hands and knees. His hair had grown thick and wooly during his long sleep. Jolie ran her fingers soothingly across his head. Conker began trembling and shaking. His skin was cold.

"I will build up the fire. Stay here. I will be back to help you in a moment."

Jolie rushed to collect the wood and uncover the coals. In minutes, the fire was ablaze.

Conker was as she had left him, still planted on his knees and still shivering. "Can you crawl?"

He did not answer, but at her urging hand, he followed her to the fire. Conker sat with his knees tucked to his chest, shaking. "Let me get you soup and tea," Jolie said. "It will warm you, and the herbs will help restore your strength."

Dashing to the small cave where she hid her food from prowling animals, Jolie brought out dried fish, herbs, and roots. As she prepared the meal, she kept her eyes on Conker. Although the well had nourished him, he was thin, his face gaunt, his body weak. She brought a wooden bowl over to him and held it up to his lips. "Sip slowly. You have not eaten in a long time. It is hot."

He gulped and, despite the heat, ravenously consumed the entire bowl in several swallows.

"Can you take this cup of tea while I get you more soup?"

Conker looked in her eyes for the first time. Recognition came over him. He nodded and held the wooden cup. Jolie spooned out more soup and brought it over.

"Take more, but try not to eat it too fast. Your stomach might not be ready for so much."

Conker sipped at the soup and the aromatic tea, his gaze shifting anxiously.

"You are in a safe place," she assured him. "It is a well used by my siren sisters. For healing. You were badly injured. Do you remember?"

Conker's bright white eyes stared at her, and he cocked his head. Then he closed his eyes, wincing. She was not sure whether he was troubled by what he remembered of the train or if he could not remember at all.

"It is okay," she said, thinking this response would do in either case. "There is much to tell, but it may still be too soon." She touched his neck and broad shoulder. "You feel as if you are warming. That is good."

Conker finished the soup and let the steaming cup of tea warm his hands. The night wore on, and Jolie was eager for Conker to speak, eager to help her friend in so many ways. He needed his hair cut. She would have to get him to try walking. But she made herself remain patient. As the faint light of dawn pushed aside the stars, she decided that the soup had not given his stomach trouble and that he should eat something more substantial.

"Conker," Jolie said. He lifted his head weakly. "I am going to catch us something for breakfast. Wait here. Do not get to your feet until I can help you. Agreed?"

He nodded, and after watching him a moment longer, Jolie took the conch shell knife and set off to hunt.

When she returned an hour later, Conker was sitting as she had left him, staring into the fire. She plucked the turkey and skinned the groundhog, and built up the fire to roast the game.

"How long?" Conker's voice was little more than a croak.

Jolie spun around. "You can speak!" She smiled tentatively.

"How long?" Conker repeated.

Jolie took a deep breath. "You were badly injured, Conker. The train . . . do you remember what happened on *The Pitch Dark Train*?"

He nodded slowly.

"You should be dead. The explosion. If you had not been wearing Redfeather's necklace—"

Conker's hand went to his chest. He clutched the copper head on the necklace, squeezing it tightly. "You look . . . different, Jolie."

Jolie stuck the game together on a spit and placed them over the fire.

"You're . . . taller." His voice gained strength. "You seem older."

Jolie prodded the logs to increase the flames.

"Jolie?"

She rose. "I need to get more—"

"How long have I been asleep?"

Jolie bit at her lip and turned. Conker stared urgently. "Almost a year," she said.

Whatever he had been expecting, she could tell he had not imagined it could possibly be that long. He sank back, his arms trembling to support him.

"Your body was broken, Conker. Only because of the well have you healed."

Conker was taking shallow, rapid breaths. His jaw clenched tight, and he ground his teeth as he tried to speak. "Where . . . where is it?"

"What?" Jolie asked, getting closer to Conker.

"The Nine Pound Hammer."

"I do not know, Conker. I did all I could just to save you."

"It's lost then?"

The roasting meat crackled, sputtered fat onto the flames. "You have been through so much, and it will take time for you to regain your strength. Please do not worry now."

Conker laid his forehead on his knees and was silent. Jolie continued to stare at him, hardly believing he was finally awake after so long. And now she felt as if she had done little to prepare herself for what to do next. Pulling her gaze away, she checked on their breakfast, rotating the spit.

"Where's the others?" Conker asked, lifting his head slightly.

Jolie shook her head. "I do not know."

"Ray? Nel? Si? You ain't seen them?"

"Not since we jumped from the train."

Conker looked at Jolie for a long time. "You've been alone, watching over me for . . . a year?"

"When I fell in the river, I found you first. I do not even know what happened to Ray. I knew only one way to save you and that was to take you here."

Conker reached out his enormous hand and Jolie took it. "I don't even know how to begin thanking you, Jolie."

"You are my friend, Conker. I am just glad you are better."

"I'm weak. I feel it. But that meat smells real good. Is it near ready?"

"Soon."

"Tell me what has happened. Tell me what you've done these many months."

"It will be a boring story, I fear."

"I want to hear it all the same."

Jolie began the story that began atop *The Pitch Dark Train*. She told how she carried Conker to the well. She told him of the passing seasons and her dreadful thoughts of losing Ray and the others and her resentment toward her siren sisters for their abandonment. She told Conker about Cleoma and of the sickness in the Terrebonne.

"What should we do now?" Jolie asked Conker. "Should we search for those pirates you befriended? They might know where Nel has gone with the others."

"I've been thinking on it while you were talking. I want to find Nel, to let him know I'm alive. He must think I'm dead. . . ." A deep sorrow broke on Conker's face. "But before that, can you lead me back to the trestle over the Mississippi?"

"I could find it again. But why?"

"We've got to look for the Nine Pound Hammer."

"Maybe Nel and the others found it."

"Maybe," Conker said. "But we don't know where they are. First, the river. I need you to search the river for it."

Jolie nodded. "Yes, when you are strong enough to travel."

"After that, Jolie, I think you ought to go back to the Terrebonne. The Gog is dead and your sisters have returned. They need you. You've spent too long looking after me."

Even after he had finished the entire turkey and the groundhog, Conker's appetite only seemed to grow. He was able to get to his feet but was still too weak to help Jolie hunt. She set off on her own, using her siren song and her conch shell knife to capture more game. Conker walked around the stream, gathering strength slowly.

That evening Jolie was amazed at how much Conker ate. No sooner had one meal been cooked than he was ready for another. She emptied every root and tuber from her cache in the cave, baking them in the coals until they were tender enough to be eaten.

By the next day, Conker was getting stronger. He tired quickly, but he was able to join Jolie to search for berries and nuts. As Jolie cut his hair with her knife, Conker asked, "What is this place?"

"The spring?"

"How did you know it was here?"

"I heard about it from my sisters. There are other springs like this—with waters that heal. This one is called *Nascuits ai Élodie,* or Élodie's Spring."

"Who was Élodie?" Conker asked as black knots of hair fell to his lap.

"My mother."

Conker looked around at Jolie, his eyes wide. "Your mother?"

Jolie pushed his head back down and continued with the knife. "Yes. I did not know her. Do you know why I am only part siren?"

Conker nodded. "Ray told me. He said your daddy was just a normal man."

"All sirens have normal men for fathers," she said. "But they are enchanted, made into husbands by our singing. My father was not like this. He was no sailor rescued from the cold sea. He gave his love freely to my mother."

"Who was he?"

"I do not know his name. My mother never had a chance to tell me, and the sisters did not remember what he was called. Élodie found him injured in the Terrebonne. The other sisters say he was an outlaw who took refuge in our swamp. My mother cared for his wounds for a time. She fell in love with this man. But after he recovered, he left her. Not long after I was born, my mother left me in the care of my sisters and searched for this man. She died here. I do not know if she ever found him again. Probably not."

"How did she die then?" Conker asked.

Jolie shrugged. "The sisters always said her heart had been poisoned by this wicked outlaw, for she had given her heart to him. This is not the way of our sisters. Love such as this is not . . . encouraged. I will not suffer the same fate as my mother."

Conker narrowed his eyes, but said nothing as Jolie continued cutting curls from his head.

"The wells are rare and secluded, as this one is," Jolie said after a moment. "They say the Spanish conquistadors sought them."

"Fountains of youth," Conker said, blowing a lock of hair from his lip.

"A siren's heart is very powerful. It bestows longevity, vitality. When a siren dies, her heart brings forth a healing spring from the roots of the earth that contains the powers of her heart. It is through my mother's death that you have been healed, Conker."

"So you reckon I'll live forever?" He chuckled.

Jolie lowered the knife and took a step out to examine Conker's haircut. She gave a satisfied nod and then grinned at Conker. "No, *Nascuits ai Élodie* can heal, but it does not bestow immortality. I would not be surprised, however—given how long you have stayed in the waters—if you live to a great old age."

Conker smiled a bitter smile as he brushed the loose hair from his shoulders. "I can only hope."

* * *

Over the next few days, Jolie hunted deer and rabbit and all manner of birds and game. She skinned and cooked and fed the fire. Conker helped her some with the tasks, but mostly he ate.

"You are putting on weight already," Jolie said one afternoon after returning with an armful of wild turnips.

"Ain't got much of a choice with all your hunting," he said.

The following morning, Jolie emerged from the well to find Conker already awake and building up the cook fire. "It's time to go," he announced.

"You feel strong enough?"

"We'll travel as far as I can, and stop to rest if I'm too tired. I've got to find the hammer."

Jolie took two bladders that she had been using for boiling water over to the well. She pulled back the bracken and submerged the bladders in the clear green spring, filling them with the well's healing waters.

"We have far to go," she said over her shoulder. "But let us hope there will not come a time that we need to use these waters."

Conker nodded. Soon they left the overgrown marsh, passing from the protective barrier that guarded the spring, and began their journey east toward the Mississippi River.

"You have pushed yourself too far," Jolie said midafternoon. They had been walking all day and the weather was warm. Conker had stumbled many times on the rocky trail along the north side of the creek.

"Just a little further." Conker got up on one knee but collapsed back again, panting.

Jolie sighed. "Rest, while I look for food."

Conker acceded with a frown.

Jolie had not been gone for more than half an hour when she returned with a harvest of Indian cucumber, sheep sorrel, and a pheasant. Where was Conker? Looking around curiously, she began to call but a hand clamped over her mouth.

"Don't say nothing."

Jolie dropped the food as she was pulled down to her knees. Conker released her and put his finger to his lips to whisper, "Quiet. There's men on the other bank."

Jolie heard the voices. She pulled the conch shell knife from her belt, as Conker pointed through the leaves.

A man with a dense black beard on a horse splashed down into the creek, his eyes searching their side of the bank and a stagecoach gun squared across the horse's shoulders.

"Alston!" another voice called from the forest on the other side of the creek. "Come on."

"Something moving over here," the man mumbled, squinting and swinging the gun around in Jolie and Conker's direction.

Two other men on horseback emerged on the far bank: one a filthy young man with longish blond hair and a pair of pistols at his belt, the other a neatly dressed black man with a tall, crisp hat on his head.

The black man spoke. "We'll have time for shooting dinner later. I want to get there tonight, even if we push on through dark."

Alston crossed a little deeper, the water splashing up onto his boots and pants legs.

The black man drew a long-barreled pistol from his jacket and cocked the lever. The gun erupted. Alston ducked and a bullet whizzed through the leaves past Jolie and Conker. His horse reared in alarm. "You hear me or do I have to send John Hardy here in to fish your body out of that creek?"

Alston grumbled, scratching at the nest on his face and turning back. "I'm hungry, Stacker."

"You'll eat when I say. Let's move."

Alston holstered the shotgun in the saddle and joined the other two on the bank with one last gaze back toward the far bank.

Jolie and Conker lay crouched in the underbrush for a long time after the men had moved on up the creek. Jolie's eyes were still narrowed as she watched the direction they had gone.

"It's okay," Conker assured Jolie. "They're bandits, but at least they're headed the other direction."

"They are headed toward the well!"

"How would they know about your well? Besides, it's protected, right?"

Jolie stood and offered her hand to Conker. "You are right. But let us travel a little farther before we stop for a meal."

QUIET DAYS RETURNED TO SHUCKSTACK. NEL'S EIGHTY-
first birthday celebration was past. The terror of the dying
man from Kansas was fading into memory. Ray and Marisol
had left with the Everetts, catching a ride on the *Ballyhoo* as
far as St. Louis. And Sally was working with the other children of Shuckstack on the chores that encompassed their
everyday routines.

With Mattias off with Dmitry hunting for game in the
mountains, Sally had recruited Rosemary to help plant the
seeds that would bring up kale and onions and radishes and
other early spring vegetables. The girls sang songs and talked
about the party as they worked with the hoes.

"What do you think of Noah's scarecrow?" Oliver called
as he came around the barn.

Sally and Rosemary turned and leaned against the hoes.

Oliver held the scarecrow's sack head, while little Noah carried the post protruding from the feet. He had a proud tilt to his chin as he helped Oliver tilt the scarecrow upright.

"Is that my blouse?" Rosemary asked.

"It was in the pile of patches in Marisol's room," Noah said. "Thought you outgrowed it?"

"That's fine," Rosemary said. "Looks better on your scarecrow anyway."

"He looks lovely," Sally said, waving a hand to the mismatch of worn-out clothes covering the scarecrow's lumpy body. "You know, I sat on my straw hat and now it's got a hole in it. You can use it if you want."

"Where is it?" Noah said, letting go of the scarecrow and surprising Oliver as the tall straw man tumbled on top of him.

Sally laughed. "Under my bed. Go get it."

Noah set off running, his brogans slapping on the wet mud where the last snow had recently melted. He nearly knocked Buck and Si from the steps as he dashed up.

"Slow it!" Buck barked, grasping the railing.

Noah sprinted past calling out, "Okay, Buck. Excuse me, Si."

Sally was about to return to hoeing when she saw Buck and Si go over to Carolyn. She couldn't hear what they were saying, but in a moment the two passed by the garden plot, heading for the trail.

Si's black braid hung tight and sleek across her shoulder, and she wore a bulging haversack. Her eyes were still darkly rimmed, but she seemed to be recovering from her injury.

Buck clamped his wide-brimmed cowboy hat over his rowdy black-and-silver hair. He hoisted a pair of waterskins over his shoulder and adjusted them to rest behind his holstered pistols.

"Where are you going?" Sally asked.

Buck kept walking, but Si stopped. "We'll be up at the Clingman's Dome for a few days."

"You're seeing Mother Salagi?" Sally asked curiously.

"Carolyn's in charge," Buck said. "She's the oldest."

"What about Mister Nel?" Rosemary asked.

"Leave Nel be," Buck grunted over his shoulder as he continued toward the trail. "He's got tonics to make to trade for a new wagon."

Si began following him. "Don't cause any trouble."

"We don't cause trouble," Sally said with a huff.

"Don't let Noah and George cause trouble," Si said. "We'll be back within the week."

Sally watched them go. As she returned to the garden, her eyes followed a circle around the yard. All the children were busy with tasks: Felice and Naomi hanging up laundry, Dale and Adam cleaning out the chicken coop, Carolyn boiling lye and bear fat in a big cauldron for soap, Preston and George carrying in wood to the kitchen stove and the fireplaces.

"Why's Si and Buck always thinking we're going to make trouble when they're away?" Sally grumbled to Rosemary.

"We can handle things without them, can't we?" Rosemary said, scattering seeds over the damp earth.

Sally brought her hoe back to the soil with a quick swipe. "They keep us too busy to do anything we want to do."

Rosemary laughed. "You just want to get back to your room so you can read that book from your pa."

Sally frowned as she brought the hoe down again and again.

When supper was over and the dishes were washed, Sally sprinted up to her corner of the loft and lit a candle.

She set the candle on the windowsill and pulled her chair close to it. With *The Incunabula of Wandering* in her lap, she opened the book and the page fell to the Verse of the Lost. She had not had a chance to read it again since Ray had left. The poem mentioned the Elemental Rose, whatever that was. It would not normally have made her curious. The *Incunabula* was filled with strange references: the Haymaker's Flute, the Toninyan, Marse Turnage's Due, and all manner of bizarre names.

But the Elemental Rose. Why had Father needed it? Sally tilted the book to the candlelight and began reading it once more:

When the storms of winter billow
at the coming of the night,
Memories shall be harvested
like the fruits of day's long light.
Lost is the potent passage.
Gone the stick of yew.
Forsaken is the wanderer's compass,
until spring returns anew.

Sealed in gold or silver vessels,
yea the taken goes,
Until the placing of the four
creates the elemental rose.
But even restoration might
in time extract a cost,
As the vessel can be made
a beacon for the lost.

In the margin, Sally saw her father's scrawling script. *The lost will be restored.* She looked up at the cobweb-cornered ceiling, thinking hard.

What was lost? she wondered. Her eyes drew up to the fifth line. "Lost is the potent passage."

She knew vocabulary well enough, and *potent* meant "powerful." What's a "potent passage" mean? She blinked hard with the inkling of an idea forming.

A passage. Like a path someone follows. Like the Rambler path. Potent passage. Yes, she thought. Being a Rambler is like following a path of power! What if the lines were like this, some hidden meaning if she could just unravel the words?

She pulled the book closer, her eyes boring into the first two lines. "Storms of winter. Coming of night." She said the lines over and over under her breath. Winter storms sounded bad, she thought. And night could be a scary time.

She kept reading. "Memories shall be harvested. . . ." Harvested, she thought. "Harvested" was like collecting crops. But *harvest* also meant to take something away, didn't it?

The meaning came to her, like several pieces in a puzzle suddenly taking shape. Ray had said that their father's memory of his Rambler powers had been taken from him. Harvested. And the attack by the Hoarhound that had severed his hand, that had to be scary, something awful like a winter storm striking at night.

And wasn't the Hound what caused her father to lose his Rambler powers, what had kept him from returning to her and Ray? He had lost his "potent passage."

She read once more the sixth and seventh lines. She had no idea what the poem meant by a stick of yew, but "forsaking the wanderer's compass" . . . A compass guides you. Her father's Rambler powers guided him. So maybe she didn't need to figure out what the stick of yew meant. They all were just saying basically the same thing. They were talking about the Rambler's powers being taken away.

She was getting it!

Sally read the ninth and tenth lines. "Vessels," she murmured. That's like a cup or something, she decided. She wasn't sure what it meant by gold and silver, or placing four of something, but "the taken," that had to mean the lost powers again. "Sealed," she mused. "Sealed in gold or silver vessels. . . ."

Her father's golden rabbit's foot.

Nel's silver fox paw.

Were they vessels? she wondered. Did they hold something? But of course they did. Her father's powers. What if his powers were trapped in the golden rabbit's foot she was now keeping safe for Ray?

Was she understanding this right? If she placed these four things—whatever they were—it would create the Elemental Rose. And the Elemental Rose could restore the lost . . . the lost Rambler powers. Was this what the poem was saying? Could his powers be restored?

She leaped up from her chair, pacing before the candle with the *Incunabula* in her hands.

She scanned the last lines. She did not know what it meant by restoration exacting a cost. Maybe there was something you had to give up to make the Elemental Rose. But the final line: *As the vessel can be made a beacon for the lost.*

Yes, the vessel, her father's hand. It had been a beacon for Ray. It had led him to her father. Maybe the cost was losing the lodestone's powers. Either way, she was certain now. The Verse of the Lost was talking about her father losing his powers. And for that matter, Nel's powers as well . . .

She gasped as she lowered the *Incunabula*.

If Nel had his leg back, his powers would be returned. If he was a Rambler again, he could cross into the Gloaming. He could destroy the Machine. Ray could come back, and he wouldn't be in any danger from the Darkness in Kansas. Maybe then Nel could help find their father.

Voices echoed from the stairs as the children came up, calling out "Good night" to Nel. Sally knelt to push the *Incunabula* under her bed.

"Mind if I read?" Rosemary said, pulling back the covers and climbing over with a book of fairy tales.

"No," Sally said, climbing into the cold linens beside her.

Sally lay back, staring at the ceiling until Rosemary fell asleep. She took the book from Rosemary's chest and leaned over to blow out the candle.

She lay in the dark thinking. She could help Nel. But she was missing the biggest piece to this puzzle. What was the Elemental Rose?

The weather continued to warm, and with it, the list of spring chores grew. Carolyn issued Sally—along with the other Shuckstack children—a busy schedule of tasks that would undoubtedly fill the day from dawn until after sundown. Patching the garden baskets. Inventorying the remaining potatoes, squash, and yams in the root cellar. Bringing out the rugs to beat the dust from them with brooms.

"What's got you in a rumple?" Rosemary asked, as she and Sally carried a heavy rug back up the stairs into the lodge.

Sally blinked, her thoughts returning to their chore. She realized Rosemary had been talking for some time as they whacked at the rug, but Sally hadn't heard a word she'd said.

"Nothing," Sally said. "Just thinking is all."

She hardly slept that night. Over in her corner of the loft, she sat up reading until long after the other children were asleep. She searched through every passage on flowers in the *Incunabula,* desperate to find something on the Elemental Rose. But when the candle melted down and flickered out, she had found nothing in the tome on roses of any sort. She crawled under the quilt beside Rosemary and stared up at the dark, her mind awhirl.

The following morning after breakfast as the children began scattering from the front porch for their daily chores, Carolyn said, "Rosemary and Sally, we need a new garden plot tilled."

Sally's shoulders sank. "We just got the seeds all planted in the other one. We'll have more vegetables than we can possibly ever eat."

Carolyn tied her bonnet under her chin, her cheeks already turning brown from the days spent outdoors again. "Not one for vegetables. We need an herb garden. For Nel's tonics. I think it'll save a lot of time in the end if we grow most of the herbs here rather than going out on foraging expeditions."

Sally opened her mouth to complain, but Rosemary grabbed her arm. "Where should we dig it?"

Carolyn started down the stairs from the front porch. "On the south side of the barn. That way it'll get the best sunlight."

Sally slumped down the stairs after Rosemary, heading for the barn. "When's a person have time to rest," Sally grumbled.

"If you didn't stay up all night reading, you wouldn't be so crabby." Rosemary smirked.

Sally rolled her eyes as she followed her inside the barn. They took down a pair of hoes and walked back out into the yard. "So which side is the south?" Sally asked.

Rosemary looked up at the sky, to where the sun was rising over the ridge beyond the millpond. She scratched a cross in the hard dirt with the edge of the hoe's blade. Kneeling down, she touched a finger to one of the points. "Well, that way's east," Rosemary said, making a little E with her fingertip.

Sally's eyes bore down at the dirt drawing. She gave a little gasp.

Rosemary marked the other points of the compass to indicate north, south, and west. She stood again, letting her eyes extend from the S to the barn. She pointed. "I guess that way's south."

Sally dropped her hoe and ran for the stairs leading up to the lodge.

"Where are you going?" Rosemary called. "What's the matter, Sally?"

Sally was through the door. A compass! As Rosemary had drawn it in the dirt, understanding burst in Sally's mind.

She took the steps up to the loft two at a time. Running past the neatly made beds, she fell to the floor at her corner of the room and yanked the *Incunabula* out from under the bed.

The Elemental Rose. It wasn't a flower at all.

She flipped through the pages furiously, stopping on some to run a finger down the lines before leafing further and further through the book. At last she found the page, the page she had seen many times but never considered long enough to figure out what purpose the diagram served.

"A compass rose!" she gasped. She set the book open on the floor and traced a finger to each of the points: north, south, east, and west. They corresponded to one of four colors. And written below the colors were four other words:

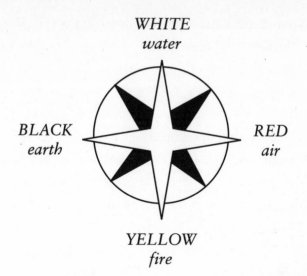

WHITE
water

BLACK
earth

RED
air

YELLOW
fire

Water, earth, air, and fire. The four elements.

A note next to it, written in her father's hand, said: Four objects are needed for the ER. Each is a stead for the four. Each brings the powers of the four into one when they are in their proper place.

ER. Her father had written ER. She was certain now this was the Elemental Rose. But what were the four objects? She scowled in frustration. The *Incunabula* could be so confusing and unhelpful sometimes!

She flipped back to the Verse of the Lost and read it once more. Yes, the tenth line said that placing the four objects would make the Elemental Rose.

But how was she to use the Elemental Rose if she didn't know what the four objects were?

The floorboards creaked at the steps, and Sally turned around.

"What in the world are you doing up here?" Rosemary asked. "If Carolyn finds out—"

"Please, Rosemary," Sally pleaded. "Just a few minutes more."

Rosemary marched across the room and scowled as she saw the *Incunabula* open on the floor. "That book is an obsession with you, Sally. Gracious sakes, we've got work to do! It's bad enough you're tired and grumpy from staying up all night reading it, but now you're shirking your chores to sneak away up here—"

"Okay! Okay," Sally snapped, shoving the *Incunabula* back under her bed and stomping to her feet. "You just don't understand what I'm trying to figure out."

"And I don't really care either," Rosemary said. "Now, come on before Carolyn gets after us."

Rosemary kept an irritable silence as the two girls began digging away the grass and weeds to clear the plot for the herb garden. Sally visualized the drawing of the Elemental Rose as she worked. What could the four objects be?

Sure, earth could be black and fire yellow, but how could air be red or water white? Well, ice was white. That could be the object for north. She supposed the sky turned red at sunset and sunrise, but that wasn't an object like dirt or flame or ice that she could use.

At that moment, Nel's voice carried across the yard as he spoke to Carolyn and Oliver. Sally set her hoe against the side of the barn.

"Where are you going?" Rosemary asked.

"I'll be right back," Sally said, ignoring Rosemary's frown.

She jogged over to Nel.

". . . Mattias and Dmitry are still out hunting," Carolyn was saying. "But they should be back today or tomorrow."

"Very good," Nel said. He smiled as he spotted Sally. "How are you today, my dear?"

Sally nodded. "Good." She watched as Carolyn and Oliver picked back up the baskets of cabbages and potatoes. Sally waited until they were nearly to the cellar kitchen door before she said, "Mister Nel, there was a Cherokee man who was at your party."

"Baxter Lowell," Nel said, taking out his pipe to light.

"He said he knew Father," Sally said. "He said something about his uncle helping Father figure out what the Elemental Rose was."

"Hum," Nel murmured as he shook out the match and drew on his briarwood pipe.

"Do you know what the Elemental Rose is?" Sally asked tentatively.

"Can't say that I do, my dear," Nel replied. "Why do you ask?"

"Just something I found in the *Incunabula*," Sally said. "I looked it up after the party and I'm trying to figure out how to make the Elemental Rose."

"What does it do?" Nel asked.

"Sally!" Rosemary called, holding up Sally's hoe.

Sally looked back at Nel. "Can I show you what it says? It will only take a moment and then I'll get back to my chores."

Nel cupped a hand to his mouth and called, "Rosemary, Sally will resume her onuses with you momentarily." He gestured with the pipe to the lodge. "Grab the book and meet me in my workshop."

Sally smiled. "Thank you, Mister Nel." She ran for the front steps.

In a few minutes, she was down in Nel's room with the *Incunabula* beneath her arm. She could hear Carolyn, Oliver, and Felice working on lunch in the cellar kitchen across the hallway. Bottles and containers with Nel's assorted roots, powders, and herbs were spread out across his table, and he cleared a little space on one end for her to put down the book.

Sally flipped through the *Incunabula* until she reached the page with the drawing of the curious compass. "It's a sort of spell, I think. Four colors. Four objects."

Nel bent over the book, inspecting the drawing.

Sally pointed to the side of the page. "And see here, my father's note. 'Four objects are needed for the ER. Each is a stead for the four. Each brings the powers of the four into one when they are in their proper place.' Do you know what the four objects would be?"

Nel chewed on the end of his pipe before saying, "Well, the note doesn't give us much to go on, does it?"

"I think each object has to be a certain color and be made

of the element listed. Like the north point. It has to be something made of water and white. Ice, maybe?"

Nel shook his head. "No, I don't think so. Look what the
note says. 'Each is a stead for the four.'"

"What's a stead?"

"A representative. I see this all the time in hoodoo lore.
It's an object that stands in for another but isn't actually that
object. See, that white object represents water, but as a stead.
That means it's not actually water, but some object that symbolizes water."

"So what could it be?" Sally asked.

"You've got me," Nel said with a shrug. He picked the
book up, reading the compass drawing again. "Hum . . . Very
interesting. It's certainly a puzzle."

"I really need to figure it out!" Sally urged.

Nel's eyebrows leaped up. "But why?"

Sally hesitated. Should she tell Nel? Surely he would want
to have his powers back. But what if he didn't, what if he
tried to stop her from making the Elemental Rose?

"It's just . . . well, because of my father . . . I think the
Elemental Rose can help find him." Sally felt this was in
fact true, even if she was leaving out a few steps in her rea-
soning.

Nel set down the *Incunabula,* his wooly eyebrows lowered thoughtfully.

Sally met his gaze with pleading eyes. "Can you help,
Mister Nel? Do you think you could help figure it out?"

Nel turned and went to a cupboard. Opening the little

doors, he rummaged inside until he brought out a tin. "It occurs I might have figured out the south point on the Elemental Rose," Nel said, still flexing his brow curiously at Sally.

"What is it?" Sally asked.

"You need a yellow object representing fire." Nel pried the top of the tin open with a fingernail.

Sally leaned close, sniffing at the yellow powder within. She drew back at the bad smell. It was like a rotten egg in the chicken coop. "Yuck, what is that?"

"Sulfur, my dear. Otherwise known as brimstone. Often used in evil works, as it's the burning smell of Dante's Hell. But there's hoodoo spells aplenty that take the approach of 'fighting fire with fire,' as the adage goes."

"Brimstone." Sally smiled.

"Only three to go," Nel said, handing the tin to Sally. "But these others. I'm not sure what they might be. Not sure we'll be so lucky as to have them lying around my workshop. Might require a little searching."

There was a knock at Nel's door, and Dmitry opened it to peer inside. "Mister Nel?"

"Come in, lad," Nel said. "Back at last. How was the hunting?"

"Fine, sir," Dmitry said, closing the door behind him. "Mattias's still up on Bee Gum. But I hurried back quick as I could."

"Everything all right?"

"We're fine," Dmitry said. "Just I've a message for you. From Buck. We ran into him and Si while we were checking the trapline. They said the seer . . . that one who lives over at the Clingman's Dome—"

"Yes, Mother Salagi," Nel said.

"She wants to see you," Dmitry said. "Something about a council. Other seers coming in a few days. I can't remember it all. Buck and Si were coming back to get you, but I said I could get back quicker and give you the message. Buck wants you to come right away."

"Thank you," Nel said. "We'll leave after dinner."

As Dmitry shut the door, Sally asked, "What about the Elemental Rose?"

"It will have to wait, my dear." Nel began to collect clothing and supplies from his dresser to pack.

"But you said yourself that we might need to search to find the other three. What if I came with you? What if we looked for the rest on the way to Mother Salagi's?"

Nel paused with his leather bag open on his bed.

"Please, Mister Nel," Sally said. "It could be fun . . . trying to figure it out. And I'll work extra hard when I get back to make up all my chores."

Nel lowered his voice. "Do you really believe this spell might reveal what's happened to your father?"

"I understand things in the *Incunabula,* Mister Nel. You know I do! Like the Gertrude's Diadem that helped Si. I can make this Elemental Rose work. I'm sure of it."

"Okay," Nel said, the wrinkles around his eyes relaxing. "Let's see if we can figure it out on the way."

LEADING NEL AND SALLY, DMITRY REACHED THE RIDGELINE, where the sun was bright but the air was still cool and the trees were not yet budding with leaves. Out of breath from the steep climb, Nel settled onto a rock and massaged his knee above the wooden leg.

"It's good to be out this far again after the winter," Nel said with a smile, wiping his forehead with a kerchief and settling his fez back on his head.

Sally rested beside him, putting down her rucksack. Inside, among her change of clothes and her share of the food, she carried *The Incunabula of Wandering* and the tin of brimstone. In the front pocket of her dress lay the rabbit's foot.

"Have you thought any more about the other objects for the Elemental Rose?" Sally asked.

Dmitry turned curiously, his blond eyebrows looking white against his face. "What are you talking about?"

Nel drank from his canteen before handing it to Dmitry. "It seems Miss Sally has yet to mention to you that we are on a hunt of sorts."

"A hunt?" Dmitry asked. "What are we hunting?"

Sally explained about the Elemental Rose and about the clues to the objects they needed. Dmitry seemed to grasp the idea right away and said, "Well, if the east one needs to be something red that symbolizes air, that's easy enough."

Getting back up to set off again, Nel asked, "What's your revelation, my boy?"

The three headed along the gentler slope of the ridgeline. "A feather." Dmitry chuckled. "That represents air, right? All we need is a red feather. From a cardinal, maybe."

"Yes!" Sally said excitedly. "Where can we find one?"

"Cardinals are all over these woods," Dmitry answered. "But I'm not sure how we'll get one of their feathers. I suppose I could catch one."

Sally winced. "You mean kill it?"

"Well, maybe not. We could try to just pluck one out and let it go."

Nel grunted. "Let's just keep an eye out for a fallen feather on the ground. How's that?"

As they followed the ridge for a time, they bantered back and forth ideas for the remaining two objects.

"White could be a quartz crystal?" Dmitry tried.

"No," Nel said. "That's white, but I don't see that it represents water."

"Quartz looks like ice sometimes."

"Still, I'm not sure that's it. Quartz seems more to represent earth."

"What about coal? That's in the earth and that's black."

"True, but coal burns, which makes it more like fire."

They went on and on like this, until Nel asked, "Will we join young Mattias tonight?"

"No, by tomorrow," Dmitry said. "I know a great campsite for tonight. Great views of High Rocks. We'll get a nice fire and I brought some yams from the root cellar to roast. . . ."

Nel stopped. Dmitry and Sally turned. "What is it, Mister Nel?" Dmitry asked.

"Hush a moment. Your mention of the root cellar gave me an idea. Let me think." Nel clapped his hand over his mouth, tapping one finger to his cheek. He murmured, "Roots . . . yes, that might be it. For the element earth. The west. See, children, these four colors, they were not just randomly chosen. Many tribes see these colors—white, black, red, and yellow—as important colors that draw on the powers of the four directions. Black and the west are the way of war. They represent might and strength. A root of the earth that gives strength . . ."

"Would the root have to be black?" Sally asked.

"Ah!" Nel barked, lifting a finger. "Yes, I think I have it. Charms that bestow strength often require Black Sampson root."

Dmitry jumped. "That's like a snakeroot, right? With those purple flowers?"

"Yes, lad," Nel said. "You've seen them?"

"They're not in bloom yet, but just ahead there's a bald. Mattias and I saw them growing all over it last fall. Come on."

Sally and Nel hurried to follow Dmitry. In less than half an hour's time, the trees broke and they reached a boulder-studded clearing of brown winter grass. A hawk cried out, and Sally turned to spot him riding on the breeze.

"Look for the shoots," Nel said. "Do you know what they look like, Dmitry?"

"I think so." Dmitry moved out across the bald, searching.

Bent forward, Nel walked around, pushing back the dead grass to expose the tiny plants coming back to life. After a few moments, Nel squatted, opened a pocketknife, and began prying the blade in the earth. The green shoot at the top was barely an inch tall, with only a couple of small leaves, but as he shook the loose dirt from the base, he showed Sally the tangle of dark roots.

"Black Sampson root." Nel smiled at Sally as he folded up the knife.

"Thank you, Mister Nel!"

"Dmitry!" Nel called. "We found it, my boy. You can come back."

As Sally put the root in her rucksack with the tin of brimstone, Nel called again, "Dmitry! What are you doing, lad?"

Sally turned to see Dmitry climbing up into a twisted pine tree growing at the edge of the bald. As she and Nel ran toward the tree, Dmitry shouted. Something was attacking him in the branches. There was a squawk and a flurry of beating wings and Dmitry jumped from the limb to tumble to the ground.

A bird swooped down, and Sally saw Dmitry bat at the bird as he ran to Nel and Sally. The bird dove one more time, striking Dmitry on the top of his head before circling back to the tree.

Out of breath and with a trickle of blood coming down from his hairline, Dmitry collapsed at their feet.

"Are you okay?" Nel asked, running his hands through Dmitry's yellow-white hair to inspect the wound. "Just a scratch. What was that?"

"A hawk," Dmitry panted. "I saw her land in a tree and I realized she had a nest there."

Nel frowned. "What in the world were you doing climbing up to a hawk's nest?"

Dmitry opened his hand. He held three bright red feathers. "I figured if she was feeding her chicks, there might be some bird carcass. Hawks catch cardinals all the time. There you go, Sally."

Sitting on a boulder in the clearing, Nel doctored up Dmitry's head. Sally had the *Incunabula* open in her lap, looking for anything to do with water that might help figure out the last object.

"Give it up," Dmitry said. "It'll be dark in a few hours. I don't think we'll find that last one tonight."

"But we've almost got them all!"

Nel dabbed the last of the ointment on Dmitry's head. "I think he's right. We've had a successful day, and aside from young Dmitry being attacked, we should count ourselves fortunate and enjoy a fire at our campsite."

Sally ignored them. "White . . . white . . . What's something white that could be water? Water . . ." She stood quickly and caught the *Incunabula* as it fell from her lap. "Water! Mister Nel, what's the name of that Cherokee elder who Redfeather is visiting?"

"Water Spider." Nel's brow twisted.

"Why is his name Water Spider?" Sally asked.

Nel said, "It's a type of spider that lives around ponds. But also to the Cherokee, Water Spider is a spirit that brings gifts to their people. I think it comes from the belief that spiders descending from their webs are like spirits bringing down great boons from the heavens like rain. . . ."

Sally's eyes sparkled. "So could—"

"Yes!" Nel bellowed. "Yes, I think you've discovered it."

"What?" Dmitry asked. "I don't understand."

"Like showers of rain falling from above, spiderwebs are connected with the gifts of water falling on fields." Nel clapped his hands. "A spiderweb. It's white. Spiders are associated with rain. That's the last one."

The excitement fell from Sally's expression. "But where will we find a spiderweb? It's still too early in spring. There aren't any spiders out."

Nel struggled for a solution. "Yes . . . but . . . well, we could . . ." Then he sighed. "I think we might be about a month or so too early."

"No, we have to find it. Can't there be any around?"

Nel tapped his hand gently on her shoulder. "I'm sorry, Sally dear. But we won't locate—"

"Actually, I think I know where we might find a cobweb," Dmitry said.

"Where?" Nel asked skeptically. "There are no webs this early in the season. Any from last year are blown away by the winds."

"Not all the webs," Dmitry said. "The webs that catch flying bugs are all gone, but not the ones that catch the crawlers. Under rocks and old logs and such. Those kinds of webs are still around. But . . ."

"But what?" Sally asked.

"But . . ." Dmitry's mouth tightened. "You never know what kind of spider it is. More often than not . . . it's a black widow. I can find us one, easy enough. But I've already risked my neck . . . er, scalp once today. I'm not up for sticking my hand in some black widow's den."

Nel frowned. Sally pulled her hand protectively to her throat.

Dmitry looked back and forth between them. "How bad do you need that spiderweb?"

"Desperately bad," Sally said.

Dmitry stood. "Well, then the good news is the spiders die in the wintertime. And their eggs probably haven't hatched yet since it's still so cold. Probably. If you want that web, chances are, you'll be okay. You willing to try?"

"Yes," Sally said hesitantly.

"Then come on."

Dmitry led them across the bald and back into the forest. After he had searched in the shadowy crevices beneath the boulders and rotting logs, he called, "Found one!"

He was squatting, his face nearly to the ground, peering under a boulder. One edge jutted out in an overhanging slab of granite. He pointed. "I see a bit of the web from here." He handed Sally a stick. "Just poke this in and twirl it around to collect the web."

Sally took the stick from him. Nel perched over her, his hands on his knees. Sally lay flat on the ground, feeling the bulge of the rabbit's foot in her dress pocket pressing against her stomach. She slowly extended the stick under the boulder. She had trouble seeing the web, but as her eyes adjusted, she spied a little bit of white in the shadows of the crevice. Her knuckles scraped along the rock, her fingers pushing through dirt and old leaves. She wouldn't get bit by a black widow, she told herself over and over. It was still too cold.

Sally circled her hand around to gather the web on her stick. When she thought she had gotten it, she pulled her hand back out from under the boulder. As the stick emerged, she saw the end of the stick covered in the wooly cluster of spiderweb.

"Great, Sally!" Dmitry gasped.

Nel whistled and stood upright, squeezing Sally around the shoulder. Sally brought the stick over to her rucksack, but before she got there, Dmitry said, "Uh, Sally. What's that on your sleeve?"

Dmitry and Nel leaned in close together to look at Sally's arm and then jerked back together.

"What is it?" Sally asked, turning her arm to inspect. Dirt and bits of leaves and such had collected on the cuff of her sleeve. But as Sally looked closer, she realized there were tiny movements as well.

"I think those are baby spiders!" Dmitry danced a frantic step.

Sally screamed, throwing the stick in the air and batting at her arm as if it were on fire. Dmitry and Nel circled around her, trying to calm her and help brush the minuscule spiders from her clothes.

After a few minutes' work where Sally insisted on inspecting and reinspecting every inch of her arm, sleeve, and dress for any signs of crawling, the three settled back down.

"I don't think the babies can hurt you anyway," Dmitry laughed, trying to reassure her.

"Quit talking about them!" Sally shivered as she went over to pick back up the stick. She looked closely at the web to make sure there were no baby spiders in the silky mass. Feeling certain it was spider-free, she took the web from the stick, rolled it into a ball, and placed it in her rucksack with the feathers, the root, and the tin of brimstone.

She had the Elemental Rose.

They camped that night at High Rocks, and the next morning, Sally woke before the sun had broken over the mountains. She started the fire and had a hash of wild tubers sizzling in the skillet as Dmitry and Nel got up from their blankets. Dmitry wandered off to refill the waterskins. Nel sipped at a tin cup of tea and asked, "I've been puzzling over this Elemental Rose of yours. I'm still not sure why you think it will help you discover your father's whereabouts."

Sally placed the breakfast to the side of the coals to stay warm until Dmitry returned. "Well, that's not really what I think it will do. Not directly anyway."

Nel's wooly white brows lowered. "What do you mean?"

Sally took the *Incunabula* from her rucksack and walked over to Nel, flipping through the pages until she found the Verse of the Lost. "It's this poem."

Nel took the book from her and turned it around. Sally backed a step away as he read it, her heart pounding. Nel squinted as his gaze moved down the page. When he at last looked up, he asked, "What does this mean?"

Sally began with the line about losing the potent passage. As she made her way through the explanation, Nel's eyes grew wide and fearful.

"Let me just try, Mister Nel."

Nel frowned. "My powers are gone, never to return. With the loss of my leg, the powers were stripped from me."

"The Elemental Rose will give you back your powers," Sally said. "That's what it does. It restores things that are lost—"

Dmitry returned and dropped the waterskins. "Ah! I'm starving. Can we eat?"

Nel pulled his gaze from Sally. "Yes, help yourself, son."

Dmitry took out the tin plates and flicked the hash with his knife onto the plates. Handing them around, he began devouring his breakfast with a pleasant smile on his face, but Nel and Sally did not eat. As Dmitry noticed, he cocked his head curiously.

Sally whispered to Nel. "Will you at least try?"

Nel picked distractedly at his plate.

"Try what?" Dmitry asked. He looked back and forth between Sally and Nel.

"We need to get to Mother Salagi's," Nel said. "We've wasted enough time already on this journey."

After covering the fire, they cleaned the campsite and set off toward the Clingman's Dome. The wind snapping atop the mountain was cool, but the bright sun warmed their skin. Dmitry led them off the ridge and through a hollow, where the woods were darker and the air moist.

"I bet we'll reach Mattias over at Bee Gum by nightfall," Dmitry said. "And then it's just a half-day journey further."

The ground beneath their feet had the crunch of the last frost of the season. Sally trudged along behind Nel and Dmitry with tears fighting to rise.

By midday they were passing through a thick hedge of rhododendron when they came upon a small pool. It was trapped in a natural dam of rocks, before splashing over into a waterfall to form a stream running down the mountainside.

"Let's lunch here," Dmitry said. "Hand me your canteens and I'll fill them down in that pool."

After Dmitry left, Nel settled on a log. Sally took out the biscuits and sliced ham from her rucksack and began making sandwiches.

"Sally," Nel said.

She looked up. Her eyes met Nel's, and within those enormous moonlike orbs she saw his expression clouded with sadness.

He leaned forward, resting his elbows on his knees. "I've walked this earth for so many years as Peg Leg Nel . . . I've forgotten what it means to be a Rambler. I've forgotten who Joe Nelson was." Nel touched a hand to the amulet beneath his shirt. "Since losing my powers, my only goal has been to keep you children safe. First Conker when he was little more than a baby, and then the children of my medicine show. And now, you dear ones of Shuckstack. There was much danger. Danger from the Gog. I was never . . . I'm not a warrior. I see myself as a caretaker. A protector. To be a Rambler again means to take up other responsibilities. Do you understand?"

"I think so, Mister Nel," Sally answered. "Someone has to watch over us children."

"I fear this Darkness," Nel whispered. "I fear what it means for you children."

"But that's no reason not to have your powers back, Mister Nel," Sally said.

Nel sat upright slowly. "Sally, I don't know of another who could unravel the *Incunabula* as you have. Mother Salagi is gifted with the vision of sight, but she could never return my powers to me."

"The Elemental Rose can," Sally said.

Nel nodded.

Sally suddenly understood what he was saying. "You'll let me try?"

Nel nodded once more.

"Thank you, Mister Nel!" Sally jumped up to hug him.

Dmitry came back with the canteens. "What are you all excited about?"

"We're going to save Mister Nel!" Sally cried.

Dmitry looked at Nel. "Save you from what?"

Nel frowned apprehensively. "Let Sally tell us what to do."

Sally was already removing supplies from her rucksack, placing the four objects beside her, opening the *Incunabula* to the drawing of the compass. She pointed to the ground. "Come over here. Do you have your fox paw?"

Nel got up from the log and unbuttoned his shirt collar. He lifted the rawhide cord until the heavy silver paw lay across his chest.

"Which way is south?" she asked.

Dmitry pointed across the pool.

"Lie down on your back with your feet toward the pool." Nel took off his fez and set it aside to lie down. Sally knelt where Nel's wooden leg and his tall leather boot rested side by side.

She put the tin of brimstone below them. Then she squinted at the *Incunabula* lying open on the ground and looked at what was next. West was black, earth. Circling Nel in a clockwise fashion, she placed the Black Sampson root next to the old pitchman's right hand.

"You're certain this is what these objects are for?" Nel asked, his lips tight as he spoke.

Sally nodded. "I'm certain." Shuffling around another

quarter turn, she positioned the bundle of spiderweb a few inches above Nel's wooly white head. She double-checked the *Incunabula* with a glance. Last was east. Red. Air. She set the cardinal feather by Nel's left hand. Finally, she adjusted the silver paw, centering it on top of Nel's chest, picked up the book, and stood.

"Okay. That's it, I think," Sally said, backing away a step with Dmitry at her side.

Dmitry's eyes anxiously flickered from Sally to Nel.

Nel's fingers clenched. He closed his eyes. His nostrils billowed with each deep breath.

"What's going to happen?" Dmitry whispered.

"Hush!" Sally hissed, pulling his arm to back away another step.

What would happen? She wondered how she would know if it was working. She looked around but nothing seemed to be happening. Then she smelled it. Rotten eggs. She looked at the tin of brimstone. Smoke was rising from the corners of the lid. She pulled her sleeve over her fingers to protect her skin from the heat and popped off the lid. Yellow flames danced up from the powdered brimstone.

"What's happening?" Dmitry gasped as she came back.

Sally squeezed his arm. Smoke began to form around Nel's legs. Water ran down from the spiderweb onto his hair. The feather fluttered, and the root twisted and began boring into the dirt. The smoke grew thicker and thicker, dancing over Nel like a phantom, covering him and clouding him from Sally's sight.

"Sally?" Dmitry gasped.

The smoke illuminated and within it she saw Nel's body shadowed as if in silhouette. He cried out. There was a flash, and she was thrown backward.

When she lifted her head, dancing lights lingered in her vision. She rubbed her eyes to clear them, and when she did she saw that Dmitry had also been thrown back. He was unhurt but looked around wildly. Nel lay still.

The silver paw was no longer on his chest. Only the leather cord remained, snapped at the ends.

Nel's wooden leg was also gone.

The boot covered his right leg, but at the left, with the pants rolled up to the knee as he had worn them to accommodate the mahogany peg, lay Nel's other leg. His calf, ankle, and foot were bare and dark brown and whole. Two legs, side by side.

Sally jumped to her feet, coming to Nel's side. "Mister Nel! Mister Nel!"

He opened his eyes. His gaze was peaceful, as if he were coming out of a gentle afternoon nap. He smiled softly and said, "Sally. What have you done?"

He took her shoulder to sit up and looked down at his feet, both of them. He wiggled his toes. "Help me stand."

Dmitry ran to his side. Nel extended his hands to the children. They pulled him until he was upright. Nel put his weight on the boot, making little circles with his ankle before touching his bare foot to the earth. Gingerly he shifted his weight to it. He walked a few steps, limping at first, but then finding the strength. He kicked his foot to the ground, and then danced, shuffling his feet in a frantic rhythm.

"Ha! Ha, ha!" he shouted over and over. Then lifting Sally in his arms, he spun her around. "Sally Cobb! You must be the greatest conjurer of our age!"

Dmitry joined them, circling around and whooping. When the three finished their wild dance, Nel cocked a hand to his ear. "The birds! Their speech," he said. "I hear them again! The jays and crows and sparrows. They're calling to one another, building their nests for their younglings. I understand them again."

Sally and Dmitry laughed with Nel, until Nel stopped to wipe his hands across his eyes. "Let's go, children. Let's get on our way to Mother Salagi's."

"What about your other boot?" Dmitry said, pointing to Nel's bare foot.

Nel broke again into a deep, roaring laughter until he held his side. "I'll have to order new ones, I suppose. At last, I'll get my money's worth out of a pair of shoes."

AFTER RATTLING OVER THE HILLS AND PAST THE FARMS
of Tennessee, Kentucky, and Illinois, the *Ballyhoo* finally
reached the massive rail yard just across the Mississippi River
from downtown St. Louis.

Back in the caboose, Ray gathered his supplies: a blanket
and a change of clothes in a haversack, waterskins, some needles and thread, a small cook set, a bowie knife sheathed at
his belt, and his red flannel toby tied to a cord around his
neck. The toby felt lighter without the rabbit's foot, although
it was a little fuller now with Nel's charms.

Before Ray left Shuckstack, Nel had given him a pouch
filled with cinquefoil, wintergreen, crushed ash leaves, and
other ground roots and herbs to protect them from the Darkness. He had instructed Ray to divide the charms into three
once they reached Redfeather.

Satisfied that he had everything he needed, Ray planted his brown felt hat on his head and headed down to the mess car.

"Ma packed us some food," Marisol said as he came in. She held up a gunnysack bulging with crackers and cheese wrapped in waxed paper, biscuits with thick slices of ham, a dozen apples, and sandwiches heavy with tomatoes and smoked meats.

"That'll last longer than the train ride to Vinita," Ray said. "Mister Everett's gone to the depot to book us passage. Should be back soon."

"How long do you think it will take us to reach the Indian Territory?" Marisol asked.

"Should be there in a day or two," Ray answered. "I suppose after we find Redfeather, it'll take us longer to reach Omphalosa. I don't think the trains run there."

Marisol put the gunnysack in the top of her leather valise and clasped the belts around the floral print of the suitcase. After neatly tying her hat beneath her chin, she held out her hand to Javidos and called him with a whisper. The fat copperhead slid up her arm, disappearing beneath her ruffled sleeve.

"Is that what you're wearing?" Ray asked.

Marisol looked down at her long blue and green dress, kicking a button boot out from the ruffled hem. "This is a good carriage dress. My boots are sturdy. I've worn them all over Shuckstack Mountain."

"What about when we leave the Indian Territory?" Ray asked. "Could be travel in the open country up to Kansas."

She scowled. "I've got other travel clothes packed for that part. What do you want me to do? Dress like a boy?"

Ray started to answer 'maybe.' But as Javidos hissed from around Marisol's arm, and she tucked her long hair under a bonnet with a venomous scowl, Ray decided to trust her choice in travel attire. It was mostly train travel, after all. "Ready?" she asked.

"Sure," Ray said.

They hopped down from the car and found Shacks and Eddie by the locomotive.

"Your pa back yet?" Ray asked.

Eddie shook his head. "Said he'd meet us up here to see you off."

The massive rail yard was a jungle of noise and activity. Train cars clattered in and out. Whistles shrieked. Workers in grimy clothes moved about busily, crossing the web of tracks and trains, emerging and disappearing in the fog of coal smoke.

Ox Everett rounded the cowcatcher with Ma at his heels. "That's fine for Ray, but what about Marisol?" Ma was saying.

Ox reared as he nearly ran into the four. "Ah, here you are. Plans have changed and it can't be helped. I've had a time, I'll tell you. Tried to purchase you tickets, but all passenger trains westbound are halted. They're rerouting trains north and south around Kansas, Nebraska, and the Indian Territory. They're saying there's dust storms out on the prairie."

"Dust storms?" Ray said.

"We both know they ain't," Ox grumbled.

Ma Everett took Marisol's hands. "It was one thing when you were planning to ride the train, but this is an entirely different matter now."

"What do you mean?" Marisol asked.

"Dear, how will you get to the Indian Territory?"

"I suppose we'll have to walk."

"Walk?" Ma shrilled. "Across the entire state? Dear, walking is fine for Ray. He's a Rambler. He understands about travel in the open country. But you're a girl."

"That means I can't walk?" Marisol's eyes flashed dangerously.

"It's different is all. A young boy traveling overland ain't going to garner much attention. But the pair of you? And a pretty girl like you at that."

Ox waved his hands between Marisol and Ma Everett. "Now, don't get all puckered, Marisol. Ma's just worried about you is all. And she's a right to it."

"Isn't there another way we could get out to meet Redfeather?" Ray asked quickly before Marisol could respond.

"Hire a stagecoach," Shacks offered.

"I asked," Mister Everett said. "None going to the Indian Territory."

"How about buy a horse?" Eddie asked.

Ray shook his head. "We can't afford that."

"I suppose you could always sneak aboard a freight train," Ox suggested. "Supply runs still going west. But you wouldn't want to get caught by them railroad bulls. They watch the cars for tramps, and those they catch . . . well, let's just say they're given a rougher sort of treatment out here."

Ma winced at Marisol, but kept her mouth shut.

"Well, we'll find a way," Ray said. "Thank you for the ride and all your help."

He and Marisol said their goodbyes to the Everetts and set off across the rail yard. Marisol turned the heads of many of the men hurrying about the tracks. Ray tried to ignore this, but couldn't help thinking Marisol was anything but inconspicuous. As they reached the edge of the rail yard, where the bridge crossed the Mississippi, Ray stopped and faced Marisol.

"I know Ma Everett pestered you back there, but you know, she might be right. Our plans have changed. You don't have to go."

Marisol put down her valise, her eyes narrowed to dagger-like slits. "You're as awful as she is! You don't think I can handle this. You don't think I can do it. Everyone thinks just because I'm pretty, all I'm good for is performing up on stage or taking care of the Shuckstack kids. I expect it from Ma Everett, but I never expected it from you, Ray!"

She spun around, snatching up her valise and swinging it at her side. With a snarl, she marched onto the plank bridge crossing the Mississippi. An old man carrying a basket of vegetables leaped to the side as if she were a wild animal. Ray ran to catch up with her.

"Marisol," he called. "That's not what I meant. . . ."

"I can handle myself, Ray," she said over her shoulder.

They wouldn't be in the city long, he thought. After that, they'd stick to the forests and less populated routes to Vinita. Hopefully then Marisol would change into her other travel clothes. Nel had urged him not to underestimate Marisol, and Ray struggled to heed his advice.

On the far side of the river, they found themselves in the bustle of downtown St. Louis. Ray followed Marisol as she pushed through the crowds of people past the storefronts and shops, dodging wagons and horse-drawn omnibuses clopping over the cobblestones.

"Do you even know where you're going?" Ray called up to her.

She pointed over the buildings. "That's the sun. It's midafternoon. Then that's west. We need to get to the south-west side of town. So we head that way. Doesn't take a Rambler to figure it out."

Ray exhaled deeply. It was going to be a long journey.

After several minutes, they left the shoppers and strolling families and found themselves in a grittier part of town. Groups of men stood around outside the mills and saloons. Pushing through one of these clusters, Marisol stepped off the curb and into a puddle, splashing her dress.

As they crossed the street, a man wolf-whistled at Marisol from the doorway of a public house. She ignored it, but Ray looked back over his shoulder, cautiously watching the man.

Ray walked in front of her as they passed into a crowd of dirty-faced men congregating on the next corner. He pushed his way politely through the group. As he looked back to make sure Marisol was behind him, he saw one of the men grab her wrist.

"You lost, doll?" The man was unshaven and churlish, and reeked with the sour stench of gin, even from several steps away.

"Get your hand off me!" Marisol snapped her arm from the man's grip. But he caught her once more and jerked her back, causing her valise to tumble into the street.

"This ain't your kind of neighborhood," the man chuckled. "You might need someone like me to escort you."

Ray knew a number of hoodoo spells that could overpower or at least persuade the man to leave them alone. But they all required Black Sampson root or coffin nails or any number of items he didn't have on him. He'd have to trust in his ability to talk their way out of this.

Ray reached Marisol's side. "That's not necessary. She's with me."

"Not anymore!" The ruffian shoved Ray off his feet, throwing him against the brick wall.

Marisol's free hand flew up to grasp the man by his greasy shirt collar. He looked down at her fuming face and began to laugh. His laugh caught abruptly in his throat as his eyes fell on the snake writhing out from Marisol's sleeve just inches from his neck. Javidos flicked his tongue from his thick triangular head, and then opened his fanged mouth to hiss.

"Yes, that's a copperhead," Marisol whispered, teeth bared. "If I want him to bite your throat, he'll do it. Does it look like I need you to escort me?"

"No," the man gulped, his entire body gone rigid. He relaxed his grip on her wrist.

Marisol retrieved her valise and helped Ray to his feet. As they hurried away, she said, "I told you I can take care of myself."

By late afternoon, they had passed the last neighborhoods and houses and were back into the countryside. Along the dirt road out of town, a farmer driving a wagon stopped to offer them a ride. His wife and two small children were lined up beside him on the bench. Marisol and Ray rode facing backward from the wagon's tail for several miles in silence.

"The look on his face . . ." Ray chuckled. "Quite a day."

"I might have been a little short-tempered," Marisol said.

"With that hooligan?"

"No, with you."

"Might have been?" Ray smirked.

"All right, I was. But you were being a . . . a gaboot."

"I didn't mean to be."

"Well, you were."

"Sorry."

Marisol sighed. "I may not know how to hunt or build a fire, but I can learn. My parents were Ramblers, too, remember?"

With the sun drifting below the tree line, Ray and Marisol hopped off the back of the wagon and thanked the farmer and his family. Soon they reached a copse of trees squeezed between the surrounding fields.

"Well, if we're to travel as Ramblers," Ray said, "then I'll need to show you how to set a Five Spot."

"What's that?" she asked, dropping her valise to the ground and pulling her hat from her head.

"Like the bottletrees. It's a protective charm. It'll keep anyone passing on the road from seeing us."

Ray handed Marisol two rocks and picked up two more. "We're going to put these stones as the corners of a square. If anyone comes along, they won't be able to get inside the square unless they know how to counter the charm. You put your two over there by the edge of the road. I'll put mine in the woods a ways."

After doing so, they met back where Ray dropped a pile of kindling sticks.

"Why's it called a Five Spot if you only use four stones?" Marisol asked.

"Our fire pit makes the fifth. As long as we keep the fire burning, the charm will work."

After building a fire ring, Ray said to Marisol, "Redfeather taught me this one." He took a small tin of saltpeter from his toby and opened it. Cupping a dash of the powder in between his hands, he blew into it. When he opened his fingers, flames leaped up from his hands. Ray shook the flames onto the kindling, and the fire was blazing within a few moments.

"Did it burn you?"

Ray held up his blackened palms with chagrin. "A little. I can't quite do it like Redfeather."

She laughed. "Price you pay for showing off."

They ate some of the biscuits and salted ham Ma Everett had packed. After unrolling their blankets on either side of the fire, they lay down. Ray cocked his hands behind his head and looked up at the dark.

Marisol leaned up on one elbow. "You know, you were right about one thing. I've never slept outside like this. Never on the ground."

"There's nothing to it, really," Ray said.

Marisol sighed and lay back down, shifting noisily a few moments. "Well, good night, Ray."

"Good night."

They woke with the sky still gray and their blankets speckled with dew.

"How'd you sleep?" Ray asked.

Her eyes puffy, Marisol grumbled, "It wasn't my bed at Shuckstack."

They rolled up their blankets and stirred the fire for breakfast. Marisol went down to a little creek with her valise to clean up. When she returned, she had changed into a more subdued cotton dress of hazel brown. The hem was still long, but Ray had to admit it was a better outfit for traveling in the wild.

As they ate, Ray spied a group of crows huddled on a branch just outside the perimeter of the Five Spot. Easing toward them, he spoke in a series of caws.

Startled, the crows scattered abruptly toward the fields.

But one crow remained, leaning his bobbing beak down and squawking. Ray held out a cracker in his fingers, which the crow swooped down to take before soaring off on midnight wings.

Marisol asked, "What did you say to it?"

"I asked where the nearest train tracks are. They're not too far. I bet it's the MKT line that runs through the Indian Territory."

Marisol got a fretful look. "You want to hop a ride on a train?"

"It would be a lot quicker."

"Are we in a hurry?" Marisol asked.

"The sooner we reach Redfeather, the sooner we find out if the Machine is causing that Darkness." Ray pulled his haversack to his shoulder.

Marisol gathered her valise and tied her hat beneath her chin. She murmured something to Javidos, who slid up onto her shoulder to flicker his tongue at her ear. Ray kicked out the fire, and they returned to the road.

Within a half hour's time, the dirt road met the railroad tracks. Ray eyed the clapboard houses nearby and said, "We'd better follow the tracks out a way. If we're to keep from being noticed, we'll need a secluded spot to sneak aboard."

They followed the tracks along the edges of the fields and farmhouses. The day was warm as Ray and Marisol trudged along the gravel of the right of way and took turns balancing on the tracks. The crow returned, swooping back and forth over their path before landing on one of the ties in front of Ray and giving a squawk.

"Get on, you beggar. You've got plenty to eat without my crackers." The crow flapped away, calling back a few complaints.

Before long they came to a forest next to the tracks. After coming down off the right of way to the forest, Ray dropped his haversack and settled down onto it. Standing in the shade of the trees, Marisol narrowed her eyes back down the straight line of track.

"How long before the train comes?" she asked as she knelt to let Javidos slither out into a warm patch of light on the leaves. The copperhead slithered a few feet and then snapped out, catching a grasshopper in his jaws.

"Who knows," Ray said, taking his bowie knife from his belt and stabbing it into the earth. "We'll have to be ready."

"What do we do when it comes?"

"Just follow me. We'll run alongside and grab a ladder or jump in an open door if a boxcar is left open."

"Won't it be going fast?"

"Take off your boots," Ray said.

Her almond eyes flashed. "Why?"

"Those boots might be good for walking around Shuckstack, but they're no good for running. Hand them over."

Marisol sat down and unbuttoned her boots, giving them to Ray with a concerned tilt to her eyebrows. Ray pulled the knife from the ground and wedged the blade between one boot's heel and the sole. With a snap, the heel popped off. Ray pried off the other one and handed Marisol back her boots.

"Try that out," he said.

She buttoned them back up and stood, taking a few skips to test them out. "I feel shorter," she said.

"At least you won't twist an ankle." He waved a hand for her to come over to him. "Now the dress."

Marisol clapped her hands protectively over her legs. "What are you going to do?"

"You'll get all tangled up running in that." He held up the knife and waved her forward again.

Reluctantly Marisol came over. Ray put the tip of the knife to the fabric between her knees. With a careful push, he ripped through, and Marisol gave a little whimper. "Come on," Ray said. "You can sew it back up."

Marisol bit her lip as Ray cut down with the knife, tearing the fabric from knee to hem. Marisol turned around, and Ray did the same to the back.

"Much better," he said, sheathing his knife. He tipped his hat over his eyebrows and lay back on the haversack to wait. The crow returned once more, watching Ray from a limb overhead. Marisol sat on her valise, running her fingers over the torn slit in the front of her dress.

They had been sitting in the cool of the forest just long enough for Ray to get sleepy when Javidos snapped his head around toward Marisol, fluttering his tongue. Marisol sat upright. "The train!"

Ray jumped to his feet and raced up to the track. There was nothing in either direction, but when he placed his ear to the steel rail, he smiled. Running back into the shadows of the forest, he said, "You're right. It's coming."

Marisol danced about an anxious turn, shifting her valise

from one hand to the other before tucking it under her elbow. "What do we do?"

"Be calm." He waved a hand at her. "We'll wait for the locomotive to pass. That way the engineer won't spot us. Then we run out onto the right of way. I'll help you get aboard."

The train was rounding out from the trees a mile away still, white sails of steam blasting out around the locomotive, with the long banner of black coal smoke behind.

"Are you sure about this?" Marisol asked. "We could trip and fall under the wheels."

"Don't trip," Ray said, watching the train move closer.

Marisol unclasped her valise, taking out the gunnysack with Ma Everett's food.

"What are you doing?" Ray exclaimed. "It's nearly here."

"Javidos. I don't want him to get hurt." She placed the reluctant copperhead inside. "I can't fit the food back in."

"Just give it here!" Ray barked.

Marisol fumbled to buckle the valise closed. She crouched with Ray behind the roots of an oak, whispering to herself in Spanish.

Within a few minutes, the train began rumbling past them. Behind the locomotive and tender were several empty passenger cars, followed by a long line of boxcars.

"Here we go!" Ray shouted, and he raced onto the right of way, kicking up a trail of dust as he built speed next to the train.

Ray looked over his shoulder. Marisol was sprinting, her jostling bag held tight to her chest. He had to admit he was

—125—

impressed with how fast she was running. Ray looked for a way to get aboard. The boxcar doors were shut, and he was about to grab a ladder when he spotted a boxcar coming toward them with the door left ajar.

"There!" He pointed.

As the boxcar moved along his side, Ray pumped his legs harder and reached for the door. It slid further open as he got a grip on the metal frame. Tossing in his haversack, followed by the gunnysack of food, and giving a quick jump, he had his belly on the boxcar's floor. He rolled over to offer a hand to Marisol.

"Come on!" he shouted.

Her eyes were darting between Ray's outstretched hand and the grinding wheels inches from her feet.

"Toss me your bag!" Ray called.

Marisol swung the valise to him, losing some speed in the process. Ray dropped the bag to the boxcar floor. He leaned back out, reaching for Marisol.

"You're nearly here. Keep running!"

Marisol widened her stride, trying to move faster. Her fingers were nearly to Ray's when her boot slid in the gravel and she fell, throwing up a cloud of dust as she tumbled end over end on the right of way.

"Marisol!" he shouted, snatching his haversack and Marisol's valise and leaping out the door of the boxcar.

As Ray ran for her with the train moving away behind him, Marisol slowly sat up. Realizing she was all right, Ray slowed to a walk. He looked back over his shoulder and watched as the train disappeared past a copse of trees. When he reached her, she was still sitting in a tousle of torn fabric and disheveled hair.

Ray knelt by her, trying to mask his frustration. "You hurt?"

With tightened lips, she shook her head.

He held out his hand. She eyed his fingers, but ignored the offer. Instead she took her valise and opened it to let Javidos out. "*Cómo estás, mi cariño?*" she whispered, rubbing his nose across her dirty cheek.

Ray abruptly spun around to where the train had been.

"What?" Marisol mumbled.

"The food. The sack from Ma Everett with the food. I left it on the train!" He flung his haversack onto the crossties and gave it a kick. Marisol flinched, holding Javidos away from Ray.

Ray ran his fingers under his hat, through his damp hair, took a deep breath, and picked back up his haversack.

"Let's go."

"Where?" Marisol asked.

"Let's just go," he said as he walked away.

They followed the train tracks on for mile after mile. The day wore on in silence but for their footsteps and chortles of the crow still following them. By nightfall, they found a stream running through a culvert under the tracks and made their way to where the stream meandered into a forest.

Marisol found several stones, which she placed to make the Five Spot. Ray gathered wood for a fire and knelt before the growing flames, poking them with a branch.

"Ray," Marisol said.

He looked up at her with a flat expression.

"I really tried to catch up. I did my best. The train was going too fast." She wiped angrily at her eye and turned away.

Ray sighed. "It's okay."

"No, it's not," Marisol said. "I told you I could handle myself, but who was I fooling? Ma Everett was right. You were right. Look at me out here with my silly bag and dress. I'm no Rambler. I should never have come." She was crying openly now, tears dripping from her long eyelashes, and Ray placed a hand on her shoulder. "And to top it all, I lost our food."

"No, I lost the food."

"But I fell and you had to get off in a hurry."

"Marisol, you couldn't help it. You were doing great. You just tripped is all. Could have happened to me."

"I was scared to get on the train. It was just going so fast. I wasn't trying hard enough, because I thought I might get hurt."

"A train's a deadly thing. I'm just glad you rolled the other way."

Her black eyes still welled with tears, but she stopped crying. "You probably wish I'd rolled under the wheel and you'd be done with me."

"No, I don't! Come on. I'm glad you're here."

Marisol wiped her nose against her sleeve. "But what about food?"

"That I can handle," Ray said as he stood. "I'm sorry to

see Ma Everett's good cooking gone, but I can find us some supper. You wait here."

Ray went out into the dusky forest, and before darkness had settled, he returned. "Get out my pan. We'll eat well tonight."

With the aroma of sorrel, wild tubers, and forest mushrooms sizzling over the fire, Marisol inhaled deeply. "This might top Ma Everett." She smiled.

Ray parceled out the hot meal and they ate, sitting side by side against the mossy bark of a fallen tree.

Ray lifted a slice of tuber with his spoon and said, "So how did you know the train was coming back there?"

"What do you mean? Javidos felt the vibrations."

"I know, but, well, how did you know he felt them?"

"He told me."

"Javidos doesn't speak. When I talk to a crow or some animal, they answer back. But snakes don't . . . speak."

"I guess I just sense what he's sensing sometimes. I always have with snakes. My grandfather taught me how. Sometimes I can even see what they see, if it's a snake I've had for a while and I really understand them well."

Ray sat quietly for several moments, and Marisol watched him as she ate.

"Why? What are you thinking?" she asked at last.

"It's just—I've never thought before about how I speak to animals, or how I understand them. Their language is not like ours. It's not made up of words, really, not like words mean to us."

"You think it has more to do with sensing their thoughts, like it is for me."

Ray nodded, still churning around the idea. His gaze went to the edge of the firelight, where on a low branch the crow that had been following them slept, little more than a shadow among the shadows.

"If I'm going to learn how to cross, I need an animal to help me." Ray narrowed his eyes. "I need to get into the thoughts of that crow."

-9-

THE COUNCIL OF THREE

"I CAN'T DO IT," NEL SAID, DROPPING TO A BOULDER and panting heavily in the cool of the forest. "The fox's form. It still eludes me."

Sally took out a canteen and handed it to Nel. As he drank, Nel stared at his returned leg, the wrinkles around his eyes deepening as he winced.

The night before, the three had met up with Mattias, where he had been hunting and trapping along the ridges around Bee Gum Mountain. Mattias pieced together a crude moccasin for Nel to wear from scraps of deer and rabbit hide. After camping again, Nel and Sally parted ways with the boys, setting off on the last part of the journey to Mother Salagi's cabin. There were only a few miles left to go.

-131-

Sally asked, "Has it not worked? Didn't the Elemental Rose give you back your powers?"

Nel reached down to the leaf-littered ground and picked up a small white feather from among the bracken. He cupped it in his palms and blew into his hands. Sally cocked her head curiously.

A low moan sounded from beyond the trees, over where the ridge dropped off sharply. The leaves on the ground began to flutter and crinkle as a breeze stirred up. Nel blew harder into his cupped hands. A roar rose—sudden and fierce, bending small trees and throwing an enormous storm of leaves and debris up around them.

Sally closed her eyes and covered her face with her hand, as the noise howled around her. She spun around, turning her back to the blast and stumbling a few steps against its force. Then just as abruptly as it had risen, the wind died. As Sally looked up, leaves were slowly settling all around the forest. The ground around where Nel sat was swept clean down to the brown earth.

Nel smiled at her as he dropped the feather from his hand. "My powers are returning," he said. "It is just that I am not yet able to become a fox."

He stood, stamping his mismatched moccasin to the ground. He gave another smile, awe evident in his curling mouth.

Nel waved a hand for Sally to follow him and they set off along the ridge. "To take animal form is difficult," Nel said, putting a hand on Sally's shoulder. "Your brother would concur. But I will remember how, Sally. Be assured. I must fashion a toby again when we return to Shuckstack. It will draw power from the wild. It will help me remember how to be the Rambler I once was."

By late afternoon, the two reached Mother Salagi's home in a cove below the Clingman's Dome. Frost-blackened moss and ancient lichen clung to the logs of the small cabin. The clapboard roof was damp with melting snow, and icicles dripped from the eaves.

In a sunny patch by the front door, Si sat on the stoop. She stood as Nel and Sally came from the tree line.

Buck appeared from around the side of the cabin. He sniffed. "Nel, your leg?"

Si's mouth widened and she ran to Nel. "How . . . how did it happen?"

"All will be explained," Nel said. He put a hand to Si's chin and tilted it up. "How are you feeling?"

"Better," Si said.

"You still look poorly," he said, inspecting her face.

Si scowled. "I'm better. It's been good to get out of Shuckstack and stretch my legs."

"She's been getting stronger," Buck said.

Nel said, "But, Si, we don't want you to overtax—"

"Hush, Nel," Si said, taking a step back to look again at his leg. "I just . . . can't believe it!" She hugged him tightly.

Buck gave a ragged smile and shook his head. "Come on. The other seers just arrived. They're waiting for you."

Sally followed Si, Buck, and Nel into the cabin. She blinked as she left the bright sunlight. The single room smelled of bear fat, drying herbs, and tangy sharp odors that she couldn't identify. Ruddy coals in the fireplace cast a dim light.

Three women sat around Mother Salagi's rough-hewn table. Sally knew right away which was Mother Salagi. The small, hunched woman rose from her seat holding a knotted root for a cane. Her hair was wispy white, and her skin brown and tough like tree bark.

"Suspect I'm a-seeing ye right, Nel?" Mother Salagi cocked a black-button eye to Nel's leg. "You're a-walking as a Rambler once more."

Buck and Si stood aside and took off their coats as Nel approached Mother Salagi.

"Ye'll have to tell us the particulars," she said, reaching out for Nel's hand with her gnarled fingers.

"I will," Nel said, squeezing her hands warmly.

"Sorry I ain't made your party, Nel," she added. "But ye know I ain't got no stomach for crowds."

"You were missed." Nel smiled.

Mother Salagi grunted before saying, "Ye turned eighty-one. Nine nines. Right potent number it is. For our likes." Then she gestured to the other two women. "Don't expect y'all know Joe Nelson, do ye?"

The first seer, a tall woman half Mother Salagi's age with long silver hair and sun-flecked cheeks, greeted Nel first. "I do in fact. We met long ago, Nel. I was a friend of Polly Ann's."

"Yes, yes," Nel said. "It has been many years then. Of

course, Josara. You've had a long journey to be here. Do you still live on Plum Island?"

"It's not so isolated as it once was. I'm rarely there anymore."

Nel nodded, then turned to the other seer. Sally guessed she was in her twenties, maybe no older than Shacks Everett. The seer's skin was smooth and black. Unlike Josara, who was dressed in a simple cotton dress and rugged boots, this young woman wore a gown of white linen with ornate gold jewelry on her wrists, fingers, and ears. And unlike the friendly Josara, she wore a cool, narrow-eyed expression.

"This here's Vastapol," Mother Salagi said.

Vastapol reached out a hand to Nel. "Your reputation is well known to me."

"It's a pleasure," Nel said.

"Who's your young friend here?" Mother Josara asked, beaming at Sally.

Sally grew shy in the presence of the extraordinary women and wanted to hide behind Nel. She said in a quiet voice, "I'm Sally Cobb."

"Nice to meet you," Mother Josara said.

"Ye Ray's sister, ain't ye?" Mother Salagi asked, her button-black eye piercing Sally.

"Yes, ma'am," Sally gulped.

"The child should not be here for our discussion, Salagi," Mother Vastapol said. "We have grave matters to consider. And Nel must explain to us how he has had his leg returned."

"It is the child who has returned my powers," Nel said.

Mother Vastapol's eyes grew wide.

Mother Josara pulled back the chairs from the table. "Come, let us all sit while you tell us what's taken place."

As Sally sat down between Si and Buck, Mother Salagi made a pine-needle-scented tea and took down wooden mugs from the jumbled shelves covering the walls of her cabin. Nel began explaining about the Elemental Rose. Partway through he asked Sally to show them *The Incunabula of Wandering*. She took out the book and slid it across the table, the pages marked for the Verse of the Lost and the Elemental Rose. Sally felt shy and nervous as the others listened to Nel and she watched the seers reading over the pages.

As Nel concluded, Mother Josara asked, "Where did this book come from?"

"Aye, Ray told it belonged to his pappy," Mother Salagi said. "The Rambler Li'l Bill Cobb."

"You trusted her to perform the spell on you?" Mother Vastapol asked. "You trusted her to have the wisdom to understand all the implications of this kind of hoodoo?"

Sally sat up straighter, her heart beginning to pound. Mother Vastapol did not meet Sally's eye, but Nel cast a quick glance at Sally before facing again the young seer.

"She has extraordinary powers," Nel said.

"She has knowledge from the book," Mother Vastapol said. "But do not mistake that for wisdom."

"Aye. Vastapol is right," Mother Salagi said. "Young Sally's a-showing a right fair aptitude, but she ain't got experience to shepherd her actions."

Sally's cheeks got hot, and she squirmed in her seat.

Nel said, "She returned my leg!"

"But at what cost?" Mother Josara asked. The seer looked over at Sally and gave a gentle smile. "The Verse itself warns of a cost. Hoodoo of this magnitude is not given so easily."

"Let's us look to ye, Nel," Mother Salagi said. "See if we can glean what might be and might not be." The ancient seer pointed a crooked finger at Sally. "Let me spy on yond Elemental Rose. Have ye the charms?"

Sally nodded nervously. She took out the four objects and placed them on the table. Mother Salagi spread the objects to their cardinal points—spiderweb north, feather east, brimstone south, and root west. She walked over to a shelf and took down a yellow tallow candle. Placing it in the center of the objects, she lit a stove match and held it to the wick.

When the candle was glowing, Mother Salagi cupped her hands around the flame and squinted her black eye at the bright light. Buck shifted in his seat, and Nel leaned closer, resting his clenched fists on the table. Si squeezed Sally's arm. Sally peered at Mother Salagi, desperate to read something from the strange expression on her deeply creviced face.

"Aye, danger," she croaked at last. "Young Sally done good restoring your powers, Nel. But the leg returned anew is a-bringing peril."

"What sort of peril?" he asked.

"It ain't clear to me. Shrouded. But some danger from abroad seeks ye."

Nel closed his eyes. Sally felt her stomach churn. But as Nel opened his eyes again and smiled at Sally, he said, "It's okay, dear girl. I am grateful to you for what you've done. As long as you children are safe and I can protect you all, what does an old man have to fear in premonitions of doom?"

Sally winced worriedly, but returned Nel's smile.

Mother Vastapol said, "Before we continue, let us speak on what brought Josara and me to the Clingman's Dome. We each received a vision of the Darkness forming in the western plains. We understand that you had a visitor who escaped from the Dark."

"It would not seem he was able to escape it." Nel explained about Mister Bradshaw. The seers were particularly interested in the man's blood, which had turned to oil.

"It is certainly the work of the Machine," Mother Josara said.

"I've been reluctant to accept it, but it must be," Nel said, wringing his hands together. "Somehow the Machine continues to grow in strength even with the Gog dead."

"Yes, a troublesome mystery," Mother Vastapol said. "Let us look to you next, Buck. Your path might illuminate our understanding of the events to come. Are you ready?"

"What are you going to do?" Buck asked, slivers of white showing from his cracked eyelids.

Mother Vastapol stood, taking a small box from the folds of her dress. She set the box on the table and opened the lid. "The raccoon has special eyes. Eyes ringed in shadow. I cast with his bones to see into the past."

Sally watched curiously as Mother Vastapol tipped the box, scattering bleached bones over the table. The room was quiet as the young seer considered the bones.

"You're a gunslinger," Vastapol said flatly.

"I spent a time with outlaws," Buck said. "I used my guns, but I'm no assassin."

Mother Vastapol touched one of the bones. "But you've killed men."

"Not without a reason."

"The bones say you've taken innocent lives."

Buck's breath caught.

"Your brother?" Mother Vastapol cocked an eyebrow at Buck.

"It was an accident," Buck snapped. "A horrible accident long ago."

"I do not doubt you." The seer scooped the bones up into the box and cast them on the table again. She traced her finger around a pair with a knowing nod. Sally could see no pattern or image from the bones, but Mother Vastapol said, "You've slain others."

"The policeman." Si came quickly to his defense. "He was trying to protect me."

"Is this necessary?" Nel interrupted, holding a hand out to Mother Salagi. "We know all this. It does no good to dredge up what's past."

Mother Salagi nodded reassuringly to Nel, and Vastapol cast the bones once more.

"See this pattern in the bones," she said, tapping what could have been ribs or leg bones. "A train. A boy with a sword."

"Yes!" Buck growled. "Seth was trying to kill Ray. I shot at him but I didn't—"

"The bones show us. Killing Ray was not his intent. He was guarding Ray from . . . a devil. Was it the Gog?"

"Seth betrayed us to the Gog," Nel said.

"I see that here. But his loyalty returned. He was trying to protect Ray from the Gog when he was shot. By your bullet."

"No!" Buck shouted. "This can't be true. The Hoarhound killed him."

"The bones do not lie," Vastapol said.

Buck flew up from his chair, knocking it backward across the floor. Sally jerked closer to Si. Buck's face was trembling, his teeth and eyes gleaming white against his ragged face. Nel took Buck around the shoulder, soothing his friend.

Mother Josara's face was gentle and sympathetic as she spoke. "You could not have known, Buck. You thought you were doing what was right. It was a terrible, terrible mistake."

Buck roared over and over, "I didn't kill Seth! It was the Gog's Hound!"

The sound of Buck shouting made Sally cold, and she looked away from him.

"Buck," Mother Vastapol said, reaching a hand across the table to take his. "I am sorry to bring this devastating news to you. But in knowing the truth, you will gain insight into your future actions. The bones have shown us this past for a reason, but only you will be able to find the meaning. Guilt is natural, but do not be overwhelmed by it. Let it guide your path to a higher purpose."

Buck calmed as Mother Vastapol held his hand, and after

a moment, he slumped back into his chair. Vastapol collected her bones into her box, her eyes lingering on the old cowboy.

"Best we continue," Mother Salagi said. "Josara, read your charms for the girl."

"Si, come stand by me," Mother Josara said, in her soothing voice. "My curios—stick and water and stone—will provide insight into your future."

Sally turned from Buck's pained face to watch Mother Josara pour water from a jug into a glass bowl. She set out a crooked stick, its worn surface polished with use. Beside it she set down an egg-shaped rock, ordinary and dull to Sally's eye.

Si came around the table to stand beside Josara.

"Reading the future is difficult and much less reliable than seeing what has passed," Mother Josara said. "Much like the waters in this bowl, what we will see will be murky. You must help me understand what is revealed. Take the stick in your right hand, the stone in your left. Hold them over the water. I will peer into the bowl."

Si picked up the stick and stone and held them over the water as Mother Josara had instructed. Mother Josara stared into the bowl, leaning closer to it after a moment.

"I see a heart," she mumbled. "Love. Are you in love, dear?"

"No!" Si said. "I mean, I love Nel and Buck and the others, of course. But 'in love' . . ."

Mother Josara smiled kindly. "It is the future, so maybe it is someone you will fall in love with. He is tall. Very tall. He holds something in his hand . . . a tool, maybe. Or a weapon."

"Could it be a hammer?" Nel asked, leaning his elbows on the table.

"Yes, yes, that is what he carries."

"Conker!" Nel gasped.

"John and Polly Ann's son," Mother Josara said.

"Conker is dead!" Si exclaimed. "This can't be the future."

"I don't claim to fully understand all I see," Mother Josara said. "These are just images, impressions. You will help determine what they mean."

She leaned back over the bowl and said, "I see something else. A crossroads."

"Is it a place where she should go?" Nel interrupted.

"No, I don't think it is an actual place. It's not a location but a symbol. A choice that Si will face. Down one path there is darkness. The other, light. The person, your love, he stands at the crossroads. He waits for you, Si. And through him something lost to you will be returned. I'm losing the image. . . . It's . . . gone."

"What did it mean?" Si asked, lowering the rock and stick back to the table. "I don't understand. Conker can't be waiting for me."

"He might be alive!" Buck said.

"I wish it were true," Nel said. "But there's no way Conker could have survived the explosion. Even the Nine Pound Hammer was broken."

"Only time will reveal who this person is," Mother Josara said. "I can offer only a possibility to explain the image. When you encounter your love, Si, you will be faced with a critical choice. Down one path lies salvation. Not just for you, but for mankind. I have seen this image of the crossroads before, but never with the two paths contrasted with such severity. The consequences are enormous and far-reaching. These possibilities are linked to the Gog's Machine. That is clear from what I saw."

"What lies down the other path?" Si asked.

"Darkness. Ruin for all humanity. Much weighs on your actions, Si. When the time comes, consider them wisely."

Si's voice sounded strangely weak. "I'm frightened."

"Aye, ye should be," Mother Salagi said. "But ye got your friends. Ye got Nel returned as a Rambler here. They will be a powerful help." As Mother Salagi's eyes settled on her, Sally jerked back in her seat. "Your turn, Sally."

"Me?" she peeped.

Mother Salagi took her little clay pipe from her pocket and lit it. "Your brother has gone to the West, a-seeking the cause of yond Darkness. What's he done with the coney foot?"

"He left it with me," Sally said. "To keep it safe."

"Aye." Mother Salagi nodded approvingly. "Have ye got it with ye?"

"Yes, ma'am," Sally said.

Mother Salagi puffed on her pipe. Then she motioned toward the far wall as she spoke from the corner of her mouth. "Shelf up yonder. Go."

Sally got up nervously from her chair and went around a straw tick bed to the shadowy corner of the cabin.

"Far end, there's a jar a-setting with powder in it. Ye see it?"

Bottles and vessels crowded the wide shelf. Some were filled with herbs and the dried organs of animals, others corked with murky liquids. At the far side, Sally saw a small jar with a screw-top lid that had what looked to be gunpowder in it. She brought it back to the seer.

"That's the one." Mother Salagi opened the lid and shook the silvery powder into the palm of her hand. "Magnetic sand," she mumbled. "From a lodestone. The pure opposite to the stone a-buried in your father's hand here. Let me see yond coney foot." She held out her gnarled hand across the table.

Sally reached into her dress and took out the rabbit's foot to give it to Mother Salagi. Mother Josara and Mother Vastapol moved closer to her to watch as the old seer held up the foot in the firelight.

Mother Salagi turned the foot in her palm as she coated it with the sand. When it was all covered, she held the foot before her with both hands. Sally watched in awe as the sand darkened until it became the deepest inky black. The light in the room dimmed, as if the powder was drawing all luminescence from the world.

The old seer hissed, "Look on, Mothers! The sand's a-turning. The Darkness. Yond Darkness to blacken the fairest heart! Help me."

Josara and Vastapol reached out to cup their hands around Mother Salagi's. Only their eyes glowed with the faint cinders from the hearth, and they began muttering and chanting together.

Mother Vastapol said, "The Machine continues to corrupt the Gloaming."

"You see the Machine?" Nel asked.

The seers did not look up, their eyes locked on the rabbit's foot, their hands clutching it together.

"It will corrupt us all!" Mother Josara gasped. "All of us who depend on the Gloaming. The Gloaming is a part of our world, too, a part of each being that lives and breathes."

"Yes, there it is!" Mother Salagi said. "It's a-ruining us. Some as more than others, but yea in the end, it'll take us one and all."

Buck cocked his head, letting his silver-streaked locks fall across his face. Si gripped the table. Sally watched the rabbit's foot as the powder made the foot disappear entirely into shadow. She feared that the foot had vanished altogether, until she saw a dull light illuminate the faces of the seers.

Then slowly the powder changed color again. What began as a bloody crimson grew and brightened into a fiery orange, lighter than the foot's golden hue, until it beamed a startling white.

Sally drew back away from the table. Mother Vastapol gave out a wail and released her hand, panting and collapsing into a chair. Josara backed away, clutching a hand to her throat.

With trembling fingers, Mother Salagi quickly wiped the sand from the rabbit's foot, extinguishing the light, and sifted the powder back through her palm into the jar.

"What did you see?" Nel asked.

"So it is true," Mother Vastapol whispered. "It has been revealed."

Mother Josara sat down again beside Mother Salagi. "The Gog's dark engine. It can be destroyed!"

"How?" Buck asked.

The three seers began talking one after the other so rapidly, Sally could barely tell which was speaking.

"A weapon must be forged."

"A spike."

"A light to pierce the Dark."

"The spike must be driven—"

"Into the heart of the Machine—"

"With the Nine Pound Hammer."

"But it's broken," Si said. "The hammer's head was lost in the Mississippi."

"Then it must be found," Mother Vastapol said.

"Can we make this spike?" Nel asked.

"It's not within our powers to do this," Mother Josara said.

Vastapol turned to Mother Salagi. "We must send the young Rambler."

"Aye, Ray," Mother Salagi said, nodding. "When he returns from yond West, I'll a-send him."

"Send him where?" Nel asked.

"To find the one who can forge the spike," she said.

"Who can do that?" Si asked.

The eyes of the three seers fell to Sally and a hush came

over the room. She shifted nervously. "What? Why are you looking at me?"

"She must not know," Mother Vastapol hissed.

"It ain't right a-keeping it from her," Mother Salagi said.

"What is it?" Sally asked.

Mother Josara smiled gently at Sally. "A vision brought Vastapol and me to seek Salagi's counsel. Besides the Darkness, we saw something else. Something we suspected Salagi would be able to explain. We've seen another Rambler."

Sally suddenly felt cold.

"He is trapped in the Gloaming," Mother Vastapol said, looking at Nel.

"Who?" Nel asked.

"The only one who can make the spike," Mother Josara said. "Bill Cobb."

Sally felt as if she might fall from her chair, and she grabbed the table to steady herself.

"I fear I spoke falsely to young Ray," Mother Salagi said. "He was a-wanting to know about his father. I searched with my charms. I told Ray I ain't seen his father in this world. I suspected he was killed. He ain't! He's living still . . . prisoned in yonder Gloaming."

Nel gasped. "We must save him."

"We don't know how to find him," Mother Josara said. "To enter the Gloaming is difficult . . . it's beyond our powers."

"Nel's powers have been returned!" Sally said. "He's a Rambler again. He can't become a fox yet, but he'll remember.

Won't you, Nel? You told me you would. Can't you cross? Can't you go find Father?"

Nel's careworn gaze flickered from Sally down to his hands resting on the table.

"No," Mother Salagi said after a moment. "Some danger seeks Nel. He must set his mind to protecting the children of Shuckstack."

"Your brother," Mother Josara said. "He will find your father. He must bring the rabbit's foot to him."

Sally could not fight the tears spilling across her cheeks. "But Ray is going to Kansas. Who knows how long it will be before he's back. If . . . if he ever comes back . . . from the Darkness. That awful Darkness! Why did you have to send him there, Nel?"

Nel got up from his chair and came around to Sally, bundling her in his arms. She sobbed against his shoulder as he whispered to her, "Ray will be fine, dear girl. Don't you worry. And he'll find your father, Sally."

"Aye," Mother Salagi said, carrying the rabbit's foot around the table to Sally and putting it in her hand. She touched a gnarled hand to Sally's face, wiping away her tears. "Your brother will come back. Until then, ye must keep the foot safe."

THE FOLLOWING MORNING NEL, BUCK, SI, AND SALLY
set off on the two-day journey back to Shuckstack. Sally was
not the only one in a somber mood. The words of the seers
weighed greatly on each of them. Most markedly changed
was Buck. While dourness was not unusual for the sharpshooter, deep melancholy bent his frame as he walked. Sally
watched with concern as Nel had to help Buck to his feet
when they took breaks along the trail.

By evening they made camp near Two Eagle Mountain.
Usually Sally loved a trip to the tall citadel of rocks, but that
evening none had an interest in the view. After making dinner,
they rolled out their blankets before the fire and lay struggling to sleep.

Sally woke to Si's voice with the dawn not yet broken.

"Buck!" she called. "Buck!"

Nel threw off his blanket. "What's wrong?"

"I woke just a moment ago, and Buck's not here."

"He probably just couldn't sleep and is taking a walk," Nel said, rubbing his eyes with his fist.

"That's not like him, Nel," Si said. "You know that."

Nel's brow furled. "Where is he, then?"

Si held up her hand, and Sally watched as the luminous shapes fixed into position along her fingers and across her black knuckles. She turned in a circle until she located Buck. "He's up on the peak."

"Let's go," Nel said, getting up.

Sally scrambled to her feet to follow them.

Guided by Si's hand, they headed up toward the rocks atop Two Eagle. The climb was steep, but they reached the peak in a few minutes. Dawn teemed with a ruddy orange. Ahead the expansive scope of the Smoky Mountains stretched out before them.

Coming over the top of a boulder, Sally saw him. Buck sat at the edge of the cliff, his head slumped and his arms resting on his knees. In his hands were his pistols.

Nel exchanged a look with Si and then called out, "Buck, what are you doing up here?"

Buck lifted his head slightly, his tangled hair spilling over his face, but said nothing. They slowly approached him. Sally stopped a few paces behind Nel and Si as the two sat on either side of Buck.

"What's going on?" Si asked.

"I've been up here thinking," the old cowboy murmured in his gravelly voice. "Thinking on all I done."

"What have you done, Buck?" Nel asked.

"All them . . ." Buck choked. "All of them that I cut their lives away."

Nel put a hand to Buck's shoulder.

"I can say that my brother, that policeman, those were just accidents," Buck said. "I should have known better, but they were just accidents. But Seth! That was something different."

"I was there beside you," Nel said. "There was so much smoke, but I saw Seth holding his sword over Ray. We all thought Seth was going to kill Ray."

"But I shot him!" Buck roared. "It was my bullet! If I hadn't fired that shot . . . He was a troubled boy, but he didn't deserve to die. I was the one that killed him. I . . . I can't trust myself not to make that mistake again."

Buck held up the pistols, their silver casings catching the bloody tint of the morning light. "My pa, he gave me these guns when I was just a boy. What would he say to know what I've done with them?"

Nel squeezed Buck's shoulder.

"I can't trust myself . . . ," Buck said, turning his pale eyes to Nel. "I can't trust the guns not to kill again." Tears spilt down his ragged face. He stood, whispering, "Never again."

Nel and Si scrambled to rise. "What are you doing, Buck?" Nel asked, taking Buck's arm.

Buck held the pair of pistols before him, the barrels upright.

"That seer, Vastapol," Buck said. His brow trembled and he spoke through gritted teeth. "She asked me a question last night after everyone else was asleep. She asked, 'Buck, why did you never become a Rambler?' The guns. Being a gunslinger always came easy to me. It was what I was good at. Learning to be a Rambler, that would have been hard. So she told me to 'cast off the gunslinger—cast away the guns.' I'm giving them up. I can't live with them anymore, Nel. I'm finished with being a gunslinger."

Nel's wrinkled face tightened.

But calm came over Buck's expression. "Sometimes, Nel, you have to do what scares you most to protect the ones you love."

He took a step closer to the edge of the cliff. Nel let go of Buck's arm and watched as the old cowboy heaved the pair of pistols from the mountainside.

Over and over, the shining silver of the guns sparkled and spun in the rising sun. Down they fell, disappearing onto the rocks far below.

The following evening, the four returned to Shuckstack. Nel fixed Buck a tonic to help him sleep. The others ate supper, and after cleaning up, the children scattered about the den, reading or playing games. Si, who had gone out into the mountains to build her strength, returned weaker than when she left.

"You'll need to stay in bed the next few days," Nel said to her. "Come down and I'll make you a new medicine. Carolyn, make sure everyone is in bed within the hour. Good night, children."

"Good night, Mister Nel," they chorused.

Sally watched them go from where she sat sideways in the rocking chair. Her thoughts swirled and tangled around her head.

Ray. Her father. Nel. Buck.

Sometimes you have to do what scares you most to protect the ones you love.

Buck's words returned again and again in her thoughts. Sally was scared. Scared for Ray out in Kansas. Scared for her father, lost somewhere in the Gloaming.

Someone had to return his powers so he could forge the spike that would destroy the Gog's Machine. But how would he ever be found?

Her hand rested against the rabbit's foot in her dress pocket. The rabbit's foot. She turned quickly in the rocking chair, letting her feet drop to the floor.

Buried within the rabbit's foot was the lodestone her father had given to Ray. It had guided him; it had led Ray to their father trapped by the Hoarhound. What if the lodestone worked again?

Sally stood up.

"Sal," Rosemary called, squatting on the floor with Naomi and Oliver. "Come play jackstraws with us."

"Not just now," Sally said. "I'm . . . going to bed."

"Nel said we could stay up a little longer."

"I'm tired."

"Suit yourself."

Sally climbed the stairs to the loft.

The lodestone. When it became the golden foot, its power to guide vanished.

The Elemental Rose could restore lost powers. Could it also restore the lodestone's powers within the rabbit's foot?

She would need to wait until the others were asleep before she found out.

Sally listened to gentle breathing and occasional snores filling the loft. Rosemary grumbled with a dream in the bed next to her. Open across her stomach was the book of Greek myths Sally had given her as a Christmas gift.

Sliding out from under her quilt, Sally pulled the rucksack from under her bed and took out *The Incunabula of Wandering* and the four objects of the Elemental Rose. She tiptoed down the stairs to the den and knelt before the dying embers. First she placed the rabbit's foot on the floor. Then she flipped through the *Incunabula* until she found the page showing the drawing of the compass.

She read her father's note again. "Four objects are needed for the ER. Each is a stead for the four. Each brings the powers of the four into one when they are in their proper place."

The proper places. Sally looked around the dark room trying to remember how the light changed with the time of day. The morning sun always came through the front door, she thought. So that was east, wasn't it?

Hoping she was right, she lined the cardinal feather with the door. She moved around the rabbit's foot clockwise. South was yellow, fire. She opened the lid to the tin of brimstone and set it down. Making another quarter turn, she put the Black Sampson root across from the cardinal feather, the symbol of earth opposite the symbol of air. At last, she turned to put down the last object, the white spiderweb—water opposing fire.

Once they were placed, she sat up on her knees with the rabbit's foot before her, her breath coming in shallow pants.

The brimstone ignited and smoke rose. Sally ran to open the front door, ushering in a cold breeze. Hopeful it would keep the smoke from waking anyone.

Sally turned back to the rabbit's foot.

The cardinal feather fluttered. The Black Sampson root writhed on the floorboards. Water puddled from the spiderweb. Smoke covered the rabbit's foot, hiding it from her sight. Sally held her breath until she thought her lungs would burst.

There was a flash, and Sally toppled back. Scrambling forward, she batted at the smoke to clear it. The rabbit's foot lay on the floor. Nothing looked different about it.

She picked it up, touching a finger curiously to the metal. The paw began slowly turning in a circle until the tiny golden claws at the tip pointed in the same direction as the Black Sampson root. She moved the paw around in her palm until it pointed east. Again, the rabbit's foot rotated until the claws pointed west.

"Sally?" A voice came hoarsely from the stairs to the loft. Little Noah stood rubbing his puffy eyes. "What's that smell?"

Sally scattered up the feather, the root, and the spiderweb. Instantly, the flames died in the tin of brimstone.

"Nothing," Sally said. "Sorry. Er . . . just go back to sleep."

Noah blinked sleepily and slumped back up the stairs.

Sally picked up the tin of brimstone, strangely cool now to her touch, and closed the lid before putting it, along with the rest of the Elemental Rose, back in her rucksack.

She paced around before the fireplace, her mind twirling with thoughts. The lodestone within the rabbit's foot was working again. It had turned to point to the west. It was pointing to her father.

Her father—whom she had always dreamed of but had never met. Her father had never even known that she had been born. He was alive and she had the means to find him where he was trapped in the Gloaming.

Sally ran for the steps down to the cellar. She reached the bottom and turned to the door for Nel's room. She had to tell him. He could take the rabbit's foot and . . .

She stopped with her hand on the door handle. No, she thought. Nel wouldn't use the rabbit's foot to find her father. He wouldn't leave Shuckstack. He wouldn't leave the children.

Sally began trembling as she realized what she had to do.

She gathered food from the kitchen larder and quietly ascended the stairs back to her room. After dressing quietly by her bed, she stuffed some clothes into her rucksack. She stood, trying to think if she was forgetting anything. Sally looked down at Rosemary curled up under the warm quilts. Should she tell her friend that she was leaving?

Sally picked up the book of Greek myths from Rosemary's chest. Sally's favorite story had always been the story of Orpheus, who ventured into the Underworld to save his wife, Eurydice. Hades told Orpheus he could return with his wife only if he walked in front of her and did not look back until they had reached the world of the living. But Orpheus was too anxious and could not help himself. He looked back. And Eurydice was lost to him.

Sally closed the book and set it on the floor. She wiped at her eyes as she hoisted the rucksack onto her shoulders. It was heavy with the *Incunabula,* the four objects of the Elemental Rose, and the scant supplies she had taken from the kitchen.

The moonlight coming in through the window reflected off the cool surface of the rabbit's foot. The foot turned slowly in a half circle in her palm until the tiny claws pointed west.

Sally headed for the stairs.

She would not make any mistakes. She would not look back.

A WEEK OF SLEEPING BY CAMPFIRE AND FORAGING FOR food, tracking game, and navigating through the rugged forests gave Ray the familiar delight of being immersed in the wild. Marisol was not so smitten with their journey.

"Shouldn't we be coming on Springfield soon?" she asked, the valise hanging heavily from her arm as she walked.

"Tomorrow," Ray said.

"Will we be stopping for the night? In a hotel or any sort of lodgings."

"We won't stop in any towns."

Late spring had brought long, hot days, and Marisol wiped a kerchief along her neck. Her already golden cheeks were brown from the sun. "Really, I don't mind paying."

Ray laughed. "Why pay for rooms when we can sleep for free?"

"Because I'm days overdue for a bath and a soft bed."

Ray smirked. "I'm sure when we reach the Indian Territory, Redfeather will be able to arrange something nice for you."

"Yes, I hear the accommodations rival Paris." Marisol snorted. "Probably lucky if we aren't stuck in some lice-infested wigwam."

A shadow crossed Ray's path, and he shielded his eyes from the sun to look for the crow soaring overhead. Ray stopped, closing his eyes to concentrate on the bird. Marisol dropped her bag, grateful for a break, and took out some water.

"Did you do it yet?" she asked.

Ray opened an eye. "Not with you talking." He tried again to focus on the bird, to see through his eyes. Quieting his thoughts, he attempted to forget his own body and to put himself high above the earth.

The crow landed on Ray's hat, knocking it forward over his nose. He gave a caw and pinched at Ray's ear with his beak. "Ow! All right," Ray said, shaking the crow from his hat. The crow flapped to resettle on his shoulder. "I've only got one piece left, you know. After that, you'll have to learn to bake them yourself."

Ray slipped his hand in his coat pocket to take out the fold of waxed paper. He held up a corner of some fry bread they'd made from acorns. The crow snatched and ate it in one gulp. He shifted on Ray's shoulder and squawked at Marisol.

"She ate all hers already," Ray said.

"Even if I hadn't, I wouldn't share with you."

The crow beat his way off Ray's shoulder, casting a series of abusive caws as he took flight.

"I don't even want to know what he called me." Marisol rolled her eyes.

"He's got a mouth on him." Ray offered Marisol a hand as she stood. "Reminds me of the b'hoys back in the city when I was a kid."

"What's a b'hoy?" Marisol asked.

"Oh, these tough guys who always started trouble. They said funny things like 'cheese it, lads' after they'd rob some grocer. They greased their hair up so they had these soap-locks at their temples." Ray pulled a couple of brown curls down from his ears to demonstrate.

Marisol laughed. "B'hoy. That fits him," she said, watching B'hoy circle once more over their heads and call out before sailing over the trees. "What'd he say?"

"Storm coming." Ray frowned.

"Sky looks clear to me."

"For now."

B'hoy was right: as dusk came, dark clouds filled the western sky. Ray tried to find a suitable shelter, but the only buildings they passed were for a logging camp that echoed with the shouts and curses of men felling a tree.

"Should we ask if we can stay?" Marisol asked.

"We're not staying with a bunch of loggers!" Ray continued walking. "There'll be an abandoned cabin if we keep going. I'll get us a better spot."

As they sat that evening before their sputtering fire, the

down-pouring rain ran rivers across the small piece of waxed canvas over their heads. Marisol growled, "You call this a better spot?"

Lightning shattered the night. B'hoy gave a croak from a tree nearby.

"Don't you start, too," Ray warned. He ventured forward to pick the pan from the coals, offering the last of the meal to Marisol. "Want any more?"

"More like stew now."

"Mind if I?"

She eyed the pan with disgust and shook her head. "I take it back, by the way."

"What's that?"

"Everything bad I said about where we'll stay when we meet up with Redfeather. I'll take any wigwam, teepee, or dugout as long as it's dry. Javidos can fight off the rats."

Ray took a few bites and shook the rest into the fire. Still hungry, he remembered he had a couple of crumbs of the fry bread still in his coat pocket. It was hardly enough for a bite and as Ray started to reach for it, he stopped.

He looked up at B'hoy, head tucked into his wing and seeming to try to sleep in the storm. Ray turned a bit on the log to put his back to the crow.

"What are you doing?" Marisol asked, fidgeting with her side of the canvas.

"Quiet a moment," Ray whispered.

He closed his eyes, feeling the cold rain plastering his clothes to his back. There was no need to try to ignore the rain or be frustrated with it. The rain was part of the wild, just as were the trees around him and the crow sitting on the branch. Ray concentrated, letting his thoughts fill with his surroundings. He didn't consider whether he hated the rain or liked the rain, but simply noticed that the rain was there. The forest was there. The crow was there. And he was among them.

He then focused on B'hoy, shutting everything else out as he tried to make the link with the bird.

Ray generated an image in his mind. The bit of fry bread in his pocket. B'hoy was welcome to it if he wanted it. All he needed to do was fly down and pluck it from the pocket by his right hip.

Ribbons of water curled down his face and dripped from his nose and chin. The fry bread. Come on, B'hoy, he thought. Take it.

Feathers fluttered, beating wings against the pouring rain. B'hoy's talons clutched his leg. His beak prodded against his side, nudging open the pocket flap.

Ray opened his eyes. The crow looked up at him, the soggy bit of fry bread breaking in half as B'hoy turned and flew back to the branch.

Ray smiled and let out a sharp exhale.

"That's a start," Marisol said. She peered up from the canvas cover at the dripping, dark forest. "Hey, the rain. I think it's stopping."

Ray stood, excitement welling in his chest. "I'll build up the fire so we can dry out."

* * *

As warm, sunny weather returned, Marisol became more comfortable with the journey. She complained less and did not try more than twice to persuade Ray to stop in Springfield.

Occasionally as they walked, Ray practiced over and over speaking to the crow with his thoughts. B'hoy was stubborn, and half the time he ignored Ray's requests to land on that log or pick up that piece of food. But Ray could hear B'hoy's thoughts too if he concentrated really hard, and he knew the crow understood him. Ray began to turn his attention next to trying to see through B'hoy's eyes.

"That's pretty hard," Marisol said, after watching Ray walking with his eyes closed. "Even when I can see what Javidos sees, it's only snippets of images. Hardly anything, really."

Ray sighed and looked up as B'hoy sailed a hundred feet over their heads. "You think he's too far away?"

"I don't know," Marisol said. Her copperhead slithered up from her collar to sprout from her hat like a flickering pompom. "Javidos is never more than a few feet away from me."

"You know, speaking to Javidos like you do," Ray said. "And seeing what he sees. That's pretty complicated hoodoo, Marisol. From what Nel says, not even that many Ramblers could do it."

She laughed as she shrugged. "I learned when I was so little, it's hardly impressive."

"But you can do it," Ray said. "Maybe there's other hoodoo you could learn—"

Marisol stopped and pointed. "Look. More travelers."

Ray and Marisol had kept to the rocky woods, but often they passed near roads. It was not surprising to see men on horseback, mule-drawn carts, or even the occasional buckboard. But what they now saw seemed to be a caravan traveling east. A large group of people were riding in wagons, loaded down with supplies, livestock, and even furniture.

That night, a family stopped near their Five Spot to make camp. The travelers were unaware that Marisol and Ray were not more than a hundred feet away. Ray crept to the edge of the protective perimeter to investigate.

"They're from Kansas all right," he reported after returning.

"How do you know?"

"More than half are sick. Coughing and some delirious. Heard a man mention the Darkness. Also they're digging three graves."

Marisol's brow knit. "I hope they reach where they're going before . . ."

Ray nodded. "I feel sad for the little ones especially. Do you think if we shared Nel's charms with them, it might help?"

"Nel did everything he could to save Bradshaw," Marisol said. "I think once you've been in contact with the Darkness too long, nothing can be done."

Ray watched the shadows of the refugees moving before their fire. He could hear someone crying. "There must be something."

"But what?" Marisol asked.

"Something."

They climbed gradually, edging the foothills of the Ozark Mountains to their south. Their journey led them through a vast forestland punctuated now with only occasional farms, sawmills, and cabins. Ray guessed it would not be more than a few days' travel to the Indian Territory. As they occasionally neared the roads, they saw more of the hastily dug roadside graves.

They made camp in the woods not far from a small farm that was bordered on one side by a quiet road. Marisol had become comfortable making the campfire, and she stacked twigs in a pyramid. "It's so quiet out here," she said.

"Nice, isn't it," Ray said.

"I guess," Marisol said. She fed pine needles into the glowing kindling and blew into it until it flamed. "I'm so used to all the children of Shuckstack. All their voices. When you go out on your own, Ray, don't you miss talking to people?"

Ray took out some watercress and wild sorrel from his haversack. "I don't really mind not talking."

"Isn't it lonely?" she asked.

"Sometimes."

"Do you ever think of Jolie?" she asked.

This surprised Ray, and he turned his face quickly to hide his reaction. "Often," he said.

"Do you miss her?"

"Certainly."

"Me too." Marisol rested on her heels, watching the flames dance in front of her. "I wonder what happened to her."

Ray got to his feet, gathering the waterskins. "I'm going to look for some water."

Marisol pushed her black curls from her face as she looked at him over her shoulder. "You okay, Ray?"

"Yeah," Ray said. "I'll be right back."

Her brow pinched a little as she turned back to prod a stick into the blaze. "I'll get supper ready," she said.

Ray climbed over a downed pine and headed through the trees.

He had thought often about Jolie over the past year. Many times when he was traveling—down in the marshlands along the Carolina coast to visit some root worker or journeying along a slow, moss-dappled river—he wished she were with him. It was true, he rarely felt lonely when he traversed the wild, but when he did it was not for Shuckstack or his family there. He missed Jolie.

Where had she gone?

Ray scanned the forest. He had a good sense for reading the landscape to locate water, and after some walking, he found a creek. As he filled the waterskins, he called out for B'hoy with his thoughts, but the crow was elsewhere. "What's he up to?" Ray muttered.

Slowly winding his way back toward their camp, he concentrated, calling to B'hoy with his mind—

A gunshot erupted, reverberating through the trees. Ray crouched, not sure which direction it came from.

"If you know what's best for you, you won't move," a voice called.

Ray spied him in the falling light: a gray-bearded man

with a rifle aimed his way. The man cautiously approached, and Ray reached for his toby. The ball of bluestone. The Indian-head pennies. They could protect him temporarily from gunshots.

"I can take down a bear three times as far as you are," the man warned.

Ray lowered his hand, knowing the man would give him no time to prepare the charm.

"That there last shot was a warning. Next won't be. Go ahead and drop that Arkansas toothpick I spy on your belt."

"I mean no harm," Ray said, pulling his knife out and dropping it on the ground. "My friend and I are camped over there a ways. Might be your property and if it is, I apologize for trespassing."

"Trespassing is only the half of what you Jayhawkers is capable." The man had reached Ray now, and he kept the rifle squared against his shoulder.

"Jayhawkers, sir?"

"Don't play me the fool!" he spat. "I'll no more ignore you Kansas trash coming through stealing and spreading your plague."

"Please," Ray said, "I think you're mistaken. We're not from Kansas. We're heading west."

"West is Indian Territory. Think I'm an idiot?" The man tilted his head to shout, "Danny! Over here!"

"Really, we are," Ray said. He flicked a glance to the high branches of the trees behind the man, looking for B'hoy in the falling light.

"Just last week, bunch of you Jayhawkers turn up. First

asking to water your jennies. Next thing, you got a knife to my old woman's throat." He shook the barrel at Ray, causing Ray to back a few steps. "Tearing the house up! Took the last of our cans and jars."

"We're not like that," Ray said. "We're just passing through."

"Danny!" the man shouted. Then he growled at Ray, "Was a time I felt right sorry for you people. But no more!" His voice pitched higher. "I see now the lot of you are wicked. I'm tired of you thinking your ills give you a right!"

Ray closed his eyes, struggling to ignore the shouting man, struggling to find some link to the crow. He called out in his thoughts for B'hoy to help.

The man hollered, "Danny!" He grumbled under his breath and then shouted again, "Danny! Quick, I got one!"

With his eyes still closed, Ray saw for a fraction of a moment the forest floor from a great height. Moving. Passing swiftly among the tall trees. The shadowy bracken and leaves stretched out like an enormous quilt.

A wave of dizziness hit Ray, and he staggered a step, opening his eyes.

A black comet dropped from the sky. A flurry of wings and scratching talons whirled around the man's face. The man shouted, dropping the rifle to beat off the crow.

Ray grabbed the man's rifle and speared it barrel-down into the soft earth. Picking up his knife, he hurled the waterskins across his back and ran. He could hear the man's curses, and hoped it meant the man wouldn't be able to use the rifle now. B'hoy flew past Ray as they raced toward the Five Spot.

From the edge of his vision, Ray saw another man come around through the trees, a long-barreled Henry rifle following Ray's movements. He fired, but Ray cut wide, moving in a zigzag as he ran.

Ray spied the first cornerstone of the Five Spot. He was almost there.

Then his shoulder was aflame and he tumbled end over end, the echoes of the shot peeling across the forest.

Ray cried out and clutched his shoulder, spirals of pain coursing down his arm.

Marisol jumped from the Five Spot's perimeter. "I've got you! Can you stand?"

Ray staggered to his feet, and they passed the protective line. Ray felt dizzy and stumbled again, his arm hot and wet with blood.

The shouting men came toward them, but their eyes passed over Ray and Marisol, unseeing. Repelled by forces they could not sense, they continued around the edge of the Five Spot and disappeared into the forest.

"A SECOND SHOT," CONKER WHISPERED. HE LAY IN THE crowding ferns at the entrance to a cave, a club of knotted ironwood in his hand.

Jolie drew Cleoma's shell knife from her belt. She crouched beside Conker, peering out at the dark forest. "Are they shooting at us?"

"No. They're a long ways off. I suspect we're safe."

They camped without a fire, as they had done every night for weeks. "These the headwaters?" Conker asked, looking at the water that flowed from a spring within the cave, running out to form a creek.

Jolie was still peering in the dark, listening for approaching voices but hearing none. She turned back to say, "No. But we should find them soon. I worry we might not have taken the quickest route."

Conker dismissed her doubts with a shake of his head. "You said that other way was past a bunch of towns. We're right to be cautious. This way's good."

Jolie had led them north across the Ozark wilderness. Soon they would turn east following the rivers to the Mississippi, where the Nine Pound Hammer had been lost. Following the rough country to the north seemed the safest. A black boy traveling with an oddly dressed white girl might draw unwanted attention otherwise.

"You go rest," Conker said, finishing the last of the river mussels. He leaned back against the lichen-covered entrance. The ironwood club crossed his lap. By his side lay a sack, containing their store of food and the bladders carrying the water from the siren's well. "I'll listen out for a while, before I sleep."

"You will wake me if you hear those men?"

"Don't worry about them."

"But if you do . . ."

"Go on. Rest. We got far to travel yet."

"I think tomorrow we will find the headwaters."

Conker nodded. "Okay. G'night."

Jolie slid into the waters gurgling in the dark recesses of the cave and slept.

Stacker Lee held up a hand, and his companions banked their horses beside his. Sunlight pierced the forest in a hundred glimmering shafts. He got down from his horse and kicked at a stone with his boot.

"What's it?" Alston asked, watching as Stacker walked a dozen yards to a second stone.

Stacker then led his horse on foot until he came to a fire pit, cold several days now. "Hoodoo magic," he said. Kneeling, he touched a finger to the leaves. "Blood. A man was shot near here. His wounds were tended. They put the fire out proper to break the charm, so he must have survived."

"John Henry's boy?" Hardy grunted, still sitting atop his horse.

"Have they set a hoodoo charm before?" Stacker scorned.

"Nope."

"They ain't built a fire neither." Stacker then stiffened and added, "Two men are approaching."

Hardy and Alston rustled to draw their weapons, circling their horses.

"Be still and keep your guns beneath your coats," Stacker hissed. "I'll speak to them."

Stacker looped the reins of his horse around a tree and removed his Stetson to neatly crisp the folds. He waited, his eyes lowered to his hat as two men—one older with a gray beard who seemed the father of the other—approached with rifles leveled.

"This here's my land," the older man called out.

Stacker placed his hat back on his head and kicked at the cold coals, his back to the two. Stacker could sense things, and he smiled to himself as he noticed their caution, although not yet true fear. They were sizing up the three horsemen: the calm black man with the fine clothes, the massive man with the dense black beard, and the younger one, filthy and long-haired.

"It's always someone's land," Stacker replied, still not facing the two.

"My meaning is that you best get off it," the old man said.

"Well, you heard the rube, boys," Stacker said. "We best get off."

Alston and Hardy did not move. Neither did Stacker. The forest was quiet.

"Don't they speak?" the old man asked.

Stacker smoothed the fine hairs of his mustache. "When I want them to," he replied.

The son jerked his Henry rifle at Hardy and Alston. "You take orders from a darkie?"

"Danny!" The older man waved a hand low at his side to his son. Alston and Hardy did not respond, their faces cold and still. The son narrowed his eyes and spat on the ground.

Stacker looked down at the fire pit. "You shot a man here?"

"That's right. Jayhawkers' filth," the old man said. "We've had right trouble with them that come out from Kansas."

"A Darkness drives folk from the western plains," Stacker said.

"Storms, they says," the old man corrected.

"They're no storms," Stacker murmured.

The old man cocked his eyebrows, but then seemed to remember his intent. "Well, you'll move on now. I claimed this land near thirty years back. Cleared it. Built my home there with my own hands. I won't have it overrun now by Jayhawkers and . . . highway robbers."

Stacker smiled down at his feet, his expression dissolving from amusement to disgust. "You may try to defend your wretched sty, but it will be in vain. This land is changing. Darkness and tribulations are coming. Not only to the western plains, but all this land. All this country. All will be smitten and plagued."

"You sound more to a preacher than a road agent," the son said, flicking his eye at the older man. "Is it Armageddon you speaking of?"

Stacker turned at last to face the two, his eyes aglow with sinister mirth, the clockwork buzzing from his chest. "No, of Eden. A new Eden. A paradise born of the engine and the furnace!" He raised his hands in the air, and the old man and his son backed a step, clutching tightly to their rifles aimed at Stacker.

"Hearken the Machine, fueled by the souls of the meek," Stacker continued.

Alston's horse whinnied and stamped his feet. Hardy circled his horse away.

"And a new world will dawn!" Stacker shouted at the two. "Baptized in the blood of the ignorant."

Alston and Hardy threw back their coats.

Jolie and Conker traversed the wilderness eastward. They followed rivers walled with tree-crested limestone cliffs and slept near blue springs and in darkly weathered caves. Bluffs and boulders gave way to an alluvial flatland, and after a week, they reached the meandering banks of the Mississippi.

Jolie slipped into the river while Conker waited on the sandy shore. "We are not far," she announced when she returned. "I remember these waters. The trestle is several miles to the south."

"You can take to the river if you want," Conker said. "I'll walk the shore and meet you."

After Jolie dove back into the water, Conker continued on, walking the remainder of the day along a fisherman's path that weaved back and forth from the river's edge into green forests and through quiet clusters of houses. Barges and steamers moved about the river, spewing columns of black coal smoke. Late in the afternoon, the path met a railroad track and he followed it to the trestle. Descending the bank to the shadows beneath the high wooden supports, he found Jolie at the river's edge.

"You sure this is it?" he asked, as a locomotive roared above.

"I am," she answered.

Conker eyed the coppery-black waters moving swiftly to the south. The river was wide—nearly half a mile—and Conker whistled. "Then maybe it's out there somewhere. But how you ever going to find it?"

Jolie smiled and placed a hand on his arm. "The river will help me."

The following morning, Jolie began her search. Conker sat all day in the shade of the trestle, watching the river and waiting. She emerged at twilight empty-handed. "The bottom is

muddy and there is much debris. I suspect some are the remains of *The Pitch Dark Train.* Do not worry. If it is here, I
will find it."

At the end of the second day, Jolie had still not found the
Nine Pound Hammer. She came up from the river feeling dis-
couraged and was surprised that Conker was not on the
bank. She settled back beneath the surface, considering
whether she should search for him. But Conker came out
from the trees after dark.

"Where were you?" she asked, climbing up on the shore.

"We had visitors. You remember those three horsemen,
the gunmen we saw just after we left the spring?"

"Why would they be here?"

"I been asking myself that too," Conker said. "They
came up on the tracks, but I was able to take to hiding before
they saw me. They spied all about before they moved on."

"It could have been different men," Jolie said.

"They weren't."

"A coincidence then?"

Conker ran his palm across the heavy knotted end of his
ironwood club. "Maybe, but I doubt it. If I see them again,
I'm assuming they got reason to be tracking us. And I ain't
going to sort it out first." He nodded to the river. "No luck
today?"

Jolie shook her head.

"I feel the hammer's presence. It's out there. You'll find
it." Conker shouldered the ironwood club. "I best sleep in
the woods tonight. I'll stick there tomorrow too. Be watching
for you."

As he turned, Jolie said, "Conker."

"Yeah."

"There." Jolie hesitated. "On the opposite bank. I found . . . a grave marker. Fashioned from a sheet of steel. It bears your name."

He looked at her and then nodded, disappearing into the trees.

Jolie woke the following morning from where she had slept on a submerged sandbar. She rose to the surface and startled a heron into the pink-speckled dawn. Gazing at the forested shoreline, she imagined Conker already awake, waiting for her to return with the Nine Pound Hammer.

She sighed and spoke to the river, "Have you not heard my plea?"

She dove, pushing her way against the swift current to search the tangled grasses and murky depths. Over the past few days, there had been a strange voice, low and distant, mingled in the water of the river. Cleoma had told her of the call that had led the sirens up the Mississippi and along rivers to the west. It was not the voice of the ancient grandmother of the waters, for she never spoke. But it was as if someone was calling from far away. Jolie could not hear the words, but it compelled her to seek its source.

She shuddered and turned her attention back to finding the hammer. As the sun drew high, the brown light filtered down to Jolie. The day was not half spent, but she was already weary. Her wrists were sore from digging through the mud. Her muscles ached from fighting the water's incessant tug.

How many days did she have to search before she accepted that it was lost? Frustration overcame her, and she shouted a boiling stream of bubbles. Jolie quit struggling against the current and curled into an angry ball. She tumbled along, through the reedy bottom, until her hair tangled in a submerged log. Cursing, Jolie grabbed the branches to keep her hair from being pulled further and snapped at the skeletal branches until she freed her hair.

Something shone a moment in the wavering light. Jolie started breaking the branches again from the log, getting down to where the silt had piled against the trunk. In the soft muck, her fingers met something hard. Digging with her nails, she dislodged a molded square of iron as large as a brick. An oval opening pierced the body.

The Nine Pound Hammer.

But where was the handle? She scattered the mud until a brown cloud surrounded her. Her palm was nearly speared by a jagged piece of wood. Brushing the muck from it, she saw that it was the narrow top of the hammer's handle.

The handle was broken.

Conker came from the trees as soon as he saw Jolie's head break the surface. "Did you find it . . . ?" he began, but stopped as Jolie held up the heavy head of iron and the broken end of the handle.

"I am sorry," she said. "I could not find the other half."

"It doesn't matter," Conker murmured, relief and disappointment mingling in his expression. "You found it. That's what counts. I . . . I'll make a new handle from this club."

"That would be no better than loading acorns in a gun," a voice said.

Conker spun around to see the three men. They were on foot, emerging from the shadows beneath the trestle.

Conker swung the ironwood club against Alston's chest. The hard wood met steel, and the shotgun hidden beneath his long coat fired downward into the earth. Conker brought the club around to Hardy. It struck the man's chin with a horrible crack.

Alston had thrown open his coat and drawn up the stagecoach gun, but Conker snatched the gun by the barrel and pummeled Alston across the shoulder with the club. Alston dropped to his knees. No sooner had he fallen than Conker had him aloft by his throat. He threw the large man several yards. He broke the barrel from the gun with a snap and scattered the two pieces, then turned to face Stacker.

A shot fired so close to his shoulder Conker felt the fabric of his shirt move.

Stacker's long-barreled Buntline smoked. He had a razor squared against Jolie's throat.

"You mistake our intent," Stacker said. And then with a whisper to Jolie he added, "No need to sing, siren." Stacker motioned with the gun toward Conker's club.

Conker dropped it. Stacker lowered the razor from Jolie's throat. She ran to Conker's side and wheeled around with a scowl. Stacker holstered his gun and looked around at his men. Alston lay groaning on the ground, while Hardy was unconscious and splayed in the dirt. Stacker shook his head with disappointment.

"At last I find the mighty son of John Henry," he said.

"You have followed us," Jolie snarled. Her hand brushed the wrapped whorl of Cleoma's knife.

"I've been looking for you, you could say. I've been looking for those that seek the Nine Pound Hammer, and here you've found it."

"How do you know about it?" Conker asked in his deep, rumbling voice. "How do you know who I am?"

"I know many things. Was born with the fey's gift, you see," Stacker said. Pointing to the hammer's head in Jolie's hand, he added, "You can't fashion a new handle for the Nine Pound Hammer from that stick of ordinary wood."

Conker glared suspiciously.

Stacker gestured to the broken bit of handle Jolie held. "Look closely at it. The original handle is of no wood you could find in any forest."

"Why are you telling us this?" Jolie asked.

"I want to see the powers of the Nine Pound Hammer restored."

"Why?" Jolie growled.

"Your mistrust doesn't serve you, siren. Listen to what I have to say and then do what you wish. To make a new handle that will return the Nine Pound Hammer's powers, you must find the Wolf Tree. Only from its wood can the handle be made."

"A Wolf Tree?" Conker asked.

"No ordinary tree," Stacker said. "Some say it's a pathway. Others the source of man's spirit. But I wouldn't know.

Go west onto the Great Plains. Avoid the Darkness. It's driven the tree from its original home."

"How can a tree move?" Conker's brow rippled with apprehension and confusion.

"I can't explain the workings of the cosmic, but if you find the Tree's guardians, they'll guide you."

Jolie glared at him a moment before asking, "How will we know them?"

Alston was dizzily taking to his feet, and Stacker motioned toward Hardy. Alston lifted his limp body and slung it over his shoulder. Stacker touched his fingers to his hat and answered, "They will know you, those who carry the Nine Pound Hammer. Good luck."

Conker and Jolie watched, perplexed, as the men went back under the trestle. They heard the whinny of horses and the clop of their hooves galloping away. Conker took the Nine Pound Hammer's head from Jolie, holding it squarely between his hands.

"I do not trust him," Jolie said.

"Me neither, but whatever purpose he's got, I think he's right. I can feel it in the iron. The powers are gone. A new handle must be made. I'll have to find this Wolf Tree."

Conker took the pair of bladders of well water from his sack and handed them to Jolie. "I ain't asking you to come. You've got your sisters to think of."

Jolie held the bladders and watched quietly as Conker packed the iron head and the broken handle in his sack. When he was finished, Jolie said, "I am coming with you."

Conker's eyes drew with concern. "You've done your part for me."

"It is not for you alone that I will go," she said. "That man said, 'Avoid the Darkness.' My sister Cleoma told me of a strange darkness that she believes might have caused my sisters to grow ill. You may have killed the Gog, but his Machine is still out there. Ray and Nel and the others will be looking for the Machine. Maybe this Darkness has something to do with the Machine. Whatever it may be, the Machine must be destroyed. You must restore the Nine Pound Hammer if that is to happen. I am tangled in this web with you and will do my part."

Conker knew there was no changing Jolie's mind and said, "I'm glad. Glad you're coming. Since the well, I feel like a ghost wandering this world."

Concern creased Jolie's face. "The waters of the well have a strange effect on those who are not sirens. You were in them for a long time. You will feel yourself soon. You need a friend to remind you of that."

Conker smiled. "So. We turn back the way we came."

"And then on west," Jolie said, "to the Great Plains."

RAY WOKE. HE BLINKED SEVERAL TIMES AT THE BLAZ-ing fire. When he tried to sit up, his shoulder erupted in pain. Marisol came over to lay the back of her hand on his fore-head.

"I think your fever's broken," she said. "That's good."

"Where are we?"

"I don't know. It all looks the same. Forest. Hills. Let me help you up so I can look at your wound."

The days since he'd been shot had passed like a dream for Ray. Despite the fever, he'd been able to explain to Marisol what herbs would fight the infection. After gathering them, she had prepared and pressed them in a moistened plug into the wound.

Ray unbuttoned his shirt and slipped it from his shoulder. Marisol untied the bandages and adjusted Ray toward the firelight. She gently touched the herbs packed against the wound. "I'm going to put fresh ones on it."

Ray nodded and gritted his teeth as she worked on the injury. After tying a new bandage around his shoulder, Marisol sat back, exhaustion and worry in her eyes. "It's getting better."

"The bullet will have to come out," Ray said.

"We've got to get you to Water Spider first."

Ray drank some water and lay slowly back to the ground. "Are you wearing pants?" he asked incredulously.

Marisol laughed and slapped at her knees. "They're yours. I took them from your pack. I've been wearing them for two days now, thanks for noticing."

"I wasn't very clearheaded. What happened to your dress?"

"It's bandages, I'm afraid."

"I'm sorry."

"Wasn't very practical anyway, remember? Sleep. You need it."

The following day, Ray sent B'hoy out to scout as they continued their journey west. With the low mountains behind them, they reached a drier land, a hill country forested with rugged post oaks and dense swatches of cedar and pine. B'hoy landed on Ray's arm and began croaking.

Ray had had little time to work further on linking with B'hoy. He had seen the one image through the bird's eyes, when the crow rescued him from the Ozark man. Ray was eager to keep trying, but for now, his attention was on reaching Redfeather.

"What's he found?" Marisol asked.

"He says there are two men, not far from here."

Within half an hour they came upon the pair, tying a downed boar to the back of a horse. A second horse grazed nearby. The two men turned as they heard Ray and Marisol approach. They both wore tall buckskin boots, up to their knees. Their long hair fell over loose shirts of homespun cloth dyed a butternut yellow. They were Indians, or so it seemed, but as Ray got closer, he noticed one was actually a black man—or of mixed heritage. He carried a flint-blade hatchet, and both had hunting rifles.

"Hello," Ray called.

The pair watched without expression until Ray and Marisol reached them.

"Are we near Vinita?" Ray asked.

The black Indian looked at the crow sitting on Ray's shoulder.

"Do you think they speak English?" Marisol muttered to Ray.

"Where have you come from?" the other Indian asked suddenly. He was big and had a wide face and heavy brow. As he peered at Ray with small black eyes, it reminded him of a bear, curious but menacing.

"Missouri, but we set out from the Smoky Mountains several weeks ago," Ray answered. "Are you Cherokee?"

"We are," the black Indian replied, his eyes still on B'hoy.

"We're looking for a man named Water Spider."

"*Ga-nv-hi-da Di-ga-ga-lo-i,*" the black Indian whispered urgently to the other.

He scowled and shook his head. *"Tla!"*

The two began to argue back and forth in Cherokee, and although Ray had learned a few phrases, he could not follow the men's rapid speech until one said *"go-gv."*

"Go-gv?" Ray interrupted. He gestured to B'hoy. "That's crow, right?"

"How did you get this crow?" the black Indian asked, despite the glowering from the other.

"I didn't really get him. He just follows me."

"Can you speak to him?"

"Yes," Ray answered tentatively.

The two broke back into their incomprehensible argument. At last, the black Indian shouted *"Ha-le-wi-s-ta!"* at the other. Then he turned back to Ray. "Are you friends with Redfeather?"

"Yes, Redfeather!" Marisol answered. "You know him?"

The black Indian looked from Marisol back to Ray, a smile forming. "Then you are the *Ga-nv-hi-da Di-ga-ga-lo-i* . . . the Rambler, right?"

Ray opened his mouth, surprised, but before he could collect himself to answer, the bearlike Indian said, "Come. We'll take you to Redfeather."

He helped Marisol get behind him on his horse, and Ray got on behind the black Indian, wincing as he was pulled up. "Is something wrong with your arm?" the black Indian asked.

"I was shot." Ray briefly told them about his encounter with the two men in the Ozarks. As they traveled, Ray and Marisol learned that the black Indian was Crossley and the other was Mulberry. Crossley's grandparents had come out long ago during the Removal, slaves to a Cherokee chief, but over time they, along with the many other black families, had become as much a part of the tribe as any other Cherokee, strangers in a new and unfamiliar land. Neither Crossley nor Mulberry had ever been to their ancestral home in the east. Oklahoma was their home now.

Water Spider was Mulberry's great-uncle, and both he and Crossley spoke fondly of Redfeather.

"Redfeather is becoming a good *di-da-nv-wi-s-gi*," Crossley said.

"A medicine man?" Ray asked, impressed. "Are you sure this is the same Redfeather?"

"Of course," Mulberry said. "Redfeather has great powers. And Great-Uncle likes him."

"We like him too," Crossley added. "He tells good stories about you all."

After a time they reached a road that passed many clusters of houses, a mercantile store, and even a small train depot. Everyone they encountered was Indian, a few in traditional clothes, some dressed in store-bought dresses, overalls, and wide-brimmed hats, but most in some combination of the two. Crossley and Mulberry greeted this person or that, who curiously eyed the boy with the crow on his shoulder and the girl wearing pants.

They eventually stopped at a cluster of cabins and outbuildings, a cornfield on one side and a fenced garden on the other. B'hoy rose from Ray's shoulder, gliding off across the green stalks.

"We're here," Mulberry said, and then he called out, "*O-si-yo!*"

A woman with touches of gray in her hair stood up from the garden. The door opened from one of the cabins, and Redfeather stepped out on the porch. He was wearing a long linen shirt, deerskin leggings, and moccasins. His hair was plaited and capped on the ends with bright red beads.

"Ray! Marisol!" he called, rushing to greet them. "I got Ox Everett's telegram that you were coming. How was your journey?"

Marisol slid down, saying, "Weather was fine. Took in the sights. Ray was shot. But otherwise . . ."

"What?" Redfeather gasped, helping Ray off Crossley's horse.

"I'm all right."

"Thanks to me," Marisol said.

"Thanks to Marisol." Ray smirked.

"Water Spider will be back soon," Redfeather said. "He can look at the wound. Did the bullet pass through?"

"No, unfortunately," Ray said.

"Water Spider will get it out."

Ray winced at the thought. "It seems to be healing. That might make it worse."

"He's a powerful healer," Redfeather assured him. "He can do it without even opening the wound."

"How's that possible?" Marisol scoffed.

"You'll see."

The woman approached and spoke in Cherokee to Crossley and Mulberry, who were still on their horses. They smiled and shook their heads. Then Crossley said to Ray and Marisol, "Sorry we can't join you for dinner. We've got to get this razorback butchered."

"Thank you for your help," Ray said, reaching up to shake their hands. They waved to Marisol and kicked their horses to set off down the dusty road.

Redfeather gestured to the woman. "Ray, Marisol, this is Little Grass. Water Spider's wife."

Little Grass smiled at the two, then her eyes went from Ray's blood-crusted shirt to Marisol's ragtag attire. "You two look like you've walked a rough road," Little Grass said. She cocked her head toward the cabin. "Come inside. Let's get you fed. Water Spider will be home soon."

The cabin was small, half the size of the den back at Shuckstack. It was simply furnished: a table, a few chairs, and a rope bed in the corner. Little Grass filled a large basin in the backyard with hot water for Marisol to bathe in. She then began preparing a meal at the fireplace while Ray and Redfeather talked together.

"Water Spider is an amazing man," Redfeather said. "He tries to live by the old ways. That's pretty rare out here nowadays. He's one of the last still living who came out when the Cherokee were forced from the Appalachians."

"I hear you're a medicine man," Ray said with a smile.

"Who told you that? Mulberry?" Redfeather shook his head. "I'm learning, but I'm no *di-da-nv-wi-s-gi*."

"But you want to be?"

"Sure." He leaned closer, an intensity in his eyes. "I'm Kwakiutl, but you know how I was never really a part of my tribe. I was so young when I was taken in by Nel. I grew up in the medicine show, traveling around. I had no idea the sort of hardship the tribes faced. The old ways are being lost."

"So Water Spider is teaching you," Ray said.

"He's been very kind to accept me," Redfeather said.

Little Grass sat up from where she was cracking small bird eggs into a cast-iron pot of soup. "Redfeather can help the tribes," she said.

"What do you mean?" Ray asked.

She didn't answer, but instead nodded to the door. "Water Spider is back."

Ray stood as the door opened. Water Spider was tall, over six feet, and stood erect and strong. Only his long white hair and deeply lined face suggested his age. When he entered, he spoke softly in Cherokee to his wife before looking at Ray and Redfeather.

"*O-si-yo. Tsi-lu-gi.*" Water Spider had a deep voice like distant thunder. His eyes sparkled brightly.

"He welcomes you," Redfeather said.

Little Grass said, "You will have to forgive my husband. He does not speak English. He says he will take it up when he is a hundred."

Water Spider seemed to know this joke, for he chuckled, and then motioned for Ray and Redfeather to sit at the table. Little Grass had the table already set with bowls and began to serve them the soup and delicious-smelling bean bread.

Marisol came in from the back door, her thick black hair

still wet, and looking pleased from the bath. "Little Grass, were these meant for me?" She waved her hands at her outfit: a loose-fitting ribboned shirt of dark blue, an embroidered skirt, and leggings.

"I hope they fit you," Little Grass said. "Your clothes were a mess. I will try to repair them."

Marisol shook her head, "No, please don't bother. I'll get new ones."

"Then you keep those," Little Grass offered.

"I couldn't."

"You will. Now sit, and . . . what is that?" Her eyes grew wide.

Javidos slithered from under Marisol's sleeve. Marisol hastened to allay her fear. "He's perfectly harmless, I assure you. I can leave him outside if you want."

"I think I'd rather he was not somewhere he'll surprise me." She sat, her eyes cautiously following the copperhead's movements.

Marisol smiled politely to Water Spider as she took her seat. He smiled back at her and then turned to say something to his wife and Redfeather that was clearly about Marisol. After some back and forth, Redfeather said, "Water Spider was asking what tribe you came from. I explained that you weren't Indian."

"My mother was," Marisol corrected.

"Really?" Redfeather muttered skeptically.

"She was Hopi. My father was Mexican."

"But you didn't grow up with her tribe," Redfeather said.

"So?" Marisol scowled. "You didn't grow up with yours."

Little Grass placed her hands on the table, which was enough to stop the argument. "Where did you grow up then, Marisol?" she asked.

"In Sonora for a time. Along the San Miguel River. I did visit my grandparents once in their village on the mesa. It was beautiful, from what little I remember."

Little Grass translated this to Water Spider, who nodded with interest. He was curious about Javidos and her ability to speak with him.

"He's little more than a pet, really. I'm no Rambler."

"But you're learning," Ray said.

The food was delicious, and Ray had several bowls as they talked. He told them about Mister Bradshaw's visit to Shuckstack. Both Water Spider and Little Grass, who knew the man, were sad to hear of his death. Ray then recounted their journey from Shuckstack, and Water Spider asked Ray about B'hoy.

"I'm beginning to speak to him from a distance, with my thoughts. Does Water Spider know how to take animal form?"

Redfeather answered after translating Ray's question. "He says he has heard of some who have. It's a rare ability. He says you are on the right path and to keep trying."

Disappointed not to get more guidance, Ray thanked him and then asked, "Have you seen the Darkness yet, Redfeather?"

"No. Water Spider says it's cursed. And it sounds like from what happened to Bradshaw, he's right. You shouldn't go there, Ray. It's too dangerous."

"Nel made us protections," Ray said.

After this was translated to Water Spider, the old man asked if he could see the charms. Ray took them from his red flannel toby and handed the small pouch across the table. Water Spider opened the string and sniffed first. Then he shook the bundles of cinquefoil and wintergreen, crushed ash leaves, and other bits of roots and herbs into his palm. After examining them, he returned the contents to the pouch and handed it back to Ray nodding appreciatively while speaking.

"He agrees they will help," Redfeather explained, "and said only Nel could make such a charm."

"Nel made enough for three," Ray said to Redfeather. "Will you come with us?"

Water Spider seemed to already know what was asked. He exchanged a glance with Little Grass, who dipped her eyes. Redfeather spoke in Cherokee before turning back to Ray.

"Little Grass does not like the idea, but Water Spider has a reason for wanting me to go."

"What's that?"

"To find the *Wa-ya Tlu-gv* . . . I'll let him explain. He said he will talk to us later. First he wants to remove that bullet from your shoulder."

Ray put down his spoon, his appetite gone.

* * *

Ray bathed first in the large basin in the backyard. B'hoy watched from the eaves of the cabin. "We'll be here a while," Ray said. "You're on your own for meals." The crow cawed several times, and Ray said, "Because you're getting too tame, that's why." The crow landed on the edge of the tub to peck Ray's hand sharply, before taking flight. "Ingrate!" Ray called.

Ray stepped back inside wearing a clean union suit and feeling too nervous to be modest. Marisol was helping Little Grass clean the dishes on the porch. Water Spider and Redfeather stood by the fireplace, where a single chair was waiting for Ray.

"Come over," Redfeather said. "Have a seat."

Water Spider smiled reassuringly and motioned for Ray to unbutton the top of his union suit. Ray sat stiffly and slipped his arms from the gray sleeves. Ray looked around for a knife or surgical instruments, but there were none. Water Spider held a long piece of red string. He tied it around Ray's wrist and slid his fingers along the string, from the knot to the loose end, muttering softly as he went.

Ray turned to Redfeather, who nodded at him and said, "Go ahead and close your eyes. Just relax."

Ray glanced once more at Water Spider, who seemed to be in a trance, and then closed his eyes. Water Spider continued whispering. What sort of spell was this? The bullet was lodged deep in his shoulder. Although the wound had closed and the infection was gone, he could feel the dull ache where the muscle was still injured.

The string grew taut. Ray felt Water Spider's fingers clasp

about his wrist. A tingling began, first in his hand, moving its way up his arm with a strange hot-cold sensation. Ray became dizzy. His thoughts quieted.

An intense pressure squeezed at his shoulder. Ray jerked forward and found hands over his eyes and Redfeather whispering, "Be still!"

Water Spider began chanting loudly, almost as if he were singing. Redfeather had to brace Ray as the pressure on his shoulder grew unbearable. Ray shouted, but just at that moment, the pressure ceased. The hot-cold tingling moved back down his arm, to his wrist, his hand, and finally became just little prickles at his fingertips.

The room was quiet. Redfeather released his grip. Ray slumped back against the chair, drained of all his energy. Water Spider breathed heavily as he mumbled something to Redfeather. "Are you okay, Ray?" Redfeather asked.

Ray opened his eyes. Perspiration dripped from Water Spider's forehead as he rolled up the red string, no longer on Ray's wrist. "What happened?" Ray asked.

Water Spider nodded to Ray's hand. Ray realized it was closed in a tight fist. He felt something hard pressing into his palm. He uncurled his fingers to expose a small piece of mashed lead. Bits of blood still clung to it.

"Is . . . this is the bullet?" Ray gasped.

"It's out." Redfeather grinned. "I told you he was powerful."

Ray looked up at Water Spider with amazement and gratitude. "*Wa-do,*" Ray thanked him.

"*Gv-li-e-li-ga,*" Water Spider answered.

Marisol and Ray lodged in vacant cabins that had once belonged to Water Spider's children. Ray was so exhausted from the night's events, he slept until nearly noon the following day and spent the afternoon helping Marisol and Little Grass in the garden. Redfeather was away with Water Spider attending to a family with sick children. They did not return until evening. After they ate, Water Spider motioned for Ray, Marisol, and Redfeather to follow him outside.

They walked together in the dusk until they came to a bluff overlooking a creek. Beyond, the patchwork forest extending to the north was illuminated by the falling yellow light. Water Spider watched the distance for a time before speaking to them in Cherokee. Redfeather translated for Water Spider.

"He says it was long ago when he was taken from the place of his ancestors out to this dry land. He has made it his home. He has had many wives, outliving each of them . . . but thinks Little Grass might beat him yet. He's traveled among the other tribes of the Indian Territory—Arapaho, Kickapoo, Apache, and Comanche. He has tried to learn their ways.

"He's also met people from the tribes of the High Plains—Lakota and Blackfeet. They have taught him much and he has listened. He kept up with the struggles of the various people to hold on to their homelands in the face of the White Man's unquenchable desires. The Ghost Dance failed to bring peace to the tribes. It failed to renew the Earth as the Paiute holy man Wovoka had preached. Lakota men, women, and children were massacred trying to hold on to the old ways."

Water Spider quietly collected his thoughts before speaking again and then allowed Redfeather to translate. "There was once a time when men spoke with great spirits and some men were able to cross into the spirit world. Water Spider met some of these spirits long ago out on the open prairie. They were guardians over a pathway to the next world."

"What does he mean, the next world?" Ray interrupted.

Redfeather asked Water Spider. "He says he has not been there, although he hopes to one day. But it is a wondrous place. A place where the old ways are still followed and respected."

"Is it the Gloaming?" Ray asked.

"I'm not sure," Redfeather said, and then spoke with Water Spider. "He does not know what the Gloaming is, but maybe it is the same."

"Who were these spirits?" Marisol asked. "Are they like ghosts?"

"No!" Redfeather scowled. "These aren't wicked or scary. They aren't the dead. Spirits are protectors."

"But are they like men?" she asked.

Water Spider said something that caused Redfeather to wrinkle his brow in confusion. They spoke back and forth for a time before Redfeather explained. "He says these spirits he met were rougarou."

"What's a rougarou?" Ray asked.

"I'm not sure. I don't know how to translate it; it's not a

Cherokee word. But they seem to be some sort of wolf and not a wolf at the same time. They're spirits and something altogether more powerful than any creature of this world."

"Why is he telling us this?" Marisol asked. "These are just old stories and superstitions."

Redfeather's cheeks reddened defensively. "They're not! If you're going to insult Water Spider—"

"I'm not insulting him. I just don't see what this has to do with us."

Before Redfeather could continue arguing, Water Spider held up his large hands and spoke. Redfeather kept his eyes from Marisol as he translated. "First White Men came on wagons to the west. Then soldiers and then the trains. More and more White Men came, until the tribes were driven onto the reservations. Water Spider thought he had seen and heard of the worst of it. But now a great Darkness has fallen.

"Some say it is a punishment for the crimes of the White Men. But Water Spider does not believe this. The Darkness sickens the hearts and the bodies of all who are in it—white, red, black, everyone."

"What does he think has brought this Darkness?" Ray asked.

Redfeather asked and then replied, "The rougarou once guarded a pathway to the next world. A sort of tree." Redfeather broke into Cherokee to get further explanation. "He says this tree—that some call *Wa-ya Tlu-gv,* the Wolf Tree—was once of great importance and only the most powerful warriors and medicine men could find it. Those that did spoke in wonder of the tree's size: its roots were larger than a mountain, and it extended up beyond the clouds. Only those blessed by the rougarou could see it, but the Tree was what connected men to their true selves. It gave us our hearts, our goodness, our spirit. Now the Wolf Tree is lost. The Darkness has driven it away."

The last rays of color lingered only on high clouds in the west. A cool wind blew across the bluff. Water Spider looked at each of them. He spoke.

Redfeather said, "Mankind is suffering. The Wolf Tree and its stewards, the rougarou, have gone missing. Water Spider says he has been waiting for you."

Ray startled. "For us! Why?"

"You're a Rambler. You can help return the Wolf Tree."

"How?" Ray asked. "I can't go looking for this Wolf Tree. We've got to go to Omphalosa—"

Water Spider then spoke, stilted at first, but in English. "Yes . . . go to Darkness. Drive it away. If Wolf Tree . . . not found. Man . . . will be lost."

Ray looked up into Water Spider's creased and worn face, his eyes black and boundless. "We don't know how to end the Darkness."

"To end Darkness," Water Spider said. "Face Darkness. Out there." He pointed a finger out at the horizon and then approached Ray, planting his large hand on Ray's chest. "And face Darkness in here."

"I DON'T SEE THE POINT," REDFEATHER ARGUED. "BE-
sides, it sounds dangerous."

Ray licked the end of the string and threaded it through a
needle to finish sewing the last of two pouches. "We can handle ourselves. I'm not planning on drawing a lot of attention
in Omphalosa. We just need to look around."

A lantern cast warm yellow light around Redfeather's
small cabin. Javidos was coiled in Marisol's lap. She stroked
his thick back and shifted uncomfortably.

"But you heard Water Spider," Redfeather said. "It's not
the town that's causing the Darkness, but the fact that the
Wolf Tree has disappeared."

"We can't go looking for this Tree," Ray asked.

"We have to, Ray! Didn't you hear Water Spider? The
Wolf Tree can help the Cherokee. It can help all the tribes.

These rougarou can lead people to a world where the old ways are respected. I want to help them. I want to help them reach this place of peace."

Marisol leaned forward. "Look, I made a promise to Nel. Ray and I are supposed to investigate Omphalosa and return to Shuckstack to tell him what we've discovered. Not solve lost Indian legends."

"This is no legend!" Redfeather shouted. "You don't believe Water Spider."

Javidos hissed from her lap, but Redfeather ignored his threats.

"I believe he met these rougarou," she said. "But that was a long time ago. There could be a million other reasons they've disappeared. And how do we know they have anything to do with the Darkness?"

Redfeather said, "Because Water Spider said—"

"Look," Ray interrupted. "Water Spider might be right. There might be a connection. Let's go to Omphalosa first. It might help us understand what's happened to the Wolf Tree."

"But Nel said for us to return afterward," Marisol argued.

Ray frowned as he tied off the last stitch. He tossed the small pouch—no bigger than a coin purse—to Marisol. It had a long cord for her to wear Nel's protective charm as a necklace. Ray gave the second to Redfeather, and slipped the last back into his red flannel toby.

Redfeather leaned forward, speaking urgently to Ray. "If we don't discover the source of the Darkness in Omphalosa, will you go with me?"

"We promised Nel," Marisol said.

Redfeather snapped at her, "You go back to Shuckstack! We don't need you." And then he said to Ray, "Why did you bring her anyway?"

Marisol flung Javidos onto her shoulder and stormed out of the cabin. Ray watched the door slam. "What's the problem with you two?"

"There's no problem."

Ray raised his eyebrows.

"You know how she is," Redfeather said. "She's spoiled. She thinks everyone is beneath her."

"She's not like that . . . not anymore. We have to work together."

Redfeather rolled his eyes. "If I try to be nice to her, will you help me find the Wolf Tree?"

Ray looked down at his toby. It felt so empty without the weight of the rabbit's foot. He had to find the source of the Darkness if he was going to at last track down the Gog's Machine.

"I'll help you. But first we go to Omphalosa."

The sun was breaking over the trees when Ray, Marisol, and Redfeather gathered their belongings and prepared to leave. Water Spider waited for them by the garden, holding the reins of two horses.

Marisol had left her valise with Little Grass as a thank-you for the new clothes. She shouldered a leather satchel as she came forward to rub her fingers into the dappled silver fur on the roan's chin. "He's beautiful."

"That's Unole," Redfeather said. "He belongs to Mulberry. I promised we'd take good care of him. This one's Atsila. She's mine." Atsila was a golden palomino, a hand smaller than Unole, but she looked strong and fast. Redfeather climbed onto her with an easy slide, dropping an iron-headed tomahawk into his belt and taking up the reins.

"I don't care much for horses," Ray grumbled, looking up warily at Unole.

"Oh, you just don't know how to ride," Marisol said, jumping to the roan's back. She offered her hand to help Ray up. "I'll lead him."

Ray sighed and hopped unsuccessfully several times before getting on behind Marisol. B'hoy glided overhead, his caws remarkably close to laughter. "Shut up," Ray murmured.

After bidding Water Spider and Little Grass farewell, they set off northwest toward the Verdigris River.

As they journeyed that first day through the pine forests north of the Indian Territory, Ray turned his attention again to trying to see through B'hoy's eyes. Riding behind Marisol, Ray closed his eyes and searched out for B'hoy.

An image flashed before Ray's eyes. He was high over the earth. The forests and hills swam below him. B'hoy banked and Ray gasped at the dizziness, losing his balance. As he slipped from the horse, Marisol reached out to catch him, grabbing his arm, but she tumbled to the ground on top of him.

Redfeather pulled back on Atsila's reins. "Are you okay?"

Marisol and Ray laughed in a heap. "Get off me." Ray pushed.

"What happened?" she asked, getting to her feet.

"B'hoy. I saw through his eyes again. But I couldn't hold it."

Marisol remounted and waited for Ray to get back on. Just as Ray got his foot up, she shook Unole's reins and Ray danced a step before falling again.

"Come on, Ray," she teased. "It's like hopping on a train."

"What would you know about that?" Ray laughed as he caught the back of the saddle and pulled himself behind Marisol.

"Quit joking around," Redfeather growled.

Marisol turned, the smile still on her face. "Why don't you use your medicine man powers and conjure a sense of humor."

Redfeather tried to mask his frown. "It doesn't work like that . . . besides, I have a sense of humor."

Two days of journey, and the forests were no longer the endless sea of trees. Ray kept trying to see again from B'hoy's eyes, but for whatever reason he had trouble making the link. On the third day, they crested a hill to view with awe the expansive prairie. Clusters of trees clung here and there, marking creeks and rivers, but the country stretched wide and open to the horizon and was dominated by an enormous sky.

And ahead, in the distance, they saw the Darkness.

At first the Darkness appeared as an intense band of storm clouds, a sliver of shadow far away. But as they rode further, it became clear that these were not storms, for there were no clouds. It was as if some gigantic shears had cut away the blue fabric of the sky, exposing the blackness of night beyond. Except there were no stars. No moon. Nothing but emptiness and dark.

Each day, the sun rose later and set earlier. It was disorienting, like winter was racing forward in time at a pace of a month each day. The weather grew winterlike as well, and Ray worried that they might not have brought adequate clothing for the cold. The prairie grass and earth soon crunched beneath the hooves of the horses. Rivers became edged in ice, and the trees on their banks were bare, some of them dead from their long dormancy.

When they forded the Smoky Hill River a week later, the sun disappeared for the last time. Darkness, oppressive and complete, closed around them.

They camped when they were tired, slept a few hours, and not knowing day from night, broke camp after a time and continued. Redfeather carried cinders from the campfire in a tin-lined box. Holding a cinder, he could envelop his hand in flames. It only illuminated a few dozen yards in any direction, but it was enough light to guide their way.

Ray was used to listening for animal noises. But there were none. No howling coyotes or deer snorts or birdcalls of any kind. Only the whipping wind whistled against their ears.

"I'm going to lose this hat," Ray grumbled, catching

ahold of the brim before it blew from his head. Shivering, he pulled his collar tighter around his neck and adjusted his legs to try to find a more comfortable way to sit behind Marisol.

B'hoy beat his wings as he gripped his talons tighter to Ray's shoulder. The crow, unable to see anything from the air, had given up flying.

Abandoned homesteads appeared every so often like ghosts on the empty prairie. Ray thought of the travelers he and Marisol had seen in Missouri, Jayhawkers desperate to escape the Darkness. He could see why they had left. Who could stay in the oppressive dark?

Then he remembered the travelers burying their dead by the roadsides in Missouri. How strange—now that they had entered the Darkness—that they saw none of the hastily dug graves.

When Ray mentioned this, Redfeather whispered, "We haven't seen anything living in days either."

Redfeather spread a map against Atsila's neck and nearly lost it to the vicious wind. Since they were unable to see the landscape around them, their travel had been slow. Marisol brought Unole close to Atsila's side and reached over to help Redfeather hold the map. Redfeather cupped his flaming hand near the map to read it.

"Well?" Ray asked, leaning around Marisol's back to see.

Redfeather ran his fingers along the tattered paper. "That was the Saline River we crossed earlier. We should be there."

"Maybe we missed it in the dark," Marisol said. She stroked Unole's ears to calm him.

"A whole town?" Ray asked.

Redfeather folded the map and peered out at the blank Darkness. "It's possible."

A few hours later, a glow formed in the distance. They traveled toward it, fear growing in their hearts. When at last they reached the top of a rise, they saw that they had reached Omphalosa.

The windows of buildings were lit, outlining a single main street nearly a quarter of a mile long. Beyond the western edge, an enormous factory reared over the small town like some predatory beast. Half a dozen smokestacks belched great clouds, glowing with otherworldly flame. The illuminated smoke formed a sort of canopy, reflecting its light across the large brick buildings.

A fence encircled the entire factory except for two entrances. One led to the town; the other to train tracks stretching out to the north, disappearing on the dark prairie. Between the factory and town was a city of tents punctuated by campfires and the shadows of people moving about the yard.

Ray exchanged a look of worry with Redfeather.

Marisol shivered and said, "We need to buy coats and some warmer clothes. Probably extra blankets, too."

"We'll look for a store before finding a place to camp outside town," Ray said.

"Okay," Redfeather said. "But let's try not to draw any attention. Buy what we need and get back out until we have a plan."

Riding toward the eastern edge of the town, they crested

a hill crowned with a solitary tree. A gasoline torch was speared in the ground beneath the tree and something hung from the tree's branches: all shadow and creaking rope. As the horses passed the tree, Ray gasped.

An elderly black woman, open-eyed but dead, dangled from a noose. In the oily light of the torch, Ray read a sign pinned to the old woman's tattered dress.

"Witch."

Nausea welled up in Ray's throat. Marisol began breathing heavily and trembling. Ray leaned closer to her back, tightening his grip around her waist. "Look away," he whispered. Redfeather slid his hand down to rest on his tomahawk as he shook Atsila's reins to hurry from the tree.

"Keep a distance," Ray said to B'hoy. "A crow might seem a little out of place."

B'hoy swept from his shoulder, circling the horses before flying ahead to perch on the shadowed far end of a corral's split rail fence. The corral marked the eastern entrance to the solitary street leading down Omphalosa. Skittish, snorting horses clustered together in the pen. Ray cast one horrified glance back over his shoulder before facing the town.

Riding down the street, Ray felt some relief that they drew little notice. The town was swarming with all manner of people. Most were immigrants—Chinese, Italians, Russians, and others Ray could not recognize—who Mister Bradshaw had said were brought in as workers for the mill. They moved about with the tasks of ordinary townsfolk: shopping, speaking together, coming in and out of homes and buildings. But their movements were strangely stilted. Ray could not place what was odd about them, but these ashen-skinned people unnerved him.

The horses kept to a slow pace, often stopping in the thickest crowds. The thoroughfare was illuminated by kerosene torches mounted on the porch rails of each building.

Ray and Marisol rode beside Redfeather past the saloons, shops, and offices. A store advertised "Johanson's Haber-dashery: Gents' Clothing—Boots—Tobacco—Supplies." Stopping here, they tied up the horses. Redfeather kept a cautious eye to the street. "I'll watch the horses while you two go get blankets and coats."

Ray and Marisol stepped onto the planked sidewalk, where the strange townsfolk moved away from them with wary glances. Marisol nodded to a line of pine coffins propped in a grim display against the front of another store. "A furniture store selling coffins?" Marisol whispered.

"Not a good sign, is it?" Ray replied as they went into the haberdashery.

A man behind the counter asked if he could help them as they came through the door. The shop was empty but for the sallow-faced shopkeeper.

"We're in need of warmer coats," Ray said. "Blankets, too, if you have them."

The man nodded with an expressionless face. "Over there." He pointed to the far wall.

Ray followed Marisol past racks and displays of boots, shirts, coats, and hats of only the most functional designs.

They tried on a few pairs of heavy, wool-lined frock coats before selecting three. Marisol grabbed the blankets and they headed to the counter.

As the shopkeeper tallied up the cost, Ray stared at the man's hands. They were pale gray, much like Mister Bradshaw's skin. But this man did not seem sick. He was not coughing.

"Eight-fifty," the shopkeeper said with a dull voice.

Marisol paid him from her coin purse, and they hurried out the door with the bundles in their arms.

They met Redfeather and began putting on the coats. As Ray rolled the blankets and tied them to the back of Unole's saddle, Redfeather asked, "What's going on over there?"

Ray came around Unole and looked across the street. A burly man in a woolen cap snatched an envelope from a boy before shoving him down into the mud. Several other men, pitiless and dark-eyed, watched from the sidewalk. Passersby did little more than glance down at the boy before moving on.

"I don't know," Ray murmured.

The boy sprang to his feet and rushed at the burly man, clambering for the envelope that was held from his reach. "Give it to me! Give it back!"

The man shoved the boy back again. "I done told you, you little wop."

One of the men on the sidewalk said, "That boy runs letters for the Pinkertons, Gatch. I wouldn't mess with him."

Gatch snarled over his shoulder, "Well, his pa owes me

five dollars lost fair in a hand of poker. Been two weeks, and he ain't paid me yet."

"I don't have five dollars," the boy pleaded. "But I can pay you later. Please, just give me the telegram. It's for Mister Muggeridge."

Gatch looked hesitantly at the envelope in his hand. Then he reached down and grabbed a rusty chain from the boy's pocket, pulling out a tattered watch.

He dropped the envelope as he snatched up the watch. "I'm hanging on to this then," Gatch growled. "Run, get that money from your pa, and I'll give it back."

"But Mister Muggeridge. He gave me the watch. I need it for my errands." The boy clawed at Gatch's coat, until Gatch grabbed the boy by the back of the neck, squeezing until the boy dropped to his knees, pleading and crying out in pain.

"He needs help," Ray muttered.

"What are you going to do?" Marisol asked.

Redfeather put his hand on Ray's shoulder to stop him. "I don't like it either, but see all those men on the sidewalk?"

"I see them." Ray turned to step back up to the line of coffins displayed before the furniture store. With the blunt end of his knife, he pried out a nail. He strode across the street toward Gatch and the boy. As he did, he sent his thoughts out to B'hoy. The crow was there in a moment, settling on a rooftop.

The boy was beating his hands helplessly against Gatch's grip. The burly man squeezed harder, shouting, "You had enough? You going to get that money now?"

Ray stopped before Gatch and said, "I've had enough. Let go of that boy."

Gatch looked at Ray. His snarl melted into a smile of savage mirth. His gray skin and black eyes gave him the look of something dangerous and wraithlike. "What you got to say about it?"

"Give the boy back his watch."

The other men on the sidewalk stepped forward with interest. Out of the corner of his eye, Ray saw Redfeather and Marisol moving around to the sidewalk, positioning behind the men.

Ray guessed Gatch to be three hundred pounds or more. He had no chance of overpowering the man normally. But a root doctor, who had lived for a time on the rough streets of Baltimore, had shown Ray a spell he used to even the odds in a fight.

"And what if I don't?" Gatch sneered, and drew a knife from his belt.

B'hoy launched from the rooftop, knocking Gatch's cap from his head and clawing and pecking at his face.

Ray lunged forward and knocked the knife to the ground. He grabbed Gatch's hand, twisted his arm behind his back, and pierced the calloused skin of his palm with the coffin nail.

One of the men on the sidewalk drew a revolver and fired it in the air. B'hoy took flight, cawing and cursing his way back to the rooftop. The man brought the revolver around to aim at Ray.

Ray pulled tightly on Gatch's arm, securing it against the man's wide back. Gatch was pitched forward, with Ray locked at his side. The big man did not struggle—he could not struggle. "Tell that man to put away his gun," Ray said.

Gatch grunted but did not reply. Ray punched the coffin nail a little further into his hand. "Tell him!" Ray said.

"Put that gun away, Curtis," he called.

The men on the sidewalk blinked in confusion. "He's bewitched Gatch," one of the men hissed. Curtis continued to hold the revolver outstretched. Another man growled and stepped from the porch, drawing a derringer from his coat pocket.

Redfeather appeared beside him and reached a hand out to a kerosene torch mounted on the porch. He extinguished the torch in his palm. Redfeather turned to face the man, flames glowing vaporously from his clenched fist. "Drop your gun."

The man stared a moment at Redfeather's hand, but then he raised the derringer. Redfeather wheeled around with his tomahawk, clipping the barrel before the gun fired and throwing the little derringer into the air. He flicked out his other hand as if lashing a whip. A tongue of flame sprouted from his hand, catching the man's pants leg on fire.

The men on the sidewalk erupted with angry cries, some scattering away. But two charged for him, one with a long hunting knife and the other grabbing a pickax from a display of tools.

Redfeather flicked his hand once more. The man with the knife yelled as his coat caught on fire. He fell into the street, rolling back and forth. The other man sprang forward and raised a pickax over his head. Redfeather caught the handle with his tomahawk, pushing the man back. But the man was quick and before Redfeather could hit him with the flames, the man swung again. Redfeather blocked with his tomahawk, and continued trying to drive the man back.

Curtis leveled his revolver on Redfeather, closing one eye to get a clear shot. Marisol clutched his wrist. The man sneered and drew back his other hand to strike her. But Javidos lunged from her shirt sleeve and bit into his knuckles. Curtis screamed and dropped his revolver.

Redfeather chopped the pickax handle in half and kicked at the man's knee. He fell, and as Redfeather held up his flaming hand, the man scrambled backward into the street. There were other men waiting on the sidewalk with weapons drawn, but after seeing what had happened to the first four, they hesitated.

Ray pulled Gatch tighter and shouted, "Tell them to back away!" Redfeather and Marisol joined Ray on either side, the tomahawk and Javidos threatening any who would attack.

Gatch roared, "That's enough. Y'all put down your weapons and get back." Guns, knives, and tools thudded to the ground.

Then Ray turned Gatch to face the boy, who was still crouching with wide eyes. "Hand him the watch." Gatch extended his free hand to the boy. "Go on. Take it," Ray said.

The boy looked nervously at Gatch's face as he took the old tarnished watch. Marisol dropped a few coins in the dirt by Gatch's feet and said, "That should settle his father's debt. Leave the boy alone from now on."

Gatch glared first at Marisol and then at Redfeather and

finally down at the money. Ray slid the coffin nail out of Gatch's palm and released him. The huge man turned, rubbing his hand and looking at Ray with anger and fear. Oily black blood smeared across Gatch's meaty palm.

"Get on out of here," Ray muttered to the boy. The boy looked once at Ray and ran, cutting between two buildings into the dark. Ray, Marisol, and Redfeather backed toward their horses.

People on the street had stopped. Ray realized everyone had gone quiet, but now the staring crowd began murmuring. "Had a snake for an arm." "Breathing flames." "Red devils!" "Witches!"

Ray, Marisol, and Redfeather mounted the horses and hurried through the parting crowd back down the street. "So much for keeping from being noticed!" Redfeather said.

They'd just reached the corral when Ray saw the boy waving to them from around the side of the last building. Ray pointed, and Marisol steered Unole toward the boy.

The boy panted, "They'll be after you soon. A lynch mob surely. They kill anyone suspected of devilry." The boy pointed to a hill north of town. "There's a soddy up there where you can hide. It's empty. No one goes there but me. Look for the windmill and you'll find the soddy. I'll meet you there in a few hours."

As Ray looked at the boy, he realized he was not so discolored as Gatch and the others. His skin was grayish but still a little ruddy pink. And his movements were not so jarring and haunted.

"Thank you," Ray said.

The boy nodded and sprinted away.

Redfeather led them down the road heading east out of Omphalosa. When they were out again in the dark, away from the town's lights, they stopped.

"Are they following?" Marisol asked.

Ray cocked his head. "I don't hear horses."

"Then let's cut up that way," Redfeather said, pointing to the north.

They led Atsila and Unole up into the low hills and circled back around, searching for the windmill in the dark. The town's lights were dim in the hills, but eventually they spied the spinning battered blades of an old windmill over a rise. When they reached it, they looked back down at the glow of the town and the brighter glow of the hissing, smoking mill about half a mile away.

"Think we're safe out here?" Ray asked.

Redfeather slid his tomahawk out. "We won't be safe until we're away from this place. Even with Nel's charms, I feel the Darkness sapping at me. We shouldn't stay here."

"I feel it too," Marisol said. "But we haven't found anything out yet."

"And it won't do us any good when we're hanging by our necks from a tree," Redfeather snapped.

Ray climbed down from behind Marisol and helped her off Unole. "Just wait until the boy comes back. Maybe he'll be able to tell us something."

They tied Atsila and Unole to the windmill's frame so the horses could water at a rusting trough next to the well. Ray found a few bundles of hay and rolled them over for the horses to eat. B'hoy perched at the top of the windmill, and Ray told him to keep a watchful eye.

Redfeather held up his flaming hand. "Over here," he said.

The soddy was a house burrowed into the side of a hill, with only a wooden door and a short section of vertical wall exposed. Redfeather clutched his tomahawk in one hand as he pushed open the soddy's door. There was a scuttle of mice, but otherwise the soddy was vacant. Redfeather lit an oil lamp that hung from the ceiling.

Whoever had lived in the sod house must not have left very long ago, for there were still tins of fish, sacks of grain, and crocks of liquid on shelves built into the dirt wall. There were only two beds with dusty, straw-filled mattresses. "No thanks," Marisol sneered.

Redfeather pulled the infested-looking mattress off one of the beds and tossed it to the floor. "There you go, your highness," he said, motioning to the rope frame beneath.

"Charming," Marisol said, letting Javidos slither from her sleeve to hunt in the corners for a meal. "At least I'm above the mice."

Redfeather looked back at her as he leaned against the door frame. "Nice work back there, by the way."

She nodded as she lay back uncomfortably on the bed. "You too."

Ray took off the other mattress, uncovering the corpse of a cat lying dried among the cobwebs. He grimaced and removed it before lying down on the frame. While Redfeather sat in a chair in the doorway watching the dark, Ray and

Marisol tried to sleep. After a few hours, Ray and Redfeather switched places. It might have been midnight or it might have been noon, for all Ray could discern. When B'hoy gave a low caw, Ray stirred from his thoughts and saw the boy, silhouetted against the mill's glow, coming up toward the soddy.

"Here he is," Ray said, waking Redfeather and Marisol. Would the boy know anything about the Machine? It was doubtful. But he might help them understand why this strange mill was built out here in the middle of nowhere.

The boy stopped when he was close enough to see the three waiting for him in the door of the soddy. "I'm alone," he said. "Nobody followed me, so don't worry."

"We're not," Ray said.

The boy came inside, looking curiously at each of them, and unloaded several dark biscuits from his pockets onto the table. "It was all I could bring to you. But you can open some of those tins if you want." He motioned to the wall.

"That's okay," Ray said, picking up one of the biscuits. He handed one to Redfeather but he shook his head, standing in the doorway and keeping an eye toward the town. Ray bit into the biscuit. It was hard and tasteless, but he continued eating it, smiling courteously at the boy.

"Who are you all?" the boy asked, sitting in one of the chairs and unable to stop staring at them in turn. "How did you do all those things?"

"It's not what it seemed," Marisol said. "We're performers, from a traveling show. They're just tricks. What's your name?"

"Gigi Fochesato. Where's your snake?"

She smiled and let Javidos slip out from her sleeve. "Don't worry. He won't hurt you. He only bites bad people."

Gigi reached out a tentative hand to touch Javidos's head and then pulled it away when the copperhead flicked his tongue.

"I'm Marisol, and my friends are Redfeather and Ray. Nobody knows about this place?"

"Some might, but nobody ever comes here," Gigi said. "When I need to get away, I like to sneak out. Sometimes I'll sleep here. It's a good place to hide."

"Who do you need to hide from?" Ray asked. "Those men?"

"They don't usually bother me. I just like to be by myself. This town. I hate it here. It turns people all wrong."

"We know," Ray said, noticing again that the boy wasn't the same strange color as the others.

"Everyone's frightened of the Darkness. They think there's some sort of curse on the town. They're always looking for someone to blame for the Darkness. Anybody people suspect of witchcraft, they beat up or kill."

Ray said, "We passed a woman who was hanged. Just outside of town. She was a witch?"

Gigi furrowed his brow. "Granny Sip weren't a witch! She was nice."

"What happened? Why did they hang her?" Marisol asked.

"I guess 'cause she made root medicines. They thought she caused the Darkness, but it's still here. I guess they know now they were wrong, but they don't care. They're horrible!

Just yesterday, a bunch of men who work with my papa killed a Chinese man 'cause he made herb potions. But the Darkness is still here. They don't seem to learn. I'm just glad Hethy got away."

Marisol asked, "Who's Hethy?"

"Granny Sip's granddaughter. She was my friend." Gigi dug around in his pocket until he pulled out a strange black seedpod that looked something like a bat. "Hethy gave it to me. She said it would protect me from the Darkness. Said Granny Sip told her it would keep the Darkness from making me turn out like everyone else."

"Can I see it?" Ray asked.

Gigi handed it to him and as Ray inspected the pod in the lamplight, Marisol whispered, "Was she right? Will it protect him?"

He muttered to her, "Hopefully. I think it's what's called a buffalo pod. I've seen them before and if I'm remembering right, it's a powerful charm that wards off evil. It seems to work for him. His skin . . ." Marisol nodded, and Ray handed the pod back to Gigi, thanking him.

"What happened to Hethy?" Marisol asked.

"She ran away before the men came for Granny Sip. I hope she's okay. I don't know where she went. I miss her. She was the only friend I had here. I wish I had gotten more of those charms for my papa and brothers before she left."

Gigi sighed, kicking his feet against the leg of the chair. "My papa. My brothers. They're different too since they came out here. They traveled out here two years ago. I ran away to find them. I just came out here a few weeks ago from

Pennsylvania. My papa and my brothers, they act strange now. And you've seen how everyone looks. It's like I hardly know them anymore and they hardly know me."

"What do you mean?" Ray asked.

"The Darkness changes people," Gigi said. "Many left, mostly the folks who settled this town. But the ones brought to work in the mill, they can't leave. Some get mean, like Gatch and those men. Some get real scared and do terrible things 'cause they're so frightened, like the ones who killed Granny Sip. But most just turn . . . I don't know. Like they're not alive anymore. Like they're just ghouls or something. That's how my papa's got."

Ray looked at Gigi, young and full of sadness. He pitied the boy. To have traveled all this way to find his father and his brothers, who now were little more than strangers to him.

"You work in the mill also?"

"Not on the floor with my papa and brothers. I deliver messages for Mister Muggeridge, around the mill, into town, to the telegraph office, wherever he needs."

"I heard those men say earlier that Muggeridge is a Pinkerton."

"There's a lot of Pinkerton agents here. They keep the peace, at least enough so that work in the factory isn't bothered."

Ray exchanged a look with Redfeather and Marisol. "Pinkertons," he mumbled.

"Think they're Bowlers?" Redfeather mumbled.

"We'll find out."

"What's a Bowler?" Gigi asked.

"Security agents. Like a Pinkerton, but worse," Ray said. "Tell me more about the mill. How long's it been here?"

"I don't know. But it won't be here much longer. Mister Muggeridge's closing it. They're loading everything up on trains. I guess I'll be going soon, too. All the workers are being sent. I can't wait to get out of this town! Things will be a lot better."

"Why?" Ray asked. "Where's all this going to?"

"To the Expo."

"The Expo?" Marisol said.

Gigi sat up in his seat excitedly. "Yeah. Haven't you heard? Everybody's going. People from all over the country, maybe all over the world. I hope my ma and sister will come out to work for the Expo. It's a fair, see? A World's Fair. They've had them in wonderful places like London and Paris, but now they're putting one here, in America."

"Where?" Ray asked.

"I don't know." Gigi shrugged. "Who cares? Anywhere's better than here."

"So, what'll your father and brothers and the other workers do there?" Ray asked.

"I guess help set up the display. They say there's a whole building just for what the mill's been making. Lots of people will want to see it."

Ray looked anxiously at Redfeather and Marisol.

"But what have they been making at the mill?" Ray asked. "What will the display be?"

"That's what's strange," Gigi said, puzzling his face up. "I can't figure out what they build. When we were in

Pittsburgh, Papa and my brothers worked in a steel mill, but that's not exactly what they do here. I see it when I'm delivering messages. It's a lot of metal parts. They're building all these huge bits of machinery, but Papa's never heard what it's all for. They assemble and store it somewhere else, underground."

Ray leaned forward. "Here! Under the mill?"

Redfeather leaned over to Ray. "You don't think . . ."

Ray spoke in a low voice, "It must be! The Gog built this mill to hide his Machine as it's being built. It's here! And we have to find out where they're sending it."

"What are you talking about?" Gigi asked.

"Gigi," Ray said, looking urgently at the boy. "We need your help."

"For what?"

Ray let his eyes fall to the dried corpse of the cat. He rose and took out his knife, kneeling before the cat and poking at it.

Marisol wrinkled her nose in disgust. "What are you doing?"

Ray held up a small bone. "A good charm. It'll need this." Then he looked at Gigi. "We're going to sneak into the mill."

-15-

THE MILL

RAY CROUCHED WITH THE OTHERS ON A HILL OVER-looking the mill. This close, it was even more ominous with its rumble and cacophony, its massive towers, spewed smoke, flames, and shadows.

"That fence is too tall to climb," Ray said.

"We could do it," Redfeather said. "But there'd be no way to keep from being noticed. Look at those guards."

Hundreds of people moved around the city of tents. Some were going to work in the mill. Others pushed carts from one building to the next, while still others ate meals by cook fires. Moving among them and patrolling the interior edge of the fence were men carrying rifles—men wearing bowler hats and black suits.

Ray turned to Gigi. "Is there just the one entrance?"

"The one leading to town," he replied. "And the train

tracks. But there's a gate they keep locked until the train comes. Why do you want to go in there anyway? I thought you were performers."

Ray exchanged a glance with Marisol. "We were. Once. It's too much to explain, but we're trying to find out what's creating this Darkness. We think there's a machine hidden in the mill that's causing it."

Gigi looked puzzled. "A machine can't cause darkness."

"Makes as much sense as a tree causing it . . . ," Marisol muttered. Redfeather scowled.

"Can you take us in with you?" Ray asked Gigi. "Would that put you at any risk?"

"Nobody would notice you." He looked at Marisol and Redfeather. "But *they* might stand out. I haven't seen any Indians in the mill."

"She's not an Indian," Redfeather said.

Marisol opened her mouth to argue, but with a look from Ray changed her mind. "We can wait for you here," Marisol said. "You can always send B'hoy to us if you have trouble."

"Not like you'd be able to help much once I'm inside," Ray said, studying the dozens and dozens of Bowlers. And those were only the ones on duty outside. Surely there were more inside the buildings. If the Gog was dead, then who were they working for?

He asked Gigi, "Do you know who owns the mill?"

"I've never seen him. Everybody answers to Mister Muggeridge. But he sends the telegrams to someone else."

"You've never seen the name?"

"I'm not crazy. I don't read them."

"But are they sealed?"

"No." Gigi looked nervous as he read the expression on Ray's, Marisol's, and Redfeather's faces. "I don't want to get in any trouble."

"It's okay," Ray assured him. "You've done so much already to help us. Can you just get me inside the gate? Then I'll be able to explore on my own."

"Without getting noticed," Redfeather said.

"Of course," Ray said, pulling out the toby from beneath his shirt. "I wish I had agar-agar."

"What's that?" Redfeather asked.

Ray opened the toby. "A type of powdered seaweed. Keeps you from being noticed. Almost as good as being invisible."

"Are you sure about this, Ray?" Marisol pleaded. "What if someone who saw you earlier recognizes you?"

Ray took the cat bone from the toby and held it up. "They won't. But I'll need someone's clothes. Someone who works in the mill."

"There's extra clothes in our tent," Gigi said. "Papa and my brothers are all working now. You could borrow them."

"Good," Ray said. "I just have to keep from being noticed until we get to your tent. If something happens to me in there . . ." He raised his eyebrows, not sure what to tell Marisol and Redfeather to do.

"Just be safe." Marisol put her hand on top of Ray's.

He nodded and turned to Gigi. "All right, let's go."

Ray followed Gigi down to the town. They snuck between two of the buildings to merge with the crowd moving along the main street. Ray pulled his hat low over his eyes and kept his head down. They reached the gate leading to the mill. Four Bowlers stood guard, lazily watching the people moving in and out.

Once they were past, Ray beckoned to B'hoy with his thoughts to stay close by. B'hoy scoffed. He had almost been shot once today trying to help him. Ray thanked him for his bravery, and B'hoy called Ray something unpleasant. But Ray soon saw the black shadow of the crow glide down to perch on the fence, turning his head back and forth with annoyance.

The eerie orange half-light fell over the yard and the tops of tents. Ray and Gigi moved into the crowded lane winding through the tent camp. Many of the workers wore denim smock coats or leather aprons to protect their clothing from the machinery. That's what he'd have to borrow from Gigi's tent.

Ray realized with surprise that a little girl was walking in front of him. He looked around. Many of the workers were children. He asked Gigi about them. "They're called the 'wispies,'" Gigi explained. "They've got no parents or family watching over them. I've seen them getting off the trains. Where they come from, I have no idea."

Ray watched a pair of thin boys pass, their ashen faces rawboned, a frail look in their eyes. They walked with the strange affected movements all the people of Omphalosa had. These could have been the Shuckstack kids, Ray thought with a shudder. This must have been where Grevol was taking them. Sally could have been one of these wispies. And if things had worked out differently, Ray might have been one of them too.

"It's just up here, ahead a bit further," Gigi said, pointing.

A voice boomed, "Boy!" and a hand reached out to clutch Gigi. Ray instinctively swiveled to defend Gigi, but two things stopped him: the brusque way Gigi shook his head at Ray, and the fact that the man was a Bowler.

Ray turned back with his head ducked to keep walking as if he were not with Gigi. When he got a few steps away, he slipped between a pair of tents to look back. The Bowler wore a neat, dark suit, a black waistcoat, and the distinctive round hat.

"Mister Muggeridge sent me to find you." The Bowler nudged Gigi forward. "Get on to his office right away. He's got a message for you to take."

Gigi hustled through the crowds, giving Ray a cautious glance. "Third tent on the left," Gigi mouthed as he walked past him.

Ray kept his eyes on his feet until the Bowler had moved on. Ashen-skinned workers parted as the Bowler walked down the lane. Third tent on the left. Ray walked across the lane until he reached the simple canvas tent.

"Hello," Ray said. "Anyone in here?" He pushed open the flap and peered inside. There were five cots, a couple of trunks, and a chipped basin with a shaving mirror and a razor. Otherwise the quarters were sparse. Ray opened the lid of a trunk and found a stained smock. He threw it on and took out the cat's bone. Holding it, he held up the shaving mirror from the basin. The gray face in the mirror was not his, but a young man's with a long nose and wide-set eyes. Ray guessed it must be one of Gigi's brothers'. Hopefully they wouldn't run into each other.

Clutching the bone, Ray slipped back out onto the lane.

Two enormous brick factories crowned with smokestacks loomed above smaller wooden offices and storage buildings. Beyond was a long warehouse, with a loading platform for the trains. Hundreds of people moved in, out, and around the buildings. Adopting the stiff, dull gait of the other workers, he went through the wide doors of the first brick factory.

Inside, the heat blasted him. But worse was the noise. It was unearthly, and Ray had to fight the urge to cover his ears. Whistles shrieked. Vents hissed with steam. Men beat hammers and dragged heavy carts. And beneath the grates, screeches, and clatters bellowed a deep, skull-jarring rumble.

Ray made his way through the maze of machinery with as much purposefulness as he could show. The walkways were packed with soot-faced men, women, and children of a dozen different nationalities. Ray had to squeeze, duck, and occasionally graze moving machinery and flaming furnaces to let others get by.

After wandering for a while, Ray was not sure he had investigated the entire building, as each place within seemed like any other. Half the time, he felt lost. This was clearly not where the Machine was being stored. He found an exit and stepped back outside to a corridor between the immense buildings. The cold air felt refreshing after the sweltering factory floor.

Again Ray walked, mixing in with the crowd of workers

between the buildings. A voice behind him caught his attention: ". . . attacked Gatch in the street earlier. This boy and two Indians . . ." Instinctively, Ray turned. A woman was talking to a group of other workers. Grateful for the cat's bone, Ray quickly moved on.

Ahead, workers on foot stopped as men drove a small train of carts along a track from one building to the next. Loaded with partially constructed pieces of machinery, the carts went through a large doorway into the building on Ray's right, into a warehouse.

He reached the doorway and looked inside. A pair of Bowlers had stepped aside for the cart-train, and Ray kept his gaze low and casual. It was a cavernous space, full of echoing clanks and clatters. Workers shouted as they busily moved about. The cart-train reached a point midfloor and began descending down a ramp into a tunnel.

A tunnel!

He watched Bowlers from the doorway, waiting for a chance to slip past. One of the Bowlers was saying to the other, ". . . being that I'm going with Muggeridge."

"Where are you going already?" the other agent asked. The men had their backs to Ray and it was hard to hear them over the noise. Ray leaned closer, getting his head far enough around the doorway to listen better.

The agent shrugged. "Yeah, I don't know. But I'm sure I'll meet back up with you in Chicago."

"I positively can't get there soon enough," the other said. "Am I ever ready to go! Just a few more days and then operations will be shut down here and we'll . . ." The agent began to turn his head as he spoke, and Ray stepped back quickly away from the doorway.

As he did, a man accidentally knocked into Ray and he fell to his knees. The bone skittered from his hand and was kicked away by another man's boot, landing at a woman's feet. As Ray rose to rush for the bone, the woman picked it up. It was the woman who had been telling the others about the attack on Gatch.

Her eyes widened as she saw Ray. "That's him! He's one of them devils!"

Heads turned as Ray dashed past the woman. Two men in leather aprons left their wheelbarrow and rushed toward Ray. Ray snatched a set of metal rods from a passing worker and threw them. The approaching men tripped as the rods clattered and rolled under their feet. Pushing through the workers around him, Ray raced for the corner of the warehouse.

Which way to go—right or left?

To the left, a swell of workers was waiting as another cart-train moved along the tracks between two of the brick factories. To the right was the loading platform for the trains, including a strange locomotive, something like a stagecoach but with the engine parts of a small train. Ray had no time to wonder about it. He needed a way to escape. There were fewer people to the right, but he knew it was no good. He'd get trapped by the fence.

Angry voices rose behind him. Ray ran to the left.

He tumbled into a man, knocking the crate of parts he was carrying. Ray scrambled back to his feet with the mob close behind shouting "Stop him!" and "He's one of the witches!" Ray dove into the crowd that was waiting for the cart-train.

"Where you going?" a young man snarled as he grabbed Ray's arm.

Ray shoved the man hard in the chest and he toppled into others behind him.

"Hey!" A beefy man growled and grabbed the young man by the collar. The young man knocked his hands away, and the beefy man slugged him in the chin.

Pushing and wedging his way to the cart-train, Ray could hear the cries as the chasing mob crushed into the back of the waiting crowd, where more fights soon broke out.

Ray leaped onto the metal coupling between two of the carts and slipped into the crowd on the far side. The tent encampment was ahead, and beyond that was the gate. Faces around him turned from the angry shouts by the cart-train to look curiously at the running boy. Could he reach the gate before the mob's call to arms spread through the camp?

B'hoy!

The crow was already gliding over the tents, joining Ray. B'hoy could not defend him against so many, but the crow seemed to have another plan in mind. Swooping ahead of Ray, he croaked loudly, parting the crowd as they startled away from the flapping bird.

Ray followed B'hoy, past the tents, down the lane. The mob was not far behind. The Bowlers guarding the gate turned toward the commotion. Other Bowlers, rifles at their sides, were charging from their positions toward the gate. He was going to be cut off!

A Bowler raised a hand to halt Ray, a tin whistle shrieking from his lips. Ray ducked beneath the agent's outstretched hands and rolled into a tumble. He caught the Bowler in his legs, knocking him forward. Ray's elbows and knees stung, but he continued his roll until he got back to his feet.

Another Bowler rushed toward him, but Ray was already out the gate and into the street.

The group of Bowlers descended on the mob. "Back to work! That's enough!" Whistles blew. Some Bowlers brought the stocks of their rifles down to beat back the rushing workers. Arms outstretched, the Bowlers formed a line and pushed back the mob, stopping their pursuit.

Jumping and pointing and crushing against the Bowlers, the mob cried: "He's the one!" "We've got to get him!" "Witches brought on this dark!" "You out there, stop that boy!"

But if anyone in the street understood, they were too surprised to react. Ray launched past the perplexed faces and followed B'hoy far enough away to slip between the buildings and escape into the dark.

Redfeather was waiting for him in the soddy's doorway. "Are you okay? We saw you being chased. What happened?"

"They recognized me."

Redfeather frowned. "Not much of a charm."

Ray pulled the smock over his head and followed him inside. "Gigi," Ray said. "What are you doing here? I thought you had a message to deliver."

The boy held up a folded piece of paper. "I'm to take this to the telegraph office for Mister Muggeridge." He extended it slowly toward Ray.

Ray reached for the letter, but then stopped. "Are you sure?"

"You can read it," Gigi said, a hint of anxiety in his eyes. Then he added, "I want to go with you. When you leave, will you take me with you?"

Ray looked at Redfeather and Marisol. They all pitied the lonely boy—alienated from his family, caught in this terrible place.

"Of course, we'll take you."

Ray opened the letter. Marisol and Redfeather leaned over his shoulder to read it.

ON THE SCENT STOP SETTING OUT TOMORROW MORNING STOP LOADING THE STEAMCOACH FOR PURSUIT STOP WILL LOCATE ON THE PLAINS STOP

They looked at one another. "What's that mean?" Marisol asked.

Redfeather added, "And what's a steamcoach?"

Ray read it several more times to commit it to memory

and then folded the letter, handing it back to Gigi. "You should hurry to deliver this. Thank you."

"You won't leave without me?" Gigi asked from the doorway.

"No. Be ready tomorrow morning," Ray answered, and then wrinkled his brow. "I'm so confused by the Darkness. What time is it anyway?"

Gigi took his watch from his pocket. "Nearly midnight."

"Thanks," Ray said. "We'll see you in a few hours then."

Gigi nodded and ran off.

Ray settled into a chair as Redfeather took food from the bag Little Grass sent with them.

"Did you find anything out?" Marisol asked.

"Chicago," Ray said. "They're taking the Machine to Chicago. I heard these Bowlers talking. And there was this tunnel. It was enormous! The Machine's being built here. It's working."

Redfeather frowned. "Isn't the Machine in the Gloaming?"

Marisol puzzled up her brow. "Ray, you said wherever you cross in our world brings you to a specific place in the Gloaming. Why would they take it from the Gloaming and move it?"

"I suppose," Ray said, "because the Machine in the Gloaming only makes the Darkness where it's been placed in our world."

"But why Chicago?" Redfeather asked.

"The Expo," Marisol answered. "Gigi said there are

thousands and thousands of people going there. If the Gog wanted to draw people to his Machine, that would be the best place."

"But the Gog's dead!" Redfeather said.

Ray exchanged looks with Redfeather and then Marisol.

"What are we going to do?" Marisol asked.

"Look, who's in charge of this mill?" Ray asked.

"Muggeridge," Redfeather said.

Ray nodded. "Well, one of those Bowlers I overheard said he was going with Muggeridge somewhere. I bet it's on that steamcoach. And if Muggeridge is pursuing something on the plains, then it must be important, right?"

"We need to go to Chicago," Marisol said. "We need to stop the Machine!"

"What happened to going back to Nel?" Redfeather asked with a sneer.

Marisol frowned at him. "This is too important."

"It'll take a while for them to get the Machine loaded and hauled to Chicago," Ray said. "We follow Muggeridge for now. He's going back to Chicago anyway after they find whatever it is they're after on the plains."

"So what do you think they're after?" Redfeather asked.

"I don't know," Ray said. "But we're going to find out."

They each took turns sleeping in the two beds while one kept watch—afraid that the mob would locate them in the soddy. After a few hours, they began gathering their belongings. Ray noticed a glum mood had overtaken Redfeather.

"You all right?" Ray asked.

Redfeather looked up from where he sat at the table. "I'm fine." His fingers twisted at the necklace of Nel's charms hanging at his chest.

Ray and Marisol exchanged a glance, then Marisol said, "You've hardly said a word all night."

Redfeather lowered his hand. "It's this place."

"Omphalosa?" Ray asked.

"Yeah." Redfeather shook his head slightly, almost as if shivering. "The Darkness here. The mill. These people. It's like being a seer and having a premonition of the future. We're seeing the future. It's Omphalosa."

Ray stood up from where he'd been going through his haversack. "No, it's not. We're going to stop the Machine. We're going to—"

"Don't you see, Ray," Redfeather said. "Even if we do, the world is changing. The old ways are gone. Not just for the tribes of the Indian Territory, but the ways of the Ramblers and Mother Salagi's kind. They're dying. They'll be lost." He waved a hand out at the dark doorway. "The world is moving on, and they . . . we have no place in it."

"What about what Water Spider said?" Marisol asked. "The Wolf Tree connects us—"

"The Wolf Tree!" Redfeather choked and squeezed his eyes tight. "Don't you see, the Wolf Tree is gone."

Marisol drew in a sharp breath, and Ray watched Redfeather as he struggled to continue.

"I realize that now," Redfeather whispered. "After seeing Omphalosa I understand that the Wolf Tree will never return. Water Spider . . . he was wrong. We'll never find it."

Ray scowled and moved closer to Redfeather. "Listen, we don't know what lies ahead. But we're going to do whatever we can to destroy the Machine."

"We don't have the means to destroy the Machine," Redfeather said.

"But we can stop them," Marisol said. "Whatever that steamcoach is after, we've got to get to it first. It might be the key to stopping the Darkness."

B'hoy cawed from the windmill and they turned to look out the door. Gigi was panting up the hill, carrying a small suitcase.

Ray held out a hand and helped Redfeather to his feet. "Come on. Let's go."

They untied the horses and led them out around Omphalosa until they reached the hills on the far side of the mill.

"Where's this steamcoach?" Redfeather asked, peering down at the backside of the warehouse. Workers were busy on the other end of the mill's grounds, but otherwise only a few agents stood guard at the back gate.

"I don't know," Ray said. "Think we're too late?"

Gigi snapped open the watch. "It's only a little after five."

"Let's keep waiting," Redfeather said, crouching on the ground to watch. Gigi sat in the dry grass, double-checking his bag.

Marisol came over between Ray and Redfeather. She gave Gigi a glance and then whispered, "I've just thought of something."

"What's that?" Ray asked.

"Remember in Missouri? We saw all those roadside graves."

"People dying from the Darkness, like Mister Bradshaw." Ray nodded.

"Right, but have you seen any graves here?"

"We saw those coffins in town," Redfeather said.

"Coffins, sure. But if the Darkness kills people here, then wouldn't there be lots of sick and dying people in Omphalosa? I haven't seen a single person even coughing."

Ray scowled hard. Marisol was right. Why wasn't anybody sick here? "It doesn't make sense," Ray said. "We know the Darkness kills people. But why not the ones here?"

Marisol's brow wrinkled as she thought. "What if these people only get sick and die from the Darkness once they leave? Bradshaw said he didn't get sick until after he left."

"Then what will happen to Gigi if he comes with us?" Redfeather asked.

They looked fearfully over at the boy as he clasped his suitcase and smiled up at them.

"He's got that buffalo pod," Ray said.

Marisol shook her head. "You said yourself that you weren't sure if it would save him. His skin, it's gray. Not like the others', but still the charm doesn't seem to protect him fully. Are we willing to take that risk?"

"You're right." Ray looked down at the ground, resting his elbows on his knees as he squatted.

"What about us?" Redfeather asked, his voice pitched with concern. "Will we be okay?"

"Of course," Ray said. "We've got Nel's charms."

Marisol exhaled deeply. "Oh, poor Gigi. We promised we'd help him—"

"Look!" Gigi called, pointing to the mill.

Ray turned. A group of Bowlers were opening a large door at the back of the warehouse. Swinging the massive frames wide, they stepped back as clouds of smoke billowed from within. Pistons chugged and a vehicle pushed through the smoke to stop in the yard.

The steamcoach looked like an oversized stagecoach, boxy and unadorned. Instead of horses, extending from the front was a barrel-nosed engine topped with a smokestack. On either side, a pair of large, diagonal cylinders were mounted to the frame. In between sat the driver's bench with its steering handle and levers. The front wheels were large with grooved metal tires. Behind a water tank, the steamcoach pulled a car, as boxy and large as the coach but with no windows.

Several Bowlers talked together as others, armed with Winchester rifles, boarded the steamcoach. Two Bowlers sat at the driving bench. Six got inside, and two more sat on the top of the car at the back. Four agents mounted horses.

"Whatever they're carrying," Redfeather said, "needs a lot of protection."

Gigi came over between them and looked up at Ray. "Are we going? Are we following that car?"

Ray dipped his eyes before speaking. "Gigi, I'm sorry, but you can't come with us."

"But you promised!"

"I know, but we have something very dangerous to do.

Also, we've met people who have lived in the Darkness and then left. They get a sickness. That pod your friend Hethy gave you, we're hoping it'll protect you, but we don't want to be wrong. If you get sick from leaving the Darkness, there's nothing we could do to save you."

Gigi looked tearful, but he firmed up his lip. "I don't care. I've got to get away from this town."

Marisol put a hand to his shoulder. "Do you want to help us?"

"Yes!" he said. "Anything."

"We've got something different we need you to do," Marisol said. "We're going out after that steamcoach onto the plains, but we'll end up in Chicago at the Expo. That's where you're going with your family. We need you to watch things for us. Keep an eye on what happens with this machinery they're taking to the Expo. When we get to Chicago, you can fill us in. Okay?"

Gigi looked reluctant. "I want to go with you."

"They're leaving," Redfeather said urgently. The steamcoach was moving through the gates, crossing over the train tracks, its headlamp blazing out at a swatch of frozen earth. The horsemen followed behind.

Ray turned back to Gigi. "I'm sorry, but you've got to do like Marisol asked. We'll find you soon."

Gigi stared at them. "You'll find me in Chicago?"

"We will." Marisol smiled, climbing up into Unole's saddle. She held a hand out and Ray climbed on behind her.

They circled the horses around and waved to Gigi. The boy watched them with welling eyes.

The wind whipped Marisol's long black hair about her face. She held it down as she turned back to Ray. "I hope we're not making a mistake leaving him here."

"Me too," he said.

Shaking the reins, Marisol headed off into the Darkness after Redfeather, following the steamcoach as it rolled across the prairie.

SALLY WAS COLD. AND SHE WAS TIRED. BUT MOSTLY
she was hungry.

The sun was setting over the prairie. She tucked into the
windbreak of a hill to escape the lonely vastness. Opening
The Incunabula of Wandering, she angled the page to catch
the last red rays of sunlight.

The *Incunabula* had been enormously helpful on her journey so far. When she reached Knoxville, she decided the
quickest way west would be by train. But she did not have
enough money and knew that a girl riding so far by train
would attract attention from the conductors and porters.

The *Incunabula* provided the answer.

She had marked the page long ago describing how agar-
agar could make you completely unnoticed by those around
you. It was as good as being invisible. After inquiring in

several stores, she found a pharmacist who stocked the powdered seaweed. Holding a bit in her hand and concentrating on being like a shadow, she simply walked past the ticket collector and onto the train.

But the effect was temporary, and by the time she reached Iowa City, the powers had waned. She could find no shop that sold agar-agar anywhere in the town. She had no idea how much farther she would have to go. The rabbit's foot simply pointed toward the west. How was she to find her father? She needed another way to travel.

Again the *Incunabula* had an answer.

Sally remembered Ray using a "foot powder" charm to command a panther. Searching through the *Incunabula,* Sally found instructions for collecting the dirt where a person's foot made an impression on the ground. Sally wandered around the town, looking for someone to try the charm on. At last she spied a tinker, with a wagon full of goods, speaking to a woman. While the tinker was busy selling the woman a skillet, Sally scooped his footprint from the dust in the street into a wide-mouthed bottle. When the little, gray-whiskered man finished his sale, Sally sidled up to him and said she needed a ride. He asked in a friendly voice where she was going. When she said west, he said he had a sister in Neligh, Nebraska, he'd been wanting to visit.

For nearly a week, she rode with him and his clattering orchestra of swinging pots and pans. Sally tried not to feel guilty about forcing the man to take her so far. After all, he had said he wanted to visit his sister—but would he have decided to do that if Sally hadn't trapped his footprint in the jar? She had to keep going west, and she couldn't risk riding with a stranger without some assurance for her safety.

Once she reached Neligh and said farewell to the tinker, Sally decided against using the foot-powder charm again. Besides, the rabbit's foot—turning slowly in her palm until the tiny claws were pointing out the direction—told her to go west. There was nothing in that direction but open prairie. She would have to walk. That's what Ray would have done. That's what her father would have done. If she was to be a Rambler, she would have to act like one.

Seven days later, huddled alone on the darkening prairie, she wished Ray were there to help her. She slammed the *Incunabula* closed. She could uncover lost spells and obscure charms from her father's book. But what the *Incunabula* didn't tell her was how to make a fire, how to find food, how to keep warm.

She was not a Rambler.

She reached into her rucksack and took out her bag of food. Only an apple, a biscuit that had gone stale, and a sliver of cheese remained. She bit into the brick-hard biscuit and chewed until her jaw felt like it would fall off. Even after she finished it, her empty stomach felt tight as a fist, but she knew she needed to save the rest of the food. Who knew how much farther she would have to go.

Shivering beneath her blanket, Sally suffered through another sleepless night.

* * *

She walked all day and did not see a single homestead. Nor a single tree. Where was she going? Where was her father?

The day was warm, with a blue, cloudless sky overhead. Cresting a hill, she looked to the south as she ate the last apple. She could still see the strange dark band covering the sky.

The Darkness.

She wondered about Ray and Marisol, hoping they had reached Omphalosa safely. An unpleasant knot formed in her throat. She had promised Ray to keep the rabbit's foot safe at Shuckstack while he was away. He would be furious if he found out she had broken her promise. But wouldn't he be happy when she found their father? That would make up for it, she assured herself.

But how was she going to reach her father anyway?

She had been in such a hurry to sneak away from Shuckstack, in such a hurry to find her father, she had overlooked the obvious question. She might be able to find her father with the rabbit's foot, but how would she cross into the Gloaming to reach him?

The Incunabula of Wandering, she reminded herself. The book had shown her how to do so many other things, surely it could help her reach her father. She had to find him. She had gone too far to turn back.

The rabbit's foot still pointed to the west. She followed it all afternoon, past endless swishing grass and tumbling sun-dappled hills.

As the sun set, she ate the last of the cheese and began dreading another miserable night. "Why can't I just find some cowboys on a cattle drive? Why can't I find some Sioux hunting party? Why can't I just find someone, anyone, in this horrid wasteland cooking a hot meal?"

As she shouted this, something moved in her pocket. The rabbit's foot! Sally took it out and held it in her palm. The foot twitched slowly toward the south.

Had she gotten off course somehow? It didn't seem likely. She had traveled halfway across the country, weeks and weeks, and the rabbit's foot had always been pointing to the west or slightly in a northwesterly direction. And now, all of a sudden, to the south? But it wasn't turning and pointing— it was twitching. Like it had done back when she and Ray were in the city.

She continued walking into the twilight, and the golden foot began to tremble slightly and then nearly leaped from her hand. Had she reached her father at last? She picked up her pace, stumbling as she went up and down, up and down, hill after hill. The prairie grew dark. The stars appeared. A corn-yellow half-moon rose. A coyote yapped and another answered.

Exhausted, Sally was ready to stop for the night—for the dozenth time—when she saw a glow beyond the next dune. Fire! Sally quickened her step. As she crested the rise, she could see a cook fire blazing from the dark in the wide bowl below. There was a small bundle covered with a blanket at the edge of the firelight. But no horse, no wagon, nobody.

The campsite seemed empty, except for a pot sitting on the ground with a wooden spoon protruding from beneath the lid.

Sally could smell food. Whatever it was, it smelled delicious. She didn't really care if it wasn't delicious. It was food, and she wanted it.

Moving closer, she peered about in the dark to see if the travelers were still there, maybe hidden somewhere out of the firelight. She saw nobody. She inched to the fireside. Her stomach whined as she lifted the lid to the pot. Beans. Her mouth watered.

As she reached for the spoon, the bundle moved. A shrill cry burst forth and the blanket rose in a whirling tangle. A hand came out from under the blanket holding a hatchet. Sally screamed and threw the lid in a hard spin. It struck with a clank, and the attacker doubled over, dropping the hatchet.

"Ouch! Hey!"

Sally scrambled to her feet, watching cautiously as the person pulled the blanket off. It was just a kid! She was no older than Sally, a black girl in several layers of tattered and patched-up dresses and shirts.

The girl winced as she touched her fingers to her cheek, a welt already rising. "That hurt!"

"Well, what were you doing hiding under there?" Sally snapped. "You scared me out of my wits!"

"This here's my camp!" the girl said, giving Sally a fierce jut of her chin. "What're you attacking me at my own camp for?"

"You can't expect a person to just stand around and let herself get hacked up by some ghost-blanket-maniac."

"You was about to eat my supper!" the girl shouted.

"I thought nobody was here," Sally said. "Why were you hiding under that blanket anyway?"

Still rubbing her face, the girl walked back to the fireside and sat down. "I thought you was a coyote. Every night I go to sleep, there's this coyote that keeps raiding my food. I had it with that coyote! 'Tonight,' I said to myself, 'I'm going to set a trap and chop that coyote to pieces when he tries to take my supper.' "

"Sorry I ruined your plan," Sally said. "And I'm sorry I hurt your face. I've barely eaten in days and I'm starving. Would you mind if I had some of your beans?"

The girl narrowed her eyes, inspecting Sally. Then she let her eyelids close. Moments passed. Was she falling asleep? Was she trying to pretend Sally wasn't there, hoping she'd leave? Sally began to think the girl was possibly insane.

"Excuse me," Sally said.

"I'm beholding you," the girl said without opening her eyes.

"You're what?"

"Hush."

Sally waited, watching the strange girl until finally her eyes opened.

"Okay, you can have some," she said, pushing the pot over to Sally. "I ain't got but the one spoon. You can use it. Or your fingers if you like."

Sally took the spoon and ate. The beans were delicious and she shoveled them into her eager mouth.

"You like them?" The girl smiled. "I've got corn cakes,

too." The girl unfolded a kerchief wrapped around the cold but enticing brown cakes. They were sweet and buttery and Sally ate them with her mouth half-filled with beans.

"Where're you come from anyway?" the girl asked.

"North Carolina."

The girl's eyes widened. "I ain't so good with geography, but that's a fierce ways off!"

"It's been a long trip. What's your name anyway?"

"Hethy. Hethy Smith. You?"

"Sally Cobb. Nice to meet you, Hethy."

"Uh-huh," Hethy said as she watched Sally finish the rest of the beans.

"Do you live nearby?" Sally asked.

"Think I'd be sleeping out here? No, I'm from Kansas."

"Are you visiting family somewhere?"

"Nope, I got no family . . ." She paused, her face twisting up. "I got . . . no family left, I guess,". she said, and then Hethy began crying.

Sally moved closer to her, patting Hethy on the shoulder. "That's okay. That's okay," she said. "Did something happen?"

Hethy wiped her face and said, "My granny, I think they killed her. I do. Them men, they was coming for her. She knew it. She told me to get. Packed my bag for me quick like and said, 'Run, Hethy. I don't know where to tell you to go, but just run, girl.' "

"That's awful," Sally said. "But maybe they didn't—"

"They did. I know they did," Hethy sniffed. "My granny

and I, we're seers. Granny Sip more than me. I got a touch of the beholding. If she was living, I'd know."

"What do you mean, 'beholding'?"

Hethy sniffled as she said, "Granny Sip, she can't see the future or nothing like that, but she can see the secrets in people's hearts. Started when she was just a little girl back in Alabama. She can behold things others can't. Heal folks, too. People used to come to her to find out if their sweetheart was doing them wrong or why their child took sick. That's why them men done killed her. 'Cause she's a witch, they reckoned. They said she caused the Dark that won't never break."

"The Darkness!" Sally said. "That Darkness to the south. I know about that. I saw it too. My brother is going to find out what's causing the Darkness. He's going to a town called . . . Ontha . . . Ompa . . ."

"Omphalosa?" Hethy's tears had stopped and she spoke earnestly. "I sure hope that ain't where he's gone. That's where I'm from. Town's turned wicked, for sure."

"My brother has powers also," Sally said. "Not like your beholding, but he can take care of himself there, I know."

"I hope so. I really do. Is that why you're out here? You trying to find him?"

"No," Sally said. "I'm looking for my father."

"I knew it," Hethy said, turning her eyes down. "I just wanted to see if you'd tell me straight."

"What? How'd you know?"

"When I beheld you a bit ago. I looked in your heart. I seen you was looking for your daddy and you're carrying something that's leading you to him. What is it? What're you carrying?"

Sally's mouth hung open a moment. Tentatively, she took out the golden rabbit's foot.

Hethy whistled. "Ain't that a pretty one," she said. "Where'd you get that?"

"I don't know if you'll believe me if I tell you."

"Try me," Hethy said, wiping her nose on her sleeve.

"My father lost his hand to a mechanical hound, called a Hoarhound."

"Hoarhound?"

Sally nodded. "This is his hand now. It points to tell me which direction to go. If I keep following it, it'll lead me to him." The foot had twitched to the south. Had it meant to lead her to Hethy? She felt the rabbit's foot stir, and this time it turned to point again to the west.

"What in the world?" Hethy muttered as she watched the paw move. "You're right. That's hard to stomach as the truth. But I believe you. When I was beholding you, I seen you was good, good in your heart. You didn't venture into the Dark, did you?"

"No, why?"

"People turn bad from the Dark." Hethy reached over to her bags and took out a dried seedpod, strangely like a bat in shape. "Granny give me this to carry and these other charms, back when the Dark started. Said it would protect me and I reckon it has. If she had only had enough for the whole town . . ." She squeezed her eyes against her tears, but then calmed herself with a few deep breaths.

Sally looked at Hethy. She had thought the girl was crazy at first, but now she found Hethy fascinating. She could see into people's hearts. She could build a fire on the prairie. She set traps to kill marauding coyotes. She was tough and honest and kind.

"Where are you going to go?" Sally asked.

"I don't know," Hethy sighed. "I ain't got no family left. I hear there's work in Chicago for those that want to work for the big Expo there. Or I could take a job root working. I know a bit from Granny Sip. How to heal and how to behold people. But that's what got Granny killed, so I don't know where folks would look kindly on that kind of work."

The girls sat for a time watching the fire send sparks up to mingle with the stars. Then Hethy began chuckling.

"What?" Sally asked.

"I was just thinking how funny it was, I thought you was a coyote and I jumped out under that blanket with my hatchet to chop your head off. I ain't never figured it'd be no little girl like me." She erupted into laughter. "Thought . . . I thought . . . you was a coyote!"

Watching Hethy's face, her expressive mouth curling wide, her bright eyes flashing in the firelight, Sally was grateful to have found her. She felt Hethy was glad she had found Sally, too. Sally began laughing, laughing with relief, laughing with joy, laughing with puzzlement over how strange and terrible life could be.

"Coyote girl," Hethy said, pointing at Sally.

"Lumberjack!" Sally said, pointing at the hatchet.

The two girls laughed for a long time.

In the morning there was no discussion of whether the girls would part ways. They simply hoisted their packs to their shoulders and set off together, west across the empty prairie.

Hethy was nearly a head shorter than Sally, though they were the same age. But trudging along in the warm sun, Sally found it hard to keep Hethy's pace. "Slow down," she said. "You're walking too fast."

It was nearly midday, and Hethy stopped to let Sally catch up. "I'm thirsty and I think I seen something sparkling up ahead. Might be a creek or something."

As the girls headed on, Sally looked at Hethy. She hadn't noticed it the night before in the dark, but now in the full daylight, she saw how oddly gray Hethy's skin was tinted. It was still brown, but faintly, as if the color was fading from it. And her hair. It should have been black, but it looked as if it had been dusted with flour.

"Hethy, why's your skin look like that?"

Hethy turned her hand before her. "We're all like this. All that lived in Omphalosa. That's how come Granny Sip gave me that bat-looking pod. If I ain't had it, my skin would be gray as a river stone."

"Do you know Mister Bradshaw?" Sally asked.

Hethy's lips pursed a moment. "Can't say as I do. He from Omphalosa?"

"Yes," Sally said. "He came to Shuckstack. He was awfully sick. Ray said the Darkness made him sick." Sally hesitated before saying, "He died."

Hethy cocked her chin at Sally. "I ain't sick. Granny Sip's pod'll make sure of that. So don't go on trying to scare me like that, Yote. I'll be all right."

"Yote?" Sally asked. "Why'd you call me that?"

"Like a coyote," Hethy said with a grin.

Sally laughed and put a hand to her brow as she peered around at their surroundings. A big blue sky. An ocean of green. There was not so much as a windmill or sod house in sight. Nothing between the girls and the distant horizon but miles and miles of windswept grass and the black drifting specks of faraway birds.

"Okay. Where'd you think you saw that water?"

"Just over that hill, Yote."

Soon they found a small pond, tucked into a depression and bordered by tall grass. The girls dipped their flasks and drank. The water had a funny, salty taste, but they drank anyway.

"So how much food do you think you have left?" Sally asked.

"Maybe for a few more meals if we're skimpy."

Hethy took a corn cake out for each of them, and when they had finished them a moment later, they looked at one another, still hungry. "Want to eat another?" Hethy asked.

"No, we'll wait until supper."

When they stopped that night, Sally looked through the *Incunabula* again, hoping to find some reference to wild foods. It mentioned medicinal herbs and roots that could be ground up for potions, but they were mostly found in the eastern forests back home. There was little more than grass out here. And she did not recognize any of the plants growing around the ponds they continued to pass.

Sharing the spoon, Sally and Hethy passed the pot back and forth until they had finished a small batch of beans they had cooked from the remaining sack. Sally continued reading the *Incunabula,* hoping to find a way to cross into the Gloaming when she reached her father.

Hethy leaned back against her pack with her hands cocked behind her head. "What's that book you're always reading, Yote?"

The sod fire crackled and gave off a pungent smoke.

Sally closed the page, her eyes sore, frustrated that she had found nothing helpful. "Do you read?"

"I learned my letters a bit."

"This book was my father's. Have you ever heard of the Ramblers?"

"You mean like in the old stories about John Henry and such?"

"Yes!" Sally said. "My father was Li'l Bill."

"John Henry's shaker? Those stories ain't true, are they?"

"They are. Mister Nel, that root worker who takes care of us back home, he was once a Rambler, too. He and my father and John Henry and all the other Ramblers, they destroyed the Gog's Machine."

"Gog?" Hethy asked. "Ain't heard that part of the story. I heard it John Henry beat a steam drill."

"No. It wasn't a steam drill." Sally told Hethy the story of the Gog and how her brother and Conker and the others from the medicine show had destroyed the Gog and his train.

"But they never found the Machine," Sally said at last. "That's really what my brother's looking for in Omphalosa. He thinks the Darkness is because of the Machine."

"Hum," Hethy wondered, her expression darkening.

"What?" Sally asked.

"Granny Sip used to say she reckoned there was something in the mill that caused the Darkness. A wicked and enormous clockwork buried beneath the town. She'd know if there was."

"So maybe my brother will find it," Sally said excitedly. "Maybe he already has and—"

In the distance, they heard a howl.

Sally looked nervously into the shadows. "Was that a wolf?" Sally asked.

Hethy cocked an eyebrow at Sally. "You scared?"

"Aren't you?"

Hethy waved a hand dismissively at the dark. "Nothing out there's going to hurt us. We're all right. It's just a coyote or something is all. There ain't no wolves left in these parts. They've all been shot or run off."

The girls lay down beneath their blankets.

After a time, Hethy rolled over on her elbows and asked, "You reckon that noise could have been a Boo Hag?"

Sally flipped over to look at Hethy. "What's that?"

Hethy narrowed her eyes seriously. "An old witch, except she ain't got no skin. She's just blood red. She catches you, she'll tear your skin off and wear it."

"That's not true," Sally said. "Is it?"

Hethy kept her brow lowered but couldn't hold it for long

and gave a wide smile as she rolled onto her back. "People tell about them Boo Hags though."

Sally laughed, scooting a little closer to Hethy. "Have you ever heard of a Wampus Cat?"

"Never. That some kind of bobcat?"

Sally told the story she had heard from Mattias and Dmitry about the half-panther, half-woman. Then Hethy told her about hodags and the Tailypo and the ghosts of Pony Express riders who haunted the prairies. Soon they were out of stories, and Sally lay listening for wild animals or Boo Hags or whatever it was they had heard howling. After a time, she curled closer up against Hethy and fell asleep.

The girls continued to follow the rabbit's foot. It led them further into the desolate expanse of great grassy dunes. Hethy had been making their campfires by cutting sod from the earth, but this soil was too sandy and too moist to burn. Sally did not mind sleeping without a fire as much as she did the meager meal. Without a fire, there was no way to cook Hethy's beans. There was little more left in Hethy's bag than a few pieces of dried beef and some rubbery carrots, which the girls nibbled at sparingly.

Fortunately there was plenty of water. Some of the ponds were as big as lakes and thick with ducks and swans and strange birds she'd never seen, with red eyes and black tufts on their heads. If they could only catch one, Sally thought. But then she remembered they had no way to make a fire, and besides, it was hopeless; she couldn't catch a bird. She wasn't Ray.

Sally pored through the *Incunabula* for some charm to help ease their rumbling stomachs or produce a fire. She found nothing helpful, but she did come across a passage she had not read before. It concerned sacred stones used by some medicine men. The stones could locate misplaced objects of importance or lost horses and even missing people. In the margin, her father had written "lodestone" in his scrawling cursive.

The lodestone!

Sally looked back at the *Incunabula*. More writing in her father's hand was further down the page: "Place what is lost in your thoughts and follow."

What had she been thinking when the foot led her to Hethy? She hadn't been thinking of Hethy. She hadn't even known her then. She'd been cold and hungry and tired and wanted nothing more than to find . . .

Sally gasped. She had wanted to find someone out on the prairie who could feed her. This was like when she and Ray were in the city and the lodestone often led them to food or helpful things. Could she think this again and would the rabbit's foot lead them to a homestead or town or even a bramble of blackberries growing mysteriously on the dunes?

The sun was high overhead, and Hethy was splashing water from a pond on her neck.

"Hethy!" she called. "Come here quick."

Hethy ran back with her hatchet out. "What? You seen a rattler or something?"

"No! I think I've figured out how to find food. This rabbit's foot. It'll lead us!" Sally held the golden foot in her palms, trying to calm her excited mind. Food. Lead us to food, she thought.

The rabbit's foot turned until it indicated the west.

"Is it telling you, Yote?" Hethy asked, watching Sally with wide eyes.

"I don't know. It's pointing the same direction it has been."

"Well, maybe there's something up yonder. Let's go!"

The hope that a hot meal was just ahead brought new energy to the girls' legs. They ran up and down the dunes, across flatter expanses and around ponds. But they soon grew tired and resumed their original pace. When the sun set and nothing had been found, the girls ate another piece of the dried meat and found a spot to sleep for the night.

"You think that foot's pulling your leg, Yote?" Hethy asked.

"It doesn't do that," Sally replied. "I don't know why it's not working. Maybe we're not there yet."

But Sally remembered how the rabbit's foot had begun to vibrate urgently when it led her to Hethy. The foot was not doing that now. It would turn to point out the right direction to go, but otherwise the rabbit's foot remained motionless.

The next day, they trudged with hard, angry stomachs. As the afternoon grew late and they came over a ridge, Sally realized that Hethy had stopped several steps behind her. She was staring at some point far in the distance to the east.

"What?" Sally asked. "What is it?"

Hethy kept staring. "You see something back there?"

Sally narrowed her eyes. The undulating plain was as

wide and empty as an ocean. But then she saw it. A form—dark against the green and gold landscape—moving their way. Sally had no sense for distance and could only assume it was several miles perhaps.

"What is that?" she wondered. "Is it a buffalo?"

"Ain't no buffalo left," Hethy murmured. She squinted and then looked at Sally with tight, fearful eyes. "I'd swear that's a wolf."

"Can't be a wolf," Sally said. "It's too big. Besides, you said all the wolves are gone from the prairie."

The creature was loping at a steady pace and then disappeared in a dip in the prairie. But in that last moment before it was gone from sight, Sally knew Hethy was right. Those ears. That tail. It was a wolf, but enormous and monstrous.

Hethy looked at Sally, worry tensing her mouth. "You reckon it's following us?"

"No," Sally said, hoping that if her voice sounded brave it would make the two girls brave in turn. "Why would it be following us?"

She looked back once more before walking on. But nothing was there.

As THE GIRLS CONTINUED THE NEXT MORNING, THEIR eyes constantly scanned the prairie for the animal. The last two pieces of dried meat made a paltry lunch, and without wood for a fire, they had no way to cook the beans.

"How long do you think we can go without eating, Yote?" Hethy asked.

"A while, I think," Sally replied. "If we have water, and there's plenty of creeks and ponds and such out here. We'll be okay a little longer."

"But we've got a lot of walking to do, and I'm hungry already."

"Me too. Don't think about it."

Hethy walked silently for a time. Then she huffed, "If I don't, I start thinking on that wolf or whatever that big thing was."

"Don't think about him either."

"I can't help it. Hey! Ain't those trees ahead?"

The girls ran across the plains, the tips of green branches growing larger as they came over several more rises. Soon they reached a shallow river, with a thin band of cedars and cottonwoods running along the banks.

Exuberant at finding wood, the girls threw down their packs, broke off dead limbs, and lit a fire. Hethy quickly cooked the remaining beans, and, almost as quickly, the girls ate them, their stomachs growing full and content.

The girls sat in the tall prairie at the edge of the trees to rest before setting off. Sally worked on lacing together prairie sunflowers and prickly poppies into a necklace, while Hethy ran her ashen-gray finger along the worn stitching on her shoe.

"Yote," Hethy said.

"Hmm."

"What do you think's going to happen when you find your daddy?"

Sally didn't look up from the flowers. "Well, if I can figure out how to get into the Gloaming . . ."

"Sure, if you can do that," Hethy said.

Sally continued lacing together the flowers. "He'll help Ray destroy the Machine."

"But what then?" Hethy asked.

Sally shrugged. "We'll go back to Shuckstack."

Hethy looked up from her shoes. "You think Mister Nel would let me live with you all at Shuckstack?"

Sally smiled. "Oh, you know he will." But then she saw

that Hethy actually had been worrying about this. Hethy had lost her only living relative and had no home left. Sally had a home, and she was looking for her father. She had so much to be happy about and hopeful for. But Hethy did not.

She tied off the end of her flower necklace and put it over Hethy's neck. "Don't you worry, Hethy Smith. You're coming back with me to Shuckstack. You're going to like it there, with Si and Buck and all the others. You'll just love them." Sally laughed with remembrance and said, "Once, when Ray was off learning from some root doctor up in Virginia, I went out with Rosemary and Oliver to pick dewberries—"

Hethy squeezed Sally's hand with a painful clutch, her eyes locked on the opposite side of the river.

"What is it?" Sally asked, swiveling her head around.

"Over there." Hethy pointed. "What's on that other bank?"

Through the thin wall of trees on the other side, Sally could see the dark form lying on the earth.

"It ain't moving," Hethy said.

"Come on," Sally said nervously. "Let's go see."

The girls scrambled down the embankment and took off their shoes to wade across the river. As they came out on the other side, they laced back up their shoes and peered up over the edge of the embankment.

Several yards beyond the trees, the tall grass had been trampled and torn up in a wide swath. In places, the prairie earth was laid bare, exposed and torn apart in clumps. Blood darkened the ground in spots.

A wolf lay in the center, motionless and toppled to one

side. Its fur was silver, with highlights that looked nearly blue where the sun reflected from its coat. Black blood, crusted and tar-like, covered much of its hide and face, and its tongue hung limply from its scarred jaws in the dirt.

"It's that wolf we seen," Hethy said.

"He's huge!" Sally gasped. "I had no idea wolves got that big."

"I don't think they do."

"Is he dead?" Sally asked.

"Must be," Hethy said. "Something done him bad."

Sally pulled Hethy by the hand as they ascended the bank and walked over to the edge of the circle of trampled grass several yards from the dead monster.

"What do you think done that to him?" Hethy asked.

Sally squinted her eyes at the bare earth around the wolf's body. "There are prints. Let's go a little closer and look."

"That ain't a good idea," Hethy said.

"We'd better know what got him so we can watch out for it," Sally said, taking a few cautious steps forward.

"Come on, Yote," Hethy pleaded, but she followed Sally as she crept near the wolf's body. His skin was torn across his hip and at his neck. One ear had been nearly severed. Little streams of blood still ran, but most had congealed into thick black blobs matted into his fur. He had older scars, too, healed but crisscrossing his hide as if from a hundred past battles.

Sally knelt to touch a hand to the dirt. Prints covered the area. Whatever had happened, it had been an awful fight. Claws had kicked away clumps of earth as big as her head.

She scanned the mangled earth until she found the clear imprint of a paw. "I see a print here," Sally said. "Come over and look and tell me if you recognize it."

"I ain't coming no closer," Hethy said.

"Why? He's dead—"

The wolf convulsed, his eyes opening and his snout swinging toward Sally. *"Toninyan!"* he uttered weakly, his eyes glazed with pain. "Where—is—*Toninyan*?"

The girls leaped back, but the wolf had dropped his head heavily to the ground again and closed his eyes.

"What did he say?" Sally gasped, scrambling back with Hethy to watch the wolf from the tall grass.

"So he *did* speak?" Hethy murmured. "I about thought I lost my wits. Come on, Yote. We got to go!"

"But he's still alive," Sally said.

"He's dying, and there's nought to do but get away before he decides he wants a last meal."

Sally stared at the wolf. His sides were heaving with breath and he drew his tongue back in his mouth. Sally took the *Incunabula* from her rucksack and began feverishly flipping pages.

"What're you doing?" Hethy asked.

"We could help him," Sally said. "We could save him before he dies."

"Why do you want to save a wolf? He looks crazy."

Sally looked up from the page. "Why in the world would you think he's crazy?"

With an earnest knit to her brow, Hethy replied, "Well, a

wolf starts speaking, he must have gone crazy. He ain't safe. Don't make no sense trying to save him."

"Look at him, Hethy. That's no ordinary wolf. He can speak. We'd help him if he were an injured man."

"What? You're crazy now, too?"

Sally leaned forward. "Wolf. Can you hear me?"

His eyes opened and rolled around in their sockets before closing again.

"We can help you. Are you dangerous?"

Hethy hit Sally in the arm. "Like he's going to tell us the truth."

Sally rounded on her. "Look, behold him or whatever it is you do. You can see the truth in him, can't you?"

Hethy considered this. "All right. I'll try." She closed her eyes and after a time, a startled expression came over her face and she opened her eyes.

"What? What is it?" Sally asked.

"He ain't a wolf. You're right about that. And he turned into this wolf, but I can't tell if he's really a man. Seems like he is and he ain't at the same time. I don't quite understand what I seen. But he's good. He's got a good heart."

"Maybe he's under an enchantment," Sally said. "Like in 'Snow White and Rose Red.'"

"Ain't never heard of it," Hethy said.

"The point is he needs our help. We should heal him."

Hethy looked anxious, but said, "If that's what you want to do."

"Thank you," Sally said, throwing her arms around her

friend. "Okay, the *Incunabula* says what herbs we need, but I don't know if they grow out here. Would you recognize them?"

"Maybe," Hethy said. "Granny Sip sent me out to gather for charms. I know a few of these prairie flowers and such."

"Take a look then," Sally said, turning the book around so Hethy could read it.

After a moment, she said, "All right. Some of these is out here."

"Do you know how to use them?"

"Ain't your book teach you that?" Hethy asked.

"It just says what herbs to use, not how to heal."

Hethy sniffed. "I seen Granny Sip set some poultices. I can do it good enough, I reckon. Come on."

Hethy led Sally away, collecting yarrow and wild indigo as they went. When they returned, Hethy said, "We got to heat water. You go fetch some wood back at those trees, and I'll start getting these herbs ready."

Soon there was a roaring fire with a pot of water warming. As Hethy worked, she said, "We've got to clean him up first. You reckon you're up for that?"

"Okay," Sally said reluctantly.

Hethy gave an encouraging nod toward the wolf just a few feet away. Before Sally moved over, Hethy added, "If he bites your hand off, I don't reckon I can heal that."

Sally crouched before the wolf, keeping a safe distance. "Can you hear me?"

The wolf opened his eyes but did not reply. His eyes were a silver-blue, almost the same as his scar-covered coat. There was an intense intelligence within those humanlike eyes.

"I'm going to try to clean this blood off of you. My friend, she's putting together something that will heal. We're going to try to help you."

"Go away," the wolf said in a low voice.

"Will you hurt me if I wash your wounds?"

The wolf closed his eyes. Sally took this as acceptance, hoping she was not wrong. She tore a strip from her blanket and, pouring water onto the wolf's haunch, began to gingerly wipe away the blood and gore. The wolf did not try to stop her, but after a time opened his eyes again and said in a weak voice, "No purpose."

"What?" Sally asked.

He lifted his nose a fraction. "No purpose in helping me."

"Why is that?" But the wolf just closed his eyes and fell back asleep.

When Sally had finished cleaning the wounds on one side, she woke the wolf with a gentle prod. "Can you turn over? So I can clean your other side."

"They will only kill me. What good is being cleaned before your death?"

"Who will kill you? Who did this to you?"

"My pack."

Hethy looked up anxiously from the simmering pot. "There're others like you?"

The wolf was silent, but then said, "They will not come back yet. They left me for dead."

"Then turn over," Sally commanded in her small voice.

The wolf let out a low growl, struggled to his feet, and fell over the other way.

"Thank you," Sally sighed. The wolf said nothing.

Hethy brought over the herbs, crushed and soaking in the hot water. It was sunset before Sally finished, and the girls worked into the night, placing the compounds into his wounds and pulling his torn hide back into place. When they had finished, Hethy whispered, "I'm bone tired, Yote. Don't like sleeping here next to this wolf, but I'm too tired to go nowhere else."

"He won't hurt us," Sally said, looking at the wolf, who twitched with fretful dreams. "Let's sleep."

Hethy shared her blanket with Sally, since hers had been used to clean the wolf. As the girls lay down, Hethy said, "I hope them other wolves don't come back."

"He said they wouldn't," Sally whispered. And although a part of her was scared that they would, another part—the one that was exhausted—trusted the wolf, and that allowed her to fall into a heavy sleep.

The girls woke to find the wolf sniffing and licking his wounds.

Sally and Hethy stood, stretching and rubbing their sore necks. When the wolf looked over at them, Hethy said, "A thank-you would be all right."

The wolf growled, but not menacingly. "You have only wasted your time."

"Why do you keep saying that?" Sally asked crossly. "Do you want them to kill you?"

With eyes half-closed, he replied, "It makes no difference anymore."

"Why? Why were those wolves so terrible to you?"

"They don't understand!" He grew agitated. "They have forgotten."

"Forgotten what?"

The wolf lowered his chin to his forepaws.

Curiosity was burning in Sally, and she tried again. "What was that word you kept saying before?"

The wolf was silent.

"You were asking for something. Toniya—?"

"*Toninyan,*" the wolf growled. "But I was wrong."

"Wrong about what?"

"I thought I sensed it. I thought the man who I gave the *Toninyan* to was with you. I thought he had come back. To help us find . . . No, I was confused. Mad with desperation and my injuries."

"What is the *Toninyan?*" Sally asked. "Who is this man?"

The wolf closed his eyes but he was not sleeping. He was ignoring her.

Hethy put her hand to Sally's shoulder and whispered, "We done what you wanted, Yote. We healed that wolf as best we could. But we got nothing else to do for him. Can we go now?"

"I suppose," Sally said, casting a disappointed glance at the wolf.

She took out the rabbit's foot and watched as it turned and pointed toward the west, where the morning sun was throwing rich light across the sea of grass and wildflowers.

"Yote!" Hethy squeaked.

The wolf was getting stiffly to his feet, his blazing eyes on Sally. There was a madness again in those eyes, and Sally worried that Hethy had been right all along. She stepped back, considering whether she could outrun him in his weakened state.

He opened his savage jaws, and dry words struggled out. "The *Toninyan*."

"Get back!" Sally said, waving her hand feebly at the wolf.

"You? You are the one . . . you have the *Toninyan*. . . ." But his eyes were not on her. They were on her hands.

He was staring at the rabbit's foot.

"LET ME SEE THE *TONINYAN*," THE WOLF DEMANDED.

Sally wrapped her fingers around the rabbit's foot. "No! What are you going to do?"

"Let me see it, child!" The wolf jabbed his nose at her hands. "I'm not going to harm you."

With shaking hands, Sally opened her fingers to show the rabbit's foot to the wolf.

He inhaled great snorts with his silver nose. "No. What is this? I sense it. The *Toninyan* is here, but this . . . this is not it! What is this object?"

"My—my father's hand," Sally stammered.

"What do you mean?" the wolf asked.

"My father. He lost his hand fighting a Hoarhound and it became this golden foot."

The wolf shook his ragged muzzle. "I don't know what a Hoarhound is."

Sally cupped the rabbit's foot and held it away from the wolf. "What does it matter? This isn't your *Toninyan*. It's his hand. Now get back!"

The wolf retreated a step at the intensity of Sally's shouts. His head lowered and his entire frame seemed to sag. "I don't understand. I sense it. I'm certain I do."

"I'm sorry," Sally said. "I'm sorry you can't find your *Toninyan*. But my father is lost, trapped in a world called the Gloaming. He's lost his powers, and I'm looking for him. I'm going to find him and give him back his hand. This is leading me to him."

The wolf lifted his head, his ears flattened against his head. "Who is this man? Who is your father?"

Sally wondered at the question and answered slowly, "Bill Cobb."

"Yes. Yes," the wolf said. "Your father was with John Henry. They came to the Great Tree long ago. We gave John Henry a branch, and your father the *Toninyan*. Did he ever show it to you?"

"I never knew my father. He disappeared before I was born. What did it look like? What was the *Toninyan*?"

"The Seeker's Stone. A mere rock to your eye, but it is a powerful object—able to guide one to what has been lost."

"The lodestone?" Sally gasped.

"Yes, a lodestone. Does he still have it? If we can find your father—"

"It's here! The lodestone is inside the rabbit's foot."

Bafflement swirled in the wolf's silver-blue eyes. Then he stared down at the rabbit's foot. "But you are just a child. Why are you carrying the *Toninyan*? Child, I must find the Tree. I need the Seeker's Stone!"

"No!" Sally backed away, fearful of the manic urgency in the wolf's eyes. "I can't help you. The stone—the rabbit's foot—it's mine. I promised my brother I would keep it safe. I need it. I need to find my father."

"But the Great Tree . . . ," the wolf said. "If I don't find it . . ." He dropped to the ground, the pain of his injuries seeming to catch up with his desperation.

Sally looked into the wolf's eyes, where a deep sadness was betrayed in those silver-blue orbs. He caught her stare and said, "If you could be made to understand all that is at stake, you might help me. Let me try to explain. Please. My name is Quorl. I'm one of the rougarou."

"The what?" Hethy asked.

"The rougarou, the same as the others—the ones who attacked me. We were once the guardians of the *Sumanitu Taka Can*. The Great Tree. It is a sacred pathway. A link between this world and the world beyond. We are the stewards of the Great Tree—"

"But I don't understand what you are," Sally interrupted. "Are the rougarou wolves?"

Quorl narrowed his eyes impatiently. "We once appeared as men, although we are not truly human. We would take the form of wolves when we wished. But now—since the disappearance of the Great Tree—we remain as wolves, trapped this way. We cannot take our true forms. The other rougarou have forgotten what we once were.

"There was a time when the rougarou helped those who sought us. Men like your father and John Henry. Others were seeking knowledge that could only be found by climbing the Great Tree and following its many branches. Each branch, each limb, each twig leads to a place, either in this world or in others. There is nowhere the Great Tree's path cannot reach. We would guide these seekers on their quests. And a rare few ascended the Great Tree, passing on to the world beyond."

"What is that world?" Sally asked.

He shook his scarred snout slowly. "I do not know, child. I have never climbed all the way to the Tree's end. And those who have never return. It is a mystery."

He closed his eyes a moment to collect his thoughts before continuing. "Not long after your father and John Henry left us, the Great Tree drifted. This did not surprise us at first. The Tree is not like anything else of this world. To move its position was not so uncommon. What was surprising was that we began having difficulty finding it when it disappeared. And we had difficulty taking our true form. And as wolves, slowly—so slowly we hardly noticed—we began to forget who we were. To be away from the Great Tree weakens us.

"Each time we would eventually find the Great Tree and could again take our true forms. Our memories would return as well. The rougarou wondered at what was happening to us and to the Great Tree, but the world itself was changing so much. New people came into our land. Men built roads of iron and ran wires along tall sticks and drove strange machines. We knew that this world was in transition, but we did not realize how much it would affect us.

"Men no longer sought us. Your father and John Henry were the last to come for our help. It seemed we were forgotten. The Great Tree drifted more and more. Eventually we could not find it at all. One by one, the rougarou forgot who they were. They are becoming mere wolves, descending into common beasts. Now I am the last one who remembers. I have tried to help my pack, but they attack me and drive me away.

"I left for a time, searching for the Great Tree, because I knew that if I could find it again, the pack would return as rougarou. I traveled to the south, where the Great Tree once stood before it began to drift. I found a terrible Darkness has fallen, as if nature itself has been overturned."

"I seen that Darkness," Hethy said. "The town I'm from, Omphalosa, that's the center of all that Dark."

"Do you know why it's happened?" Quorl asked.

"My granny told me. She was killed by them people there 'cause they thought she witched up that Darkness. But Granny Sip, she said there was a terrible clockwork that brought on the Dark."

"A clockwork?" Quorl wondered.

"The Gog's Machine," Sally explained. "Have you ever heard of the Gog?"

"Yes, this creature serves the Magog. They must have taken shape once more in this age. Surely their evil is behind what has come about. And if I don't find the Great Tree, the repercussions will be terrible. Not just for me or for the pack, but for all living-kind. The roots of the Great Tree run deep. They touch and affect each living being. The Tree is a source of divine energy—of nourishment and vitality, of creation and destruction and rebirth. Mankind will be affected most by the Gog's plans, although even I can't see or even imagine all the ways."

Quorl looked urgently at Sally. "You carry the *Toninyan,* child. The Seeker's Stone can find the lost Great Tree, as it finds all things lost that one wishes found. But it is a gift for humankind, and only you can wield it. Have you uncovered how to use the *Toninyan?*"

Sally was dazzled by all Quorl had told her. "I don't know," Sally said. "The rabbit's foot turns to point the way to go. It's been leading me to the west, and I'm hoping that it's leading me to my father. But I don't know how to make it find your Tree. It's only ever pulled me toward my father. . . ."

But then Sally remembered: that was not true. The rabbit's foot had led her to Hethy because she had been lost—lost on the prairie with her pot of beans.

But did she *want* to help him? Shouldn't she continue searching for her father?

"We've hardly eaten in days," Sally said. "And we have no food left. We've had little sleep either. There's so much to consider, and I can barely think properly, Quorl."

"Yes," he said, getting stiffly to his feet. "You need to

eat. I do too. I will try to find us something. I will return soon."

The rougarou limped out onto the prairie. As soon as he disappeared, Hethy asked, "You think you could use that thing? You reckon you could find his Tree?"

"I've been thinking about it. I don't think Ray really knew how the lodestone worked. He told me how it led him to this pirate named Peter Hobnob and then to the Pirate Queen's silver dagger. But he never knew why. Now I see. They were both lost, Hethy. Ray must have wanted to find them, just like I wanted to find you."

"You ain't even known who I was."

"But I wanted to find food, and there you were. What about my father? If we help Quorl, how long will it take?"

"I know what you saying, Yote. And I know how terrible you want to find your daddy. But I reckon we've got to help this Quorl, as you're the one with that *Toninyan* and all."

"I guess you're right," Sally said soberly. "I think I know how to find his Tree. I found the answer the other day, when we were trying to find food. Remember? The rabbit's foot—or this *Toninyan* that's the lodestone—it couldn't help us because the food wasn't lost after all. We were. But I read the answer. My father wrote, *'place what is lost in your thoughts and follow.'* I suppose that's all I have to do."

"Then try, Yote. Ask the rabbit's foot—or whatever you do—to see if it'll hit on that Tree."

Sally cupped the rabbit's foot in her hands. It was pointing toward the northwest. She closed her eyes and began thinking of the Great Tree, unsure how to imagine it.

The rabbit's foot jerked. She opened her eyes to see it rotating ever so slowly around in her palm.

"It moved! I just seen it." Hethy gasped. "That ain't the same way, is it?"

"No," Sally said. "I think . . ." She looked up. "It's pointing north."

Hethy nodded. Sally put the rabbit's foot in her pocket and sat on the grass, her knees to her chest and her thumb anxiously in her teeth.

It was not long before Quorl returned. "I am still too weak to catch any game. I dug up these roots. Put them in the coals to cook. They'll nourish you." Then he sank down with exhaustion and closed his eyes.

Hethy stirred up the fire. The roots looked like small yams, yellowish and rock-hard. As they split and blackened, Sally examined Quorl's wounds. Some of them were bleeding again, and she cleaned them and put fresh compounds on him.

As she did this, she asked, "Are you sleeping, Quorl?"

"No," he said, and he opened his eyes.

"I can work the *Toninyan.*"

"You can find the Great Tree then?" he asked, sitting up.

"Hopefully."

"And you'll help me? You'll guide me to it?"

Sally tried not to let her reluctance show. "Yes, we'll help you. But, Quorl, you said the Great Tree leads to other worlds."

The hopelessness had left Quorl's eyes, and although he still had a mad glint, it was madness born of returning optimism. "Yes. It does."

"My father is in the Gloaming. Do you know this world?"

"Not by this name, but the paths of the Great Tree are as many as the blades of grass on this prairie."

"If we help find the Great Tree, can you guide me to Father using the Tree?"

"Yes! Yes, child. Who knows how far you would have to travel across this land to reach him. But crossing the Great Tree . . . I will lead you to him more quickly. I pledge this to you. What is your name? Oh, I seem to have forgotten all my courtesy. Please, tell me your names, girls."

Sally could not help but laugh—laugh with excitement at the prospect of crossing the Great Tree to reach her father, and laugh at the strange enthusiasm that animated the rougarou now. Even Hethy, who was poking the baking roots from the fire, smiled at the rougarou.

"My friend is Hethy Smith. I'm Sally Cobb."

Hethy chuckled. "I call her Yote."

"Why is that?" Quorl asked.

"'Cause I thought she was a coyote when I met her. See, Yote was out on the prairie, all alone. . . ." Hethy told Quorl about how she attacked Sally on that night, and as the girls ate, they began to tell Quorl about their lives—Hethy's sad tale of Omphalosa and Sally's pastoral life at Shuckstack. The rougarou listened intently. And although the roots weren't particularly tasty, they filled their stomachs, and the girls felt good after eating them.

Whether it was because he was energized by the anticipation of finding the Great Tree or because Hethy's compounds were helping him heal, Quorl was eager to begin their journey.

"Which way is the Great Tree? Have you asked the *Toninyan*?"

"To the north," Sally said, gathering her belongings to depart.

The two girls and the limping rougarou set out at midday. Quorl stubbornly ignored his injuries, but by late afternoon, Sally could see he was obviously tired. They camped for the night on the open plains.

"How far away is the Great Tree?" Quorl asked the following morning. They had been walking since sunrise, and the weather was warm and windy.

"I don't know how to read *that* from the rabbit's foot," Sally said. "Although, when it led me to Hethy, it began shaking and such just before I found her."

"Is it doing that now?"

Sally took the rabbit's foot from her pocket. "No."

The rabbit's foot pointed due north, and they continued for miles and miles. Quorl was healing much more quickly than the girls expected. Hethy continued to collect yarrow and wild indigo to make new compounds for his wounds each night, although she still convinced Sally to place them on the rougarou. Quorl managed to catch a few prairie dogs, but neither girl was particularly keen on eating them.

"They ain't much better than rats," Hethy scoffed. But Quorl knew the prairie plants and found more tubers and roots and wild greens to keep their stomachs sated.

Later in the afternoon, Sally looked up from her walking. "Look at those clouds," she said, pointing to the west.

"A storm." Quorl narrowed his eyes and sniffed at the breeze. "We'll have to stop soon. I'll make you a shelter."

They soon reached a creek, where Quorl began digging into the soft earth in the bank to make a shallow cave. As the storm front moved toward them, the sky darkened with an ominous green-black wall of clouds. Lightning flashed in the distance, and the thunder pealed long and low across the prairie.

While Quorl worked on the dugout, Sally and Hethy collected firewood and searched out the edible plants Quorl had shown them. Sally picked up the dry branches silently, her thoughts far away.

"Something bothering you, Yote?" Hethy asked after a time, as she dug up some turnip-like roots growing at the creek's edge.

Sally looked over at her. "I keep thinking of Father, Hethy."

"What's there to worry you? You traveling all this distance, with no way to get into that Gloaming. Now you can. Quorl's going to take you to him."

Sally hoisted the limbs in her arms. "I know, it's just I thought I understood the *Incunabula*. I thought I understood the Verse of the Lost. But what if I'm bringing danger to him? What if giving him back his hand brings him some harm?"

"Like that Mister Nel?"

"Yeah."

Hethy screwed up her nose. "But didn't you say Nel was grateful to you for doing it?"

"Yes," Sally replied.

"Then don't let it fret you none." Hethy toted the bundle of roots and corms and nuts in the skirt of her dress. "Come on, Yote, let's get on back and get a fire going and you'll feel better. You'll see."

The girls returned with the wood to find Quorl inspecting the dugout in the creek's bank. "This should protect you from the storm," he panted. "But if the creek rises too much, we'll have to leave. Let's hope the storm passes quickly."

A clap of thunder underscored his words, and the daylight dimmed ominously fast. Hethy quickly started to build the fire in the mouth of the dugout, while Sally prepared the supper to cook. The drops began—big as a man's hand and then smaller and faster, scattered with tiny, crunching balls of hail. The girls backed against the dirt wall, the fire warding away the wet. Quorl lay on the pebbled bank outside with the rain soaking him.

"Why don't you come in?" Sally called over the din. "We can try to make room."

Quorl shook his head. "Rain and cold make no more difference to me than warmth and sunshine. They are all just elements—none better or worse than the other."

Hethy raised her eyebrows at Sally. "That's good for us he feels that way."

Hethy poked at the fire with a stick, and then adjusted the pot cooking their stew of wild plants so that it sat over hotter coals. Sally opened the *Incunabula* to the Verse of the Lost and again read it.

"You still worrying on that, Yote?" Hethy asked.

"I just can't believe I didn't realize it was a warning."

"What was?"

Sally ran her finger beneath the final lines as she read aloud, " 'But even restoration might in time extract a cost, as the vessel can be made a beacon for the lost.' See, Hethy?"

"You know I don't understand that crazy book."

Sally leaned back against the dirt wall. "I thought the cost was the lodestone's powers, not some cost for Nel."

Hethy settled beside her and looked over at the book in her lap. "Hum, maybe it ain't as bad as you think. What's that last part there mean about the vessel and the beacon?"

"The rabbit's foot's the vessel. And it's a beacon because it guided Ray."

"What's a beacon?" Hethy asked.

"Like a lighthouse or something. Something to help people find their way in the dark."

Hethy looked at her. "Like the Darkness in Omphalosa?"

"No, like when Ray was trying to find our f—" Sally stopped.

"What is it, Yote?"

Sally was thinking. What if it *was* like the Darkness?

"The vessel can be a beacon for the lost," Sally murmured. "When Mother Salagi covered the rabbit's foot with that powder, she and those seers saw that a spike needed to be made."

"To stop that awful clockwork?"

"Yeah," Sally said. "They said the spike would be 'a light to pierce the Dark.'"

"Like that lighthouse you talking about."

"Yeah," Sally uttered, half-dazed.

The girls were quiet a moment. Hethy finally turned to Sally. "Is that poem in your book saying the vessel is the rabbit's foot and it's got to be made into a spike?"

"But Father," Sally said. "If I save him, if I help him get back his Rambler powers, then the rabbit's foot will be gone."

"Yote?"

Sally slowly brought her gaze around to Hethy. The whites of her friend's eyes seemed to glow from her ashen face.

"Yote, you can't give back your daddy his powers, can you?"

Panic swelled in Sally. Her hands trembled against the pages of the *Incunabula*. "I have to, Hethy! I have to save Father!"

Lightning struck the prairie nearby, shaking some dirt loose from the back of the dugout. Quorl looked up at them curiously. Hethy and Sally moved closer together, Hethy clutching Sally's shaking hands and shushing her gently. "We'll figure it out, Yote. Don't you worry. Maybe you ain't got it right."

She crawled over to lift the pot from the coals. Taking turns sharing the spoon, they ate the stew while the storm rumbled past.

Sally didn't know if she had been wrong to help Nel. She didn't know if Ray would ever return again. She didn't know if the Verse of the Lost meant that the rabbit's foot had to be made into the spike.

But she did know with certainty one thing. She had to have her father back. One way or another she had to save him.

Fortunately the storm was fast-moving and brought little rain over the night. The creek rose, but not enough to endanger their camp. They woke the following morning to clear skies and a stout wind.

As they continued north, the wind lashed the prairie in sudden gusts, blowing the girls' dresses and hair in tangles. Sally could not stop thinking about her father. Had Mother Salagi meant for Ray to bring their father the rabbit's foot so he could make the spike? What was she going to do?

They stopped midday by a pond and refilled their flasks. Quorl trotted away from the girls, going up onto a rise and surveying the plains. Hethy sat on the ground, her head cupped in her hand.

"You okay?" Sally asked.

"Feel a little dizzy is all."

When Quorl returned, he looked anxious. His ears were flattened and his tail drooped. As he approached the girls, he said, "Get on my back. I'll carry you."

"But your leg . . . ," Sally began.

"My strength is returning. We need to move faster and we can only do so if I carry you."

Sally exchanged a worried glance with Hethy. "Is something wrong?"

He lowered to allow them to get on. "Do as I ask."

Sally climbed onto Quorl's back, and Hethy got on behind her. Sally dug her fingers into his silver-blue fur and clutched the loose skin about his neck.

"Do you have a good grip?" he asked.

"I reckon I do, if Sally does," Hethy said, encircling her arms around Sally's waist.

"Hold on tightly," Quorl said, and he began to trot, eventually breaking into a faster pace on the flat expanses.

Sally was amazed at how easy it was to keep her balance. Quorl moved fluidly, despite his healing leg. Sally kept her knees firm against the rougarou's ribs. Hethy seemed to get the worst of the ride. Sitting closer to Quorl's hips, she bucked up and down, and complained endlessly in Sally's ear. But squeezing herself to Sally's back, she kept on throughout the afternoon and into the night.

The girls fell asleep at some point, and Quorl slowed to a loping gait. Sally opened her eyes occasionally, and each time the moon was in a new position against the vast field of stars.

Quorl stopped and was sniffing at the ground when Sally woke at last.

"I've got to stretch," she said, nudging Hethy, who was slumped between her shoulder blades.

The girls dismounted, stiff and sore. Quorl followed some scent along the grass. As Sally watched his circling, Hethy began coughing.

"You all right, Hethy?" Sally asked.

Hethy crouched on the ground, covering her mouth with a fist as the coughs subsided. "I'm tired, Yote. I don't feel good." She laid her head to her elbow on the earth and closed her eyes again.

"Don't sleep, child," Quorl said, returning. "We must keep going."

"But we're exhausted," Sally said. "Let us just sleep a few minutes."

"No! Get up," Quorl snapped.

"Why?" Hethy mumbled, her eyes half-sealed.

As if in answer, a long howl—a single reverberating note—rose in the distance.

Quorl swung his head around, ears and tail lowered. He turned back to the girls and through his bared teeth said, "The pack has been following us. I did not want to frighten you, but there is no hiding it any longer. They have my scent and they'll come for me. Get on and quickly!"

As the girls mounted Quorl, another howl resounded. Quorl dashed across the night prairie.

Jarred, Sally clutched tight to the rougarou's neck as she felt the tiny claws of the rabbit's foot tapping against her palm, pointing to the north. "Turn slightly to the right," Sally called. Quorl adjusted his path each time Sally checked the foot. Quorl covered a great distance, but they could still hear the calls from the pursuing rougarou.

"I see them," Hethy said. Sally looked over her shoulder. Large forms, shadowed against the moonlit plains, raced toward them.

"Faster!" Sally cried, but she could feel Quorl struggling. He might have been immune to the pain, but his leg was weakening. Fresh blood speckled the fur of his tail.

Ahead, the land seemed to disappear, as if the prairie—which had rolled on endlessly—ended abruptly not a hundred yards before them. It looked as if they were reaching the end of the world. But then Sally saw what seemed to be a cliff, and the edge was rapidly approaching.

"Quorl!" she screamed.

But Quorl did not slow. He leaped over the edge, and Sally was relieved to find that it wasn't a cliff after all. The other side was not so steep, and Quorl's paws caught on the sloping, soft earth. Keeping his balance, Quorl slid on his front paws as he descended until he reached the ground below.

Strange landforms rose around them—sharply eroded buttes, their tops flat and gleaming with grass, the edges washing down into talons of dirt. Quorl had to navigate around them and, when trapped against their walls, he scrambled up the sides, slipping in the loose earth.

The golden foot was tugging stronger now, flinching against her fingers the way it had when she found Hethy.

"Keep going, Quorl!" Sally shouted. "We're nearly there."

But this was strange to Sally. The foot seemed to tell her that the Great Tree was near, but she saw nothing around but the ghostly badlands. Where was it? Wouldn't it be visible by now?

A snarl startled Sally. A rougarou ran toward them, not more than fifty yards behind. She turned to peer back, and there they were: a dozen wolves in all. Their eyes flashed ferociously in the moonlight, and their teeth gleamed.

Even in the half-dark, Sally could see their coats were not like the gray-brown of ordinary wolves she had seen in pictures. Some were all black. Others moon-white. Still more seemed a tawny gold or bright copper-red. None had a silver-blue coat like Quorl, but like him, they were large—great monsters leaping and racing closer and closer.

The buttes surrounded Quorl, driving him into a dry canyon. The pursuing pack split into three: two groups going right and left up the sides onto the flat rim of the canyon and the third—led by a black-furred rougarou—following behind Quorl.

The rabbit's foot trembled fiercely.

"It's here, Quorl!" Sally cried. "It has to be here! Oh, where is the Tree?"

The canyon ended. And Quorl nearly tumbled as he stopped.

They were trapped.

The eight rougarou above spread out along the top of the canyon, peering down savagely and snarling.

Quorl shook his back. "Off! Get behind me."

The girls leaped from Quorl and huddled together against a cove in the canyon wall. Quorl turned, lifting his nose straight up. "It is here, my rougarou!" he cried. "The Great Tree is found!" He howled a powerful, ear-piercing sound.

The black rougarou came a step forward: ears flat, back arched, fur bristling.

"Stay back, Renamex!" Quorl growled. "You may have me, but you must let these humans go."

The black rougarou snarled.

"Renamex," Quorl said. "You are my *nata*, you are mother to our pack, and I submit to you. But listen! We are rougarou. We are not wolves. Can you still understand any of what I'm saying? Don't you remember who we are?"

Renamex pulled a paw back, her ears flickering.

Sally clutched Hethy, both girls shaking. She looked up at the eyes of the rougarou. They were not like Quorl's. They did not have the same bright intelligence that burned in his blue eyes. Their eyes were those of wolves—dark and merciless.

"The Great Tree is here, my pack!" Quorl roared. "Don't you see it?"

The moon was behind the canyon's rim, and its light shone in Renamex's eyes. The light grew brighter. Long shadows deepened along the canyon. Renamex's eyes began to transform. Her ears rose and she lifted her snout, sniffing.

Hethy was crouched on her knees, pulling at Sally's skirt,

but Sally stood. The pack whined and rolled their faces against the earth.

Quorl howled again, a singular, heart-wrenching note.

Renamex's eyes widened. The light above grew brighter, brighter, until it was as if a thousand suns burned. The *nata*'s eyes lightened into a pair of lapis gems, blue and deep against the blinding white sheen.

Sally stepped out from the cove. She turned to look behind her. There was a flash and she covered her face with her hands. When it passed, she pulled away her hands to see.

Over the rim of the canyon, somewhere beyond, Sally saw it. Glowing softly as if with moonlight, the Great Tree was towering, too tall even for the enormity of the sky. Rising, its roots alone were larger than a mountain range. Rising, narrowing to a ghostly white trunk. Rising, it filled the night. And miles above, its branches spread, distant and faint, mingling into the constellations and cosmos.

The rougarou were all now looking upward. Sally watched as, one by one, their eyes became blue.

"Thank you, Little Coyote," Quorl panted behind her. "You led me to the Great Tree. It is found, at last."

Sally could not speak. Hethy emerged from the shadows to take Sally's hand. She gasped as she stared up.

The black rougarou, Renamex, moved forward to join Quorl. Sally and Hethy hid behind Quorl, but Renamex did not look at them. She was beautiful, her fur dark and silky as a sable. She lowered her nose, nuzzling it against Quorl's throat.

"You . . . have done it, Quorl," Renamex said, hesitating as she found her voice. "You have returned the Great Tree, and you have returned us."

One by one, the rougarou howled. Lifting their faces to the Great Tree glowing in the night, they howled in a long chorus.

THE STEAMCOACH MOVED ACROSS THE DARK PRAIRIE
like a slow comet, its cacophonous engine belching smoke
and its headlamp piercing the dark with a lance of light. It
was easy to follow. Ray, Marisol, and Redfeather kept the
horses a safe distance, but the Darkness gave them little reason to worry that the Bowlers would know they were being
followed.

After what they could only guess was several days' travel,
the sun rose again. The light was brief, but it grew longer
each day. The undulating hills of the prairie kept the horses
hidden from view during the daylight.

B'hoy glided above. Ray finally understood how to see
through the crow's eyes and hear through his ears. At first
he could only get flashes of the world from the crow's vantage. It made Ray dizzy, and he would lose his concentration

easily. But he kept trying until he was able to focus. He could see what B'hoy saw and so could observe the Bowlers' progress at a distance.

The Bowlers camped each night, the fourteen men falling into duties of building a fire, distributing supper, hobbling the horses, setting up the canvas tents, and posting watch. Overseeing it all was the stout Bowler named Muggeridge.

When the steamcoach stopped each night, Ray would set up a Five Spot at their camp, close enough to see when the Bowlers prepared to leave, but not so close as to risk discovery. They were never near enough to overhear the Bowlers, but B'hoy came in handy for that.

Ray sent the crow out to spy at the edge of the Bowlers' firelight.

"What are they saying?" Marisol asked, as she laid out the dwindling store of food Little Grass had sent with them.

Ray opened his eyes. "Not much. That Pike guy is just talking about some showgirl back in Cincinnati he's in love with." Then he added with a grin, "But I can't keep my concentration when you talk to me."

"Sorry, sorry," Marisol said with mock kowtowing. "Don't disturb the great Rambler at work. Wouldn't want you to miss a word of that riveting yarn."

Although he never mentioned it, Ray had worried whether they would become sick after leaving the Darkness. And when they finally left the Darkness behind and none of them showed any signs of illness, he realized Redfeather and Marisol had been silently worrying as well. A buoyancy came over their spirits, as if they were three prisoners newly released from their dungeons. The warm weather returned. They shed their coats. Javidos crawled out from Marisol's collar to sun himself across her shoulders. Even Redfeather grew more lighthearted.

But the joy of having left the Darkness did not diminish the urgency to reach their goal. Quite the opposite: they were energized more than ever to discover what the steamcoach carried in the windowless car at the back and what the Bowlers were pursuing across the plains.

The green grass of the prairie rippled in the wind. Beyond a series of hills, a banner of black smoke rose, signaling the steamcoach's location. Riding behind Marisol on Unole, Ray watched the Bowlers through B'hoy's eyes as the steamcoach stopped.

Muggeridge got down from the driving bench and walked back to the car, unlocking the door. Desperate to see what was hidden in that heavily guarded car, Ray told B'hoy to swoop low. But the crow could not descend before Muggeridge entered and closed the door. The other Bowlers, rifles in their hands, waited placidly at their positions: two atop the car, others peering out the six windows of the steamcoach, and the last waiting on the driving bench at the front. The four on horseback sat with rifles across their knees. After a few minutes, Muggeridge came back out and spoke to Pike, the other man on the driving bench.

Ray wanted to listen, but B'hoy refused, not willing to get close again to the Bowlers and their guns. Muggeridge pointed to the north, seeming to discuss with Pike the direction the steamcoach would travel.

"Get down there!" Ray argued with B'hoy. "What are they saying?"

Irritated, the crow took a steep dive, and Ray almost lost his balance. Clutching Marisol's arm, he squared himself again in the saddle behind her.

"You all right?" Redfeather asked, wheeling Atsila around.

"Stupid cowardly crow," Ray grumbled as they rode on.

The steamcoach stopped late in the day. Ray found a lake nearby to make camp. The Bowlers were not visible, but the prairie wind carried their muffled voices. As Ray set up the Five Spot, Marisol said, "We're running low on food."

Redfeather took the bow and arrow from Atsila's saddle. "It's nearly dark. Game will be active now."

"Keep out of sight of the Bowlers," Marisol said.

"Oh, thanks for that useful tip." Redfeather smirked. "I almost forgot there were fourteen men with guns around."

Marisol laughed. "Be careful. That's all I meant."

He nodded and set off.

Ray went down to the lake to fill the waterskins. He found white-flowered arrowhead growing along the banks and dug some up to cook with the corms. Redfeather returned much quicker than either Ray or Marisol expected, a small pronghorn buck over his shoulder. Redfeather lit a fire while Ray dressed the deer, and after dark, they ate a delicious meal.

"You're pretty good with that bow," Marisol said as she cut another piece from the deer.

"Just takes practice," Redfeather said. "You want to learn?"

Marisol cocked an eyebrow. "Are you offering to show me?"

Redfeather shrugged. "Might come in handy."

As Redfeather got up to set up the pronghorn's hide for a target in the firelight, Marisol picked up Redfeather's bow and took an arrow from his quiver.

"I'm sending B'hoy to spy," Ray said. "I'll be down by the lake so I can concentrate."

Looking back as Redfeather helped Marisol notch an arrow, Ray walked over to the edge of the Five Spot. He sat down in the grass and closed his eyes.

B'hoy was catching a grasshopper. He gulped it down and then took flight. Soaring up into the night, he did not have to go far before he saw the Bowlers' campfire by the silent steamcoach. B'hoy moved lower, circling the camp before alighting on the steamcoach's smokestack.

Only ten of the men sat around the fire, talking and smoking and eating packaged dinners from tin cans. Three others were armed and on watch duty. One was missing: Muggeridge. Through B'hoy's spying, Ray had noticed that Muggeridge often went into the car after the Bowlers set up their camp.

As B'hoy turned around on the smokestack, Ray could see Muggeridge returning from the car and picking up his canned dinner. Several conversations were going at once, and he let his attention wander from group to group:

"... we'll need to find a pond tomorrow or by the latest the following day, so we can refill the water tank ..."

"... how much longer until we need to take on more coal? There positively has to be a depot or some town if we just keep ..."

"... they say the board governing the Columbian Expo denied Buffalo Bill's application for his Wild West show. How do you like that? So he's setting up just outside the Expo grounds by the Midway ..."

"... that's why he's using Stacker Lee ..."

Ray paused on this group of men. Muggeridge was talking to Pike and two other men, named De Courcy and Murphy.

De Courcy licked his spoon. "So who is this Stacker already? I heard his name before. Is he a Chicago Pinkerton?"

"He's no Pinkerton at all," Pike answered. "He's not even a living man."

"What's that mean?" Murphy asked.

Pike and Muggeridge exchanged a look, and Muggeridge nodded for Pike to go ahead and answer. Some of the other men turned their heads to listen.

"Sure, Stacker Lee was once a regular man, as regular as any St. Louis two-bit thug. He was absolutely a known killer. Sometimes for money, sometimes just for sport. Killed this Lyons kid over some hat. So after that, Stacker up and disappears. Some said he was dead. You know something? I know plenty of marshals that wished he was. And then Muggeridge hears he's working for the boss."

"The boss? Our boss? Mister Horne?" another Bowler asked.

"Not Horne," Muggeridge said, cocking his eyebrows. "*The* Boss."

The men nodded, eyeing one another and leaning forward as Pike continued. "What I heard, someone stabbed Stacker Lee in the chest with a bowie knife. Split his sternum. Burst his heart. Right! So the Boss, he somehow he gets ahold of Stacker as he's dying. He takes out Stacker's heart and replaces it with a mechanical heart. Some clockwork device."

"Yeah, like that . . . that . . ." De Courcy cocked a thumb toward the steamcoach.

"Right," Pike said. "One of them. So Stacker, he's walking, talking, breathing, killing, but he's not alive. Believe me, any shred of human emotion that once tugged at his malevolent heart, well, it's gone now. If he was remorseless before, he's ruthless now. If he was a stone-cold killer before, he's a glacier now. Yeah, he's a catastrophic blizzard."

"So he's working for the Boss?" Murphy asked.

"That's what I heard," Pike said with a shrug. "He's off looking for the Nine Pound Hammer. You know, John Henry's hammer."

Ray nearly lost his link of concentration with B'hoy. He struggled to refocus his thoughts to what the crow was seeing and hearing.

". . . that Negro boy who destroyed *The Pitch Dark Train,* yeah?"

"That's the one," Muggeridge said.

"What's the Boss want the hammer for anyway?"

"I think just to display at the Expo. Probably thinks it'll be a hit with the crowds, people are interested in John Henry and all. Guess the authentic Nine Pound Hammer will bring people to his exhibit . . ."

". . . keep seeing that crow."

Ray's attention—and B'hoy's—was suddenly drawn to two of the men on guard duty at the back of the car.

The men were looking at B'hoy. "Crows are beggars," the other man said. "He's only waiting for our scraps."

The other man scraped out the last of his meal from his tin can. "I hate beggars and bums of any kind." He heaved the can at the crow. B'hoy took flight as the can scattered out in the grass.

Ray raced into the campsite, startling Marisol, who swung around with her bow. Redfeather grabbed the arrow and pushed the bow down.

"What's the matter, Ray?" he asked. "You nearly got shot."

"The . . . the Bowlers," Ray panted. "They said there's this man with a clockwork heart and he's looking for the Nine Pound Hammer. . . ."

"Slow down," Redfeather said. "Start from the beginning."

Ray tried to sit, but as soon as he did, he was on his feet again, pacing around the fire and telling them what he had heard.

"Don't worry. He'll never find it," Redfeather said, when

Ray was finished. "The Nine Pound Hammer's head is at the bottom of the Mississippi River. There's no way he could get it."

"But who is this mysterious 'Boss' they were talking about?" Marisol asked.

"It's Grevol. It has to be," Ray said.

"Grevol!" Redfeather scoffed. "The Gog? He's scattered in a million pieces at the bottom of the Mississippi too. Didn't you see what that explosion did to *The Pitch Dark Train*?"

"But the Gog was no normal man," Ray argued. "The bottletrees couldn't stop him. He could walk through fire—"

"So can I. So could you when you had my copper. But if we'd been on *The Pitch Dark Train*, we'd never have survived the explosion. Conker didn't."

"Whoever he is," Marisol said, "someone's carrying on the Gog's work. And about this Stacker, I think Redfeather's right." Redfeather raised his eyebrows with surprise, but Marisol continued, "There's no way that anyone—even someone with a clockwork heart—could find the Nine Pound Hammer."

Redfeather nodded. "We can't stop this Stacker Lee. Besides, we're out here now. We've got to find out what that steamcoach is after."

Redfeather salted the rest of the venison, which, along with the arrowhead tubers, would last for several more days. They continued following the steamcoach, keeping the horses out of sight.

B'hoy was more wary now. Ray had to coax and flatter him into spying. At night, the crow was willing to listen in less conspicuous spots near their camp, but by day, he would do little more than circle high overhead for Ray to watch from above.

At one point, they came upon a spot by a creek where the earth was violently upturned. Ray got off Unole to examine the ground.

Redfeather watched curiously from Atsila. "What happened here?"

"There was a fight," Ray said, kneeling to look closer. "Some sort of animals. Wolves? Coyotes, maybe, but the grass is really torn apart. No, here's a good print. These tracks are some sort of canine, but they're huge. Bigger than any dog I've ever seen. I don't think wolves even get this big. Look, there's other tracks, too. Shoes. They're small. Probably just kids. Two sets. It looks like the kids camped here and left in that direction. Huh?"

"What?" Marisol asked.

"Strange. It looks like the kids' tracks follow one of the wolves."

"Or the wolf followed the kids," Marisol said.

Ray nodded and took Marisol's hand to get back on Unole. They started to ride off, when Redfeather pointed to the ribbon of black coming from the steamcoach beyond the hills.

"Look," he said. "They're turning north."

The initial relief they had felt after leaving the Darkness had been replaced by determination to discover what the steamcoach was after. But their days of travel had yielded no answers.

As the three sat around the campfire, Redfeather worked on fixing some of the feathers that had come loose from the arrows Marisol had been using for practice. "We can't keep hoping we'll sneak a glance sometime," he said. "We need to find a way."

"How do you propose we do that?" Ray said, clenching his fists. "Over a dozen armed Bowlers guarding it day and night. B'hoy's too scared to go close enough to see anything."

Marisol said, "But every night, when the Bowlers set up their camp, Muggeridge goes into the car, right? If we could only catch him when he does—the door is left cracked."

"That's suicidal," Redfeather said. "Even in the dark, we could never get close enough to look inside the doorway. We'd be spotted in a second."

Marisol leaned forward, planting her hands firmly on the ground. "But a snake wouldn't."

Redfeather opened his mouth, but said nothing.

Ray asked quietly, "You'd be willing to risk Javidos?"

With the firelight dancing off her lovely face, Marisol's eyes betrayed her terror for a moment, but then she tightened her mouth and nodded. "He'll be all right."

Redfeather said, "It's not like B'hoy who can fly over there. We'll have to leave the Five Spot to bring Javidos close; otherwise it will take him forever to reach their camp."

"We shouldn't all go," Marisol said. "I'll do it."

"No, we're coming with you," Redfeather insisted. "Just in case."

"Then let's do it."

"Now?" Ray asked.

"Now," Marisol replied, her jaw set.

Lying on their stomachs, they peered down at the Bowlers' camp. Away from the Five Spot's protection, they had to be particularly careful. Redfeather had his bow and arrow, along with his tomahawk.

The steamcoach was shadowed against their campfire. They could hear the voices of the men as they ate their meal on the far side. The horses grazed several yards outside the firelight.

Ray looked around for who was on guard duty. Murphy and another man were sitting outside the firelight, smoking cigars in the dark. Sokal, the man who had seen B'hoy, was sitting on the bench atop the car. A Winchester rifle lay across his knees.

Ray whispered, "Muggeridge is in there. Look. The door's cracked."

"Perfect," Redfeather said.

"Okay, here he goes," Marisol said. After giving him a kiss on the top of his head, she laid Javidos down in the grass. The copperhead began slithering, his thick body moving over the earth. Marisol closed her eyes.

Ray and Redfeather watched Javidos move closer and closer. From their angle, the copperhead's body caught the firelight and they could follow his progress. After a few minutes, Javidos was nearly to the car. Sokal climbed down from the car and stretched his back. His boots were not more than a few feet from Javidos.

Redfeather notched an arrow in his bow. "No," Ray whispered quietly in his ear so Marisol couldn't hear him. "Don't be hasty! If something happens to Javidos, we can't risk being discovered."

"I know," Redfeather whispered. "Just in case."

Ray looked over at Marisol. Her eyes were still closed, her face still and passive as she concentrated on seeing what Javidos saw. The copperhead moved wide around Sokal, going underneath the car to keep away from his feet. Sokal had not noticed him.

Javidos lifted his head onto the step off the back of the car. He was almost there. The door was cracked, an outline of light framing the doorway. Just as Javidos put his nose to the doorway, the light went off inside and the door opened.

Javidos dropped beneath the car as Muggeridge stepped down and turned back to lock the door. Pike came around the steamcoach to meet Muggeridge. The two talked. Sokal walked over toward the two men. Marisol gasped, and Ray looked over to see her struggling to hold her concentration.

Sokal cocked the Winchester and said something that startled Muggeridge and Pike. Ray realized what Sokal was doing. The agent had spotted Javidos.

"No!" Ray gasped.

Sokal aimed the rifle down, angling it into the shadows under the car. The barrel flashed, and if Ray had not rolled over to put his hand over Marisol's mouth, her scream would surely have given them away. B'hoy croaked and took flight.

"Wait." Redfeather waved his hand. "He missed. Javidos might be okay."

Ray took his hand from Marisol's mouth, and the three looked toward the steamcoach. There was a bit of commotion. Sokal was holding the gun toward the ground, swinging it this way and that in the dark. Muggeridge and Pike had backed away from the car but suddenly ducked and swung their arms around to protect their faces.

"B'hoy!" Ray said.

Shouting erupted, and several of the other Bowlers came around the side of the steamcoach to see what was going on. Sokal shot his rifle repeatedly into the night sky, but B'hoy had gotten away, Javidos dangling in his talons.

"Quick!" Redfeather grabbed Marisol's hand. "We'd better get back to the Five Spot."

They ran, and when they returned to their fire, B'hoy was already waiting. Javidos wriggled on the ground next to him.

"Oh, Javy! *Te pido perdón*," Marisol exclaimed, picking the copperhead up to caress and dote on him. B'hoy gave her a loud squawk and she added, "Yes, thank you, B'hoy! That was very brave of you."

B'hoy hopped around proudly and then landed on Ray's fist. "Absolutely you deserve a treat."

Redfeather brought him some of the pronghorn and held it out. "How's that? Hey! I think he likes it."

"Of course he does." Ray smirked. "He'll eat anything."

Marisol put her hand abruptly to her throat with a gasp.

"Muggeridge! I heard him. Before that man tried to shoot Javidos, he was talking to that other Bowler."

"What did he say?" Ray asked.

"They were talking about whatever is in that car; it's following a sort of scent or something. They said they were getting close. Not more than a day or two more. And then Muggeridge said what they're tracking."

"What?"

"A golden rabbit's foot. Whatever's in that car is leading them to your father's foot. They said, 'At last we'll get the boy.' They meant you, Ray. They think they're pursuing *you*."

"But . . . but that's impossible," Ray said, fear and puzzlement pounding in his head. "That can't be! How can they be after the rabbit's foot? The rabbit's foot is back at Shuckstack . . . with Sally. . . ."

Ray went cold.

The Bowlers were pursuing Sally.

SALLY AND HETHY FEASTED. THE ROUGAROU FOUND A stand of trees nearby and carried back limbs in their mouths for a fire. Others hunted fat prairie birds for the girls. The girls were treated like queens, but their treatment hardly compared to the reception showering Quorl.

Each rougarou came in turn to him, nipping at his chin or rolling and prostrating himself or herself before the silver wolf. Quorl's eyes blazed with pride, but he masked his pleasure with a demure gaze at Renamex. "My *nata*. Tell them to stop."

"You have saved us, Quorl. Let the pack honor you as you deserve."

"But we are not wolves," Quorl growled. "They should not act as such. . . ."

Sally laughed and relished the proceedings. Around her the sun was rising, washing the strange eroded land formations in warm light. She looked up at the Great Tree rising from beyond the canyon's rim, ghostly and swirled with the pink and purple colors of dawn.

Sally turned to a golden-furred rougarou who had brought them birds. "Won't others—people nearby—see the Tree? I mean, it's so huge. I think they could see it back at Shuckstack."

"No, Coyote," the rougarou said. "Only those who have been blessed by the rougarou can see the Great Tree. Do not worry. Have you eaten enough? What else would you like?"

"Oh, I'm so full," Sally said. "How about you, Hethy?"

As she turned, she found her friend already asleep, curled in the grass with her blanket under her cheek. Her skin looked grayer than usual, more faded. Sally too was exhausted from the long journey and the terrifying pursuit and the excitement of the Great Tree's return. "No. I think I'll sleep now. What is your name?"

"Coer," the rougarou replied. "The *nata* has charged me with taking care of you two. If you need anything—when you wake—I will be here."

"Thank you, Coer." Sally lay down beside Hethy and fell asleep almost at once.

When the girls woke, the sun was high. The Great Tree looked faint, like the moon during the day. As he had promised, Coer was lying nearby, ears alert and head high.

He got to his feet when he saw Sally and Hethy stir. Sally looked around and realized that there was only one other rougarou, besides Coer, still there.

"Where is Quorl?"

"There is urgent business," Coer said. "He is speaking with the pack. They have gone to the roots of the Great Tree. They are not far away. We will take you there now."

As they climbed up from the canyon, Coer introduced the other rougarou as Oultren. Her fur, like Coer's, was golden, flecked on the tips with black, but Oultren had a large whitish patch across her breast.

"What did you mean by 'urgent business'?" Sally asked.

"We are still wolves," Coer explained. "We have been this way so long we have nearly forgotten our true forms. But Quorl reminded us that, since the Great Tree has been found, our true form should have returned."

If he was concerned, Sally could not read it from his canine expression. "You mean you should be men again?"

"And women," Oultren added. "But not human, like you. Just as we are not wolves, although we may look like it. We are rougarou—neither human nor animal."

Hethy exchanged a puzzled expression with Sally. But Sally did not question them further, as they were reaching the Great Tree.

Up close, the roots rose from the prairie like an enormous rock face. The sides were gray-brown and its surface was as substantial as if it were an actual tree or a mountain. The bark of the Great Tree was like the bark of any oak or maple, but magnified, making Sally feel she was nothing more than a tiny insect. Looking closer, she could see that the grooves in the bark made enormous shelves and ridges and could easily be ascended, much as one would climb a set of wide, irregular stairs. There were any number of ways to climb the Great Tree, and as Sally let her eyes follow the rising trunk, she saw the Tree become transparent and misty, mingling with the blue sky and clouds beyond.

The rest of the pack was circled together in the shadow of the enormous roots, talking formally. They sat with the three black wolves together, then the three white, the three red, and finally the other gold besides Coer and Oultren. Quorl, with his strange blue-silver coat, sat in the center. It was as if they were following some particular etiquette or aesthetic design. The reason was beyond Sally's understanding, and she could only wonder at its purpose.

When Renamex saw the girls, she got up. "Come and join us, little ones. We have questions for you."

Sally and Hethy entered the circle of the pack. The rougarou were all grand and enormous, like the statues of lions guarding a palace gate. Hethy took Sally's hand to follow her to where Renamex was gesturing with her nose. "Go on, Yote," Hethy whispered. "You first."

"Here. Sit by me," the black rougarou said. "We are grateful to you for helping Quorl. We feel shamed by what we have done to him, but we were not ourselves. The loss of the Great Tree afflicted us. And still we have not yet found our true forms as rougarou. We have much still to discuss and consider, but for now we want to know more about you. Quorl says you carry the *Toninyan,* but it is buried in a rabbit's paw of gold. May I see it?"

Sally took the foot from her dress pocket. Renamex sniffed at the golden foot, turning her head back and forth to inspect it. Another rougarou joined her. He was surely the largest of the pack, nearly all white but with a ridge of ebony running from his nose along his spine to his tail.

"This is Mangoron," Renamex said. "He is more familiar with the magic of your people."

Mangoron gazed on the rabbit's foot for a long time before saying, "This object is very powerful. How did you come to possess it?"

Sally told about how her brother had first gotten the lodestone from their father, and how it had become the rabbit's foot. She admitted that she had broken her promise to her brother by taking the foot from Shuckstack, but as she went on to tell the listening rougarou about how her father came to be lost in the Gloaming, she explained, "His powers were trapped in the hand when it was severed. That's why I want to find him. I know how to return his Rambler powers to him."

Renamex looked once more at Mangoron before saying, "This object must be protected. There are men who would want to possess it. Whatever force drove the Great Tree from us is still at work. You are not safe traveling with it unguarded across the prairie. No, do not be afraid, Coyote. I see that you are worried that we might take it from you. We would not do that. You and you alone must hold on to the foot and keep it secret from others."

"That's what I want to ask you," Sally said. "I don't want to continue across the prairie. I want to search for my father by crossing the Great Tree. Will you let me? I know that it's difficult to find your way. Quorl told me all about it. But the rabbit's foot—my father's hand—it can show me the way. I'm sure it will."

Renamex looked around at the other rougarou. Glances and expressions too difficult for Sally to understand were exchanged between the wolves.

"It has never been done by a child," Renamex finally answered. "Even if you knew the way, the journey would be difficult. I am not certain it would be easier this way than if you continued over the land on foot."

"I would go with her," Quorl said.

The pack shifted. A rougarou whom Sally had not met said, "You are injured, Quorl. The way is too steep. It would require all your strength."

"I am bound to this girl now," Quorl said. "If any of us were to guide her, it should be me. But I understand that maybe another would make a better guide. . . ."

Sally felt a flush of excitement and pride. She had saved Quorl and helped him find the Great Tree. Now he would help her find her father.

"Quorl, I can wait while you heal. If you are really willing, I can wait a little longer."

Quorl nodded. "A few days, Little Coyote. Just give me a few days."

* * *

That night, after the girls ate, Sally and Hethy were finally alone. Half of the rougarou went out to patrol the prairie. Others slept at the roots of the Great Tree. Coer and Quorl spoke together several yards from the blazing fire.

"You sure are quiet, Hethy. Are you still afraid of them?" Sally asked.

"I ain't afraid of them. They're kind and I feel safe with them watching over us. What I'm worrying on is you."

Sally smiled halfheartedly. "What? Why are you worried about me?"

"You ain't telling them the truth is what. About that foot."

"I told them the truth," Sally said, lowering her voice. "What did I lie about?"

"It weren't what you said but what you ain't said. Don't you remember what we talked about? About that spike?"

Sally's face darkened and she grabbed Hethy's arm. "You be quiet, Hethy Smith! You don't know what that foot's for. My father will destroy the Machine, but only if I save him. If you speak a word of this to Renamex and the others, they might not let me find my father. They might not let me go after him."

"Granny Sip died 'cause of what that Machine done to those people in Omphalosa," Hethy said. "I want to know that that clockwork is going to end."

Hethy twisted to pull her arm from Sally's clutches, but Sally squeezed harder, saying, "Don't you understand? Father will know how to destroy the Machine. And I'm going to find him with or without you. You promised to be my friend. I thought you were going to help me and we'd rescue my father and then we could all live together at Shuckstack."

Hethy swung her arm and broke Sally's grip. Hethy's chest heaved as she backed from Sally, her dark eyes wide.

Sally trembled as she asked, "What if it was Granny Sip? What if there was a way you could bring her back? I have that chance, Hethy! Don't you see? I thought my father was dead. But he's not! I can bring him back."

Hethy looked frightened. Either from fear that she might be abandoned by Sally or because of Sally's vicious expression and the way she had been clutching her arm, Hethy burst into tears.

Sally reached a hand to the sobbing girl. "It's okay, Hethy. I'm sorry I shook you like that. I . . . I didn't mean to upset you."

Hethy jumped to her feet, her hands cupped over her eyes, and ran off. Quorl and Coer turned their heads curiously, and then Coer got to his feet.

"Don't worry," Sally said, her voice shaking. "She won't go far."

"Should I follow her?" the rougarou asked.

"No, she'll be back," Sally said, and lay down on her blanket.

Sally woke in the night to some sort of excitement among the rougarou. She looked around, but Hethy was not there. Had something happened to her? Sally got up and walked toward the pack, clustered together by the Great Tree.

As she moved closer, Quorl turned.

"What's happened?" Sally asked. "Is Hethy—"

But then she saw Hethy in the shadows by Coer's side. She coughed into her hand a moment, but then stopped, settling back behind Coer.

"Strangers," Quorl replied ominously. "Some of the pack patrolling found two humans. They've asked to speak to the *nata*."

"Who are they?"

"I don't know. They've only just arrived."

Staying close to Quorl's side, Sally peered through the pack to see the strangers—a boy and a girl—waiting as Renamex approached them. Everything about the pair was bizarre and frightening to Sally. And what frightened Sally most was that she thought she knew who they were.

The girl was barefoot and wore a peculiar dress that seemed woven from grass. Her skin was pale as moonlight and her dark hair hung in a single braid past her slim waist. She wore a funny shell on her belt. As Sally looked closer, she thought the shell might be a knife, but where the girl would have gotten such a weapon, she couldn't imagine.

The boy—black and nearly twice Sally's height—carried a club of heavy wood. Although he certainly was not threatening the rougarou surrounding him, his manner suggested that if it came to it, he would be a terrifying adversary, even to the rougarou.

Sally had never met either of them, but she knew them without a doubt. This was the siren Jolie and Conker, John Henry's son. But how? Conker had died destroying the Gog's train. No, she remembered. Mother Josara had seen in her bowl that Conker was alive. But how had he survived? And Jolie . . . Ray was heartbroken that she had disappeared. Sally knew this in a thousand ways that Ray had never said.

Sally tensed. If they realized she had the rabbit's foot, would they try to stop her from reaching her father?

Renamex, with Mangoron at her side, was approaching Conker and Jolie. "Welcome," she said in a near growl. "We trust that you come in peace?"

Conker laid his club on the ground, and Jolie removed her shell knife to do the same. "Yes, we come in peace," Conker said. "We're looking for the guardians of the Wolf Tree."

"You have found us. I am Renamex, the leader of the rougarou. Why are you looking for the Great Tree?"

Renamex was not unfriendly, but she was not warm either. She held her head stiff and tall before the strangers. Sally noticed that although their eyes flickered cautiously— or maybe it was curiously—to the pack surrounding them, Conker and Jolie faced the *nata* without fear.

Conker took something from a bag. Sally could not see what he showed Renamex, but whatever it was had a visible effect on Mangoron. "The head of John Henry's hammer!"

"I am his son," Conker said. "We set out from the banks of the Mississippi three weeks ago. The handle has guided us. A glowing that has increased the further west we have come. The night before, it flashed a great light."

"When the Tree returned to us," Mangoron said to his *nata*.

"The wood from the handle comes from the Great Tree," Renamex said to Conker. "They are linked. That is how it has led you to us."

"The handle has been broken," Conker said. "I've come to ask your help in fashioning a new handle and restoring the hammer's powers."

Mangoron stepped closer, his tail rising. "I remember when your father made the Nine Pound Hammer, many years ago. We went together up the Great Tree. I helped him find the branch, and together we finished the weapon. Am I right to assume that your father is dead?"

"Yes. And I could tell you about it, if you want to hear."

"We do," Renamex said. "But not now. It is late and you must be tired from your journey. The decision to allow a human to cross onto the Great Tree is never taken lightly. Nor is the decision up to me solely. The pack will discuss this request. Be assured, we respected your father. We will show you every courtesy. Tell us your names."

"I am Conker, and my companion is Jolie." Jolie nodded after Conker spoke, and as she acknowledged the other rougarou around her, her gaze fell on Sally and Hethy. Jolie's eyes widened with curiosity, but then she looked away.

"Welcome, Conker, and welcome, Jolie," Renamex said in a kinder tone. "We have food, if you are hungry. Or a fire, for you to sleep. Be patient. We will have an answer for you tomorrow." Renamex turned, and Mangoron followed her. Oultren came forward from the pack and spoke with Conker and Jolie, acting as their attendant much as Coer had done for Sally and Hethy.

Hethy joined Sally as the circle of rougarou broke. "He's the one you told me about, ain't he? He's the one you said died on that train."

"So he says." Sally narrowed her eyes. "It's very strange, Hethy. Why haven't they gone to Shuckstack? Why have they been keeping what happened to them a secret all this time? It's suspicious, if you ask me. We must keep quiet about who I am. And about the rabbit's foot. At least until we get to know them better. Will you do that?"

Hethy's face was impassive, her expression withdrawn. "Sure, Yote. I'll do like you ask."

"Thank you, Hethy. You're such a good friend. I'm glad I can trust you." She hugged Hethy and then took her by the hand, looking her in the face. "You don't look good, Hethy. Are you all right?"

"Feeling poorly," she said, stifling a cough. "Yote. I'm scared that pod Granny Sip gave me ain't working no more."

Sally frowned, feeling her heart thud with concern for her friend and with guilt at how she'd treated Hethy.

"We should sleep. You need to rest. You've been through so much. Come back to our fire."

The girls got under the blanket. Hethy coughed off and on for a time, but soon Sally could hear her breathing relax with sleep. Sally lay with her eyes closed, unable to sleep. After a time, she heard Jolie and Conker approach the fire.

"Who are the girls?" she heard Conker whisper.

Jolie answered in a hushed voice, "Oultren says they were lost on the prairie, and that one of the rougarou rescued them. Poor things."

"What's going to happen to them?"

"I suppose the rougarou will help them get back to a town. They could not be in better hands. These rougarou seem kind enough."

Sally cracked her eyelids and saw Conker and Jolie lie on the ground on the far side of the fire.

"Yes," Conker said, cocking his arms behind his head and taking a deep breath. "Yes, I expect they are. But just 'cause they're kind don't mean they'll help us."

CONKER WOKE TO JOLIE TOUCHING HIS SHOULDER. "I need to find water," she whispered. "There's a stream nearby. I'll be back soon."

"Okay," he mumbled. After she left, he could not go back to sleep. With the dawn still half an hour away, he rose and stirred the fire.

The two young girls were sleeping next to one another, and Conker wondered what they thought of the strange creatures who had rescued them. Talking wolves. He had seen strange things in his life, but these rougarou were the most fantastic.

What was this place where the rougarou lived? Conker had never seen landforms such as these. He had not noticed them last night. They were not mountains or hills, but canyons eroded from the ocean of grass. Like the world was beginning to dissolve here. Where the land was washed away most, it made sharp spires and jagged pinnacles. It was a twisted land, beautiful and desolate.

Oultren came over. "The pack wishes to hear from you."

Conker followed her over to the circle of rougarou. Renamex nodded to him as he stood at their center. "Tell us more about your purpose in wanting to restore your father's hammer."

The pack listened carefully as Conker chronicled the life and death of his father and how the medicine show had defeated the Gog but not his Machine. And he explained as best he could how vital the Nine Pound Hammer was to destroying the Machine.

When he was finished, Oultren led him back to the campfire. "We will have our answer soon. Be certain that we are wise. If the pack decides not to allow you to cross, there will be a just reason. Are you hungry?"

Conker shook his head. He had no appetite. Oultren bowed her head to him and trotted back to her brethren.

Conker hoped he had conveyed the urgency of their task. But he worried: what could the evils of the Machine mean to these beings? After a time, he heard the girls talking. They were awake, and he walked over to them. "Morning."

"Good morning," the girls answered together.

"Sorry if we woke you last night," Conker said. "Awful late to show up as we did."

"That's okay," the black girl answered. "My name's Hethy and this here's—"

"Coyote," the other girl said quickly. "Hethy likes to call me Yote, but you can call me either."

"Well, nice to meet you." Conker's gaze lingered a moment on Hethy. Her skin had a strange gray tint, and her hair looked like an old woman's, silver and white. "Y'all got lost out here, I heard."

"Yeah," Coyote answered. She was a jittery girl, her speech rapid and clipped. "We just lost our way is all. Not hard to do on the prairie."

"Where you come from?"

"Oh, it's a town," Coyote answered vaguely. "Springville. Just up to the north a little ways. Where are you from?"

Conker thought about the question. "Nowhere, I suppose. I never really had a set home. I worked for a time with a traveling show. Home was a train. But that was a long time ago."

They were quiet, Conker squatting before the fire, the girls making a breakfast from the remains of a roasted bird and eyeing Conker curiously.

Conker poked at the coals with the end of his club. "Have you seen the Wolf Tree?"

"*Wolf* Tree?" Hethy asked. "You mean the Great Tree."

"That's what the rougarou call it," Coyote added. Then she paused before saying, "It's right over there. Haven't you . . . don't you see it?"

Conker looked to where the girl was pointing. All he saw were the strange landforms. "Where? There?"

"You can't see it, can you?" Coyote asked.

Hethy shook her head. "Them rougarou said only those been blessed by the pack could see it. I guess they ain't going to bless you 'less they going to let you climb up."

Conker frowned. "But they blessed you?"

The girls looked anxiously at one another. "Well, I suppose we're just kids," Coyote answered. "They must have figured it wouldn't matter if we saw it."

Conker suspected this was a lie. He continued prodding at the fire, his face placid, while the girls ate their breakfast and then left to wander the canyon's walls.

Soon Jolie returned. "Have they decided?" she asked, her hair still dripping.

Conker looked over to where the rougarou were clustered. "No."

"Where are those two girls?"

"I don't know. Last I seen, they were playing down in one of the gullies."

"You have not eaten, have you? Let me get you something." A roasted bird, caught by the rougarou for the guests, sat untouched on a spit. Jolie took out her knife to cut away some of the meat.

The two ate without speaking. Conker felt they were alike in this way, not needing to make idle conversation, and it comforted him as they waited. After a time, Oultren broke from the pack and loped over to them. "Come," she said, with no hint as to what the pack had decided.

Conker and Jolie followed her, and when they reached the pack, they sat across from Renamex.

"Conker, we have great admiration for your father," she began. "But even if you were not his kin, we can see that both you and Jolie have great destinies in this world. You are warriors and your fight is worthy.

"The Great Tree has grave implications for humanity. It links the life in this world with a creative force that illuminates and regenerates. There is much concern among the pack for the Tree. You have come to us at a time of deep questioning. We have lost our true forms, and do not understand why. We worry what future our stewardship will take. But our task remains to protect the Great Tree at all costs.

"We are concerned that to take from the Great Tree, to allow you to sever a branch, would profane the pathway. While we are the Tree's stewards, we do not fully understand the workings of the Great Tree. Would taking a branch damage in some way the connection between this world and the world beyond? Some have argued that the risk outweighs the task you have before you."

Conker felt a vein running along his neck throb. Jolie placed her fingers on his arm.

"Mangoron, whose opinion is held in high regard by the pack, has speculated something that the rest of us had not considered. This Machine that you intend to destroy, what if it caused the Great Tree to become lost? And what would have happened if we had not found the Great Tree again? What would have happened to humanity?

"The Machine might still bring some ill to the Great Tree. And we now agree that we must help you, in whatever way we can, to bring about its destruction. Conker, you will be the first to ascend the Great Tree in a long time. You have the blessing of the rougarou."

Conker and Jolie stood as they saw the Great Tree materialize, rising from the prairie like an enormous glimmering tower.

Mangoron stepped forward, drawing Conker from his amazement. "As I was for your father, I will be your guide also."

Mangoron had explained to Conker that to reach the lowest branches could take a day and part of a night. Conker would need plenty of food and water; the ascent would be strenuous. Conker built up the fire, and he and Jolie busied themselves with roasting game that the rougarou caught for them.

Coyote approached nervously. "Quorl says it is cold up there. We have a blanket you can use."

Conker smiled at her as she laid it on the ground and quickly ran back to join Hethy.

"I'll need to rig some sort of ax," Conker said as he and Jolie worked. "You know how to make something like that?"

"That will not be necessary," Jolie replied, taking out Cleoma's shell knife.

Conker looked at the siren weapon. "It's just shell, not metal. Will it cut a branch?"

Jolie lifted a thick log from the pile next to the fire. She turned the knife so the blade was facing up and sawed into the log easily. She then held the knife up to show him the back with its ridge of irregular teeth.

"This knife is designed for hunting as well as defense. We use this edge to cut through the bones of animals. It will cut your branch."

"Thank you," Conker said. "I'll take good care of it."

"Of course." Jolie smiled as she gave Conker the knife.

Conker went to sleep before the sun set. Mangoron said he would wake Conker several hours before dawn for their departure. When he heard Mangoron's voice whisper at his ear, Conker was awake in a moment.

Jolie woke, and Conker left the Nine Pound Hammer's head with her, filling the sack now with the food and water and the blanket. He looked over at the girls sleeping by the fire. The pack watched Conker silently, reverently, their blue eyes glowing.

"Okay," Conker said to Mangoron. "You lead the way."

The rougarou nodded and trotted toward the roots of the Wolf Tree. The bark made a rough stairway circling around the vast trunk. Conker stopped, one foot on the bark, the other foot still on the earth. He looked back at Jolie, her fierce eyes on him. He raised one hand and then turned to climb.

The crude stairway did not make a perfect spiral, for the bark was broken into enormous pieces. When Mangoron and Conker came to the top of one of these pieces of bark, they had to leap onto the next piece across a gap of at least two yards. Although Conker had no difficulty with this, he realized that jumping from section to section hundreds of times—or would it be thousands of times?—would make him tired and sore.

They climbed and leaped across the chasms, up and up. There were sections where the pathway ran almost horizontally, and other times the way was so steep that Conker had to climb with his hands. He was surprised at the ease with which Mangoron could scale the nearly vertical faces. The rougarou understood where to position his hind legs and how to pull himself with his front claws, or teeth even, when the need arose.

In the dark of night, the Wolf Tree seemed to absorb the moon and starlight, so that the Tree itself looked luminous. Soon the night sky began to tint with the first wash of gray and deep blues of dawn's arrival. Conker could see how truly high they had risen.

As they rounded once more to the side facing the rougarou's camp, Conker paused to look out at the world below. How far up were they? A mile now? He could see the pack below. He could make out Jolie and even the two girls, rousing from their sleep. How strange it was to look down on them, as if he were a bird. How small they were. Then a wave of vertigo struck him, and he fell back against the Tree.

"Best not to look back," Mangoron said. "It will get easier the higher we go. I know that sounds illogical, but you'll see. That's why I like to leave before daybreak. I've found that most are more fearful when they can still see the earth clearly. The first hours are the hardest. Look ahead. Look up. You won't fall."

They went on, higher and higher. Conker's thighs burned with exertion. He was sweating, even though the wind was getting cool the farther they climbed. They stopped and ate, resting for a time on a wide ledge. Birds flew past below them. At the horizon, the curvature of the earth was visible. They continued on.

Conker did peer back on occasion. He could no longer see the pack or Jolie or the girls. Or were those tiny specks them? Mangoron had been right. It was less dizzying to look down now. Maybe it was that the distance was more abstract because of the tremendous height. How far had they climbed? Several miles surely. Conker found it harder to breathe. The air was much colder, and he draped the blanket over his shoulders.

What was most peculiar was that when Conker looked down, the trunk became semi-transparent closer to the ground, just as the top of the Wolf Tree was fading into the sky. It was as if the portion where Conker and Mangoron climbed was solid and substantial, but from a distance, the Wolf Tree could be seen for what it truly was. But what was that? What was it made of? Light? Spirit, maybe? Nothing material, he reckoned.

After a while, the lowest branches begin to appear. They were still a long way off, but the branches seemed to coalesce from the sky itself, stretching out horizontally farther than they had climbed up.

"How long will it take us to reach those branches?" Conker asked Mangoron.

The rougarou looked out at the sun, gauging its position. "After dark, I think."

They rose to such a height that clouds drifted past below them, casting enormous shadows like black sailing ships across the surface of the prairie. Conker had to stop more frequently, not so much because his muscles were weary, but because he was short of breath. Mangoron waited patiently, urging him to drink more water, explaining that this would help.

By nightfall, they were just below the lowest branches. Conker could see the trunk continuing up, seemingly infinitely, with more branches stretching out as it rose. They wound their way up until at last they stood atop a branch nearly a hundred feet thick. Mangoron suggested that they rest, even try to sleep for several hours before going on. Conker agreed, and although the air was growing bitterly cold, he covered himself in the blanket and slept a heavy, dreamless sleep.

When they woke, it was still night, although Conker could not tell how late. They began their journey along the branch. This was much easier than the climb had been. The branch slowly narrowed, and after several hours, they came to the first split.

"Which way do we go?" Conker asked.

"It makes little difference as you are not crossing the pathway to reach the other world. We'll take the narrower of the branches."

They went on like this: coming to where the branch divided and taking whichever branch seemed the smaller. A branch forty feet in width divided into two branches, each twenty-five feet in width. Soon the branch they were crossing was little more than eight feet across.

Mangoron began to move more quickly, sniffing rapidly

at the bark and growling with agitation. As Conker hurried after him, there was a great crack. The limb broke away beneath Mangoron's feet. He would have plunged to his death had Conker not leaped to the edge, snatching Mangoron by the back leg. The rougarou yipped as his hip caught the brunt of his weight. Leaning over the edge, Conker watched as the enormous broken bough dropped into the howling wind and disappeared in the dark.

Conker heaved Mangoron back onto the limb. The rougarou lay panting, his eyes wild and deeply troubled. "The Tree! How could this have happened? I've led countless across its passway and never has a branch broken."

Charged with fright-filled energy, Mangoron investigated the broken limb and others around it. "The branches, they are weak. They are cracking all around. What has happened to the Great Tree?" Distress filled his voice as Mangoron barked. "The Tree is dying!"

"No," Conker said, disbelieving. "How can it die? It's not an actual tree."

"It can die. I would never have imagined this before, but now, in witnessing it, I can see with certainty that the Great Tree is dying. These branches. They've become brittle. The bark is peeling. The wood beneath is dry and dead. That Machine! It is killing it."

Mangoron turned this way and that at the broken branch's edge, like a fox cornered by hounds and desperate for escape.

"What about the handle?" Conker asked. "Can it still be made?"

Mangoron stopped his frantic pacing, breathing in shallow gasps until he gathered himself. "Yes. Yes, I don't think all the branches are dead. We will have to find one still living. Follow me."

Mangoron led Conker back along the branch, taking careful steps and often testing the limb to make sure it would support them. When they reached where another, larger limb spread out from the branch, Conker followed Mangoron along it.

"Here," Mangoron said after they reached an area where several smaller branches grew from the one they had been following. "This limb we are on is still healthy. And look. Out there. See that branch, the one with leaves still on it. That is it. Cut that branch. Go now."

Conker had to climb out. He was glad that it was night, glad that he could not see the great distance below him. He moved slowly up the limb, taking solid holds. The limb groaned under his weight. This was dangerous work, risky, like walking out on a frozen pond, not knowing if his next move would send him plunging to his death.

But Conker was not afraid of dying, not anymore, and he was surprised as this fact dawned on him. He had died once already. He would do it again one day.

Conker eased his way out further and when he reached the limb, he could see that it was the perfect thickness. Taking the shell knife from his belt, he sawed first at the narrow end, cutting the leaves and thinnest twigs away. The limb swayed beneath him as he worked, but there was no keeping it from moving.

"Be careful," Mangoron growled.

Conker measured off a length a little longer than his arm. He took a deep breath. Leveling the knife on the bark, Conker sawed through the dense wood.

When he had finished, he secured the branch in his belt and crawled back. He had done it. He had the branch that would restore the Nine Pound Hammer.

Mangoron inspected it when Conker returned. "Yes. This is good. This wood contains the power of the Great Tree. There is life left in it yet. But I fear that if my pack does not find a way to save the Great Tree, it will die and crumble away into oblivion. What will become of the rougarou then? What will become of the world?"

-22-

GUNSHOTS

SALLY? **W**HAT **COULD SHE POSSIBLY BE DOING OUT** here?

Ray had sent B'hoy scanning wide, ahead and across the prairie to look for her, but each time he returned, he had seen no one.

As they stopped at a creek to water the horses, Ray got down and walked out, inspecting the ground. The treads of the steamcoach had cut parallel swaths across the prairie.

"What are you doing?" Redfeather called, getting down from Atsila and handing the reins to Marisol.

"There are more of those footprints," Ray said.

Redfeather came over to Ray. "They're small. Two pairs," he said, touching a finger to them. "Do you think one of them could be Sally's?"

"It must be," Ray said. "But who's she with?"

Redfeather pointed. "Look, there's that wolf print again."

Ray followed the tracks out, kicking aside the grass to find the prints in the soft earth. "This doesn't make any sense!"

Marisol rode up from the creek, pulling Atsila along by her reins. "Ray, we don't know for sure that it's Sally."

"It has to be her!" Ray shouted. "Don't you understand? No one else could possibly have the rabbit's foot!"

Redfeather and Marisol flinched. Ray's nerves were on edge. He knew he had spoken too harshly, but he could not help himself from snapping. And to make matters worse, they had not slept the night before. The Bowlers were quickening their hunt, having only stopped for an hour to eat and fill the steamcoach's water tank. The agents continued their pursuit through the night. The four Bowlers on horseback rode ahead, spread out in a wide fan.

"Ray," Marisol said as they rode on.

"What?"

She pushed aside her hair to say over her shoulder, "What if that's not a wolf?"

"What else could it be?" Ray asked.

Redfeather gave Marisol a curious look as he brought Atsila next to Unole.

Marisol glanced at him before saying, "Remember what Water Spider said about the guardians of the Wolf Tree."

"The rougarou?" Redfeather asked.

Marisol nodded and shook Unole's reins.

Redfeather's eyes remained wide as he rode after her.

The sun had already set, and darkness was falling fast. A mile ahead, they could see the black tendril of the steamcoach's smoke. Redfeather shook Atsila's reins to quicken her. "What will happen to Gigi and the other workers when they go to Chicago? Won't they all get sick?"

"No, don't you see?" Ray explained. "This is how the Gog plans on enslaving mankind. This is all part of his design. The Machine will make it so nobody who enters the Darkness can ever leave. They'll be trapped—all those workers, everyone who goes to the Expo, and after that . . ."

Redfeather grunted, a frown darkening his eyes. "I don't think they'll stop again tonight. Our horses are weary. How much longer can we keep up this pace?"

"Look." Marisol pointed. "The ground seems to fall away just up there."

Ray narrowed his eyes but could not make out what they were approaching. He closed his eyes and looked from B'hoy's perspective high above. "It's some sort of bluff, but it drops more gradually than we can see from here. And below, there's a maze of strange spikes of earth and twisting cliffs. It's an odd country."

"The steamcoach is headed that way," Redfeather said. "We don't want to lose it in the dark. Let's hurry to stay close."

The wind rattled the prairie grass. The moon rose. They kicked the tired horses into a faster gait. Marisol took the last of the salted meat from her bag and handed some to Ray and Redfeather. They ate as the sky transitioned from twilight to night, and soon they were nearly to the badland buttes and canyons.

"Maybe we should try to get ahead of the Bowlers," Ray said. "The way they're driving that steamcoach, they must think they've nearly caught Sally. If we use the dark as cover, maybe we can get ahead of them and look for her before—"

A gunshot rang out. The bullet whined past them, and Unole reared, throwing Ray from her back.

"What was that?" Redfeather shouted, trying to brace Atsila.

But Unole was startled, and Marisol could not stop him from running. Ray was on his feet, watching as Redfeather galloped after her.

Ray saw them in the moonlight.

Two Bowlers, spread at least a hundred yards apart, waited in ambush. As Marisol raced past, one of the Bowlers brought his rifle to his shoulder. The barrel flashed.

Unole collapsed in a tumble of legs and torn earth.

It was late in the day when Sally heard the first of the rougarou call, "They are returning!"

The rougarou Mangoron and the giant Conker rounded the trunk of the Great Tree nearly a thousand feet above. The pack gathered eagerly at its roots, whining and barking like pups. Hethy put down the stick she was using to draw letters in the earth, and joined Sally, watching the two make their way down. Jolie twisted her way through the pack to stand at the last step.

As Conker approached her, he held out her shell knife and put his large hand over the siren's shoulder. "I have found it."

Jolie's smile fell as she saw the somber expression on Conker's face. "What is wrong?"

Conker shook his head, continuing to follow Mangoron. "Renamex. *Nata*. My pack," Mangoron announced. "I bring dire news. I know now why we have not returned to our true forms. Our stewardship has failed. The Great Tree is dying. Its outer branches are crumbling. We were right to help Conker, for he and his father's hammer are our only hope. This Machine must be destroyed before the Tree perishes."

The pack erupted in questions. Renamex growled and snapped to settle them. Sally pushed her way through the terrified and furious pack. "What does this mean?" she asked Renamex. "Can I cross?"

The *nata* turned from the loud voices surrounding them. "No, Coyote. It's too dangerous."

Sally turned to escape the commotion and knocked into Jolie. The siren took her by the shoulders, looking down at her curiously.

"What do you mean? You were going to cross the Wolf Tree?"

But Sally broke from her grip and ran.

From the fireside, Sally watched with anxiety as the pack discussed Mangoron's news over at the Great Tree's roots. Hethy plucked the feathers from another bird, her eyes occasionally flickering to Sally or to the rougarou. Neither girl spoke.

Although she would not be able to reach her father across the Great Tree, she had the rabbit's foot. It pointed to the west, calling Sally to continue her journey. She could still find her father. But to have traveled across the Great Tree—what an adventure that would have been!

Would Quorl and Hethy and the others let her continue after her father now? Renamex would want to meet as a pack to discuss it. They would want to know more about the rabbit's foot. How could she explain whether the foot was meant to restore her father's powers or to forge the spike? She was not even certain!

But she was certain she needed to find her father. All depended on that! And if they decided she was too young to be venturing across the plains alone, then what would she—

Sally was startled from her reverie as Conker stood before her. She scrambled to her feet.

"Easy, girl," he said softly. "I've only come to return your blanket and to thank you for letting me borrow it."

Hethy stood to take it, smiling up at the giant. "You're welcome," she said. "Was it cold up there?"

Conker nodded. "Fierce cold."

Hethy gave a cough and then said, "Started on your handle?"

Conker looked over his shoulder at Jolie, who was building a separate fire a dozen or so yards away. "We're about to begin. You can come watch if you want."

"Thanks," Hethy said. "Maybe in a bit. I'm about to set these birds to cooking. I'll bring some to you when they done."

"We'd appreciate that," he said, and turned to go, letting his gaze fall once more on Sally.

Sally sat fretting for a long time. Finally Hethy stood, wiping her hands on the front of her dress. "Well, them birds'll be cooking for a bit. I'm going to go watch them work on that handle. You want to come?"

Sally shook her head dully.

Hethy turned a brow up quizzically. "Okay then. I'll be back."

Sally watched as Hethy approached the other fire. Jolie was crouched beside Conker. The giant was working intently. Moving the knife in long, controlled strokes down the branch, he shaved away the bark in thin ribbons. Hethy knelt, placing her hands on her knees. She began coughing, bending forward as it shook her frame.

Sally anxiously watched her friend a moment longer as the fit subsided. She hated what she was about to do. She couldn't call attention to herself. It was like back at Shuckstack, when she had snuck away. She had been careful then. Nobody had realized until she was gone.

She couldn't pack the blanket or any provisions. They could turn to see her at any moment. What would she eat? How would she survive? She had nearly starved before, even with Hethy's help. Well, she would have to worry about that later. Her first step was to get away unnoticed.

Sally slipped her fingers around the straps of her rucksack, picking it up. She walked slowly, making her way toward the rougarou as if she were listening to their discussion. Casting a careful glance, she saw Jolie talking to Hethy, Conker working on the handle.

Keep going, she told herself. They'll take care of Hethy.

The rougarou were too busy to notice Sally, and she kept walking deeper into the shadows around the roots of the Great Tree. Sally broke into a run. When she reached the edge of one of the buttes, she slid on her hip down the slope of soft dirt, tumbling at the end and landing hard on her elbows. Sally scrambled to her feet, touching her hand to her pocket to make sure the rabbit's foot was still there, and raced along the gully until she found herself out on the open prairie. The low moon illuminated wisps of cloud. Looking back, she could see the Great Tree behind her, ghostly and seeming no farther away than when she left.

After a time, she slowed to a jog and then walked as she made her way across the grassland. She had to keep going. She couldn't stop now; she was still too close. But she was hungry already and wished she had eaten before she ran away.

A gunshot echoed.

Sally froze. She was not used to the sound of guns and could not guess how far away the shooter was. She crouched on the ground, her heart racing. Another shot rang out. No, they were not firing at her. This much she could tell. But someone was shooting, and they weren't far away.

A pinnacle rose in the dark ahead. If she could reach it, there would be more of the buttes and canyons and places to stay hidden there. She quickened her pace, and as she did, she drew the rabbit's foot from her pocket to check the direction.

The rabbit's foot was glowing.

Sally stopped. Why was it glowing? She'd never seen that before. But Ray had.

She heard something. The beat of feet against the earth. It was growing louder. Sally turned back toward it. Something was racing across the prairie toward her.

Her legs tangled in her dress as she spun around. Stumbling only a moment, she ran, knowing she had nowhere to hide.

Over her shoulder she saw it. A shadow descended upon her, enormous and leaping. She fell backward and cried out as it landed before her.

"Where are you going, Little Coyote?"

"Quorl . . . wh-what are you doing here?" Sally stammered, her hand to her chest.

"You should not be out here alone. There are men about with guns."

She held up the rabbit's foot, letting its warm white light illuminate Quorl's eyes. "Look. The *Toninyan* is glowing. That means a Hoarhound is out there with those men. Are they after the rougarou?"

"No. How would these men know of us? They must have some other aim. But they are armed, and if this beast is with them, then you are at risk. Come, let me take you back."

"I'm not going back, Quorl. I must find my father."

"You're leaving without your friend Hethy?"

"She . . . she shouldn't come. It's *my* father. It's too

dangerous for her. I hate goodbyes and I didn't know how else to leave without making it hard, on me or her or any of you. The pack has been so kind to me, and I'm sorry I left without explaining, but I must go, Quorl. Please tell them I'm sorry."

Quorl looked curiously at Sally and growled low.

"I am bound to you, Little Coyote. You said your father could help stop this Machine. If we can find him, maybe he can join Conker and together we can fight. I am coming with you. I will be your guardian."

Sally could not help herself. She threw her arms around his neck. "Oh, Quorl."

"Get on my back," Quorl said. "Let us get away from those men. Which way does the foot tell us to go?"

After Hethy left to check on the roasting birds, Jolie watched Conker work. He had stripped the branch of its bark. Beneath, the grain was tinted a dusky red unlike any wood she had ever seen. Conker shaved the wood slowly, sculpting the handle with precision as Mangoron had instructed. He stopped on occasion to judge the balance and feel of the grip beneath his hands, and then he continued, altering here and refining there.

The pack was making noise, and Jolie stood to look. Hethy was speaking to them, and the expression on her face made Jolie wonder if something was wrong. Renamex was giving orders, and one of the rougarou raced away.

"I will be back in a moment," Jolie said, but Conker hardly heard her.

As she approached, Hethy ran up to meet her, coughing with the exertion. "You didn't see Yote nowhere, did you?"

"No, why? She is missing?"

"Quorl, too. They're gone and no one knows where they went." Hethy was wringing her dress in her hands, and she mumbled nearly inaudibly, "She's gone and followed it without me. She left me, sure enough."

"Followed what?" Jolie asked.

Hethy turned her eyes away, guilt and fear mingling. "I ain't suppose to tell you. She don't want you to know."

"Know what?"

"I promised her and I'm afraid she'll be mad. But she might be doing wrong. I just don't know."

"I want to help you, to help your friend," Jolie said. "I heard Coyote say something about wanting to cross the Wolf Tree. Is that what this is about?"

"It's her daddy," Hethy relented. "She's trying to find him. He's lost somewheres. In this other world. The Gloaming."

"The Gloaming?"

"And she thinks she can rescue him 'cause she's got this foot."

"A foot?"

"A rabbit's foot. Made of gold."

Jolie's mouth fell open. "Who is this girl? What is Coyote's real name?"

"Sally." Hethy winced. "Sally Cobb."

Jolie's mind erupted with a thousand thoughts. Sally!

What was she doing out here? Why wasn't she with Ray? And why did she have the foot? Jolie imagined all that could have occurred in the past year since she'd last seen Ray. Her heart stung as she thought of him.

"Do you know Ray, Hethy?"

"That's her brother. I ain't met him."

"But he is alive?"

"Sure. 'Less something happened to him in Omphalosa." As she saw Jolie's puzzled expression, she added, "The town, where I come from. Yote . . . Sally told me that's where Ray was going. To try and figure out what was causing the Darkness. To try and stop that awful clockwork."

"The Machine!" Jolie paced, trying to piece together what was happening and what she should do. "But we are Ray's friends. Why did Sally not tell us who she was? She knew who we were. She had to."

"She told me not to tell you. She didn't want you to know. Oh, what foolishness that girl takes to!"

"It is all right," Jolie said, calming herself and wanting to calm Hethy. "You were trying to be a good friend. You wanted to be loyal, and that is good. We have to find her. We have to find Sally before she gets too far."

Hethy gestured to the rougarou. "Renamex. She done sent out Coer. But Sally, she ain't going to want to be found. She'll try and resist. And Quorl's with her. He got a debt to her. He'll do whatever Yote asks."

"But I have a way to stop her."

"You ain't going to hurt her?"

"No," Jolie said. "I am a siren. There are powers I can use. If we can catch her, I can convince her to come back with us."

"We'll need to be quick like," Hethy said. She ran over and spoke with Oultren. The rougarou listened and then followed Hethy back to Jolie.

The rougarou crouched on the ground. "I will carry you," she said.

Jolie looked back at Conker. All his attention was focused on completing the handle for the Nine Pound Hammer. She could do this without him. They would find Sally and be back before he finished.

Jolie swung her leg over the rougarou's back and Hethy got on behind her. As they raced away, Jolie heard a rifle fire in the distance. And then another.

CONKER LOOKED AROUND AS IF AWAKENING FROM A
dream. The fire had burned down to coals. The shell knife lay
on the ground atop wisps of shaved wood. Across his knees
rested the handle.

His work was complete.

Conker took the iron head in one hand and the handle in
the other. Setting the chiseled end to the hole in the head, he
pushed. The two pieces connected smoothly, and Conker felt
them draw strangely together and lock. He sensed the deep
connection between the iron forged by his father and the
wood cut from the Wolf Tree, like the two materials had become one. The power of the Nine Pound Hammer surged
into his arms.

He stood.

Where was Jolie? He had not even noticed that she had

left. But there were her waterskins from the siren well, so she must not have gone far. The girls were not there either. At least three of the rougarou were missing, and those that remained were gazing at something out on the night prairie.

A light was moving over a hill in the distance.

Conker stared at it curiously. Was it a train? No, it couldn't be. There were no tracks anywhere around. But the dark locomotive with its single blazing eye chugged and hissed like a train.

With the Nine Pound Hammer in his hand, Conker found Mangoron. "What is that?"

The rougarou growled. "We don't know yet. Men. We heard gunfire. Look, here come Oultren and Coer now."

The two golden rougarou ran to the pack, their fur bristling. Coer limped, and as Conker looked closer he realized there was blood in his fur.

Coer lowered his head as he approached Renamex. "My *nata,* there are men coming. Men with rifles. Men driving a strange machine—"

Oultren interrupted, "I went out with Hethy and the siren Jolie. We were looking for Quorl and Coyote when we caught up with Coer. Men came from the darkness. We were attacked. I hid the two girls in a gully so we could get back here quickly. They are safe for now."

Renamex gave a long, low, steady growl. The rest of the pack joined her. "Men with such a machine. They have attacked our pack. They have no right to be here, at the threshold to the Great Tree. We must defend our charge. Rougarou!

We will face these men. We will fight! We will send them scurrying in fear before us!"

The rougarou snarled and snapped, growing into a thunderous rage. Conker stepped back. Mangoron turned to him, seeing the Nine Pound Hammer complete for the first time. "You have done it then?"

Conker raised the Nine Pound Hammer. "Yes, and I'll fight with you if you'll let me."

Renamex answered, "We will." Then she turned and ordered, "Coer, you are limping. Stay here. Guard the Great Tree with John Henry's son."

The rougarou lowered his head, showed savage teeth, and moved beside Conker.

"Follow, rougarou!" Renamex howled. "Drive away these men! Destroy their machine!"

The pack leaped away after their *nata,* their cries splitting the night as they charged. Their shadows raced across the moonlit prairie toward the dark locomotive. In moments, rifles blazed and shots popped, but they were met with terrifying roars.

Conker retrieved the shell knife and wedged it into his belt. Jolie. Was she safe? He could only hope she was. She was tough and fearless. She would protect the girl Hethy.

He threw more logs onto the fires, building up a blaze to illuminate the perimeter of the Wolf Tree's roots. Coer paced, ignoring the injured leg. The muscles along his back rippled with eagerness, but Conker could see he was weakened. He had been shot in several places, the blood running into his fur along his back and down his breast.

"You're badly injured," Conker said. "You want me to look at your wounds?"

Coer growled. "There's no time for that. We have our charge. Do you know these men?"

"No," Conker replied.

He watched the battle. The night was too dark and the distance too great for him to make out clearly what was happening. But he had no doubt who these men were. Who else would be out here, driving such an engine, but agents of the Gog's Machine?

Something emerged from the back of the locomotive. Conker could not make it out. From his vantage, it appeared large and ghostly white. There was a tremendous noise, unlike any animal or machine or weapon, and he heard a rougarou cry out in pain and go silent.

"What is that, Conker?" Coer asked.

Before he could answer, a shot sounded loudly—not in the distance, but here, not more than a dozen yards from Conker.

Conker whirled around. Coer roared, searching for the shooter, but just as quickly, another shot fired. The rougarou yipped, his back leg collapsing beneath him. Before Conker could run to him, a third shot pierced the rougarou's head. Coer lurched forward, his body tumbling grotesquely.

Then something happened to his form. The rougarou was no longer a wolf but a man, lying in the same horrible position he had died in. Long golden hair fell about his bloodied face. His skin shimmered with the same ghostly light of the Wolf Tree, then faded.

Conker held up the Nine Pound Hammer. "Who's there?" he bellowed. "Show yourself, coward."

Two men stepped into the firelight. The first was a filthy young man with long blond hair and a pair of Starr revolvers, one extended toward Conker, the second leveled at his hip. The other man was large, with a dense black beard. He had a long rifle, still smoking from the three shots that had killed the rougarou.

Conker recognized them. The river. Stacker Lee's men.

"Where is he?" Conker asked.

The young man with the blond hair rubbed the barrel of one of his revolvers along his chin. "Still got a bit of a scar. Right over here," he said, reminding Conker of the blow he had taken from Conker's club.

"Where is he?" Conker repeated.

Stacker Lee stepped out from the shadows, a cold smile splitting his face. He gripped the arms of two people, coarse sacks draped over their faces.

"You've done well, Conker," Stacker said. "I see you've finished the Nine Pound Hammer. Is the Wolf Tree here? Yes, I sense it is. Ah, a shame we can't see it."

"Are you with those men?" Conker asked, motioning to the gunfire nearly a quarter mile away. For a moment, Conker could hear how the battle had turned. He was no longer certain that the rougarou had the advantage.

"No. Funny coincidence, really. But seems they are agents of the Gog, doing their job for Mister Grevol. Just like I am."

"Grevol!" Conker's knees nearly buckled.

"You thought you'd killed him, didn't you? Well, I'm

sorry to dash your sense of grandeur. Mister Grevol is mighty resilient. Something like *that* is difficult to kill. Especially now. Especially after what he's become."

"What do you want?" Conker growled, his eyes flickering to the two hooded figures at Stacker's side. Their hands were tied behind their backs.

Stacker jerked the hood off one of his captives.

Si.

Her eyes grew wide as they focused on Conker. Tears spilt down her cheeks. She struggled to call out his name, but a cord was wrapped around her face, cutting into her cheeks, its knot in her open mouth.

Stacker swung around behind Si, pulled back her head, and snapped open a long razor. He pressed it to her throat. "We have negotiations to conduct, and if all goes well, they will be civil."

Conker could not take his eyes from Si. He fought to master the trembling that threatened to overtake him. He had not seen her since that night the Gog's train had been destroyed. Si—his oldest friend, his dearest.

He brought the Nine Pound Hammer up across his chest, finding the right grip on the handle, feeling the measure of its weight, ready.

"Let her go," Conker said in a low growl.

"Of course I will," Stacker said. "We didn't bring her all the way out here to show you the stars on her celestial tattoo. You'll have her soon enough. Just hand over the hammer."

Conker's eyes flickered to the other hooded figure.

Stacker saw this and lifted a finger as if just remembering.

"Alston," he ordered, and the bearded man walked over and pulled the sack from the figure's head.

Conker did not recognize him at first without his wide-brimmed hat, without his silver pistols. His long black-and-silver hair covered most of his face. He had a beard where he hadn't before. He looked old and weak and broken.

Alston jerked the rope from Buck's mouth and then the binding from his wrists. He pushed Buck forward to stumble onto the ground at Conker's feet.

Conker knelt, taking his old friend by the elbow, but Buck did not rise. "Buck. Are you okay?"

Buck nodded silently.

"Should have shot him when we captured them back in Nebraska," Alston said.

Stacker looked down at Buck with disgust. "Yes, one hostage would have sufficed to gain the hammer. But I just don't have the heart to shoot a worthless cripple."

Conker growled. "Cripple. Buck may be blind, but give him a gun. He's a dead-on shot. He could take down the three of you."

The men laughed. A gleam formed in Stacker's eyes—something hungry and cruel. "Really?"

"You're lucky he's unarmed," Conker said.

"Oh, well, just for a laugh, let's see," Stacker said. "Hardy, toss Buckthorn there one of your revolvers."

Hardy threw one of his Starr pistols. It slid on the grass and knocked into Buck's boot.

Buck did not move.

"Yes," Stacker said. "It seems that the former sightless

sharpshooter and sideshow freak has given up his gunslinging ways. Ain't that right, Buckthorn?" he shouted, as if Buck were nearly deaf also.

Buck slumped his head forward.

Hardy chuckled. "He ain't good for nothing but target practice." He fired twice in the ground by Buck's leg. Buck did not move, did not flinch. Hardy went over to retrieve the gun, giving Buck a kick as he walked away.

"So, as you can see," Stacker said, "Buckthorn won't help you. Si . . ." He tugged at the cord until he released it from her mouth. "She's a little too preoccupied to assist, so that leaves just you, Conker. You and the three of us. What's it going to be? Put down the Nine Pound Hammer, and I'll release the China girl."

"Don't, Conker!" Si cried. Her cheeks were raw and red where the cord had cut into them. She gazed fiercely at Conker, like the Si he used to know. "You can't give it to them."

Stacker smirked. "My razor hand is trembling. Be silent, girl, before you make it slip."

Conker looked from the razor to Alston and Hardy to Buck and finally to the Nine Pound Hammer in his hands.

"Conker," Si called. "Listen! A seer who knows Mother Salagi told me a prophecy. She said that I would come to a crossroads—"

Stacker clapped his hand over Si's mouth, pulling her neck back sharply. "You just won't listen, will you? I tried to caution you against tempting me." He began to draw the razor.

"No!" Conker held up the hammer. "Don't! Here it is. Release her."

Stacker looked at Conker and then nodded.

Conker stepped forward, past Buck. Hardy cocked his pistols. Alston leveled the rifle. Conker stopped and knelt. Slowly, he put the Nine Pound Hammer on the ground.

Stacker smiled. He cut Si's ropes and then folded the razor, dropping it into his breast pocket.

Conker stood again and took a few steps back, watching as Stacker picked up the Nine Pound Hammer. Si struggled from the last of the ropes. Before she could run to Conker, Stacker snatched her wrist.

"Ah, one last thing. We can't have you following us with your tattoo. Hardy."

Hardy squinted as he took aim and shot Si's hand. Si screamed and fell to her knees, clutching her hand to her breast.

Conker roared.

Hardy was closest to him. Conker pulled Jolie's shell knife from his belt and punched it into Hardy's chest. Hardy opened his mouth to gasp but no air came out.

Alston's rifle erupted, and Conker's shirt shredded, blood at his hip. Snarling, Conker lunged at the man, bringing his great fists down until Alston went limp.

A bullet tore into his leg, and Conker stumbled to one knee.

"Stay where you are!" Stacker shouted. He turned the long, smoking barrel of his Buntline pistol to the back of Buck's head. His other hand, holding the Nine Pound Hammer, wrapped around Buck's chest.

"I'm taking your friend with me. You just stay right here with the girl."

"You could kill me," Conker growled. "You could shoot me in the head. Why don't you?"

Stacker regained his malicious smile. "Because I need you to live. If I'm to get my heart back, I need Mister Grevol to know you'll come for me. I know you'll come for me. But I'll reach Mister Grevol first."

"Conker," Buck groaned as Stacker backed away. "Conker . . . I'm sorry." Buck's face twitched with emotion, but slowly, step after backward step, Stacker moved into the dark with Buck and the Nine Pound Hammer.

Conker watched them until they were gone, and then he turned to Si.

RAY WATCHED HELPLESSLY AS REDFEATHER RACED ATsila toward Marisol. The agents leveled their rifles at him.

As they fired, Redfeather leaped off Atsila, landing by Unole. The Bowlers ran toward him, but Redfeather whirled around, his bowstring twanging. One of the Bowlers tumbled. The other fired his rifle repeatedly, dropping to the ground to take cover.

There was a whistle, and Atsila circled around to return to Redfeather. He climbed onto the horse and pulled Marisol on behind him.

Redfeather shot another arrow, and the Bowler returned fire, driving Atsila away.

They were safe. But Ray was cut off from his friends by the Bowler. He dropped back to the ground, hiding in the tall grass.

How had they known to set the ambush? Had they seen the horses following them? Maybe B'hoy—the solitary crow trailing their steamcoach—made the agents suspicious?

After a few moments, the Bowler got to his feet and began jogging in the direction Redfeather and Marisol had gone. Ray ran over to Unole. The horse was dead, and Ray could only hope that he died without suffering. He felt sad and angry for the animal, to have been caught up in such terrible violence.

B'hoy flew down to land on Ray's wrist.

"Good boy," Ray whispered. "Fly out. See if you can find Redfeather and Marisol." The crow croaked and took flight.

As Ray crested a rise, he could see the shadows of the buttes and chasms about a mile away illuminated by the rising moon. Below, the steamcoach trudged through the darkness, casting out its funnel of light across the prairie. Something else drew his eye: a fire, small and far away, tucked against the wall of one of the buttes. Who was out there? Could it be Sally?

Before he could wonder further, he saw forms dashing across the plains, racing toward the steamcoach. Whatever they were, they were large and they were fast. It might have been men on horses, but then he heard a growl and a bark and howl. Were they wolves?

The rougarou!

Gunfire erupted. Flashes of fire lit the black prairie. The first of the rougarou clashed against the steamcoach. Others yelped as bullets hit them. The pack spread out—how many were there?—to encircle the steamcoach and the four horses.

Bowlers poured from the doors of the steamcoach, taking positions. Muggeridge's voice carried, barking orders, issuing commands.

Ray opened the toby and took out three items: a pair of Indian-head pennies and a ball of bluestone. He slid a penny into each of his boots. He clutched tightly to the ball of bluestone. It would protect him from the bullets, at least until the spell wore off. He hoped he would have at least half an hour.

Ray moved down the hill. He had to find Sally before those Bowlers did.

The rougarou scattered, moving around and away from the steamcoach, making it difficult for the Bowlers to focus their attack. Rifles cracked. Bullets whined. The area around the steamcoach looked like a fireworks display, brilliant flashes within a growing cloud of gunsmoke.

A rougarou howled a high piercing note, and the entire pack descended upon the Bowlers, using the smoke as an opportunity to strike. Agents ran in every direction, guns blazing. The men on horseback had trouble keeping their horses from panicking. The scene grew frenzied as the battle began to spread. Men and rougarou ran this way and that. Muggeridge had lost control over his men and was desperately defending himself against a dark-furred rougarou.

Then Ray saw men hiding at the back of the steamcoach. No, they weren't hiding. A tingling formed at Ray's fingertips. The agents opened the door, and when it swung wide, a shape emerged from the depths. Pale white against the dark. With slow, creeping steps it lurched down onto the plains, swinging its jaws around menacingly.

A Hoarhound!

Ray again noticed the odd tingling in his fingers, and as he brought his hand up, there was a tug, a strange pull toward the Gog's Hound.

He had no time to wonder on it. B'hoy returned but had not found Redfeather and Marisol. It was too dark and chaotic. "Thanks, B'hoy. You should stay clear of the battle. I don't want a stray bullet to get you. But if you see a girl . . . Sally is out there!" And he shooed the crow into the air.

Ray ran closer to the battle. He reached a dry gully. The walls hid him from the fight, and he moved nearer, looking for Sally or Redfeather or Marisol. With the other horses and the darkness and the smoke and the turmoil, Ray could not tell if any of the horses were Atsila. But there was an arrow perched in the earth. Redfeather had been here. Where were they?

Several rougarou leaped on the Hoarhound. It shook them away, its terrible jaws locking upon a rougarou's back. With a whine of pain, the rougarou was flung by the Hoarhound and fell limply at the edge of the gully several dozen yards ahead.

Ray started toward it, but the agent De Courcy bounded into the gully between him and the dead rougarou. He began reloading his rifle, his breath coming loudly and his fingers fumbling with the cartridges. He swung the rifle up, steadied his elbows on the top of the gully, and began firing.

As De Courcy ducked back into the gully, he saw Ray. He

snarled and brought the rifle around. Ray clutched tight to the ball of bluestone. He squeezed his eyes shut as the rifle erupted. When he opened them again, he saw the agent staring dumbfounded at Ray.

A rougarou charged, and De Courcy scrambled out of the gully, running for his life. The attacking rougarou leaped over the gap, a shadow and a blur, and pursued the man.

Ray crept over to the dead rougarou. It was enormous. Much larger than he had imagined, even from the paw prints he had seen days ago. Its blank open eyes were pale blue, so like a human eye and yet so otherworldly. Then the rougarou transformed into a woman—unlike any woman he had ever seen. Her hair was dark red, and her skin seemed filled with moonlight. The light slowly faded, leaving the rougarou's lifeless human form.

More gunfire erupted nearby, and Ray ran farther down the gully. When he reached a safer spot, he looked back at the plains. A rougarou was chasing a horseman, who was trying to fire backward. His horse was not swift enough and the rougarou leaped, catching the man in his jaws and tearing him from the horse's back. The Hoarhound, nearly twice the size of the biggest rougarou, was surrounded by at least five of the pack.

Sally was nowhere to be seen. Was she hiding at that campfire?

Ray looked for a way out of the battlefield. If he continued following the gully, he would only wind up in a more conspicuous spot. So he climbed out onto the prairie again and ran toward the campfire. A stray bullet slapped against his head and he dropped to the ground. He touched his temple, which stung, but no more than if he had been pelted by a stone.

On the moonlit earth before him, he saw a footprint. No, a pair of footprints. Sally had been traveling with another child. Had they passed here, sneaking away to escape the Bowlers? Ray had to look closely to tell which direction the prints were going. And there, the dirt was pulled up where the toes would have caught if she was running.

She was going west.

A rougarou roared not more than fifty feet away, its jaws clamping onto the shoulder of a Bowler. The man screamed, fired his rifle, but missed. The man fell, and the rougarou leaped away.

Ray followed the prints, pausing occasionally when the tracks grew faint. After searching, he found them again. He was close. He knew it. He would find her and he would help her escape. Why had she come out here? Why had she put herself and the rabbit's foot in such danger?

He followed the footprints to the mouth of a canyon. In the soft earth, the prints were clearer. How strange that one of the two travelers was barefoot. He jogged silently into the shadowed canyon.

Ray was glad to be moving away from the battle now. The canyon wound back and forth, and then the prints stopped at one of the sides. The wall of the canyon was sloped, and the dirt was broken in places where they had climbed up.

When he reached the top, he saw that the prairie continued flat and endless to the horizon. It appeared empty. Where was she? He looked back. Below, the battle was clearly displayed.

The dark shadows of bodies—men, horses, rougarou—were strewn across the plains. Several rougarou butted against the steamcoach, shaking its wheels from the ground. There were only a handful of agents left to defend the vehicle, and they fired from the windows of the locomotive. Over a ways, the Hoarhound was lunging like an enraged bear at the rougarou surrounding it. When the Hound swung one way, a rougarou would strike from behind, tearing at the frost-hardened flesh covering its clockwork, trying to wear it down like a cornered prey. But Ray knew there was no exhausting the Hoarhound. It would fight mercilessly until it was destroyed completely.

Ray heard a noise behind him. He turned, peering across the moonlit expanse. He saw nothing. But then a moment later, he spied a horse, riderless and grazing. Redfeather's horse? Ray moved closer. He wanted to call out, and he almost did, until he saw the horse more clearly. It was not Atsila. It was a dark quarter horse. One of the Bowlers' horses.

Where was the rider?

A voice whispered and another shushed it. Crouching low, Ray moved with silent steps, his knife drawn. Ahead was a taller tuft of grass, and he knew the land well enough to guess that behind that tuft was a deer wallow. The perfect hiding place on this vast openness.

Ray opened his hand to check the ball of bluestone in the

moonlight. The rock was now a ruddy orange. If he were to take the pennies from his boots, he knew they would now be blue. The protective spell had faded.

Ray cast the bluestone aside and kept low to the ground, moving as slowly as he would when hunting. He circled the wallow, his eyes trained on the spot. There was movement, shadowy figures. He could see the faint profile of faces, looking in the other direction. They had not seen him.

He could leap into the wallow. If it was Sally, he would only startle her. But if they were Bowlers, he'd have a moment to attack with surprise on his side and then escape again.

Ray drew closer. He steadied his breathing until even a rabbit could not have known he was there.

Now.

He propelled himself forward and jumped, landing behind the two figures in the wallow.

There was a gasp and a cry. And one of the figures circled with a knife. Ray grabbed the wrist and knocked the knife away.

"Ray?"

All the air rushed from Ray's lungs. He let go of her wrist.

"Jolie?"

A year. So many times on his travels, he had half-expected to find her at some river or marsh. Each time he didn't, it was like reopening an old wound. Over the months, he had come to believe that she was gone for good, and that he would never see her again.

But here she was. The last place he would ever expect to find her.

They stared at one another. He soaked in her visage like a cold stone gathering warm sunlight. She looked different, or maybe he was seeing her as he hadn't seen her before. No, she *was* different: fuller, stronger, healthier, and lovelier.

Jolie clasped his arms and shook him. "Ray. Ray. What are you doing here?" No words came to his lips. She wrapped her arms around him, trembling, whispering, "You must have thought I abandoned you in the river."

"No," Ray said, nearly into her ear. "No, I knew you didn't."

She released him, and he laughed when their eyes met. "What *did* happen to you? Where did you go?"

There was a cough. Ray turned to see the other person. It was a girl in tattered clothes, probably Sally's age or maybe younger. She looked warily at Ray as she spoke. "Reckon y'all can catch up later? We best keep moving."

"I'm sorry," Ray said, embarrassed by his display with Jolie, and that he had ignored the girl until this moment. "I'm Ray Cobb."

"I know. I'm Hethy." The name sounded vaguely familiar. Before Ray could ask anything, the girl turned to Jolie. "Suspect we should get."

Jolie looked around. "There is a horse nearby. I have not seen his rider, but I found this knife in the grass. He may be about."

Ray had been shaken by finding Jolie, but he gathered his wits again and looked around. "No. I think he'd still be on him if he were. The Bowler probably fell in the fight, and the horse is trying to escape to safety."

"So they are Bowlers?" Jolie asked, her eyes narrowing. "I thought the Gog was dead."

"I thought so too. I'm not so sure anymore. There's so much to explain. But first there's Sally—"

"We were looking for her," Jolie said. "She has the rabbit's foot, Ray."

"I know." Ray nodded. "And those Bowlers are after it. She's probably trying to bring it to me for some—"

"No she ain't," Hethy said sharply.

"What do you mean?" Ray snapped. Hethy drew closer to Jolie, her mouth sealed.

"Hethy has been traveling with Sally," Jolie explained. "Sally is trying to find your father."

"He's dead," Ray said matter-of-factly.

Jolie exchanged a look with Hethy.

"What?" Ray asked.

"Sally learned something from Mother Salagi. Your father is alive. He is trapped in the Gloaming."

Ray felt dazed, sick.

"She is following the rabbit's foot's pull," Jolie added. "It is leading her to Little Bill."

Ray could not believe this. The lodestone had been able to guide him to his father. But once it became the rabbit's foot, that power had been lost. And his father! He was alive? After all that had happened, the knowledge felt cold and abstract.

"If those Bowlers escape the battle, they'll continue after her. . . ." He shook his head to clear his welling panic. "Follow me."

Ray crept back to the edge of the butte, Jolie and Hethy behind him. The battle still raged. The remaining pack of rougarou—Ray counted seven—surrounded the Hoarhound. Most of the rougarou were limping. But the Hoarhound was weakening too. The skin was ripped from its side, exposing the black machinery beneath. Part of its jaw looked crushed.

What the pack had not noticed, and what Ray could see from his vantage point, was that the half dozen or more remaining Bowlers were using the Hoarhound as a diversion. Muggeridge was loading the men back aboard the steamcoach. One man remained on horseback, keeping between the Bowlers and the rougarou. After a few moments, the steamcoach began driving away toward the west. Some of the rougarou saw this and tried to pursue. But the Hoarhound was between them—its teeth flashing, its powerful shoulder bashing them away. The horseman fired, keeping the other rougarou back.

Hethy coughed and put a hand to her mouth to stifle it. "Sorry—" she began to say, but broke into another cough.

Ray looked from the girl back to the plains below. "They're going to get away," Ray said.

He held up his hand, feeling again the strange sensation of the Hoarhound's presence.

Jolie asked, "What is it you sense?"

Before he could answer, Hethy's coughing deepened. Jolie put her arms around her. "Are you all right?"

The girl doubled over, her eyes streaming with tears as the violent fit wracked her body.

"What's wrong with her?" Ray asked.

"I do not know."

Hethy collapsed in Jolie's arms, and Ray sprang forward to help lower her to the ground. He crouched over her, trying to see her in the pale moonlight. "Hethy? Are you all right?"

The girl was lying on her back, beginning to choke from the brutal coughing. Her eyes rolled back and her lips were speckled with blood.

Even in the thin light, Ray saw it. Her blood was black. It was oil. He had trouble telling, but he was certain her skin was ashen gray.

Hethy gasped for air, the coughs suddenly stilled. Ray pulled the girl's head to his lap, looking her in the face. "Hethy? Can you hear me, Hethy?"

The girl's mouth opened and closed and then she uttered, "Granny Sip . . . Granny Sip . . ."

"What is she saying?" Jolie asked Ray.

Ray realized who she was calling out for. Granny Sip. The old woman hanged in Omphalosa as a witch. Gigi had said her granddaughter had escaped.

Ray looked at Jolie desperately. "This girl's come from the Darkness! She's dying."

"No!" Jolie cried. "No, Hethy!" She began scrambling, looking around frantically. "The well's water! Where is it?"

"What are you looking for?" Ray asked.

"I had skins of water. Healing water from Élodie's Spring. I . . . I must have left them with—"

A rifle cocked, and Ray turned.

An agent stood over them, shadowed against the night sky. A sheen of moonlight glowed from his rifle barrel.

"I knew we'd catch you," Sokal gloated. "Yeah, De Courcy said you were nearby. And I got you. Don't move."

Struggling in Ray's lap, Hethy choked on the oil filling her lungs. Then her eyes rolled back and she grew limp.

Soft, eerie singing began. Ray had heard it before. Sokal's eyes widened and darted to Jolie. He backed up a step, turning the rifle on her. But Jolie kept singing her wordless, dark music. Sokal stared, transfixed by Jolie's spell.

Singing all the while, Jolie walked slowly toward him, her face a mask of hatred. She took the rifle from his hands and threw it aside. Then she reached a hand to her lower back. What was she doing? With slow movements, she took out her knife, never stopping her song.

"No," Ray whispered, laying Hethy on the ground to stand.

Jolie ignored him, stepping closer.

Ray grabbed her arm. "Will he do whatever we say?"

Jolie nodded again, still singing.

"Can he speak?"

She nodded, and Ray turned to Sokal. "Where is Grevol taking the Machine?"

Sokal's eyes flickered. "Chicago," he muttered.

"What's he going to do with his Machine?"

Sokal struggled, gritting his teeth as the words came out. "He's . . . setting it up . . . at the Expo."

"Why does Grevol want the rabbit's foot?"

Sokal squeezed his eyes shut. "Don't . . . know."

Then his eyes opened, and a smile struggled to his lips. "You'll all . . . be killed. Mister Grevol, he knows . . . about the others. . . ."

"*What* others?" Ray shouted.

"Muggeridge said . . . Mister Grevol . . . sending men to . . ."

"To where!"

"Shuckstack—"

An arrow sank into Sokal's chest with a heavy thud. Jolie stopped singing and turned. Stunned, Ray stared helplessly as another arrow struck Sokal just below the collarbone. He toppled backward.

"No!" Ray shouted, leaping for Sokal. He grasped the man's sodden shirt, pulling at him desperately. "How does he know? How does he know about Shuckstack?"

Sokal opened his eyes. His lips parted, his teeth darkened with blood. The grim smile froze on his face as he died.

"No!" Ray cried over and over, shaking Sokal.

"Ray. Are you all right?"

Redfeather had his bow notched with another arrow. Marisol stood behind him, looking wide-eyed from the dead Bowler to Jolie to the girl lying on the ground.

"You killed him, Redfeather," Ray said, his voice cracking.

"He's a Bowler. I thought you were in trouble."

"No." Ray dropped his gaze. He felt dizzy. "Shuckstack. Grevol knows where Nel is."

"What?" Marisol cried. "What about the children? We have to warn Nel!"

"How?" Ray asked, shaking his head and going back over to Hethy. He put his ear to her chest. He could hear the faint beat of her heart and the wet drawing of breath. She was still alive, but only barely. Ray lifted her in his arms.

Redfeather came forward. "Jolie . . . what are you doing here?"

Jolie looked at Redfeather and then at Marisol. "I came out with Conker."

Ray spun around. "Conker! He's alive?"

"I did not have time to tell you. That is where I have been. I found Conker, after the Gog's train exploded. I took him to a siren well to heal him."

Marisol stammered, "I—I can't believe he survived. We thought . . . all this time we thought . . ."

"He was wearing your necklace, Redfeather," Jolie said. "The copper. It saved his life. And listen! We found the Nine Pound Hammer in the Mississippi. The handle was broken. We came to get help from the rougarou and their Wolf Tree—"

"Those wolves . . . they're the rougarou, aren't they?" Redfeather gasped. He gazed around at the dark plains. "The . . . the Wolf Tree. It's been found?"

"Yes," Jolie said. "The rougarou have helped Conker restore the hammer."

"Then Conker can destroy the Machine," Redfeather

said. "We can stop it at last. I'm glad we found you again, Ray. You have Marisol to thank. She found your tracks, and we followed you."

Marisol dropped her gaze. "Javidos found them. He's the one to thank."

"I think you're becoming a Rambler," Redfeather said.

Marisol smiled, her eyes falling briefly on Jolie and then turning to Ray. "What do we do now?"

Ray looked down where the last of the gunfire sounded from the retreating agents. The Hoarhound was following the steamcoach, but the rougarou were no longer pursuing. Ray turned, thinking of a plan.

"We have to act quickly," Ray said. "The Bowlers will keep hunting for Sally, and she's on foot. They will catch her with that steamcoach."

"She is not on foot," Jolie said. "She has a guardian. A rougarou. He is protecting her, and if she is riding on him, they will not be easy to catch."

"With that Hoarhound, they might still catch her. We have to reach her first."

Redfeather took Atsila's reins and led her over. "There's that Bowler's horse over there. Can you ride it?"

Ray nodded.

"What about Hethy?" Jolie asked. "We must get her back to my waters. They will heal her."

Ray put her in Redfeather's arms. "Take her to Conker. Tell him to give her the siren water. I fear it's too late, but there's nothing else to do."

"What do we do then?" Redfeather asked.

"Go with Conker. Go to Chicago. We'll meet you there after we've found Sally."

Marisol clutched Ray in an embrace and then hugged Jolie before climbing onto Atsila's back.

Redfeather lifted Hethy up to Marisol and then nodded to Ray and Jolie as he climbed into the saddle in front of Marisol. "Be safe, my friends," he called.

"You too," Ray said.

They watched as Marisol and Redfeather rode out into the darkness.

THE FAINT LIGHT OF PREDAWN HUNG OVER THE SKY.
Conker sat next to Si, wiping at her temple with a wet rag. Si
stirred and opened her eyes.

She smiled painfully up at him. "You're here? You're
really here?"

"You think it was a dream?"

"I wasn't sure. . . . Most of what's happened seemed a
nightmare. My hand!"

She lifted her hand. It was wrapped thickly in bandages and throbbed so terribly that tears sprang to her eyes.
"How . . . how is it?"

"It's wounded. Awful bad, Si. But I gave you some waters
from a siren well. They'll heal you."

Si winced sickly. "What about the—"

"I don't know about the tattoo. All that matters is that you're okay."

Si pulled her hand against her stomach and rolled over on her side, crying softly. Conker ran his large hand softly over and over against her hair.

"Where's Buck?" she whispered after a time.

"He took him."

"The Hammer?"

"He took it also."

She sat up, her eyes ferocious. "We'll find Stacker Lee. We'll save Buck and get the Hammer back too."

Conker nodded. "Yes. We will." He did not want to tell her yet about Stacker's strange parting words. Si was tired. She needed to rest.

"Conker," Si said.

"Yes."

"I think I've done something terrible."

"You need to rest, Si. Don't trouble your—"

"Listen! I tried to tell you when Stacker had me. There was a prophecy. About me. This seer who knows Mother Salagi told me that I would come to a crossroads. I would have to make a choice. One way was doom. Not just for me or for you but for all mankind. And the other way, there was something good. She said the choice would require a great sacrifice."

She cringed, but Conker could not tell if it was her hand or what she was about to say that pained her.

"When Stacker used me to get the Nine Pound Hammer.

That was my crossroads. I wasn't supposed to let you give it to him. I was supposed to sacrifice myself, so you could have the Hammer."

Conker put his hand to her cheek. "No, Si. That ain't it."

"It was, Conker! I've brought danger to us all."

"But it weren't your choice. It was mine. I gave Stacker the Nine Pound Hammer, not you."

"But what about the prophecy?"

"I don't give much thought to such matters. But if it's true, that weren't your crossroads. You ain't got there. Not yet."

Si looked at him for a long time, and something like acceptance came over her face. She took his hand and pulled it close to her as she closed her eyes.

Dawn was breaking when Conker saw the rougarou return. So few! Only seven survived, and three of them carried the bodies of men and women, rougarou returned to their true form—if only now in death.

Conker was glad to see Mangoron was still alive. The rougarou limped over to him.

"Who is the girl?"

"An old friend."

"She is injured?"

"Yes. But she's healing. I'm sorry for your losses, and sorry to tell you that Coer died."

"How? I saw none of the men leave the battlefield."

"It wasn't them Bowlers." Conker told him about Stacker Lee and how he took the Nine Pound Hammer.

"This is dire news," Mangoron said when Conker had

finished. "The Great Tree depends on you as well as your father's hammer. We—"

But there were growls from over at the rest of the pack. Conker stood, ready to fight if the agents had returned. But it was not Bowlers. It was a young man and woman—both seemed to be Indian—on a horse. Renamex, injured as she was, snarled and led the others to surround the two.

Si rose and grabbed Conker's arm. "It's Redfeather and Marisol."

"They are friends!" Conker shouted as he ran toward the pack. "Do not harm them. Let them approach."

Renamex ordered her pack back, her eyes cautiously following Conker and the two strangers.

"Conker," Marisol said, dismounting the horse. She embraced him. "I could hardly believe Jolie when she said you were alive. And Si, you're here too?"

Conker's smile failed as he watched Redfeather slide off his horse with Hethy in his arms. "It can't be," Conker whispered. "The girl. Hethy. What happened?"

"She is dying from the Darkness. She might still be saved. Jolie said there were waters."

"Bring her over here," Conker said, running ahead of them to get the waterskins.

As Redfeather laid Hethy on the ground by the campfire, Conker cupped a hand beneath her head and poured a thin trickle into Hethy's mouth. He tilted her head up, staring at the black blood caked to her lips.

Redfeather knelt over him. "A man came to Shuckstack, dying from this Darkness. Nel could do nothing to—"

Hethy's lips closed and she swallowed.

"Give her more!" Si said.

Conker put the skin to Hethy's lips and spilt a little more of the siren waters into her mouth. As she swallowed, she frowned and opened her eyes a fraction.

"Conker," she whispered, giving a slight cough.

"You're all right, girl," he said. "You're going to be all right."

They huddled around Hethy, watching over her. Soon the ashen color began to fade from her skin, and as it did, Hethy's wrenched face relaxed as she slept.

Conker looked up at Redfeather, who was staring at the rougarou. "Where is Jolie? Why didn't she come back with you?"

"She left with Ray—" Redfeather began.

"Ray!" Conker gasped. "Where is he?"

"He and Jolie have left to find Sally."

Conker scowled with confusion. "Sally? Ray's sister?"

"She's why Buck and I are out here," Si said. "She ran away from Shuckstack with the rabbit's foot and we were following her. Until Stacker captured us."

"Well, she still has the rabbit's foot, at least," Marisol said. "But the Bowlers are pursuing her. Their Hoarhound is drawn to the foot."

"They can't . . ." Si frowned. "If the Bowlers get the rabbit's foot, all is lost."

"Why?" Conker asked.

"Mother Salagi discovered something about Li'l Bill.

It's why your father did not defeat the Gog. You need not only the Nine Pound Hammer but a spike as well. A spike only Li'l Bill can make. If he doesn't make it, the Machine can't be destroyed. Sally needs the rabbit's foot to save her father."

"If they catch her before Ray does, then all will fail," Conker said. "Catching Stacker and getting back the Hammer won't matter then."

Redfeather looked curiously at him. Before Conker could explain to him who Stacker was, Renamex approached.

"We are going to bury our dead."

Redfeather came anxiously toward the black rougarou. "Has the Wolf Tree been found? We've been seeking it, but I cannot see it."

Renamex studied Redfeather a moment. "Why have you sought the Great Tree?"

"Water Spider, of the Western Cherokee, sent us. He met you before—"

"Yes," Renamex said, her canine mouth curling. "I remember Water Spider."

"He sent us to find out why the Wolf Tree has been lost. Have you found it? Is the pathway to the next world open?"

"The Tree is dying. The Darkness must be stopped before we can discover what will heal it. But yes, the Great Tree has been found once more. Look, young one. Look behind you."

Redfeather turned, leaning his head back as the glowing

tower took form before his eyes. Marisol stepped to his side and clutched his hand. "Water Spider," Redfeather said. "He was right."

Marisol nodded and whispered, "It's beautiful."

"Yes. It is." Redfeather squeezed her hand.

With the morning sun warming the prairie, four holes were dug in the earth at the roots of the Wolf Tree. All but Conker gathered as the fallen rougarou were buried. He watched over Hethy. But Conker listened as Renamex and the pack sang in lonesome howling tones.

Hethy opened her eyes and looked up at him. "What they saying?" she asked.

"I don't know the words," he replied. "But I expect she's blessing the dead."

She shifted and tried to sit up, but Conker said, "Rest, girl."

Hethy lay back. "What's going to happen to me?"

"The rougarou will care for you. You have more healing to do, but I reckon whatever ill hold that Darkness had over you is passing."

"Are you leaving?" she whispered.

"Yes."

"Are you coming back?"

Conker saw Mangoron trotting toward them. "I don't know. I don't know what will happen to us. But you are safe here. Go on. Rest."

She gave him a faint smile and closed her eyes again.

Mangoron lay down by Hethy. Conker nodded to him as he rose and left to join his friends.

After bidding their farewells, the other rougarou set out to bury the dead Bowlers on the battlefield, along with Stacker's men, Hardy and Alston. Conker, Si, Redfeather, and Marisol began packing food and their meager supplies to depart.

"What are we going to do about Nel?" Redfeather asked Marisol.

"What about Nel?" Si asked.

"The Gog has not been killed. And he's learned that Nel is at Shuckstack."

"That's the danger!" Si said, terror welling in her expression. "The seer warned that something was seeking him. Grevol! How can Nel alone ever protect the children against him?"

"Then let's waste no more time," Conker said. He put Jolie's shell knife in his belt and threw the remaining waterskin from the siren well over his shoulder.

"There's a town about forty or fifty miles to the east of here," Si said. "Stacker kept his distance from it, but I remember seeing it. Redfeather, you and Marisol ride there as fast as you can. Find a telegraph office. Send a wire to Missus Maynard. She'll get it delivered to Nel. Conker and I will meet you."

Redfeather was already untying Atsila's reins. He leaped to her back, and Marisol swung on behind him.

"We'll see you there in a few days," Redfeather called.

"Ride," Conker said.

Redfeather cast one final glance back at the Wolf Tree. Then Atsila's hooves kicked up loose clods of earth as she sped across the prairie.

Conker looked down at Si. She held her hand gingerly to her stomach, but her face showed no pain. She was so courageous, Conker thought. And they were together again. He did not know what the seer had meant about Si's crossroads, but he hoped he would be with her when she reached them. He hoped never to leave her side again.

Si cocked an eyebrow. "I'd say we should ask one of the rougarou to carry us, but you're far too big."

Conker smiled. "I can walk fast. Can you keep up?"

"Have I ever not?" she asked. "You ready?"

"Whenever you are."

"Let's go."

The sun blazed over the rustling prairie in a brilliant blue and cloudless sky. The middle of the enormous country— where the Wolf Tree stood dying—was nearly empty. But small bands of travelers, hunters and hunted, were radiating east and west.

Four began their journey eastward, following Stacker Lee toward the grim and dirty industrial city of Chicago. A city where a multitude was descending to see the spectacle and promise of a better future that was the Columbian Exposition.

Westward, on the back of Sokal's horse, Ray and Jolie pursued Sally. The evergreen-crested Black Hills hung in the distance, and beyond, hundreds and hundreds of miles still, rose the great Rocky Mountains. Between Ray and his sister, the steamcoach spat its tendril of black smoke and rattled over the land. In the back—battered but having lost none of its menace—was the Hoarhound.

And its hungry clockwork innards felt the draw of the rabbit's foot.

JOHN CLAUDE BEMIS grew up in rural eastern North Carolina, where he loved reading the Jack tales and African American trickster stories, as well as fantasy and science fiction classics. A songwriter and musician in an Americana roots band, John found inspiration for the Clockwork Dark trilogy in old-time country and blues music and the Southern folklore at its heart.

Drawing on the legend of John Henry's struggle against the steam drill, John began exploring how Southern folklore could be turned into epic fantasy. This passion grew into his first novel, *The Nine Pound Hammer,* a story set in a mythical nineteenth-century America full of hoodoo conjurers and cowboys, battling trains and steamboat pirates.

John is a former elementary school teacher and lives with his family in Hillsborough, North Carolina. Visit John's Web site at www.johnclaudebemis.com.